IDYLL FEARS

ALSO BY STEPHANIE GAYLE

Idyll Threats

IDYLL FEARS

A Thomas Lynch Novel

STEPHANIE GAYLE

SEVENTH STREET BOOKS®
AN IMPRINT OF PROMETHEUS BOOKS
59 JOHN GLENN DRIVE • AMHERST, NY 14228
www.seventhstreetbooks.com

Published 2017 by Seventh Street Books®, an imprint of Prometheus Books

Cover images © sbayram/iStock (snowstorm); iofoto/Depositphotos (road)
Cover design by Jacqueline Nasso Cooke
Cover design © Prometheus Books

Inquiries should be addressed to
Seventh Street Books
59 John Glenn Drive
Amherst, New York 14228
VOICE: 716–691–0133
FAX: 716–691–0137
WWW.SEVENTHSTREETBOOKS.COM

21 20 19 18 17   5 4 3 2 1

Names: Gayle, Stephanie, 1975- author.
Title: Idyll fears : a Thomas Lynch novel / by Stephanie Gayle.
Description: Amherst, NY : Seventh Street Books, an imprint of Prometheus Books, 2017.
Identifiers: LCCN 2017014990 (print) | LCCN 2017023092 (ebook) |
    ISBN 9781633883581 (ebook) | ISBN 9781633883574 (paperback)
Subjects: | BISAC: FICTION / Mystery & Detective / Police Procedural. |
    FICTION / Gay. | GSAFD: Mystery fiction.
Classification: LCC PS3607.A98576 (ebook) |
    LCC PS3607.A98576 I38 2017 (print) | DDC 813/.6—dc23
LC record available at https://lccn.loc.gov/2017014990

Printed in the United States of America

For my father, Paul Vincent Gayle,
who gave me my work ethic and my nose and who taught me
silence is a tool (and a weapon)

CHAPTER ONE

Wind chimes tinkled, their high, golden sounds all wrong on this chill December morning. My fingertips traced my jaw to check my shave. The coffeemaker sighed, its work done. I filled my thermos. Loose linoleum tried to trip me on my way to the window. Outside there was pearl-gray sky. Hell. I'd lived here long enough to recognize a snow sky. Snow days were busy. Car accidents, medical emergencies. Not to mention the local yokel antics. Two weeks ago, a fistfight broke out at Karp's Hardware over the last snow shovel.

I zipped my jacket. Stuffed my leather gloves deep in my pockets. The glassy sound of the wind chimes grew frantic. Strong wind outside. My phone rang. I paused at the door. It rang twice more. No one would care if I were late to the station. No one but my feral secretary, Mrs. Dunsmore. I picked up the white plastic receiver.

"Get out of town." The voice was pitched low and deep, verging on Darth Vader.

"Or what?" My pulse leapt to the base of my throat.

"We don't want your kind here." He broke into a coughing fit.

"My kind?" The more he talked, the better my chances of identifying him.

"Homo," he said. "Queer." He hung up.

I dialed *69 and wrote down the caller's telephone number. Flipped a page and checked my log. Second call from this number. Darth Vader didn't know it, but he was in trouble. The log contained eight other numbers. Either most people in Idyll didn't care that their chief of police was gay, or they were smart enough not to call him at home to complain. I grabbed my thermos and whistled my way to the car. Shrieks brought my eyes up. Kids, running.

The car radio announced that Idyll's schools were closed, along with twenty others. The weatherman was excited. "This one could end up in the record books, folks. The worst of the storm will begin around 10:30 a.m., with visibility at less than a quarter of a mile." Shit. We were in for it. I might have to call in the reserves. That meant overtime. The selectmen would rant. They rated safety well below meeting the annual budget. I backed out of my driveway slowly. My neighborhood was lousy with kids excited over the blizzard-induced three-day weekend. When I reached the end of the block, my radio squawked.

The dispatcher called, "Four, 10-2."

Patrol car four answered. "Four, go ahead."

"Four, we have a 10-76." He paused. "It's a kid."

"Location?"

"176 Spring Street."

Spring Street was a mile or so away. I could be there in minutes.

"Um, what was that address again?"

I knew that voice. Hopkins. A snowflake smacked my windshield, melting on impact. Dispatch repeated the address. Hopkins was lazy. Counting the days to retirement. Probably had been since he was a cadet. Some cops are like that. But even a shiftless hump like Hopkins could find a missing kid. He was a local, better suited to the job than me.

Snowflakes fell lazily. Maybe this storm would fizzle out, like the last one. The police station's parking lot was half full. My spot was at the building's rear, my door parallel to the back stairs. The lazy clowns at the DPW did a poor job plowing. Last week I'd had to put cardboard under my rear tires.

The station's warmth was a shock after the cold. Nearby, I heard the soft snicker of crepe soles. Mrs. Dunsmore. She stood before me, her profile soft with age. Her nostrils flared. Her hand went to the silver crucifix she'd worn since they'd told her about me. I was tempted to tell her my grandmother, Rose, had owned one just like it. "Chief," she said, her voice hoarse.

I plowed forward. Her sigh was a gust at my back. I turned. "What?"

"You're late." Great. The harpy wanted to scold me. "And we've got a situation."

"Gimme five minutes." I couldn't deal with her disapproving mug so early.

My shining doorplate, *Chief Thomas Lynch*, was only a month old, though I'd been here almost a year. I reached for my phone. Punched in three digits. "Get me the address for this number." I recited the one from this morning's call.

"Will do," my part-time detective, Finnegan, promised.

I sat in my chair, tented my fingers, and stared at the ceiling. The room smelled of burnt dust. The odor would last until late spring, when the heat was turned off. The phone rang. Outside call. I snatched the receiver up. "Chief Lynch."

"Chief, it's Charles Gallagher." Charles co-owned the town's candy store, Sweet Dreams, with his partner in all senses of the word, David Evans.

"Good morning, Mr. Gallagher. How are you?"

"Not well, I'm afraid. We've had a break-in at the store."

Mrs. Dunsmore walked in. I waved her out, mouthing, "Give me ten." She scowled but left.

He said, "I went to put up a sign saying we're closed, what with the blizzard coming. Wanted to make sure the hatches were battened, so to speak. The back door was broken open."

"Cash register?" I asked.

"Intact, but inside is a mess. There's glass and candy everywhere, and there's hate speech on the wall."

"Hate speech?"

"Anti-gay." Faint crunching sounds came through the phone. "It's going to take forever to clean up this mess."

"You're insured?" I asked.

My phone lit up. It blinked and then disappeared. Mrs. Dunsmore had grabbed it. She'd been doing it more often, as if it were her job. Funny, given her feelings about me.

He said, "Oh, of course we're insured. It's not that. I can't believe that someone would do this." He sounded confused. Shock, most likely.

"I'll send someone over, to take a statement and pictures. Don't touch anything."

"You can't come?" he asked.

Burglaries weren't my patch, and he wasn't asking because it was my job.

"Detective Finnegan will be over soon."

"Thanks, Chief."

He hadn't called the main line. Maybe he worried our detectives wouldn't be sympathetic. I hoped that wasn't true, although Wright would walk six feet around the coffeepot, empty mug in hand, if I stood in its path. It shouldn't have surprised me. Black guys are more homophobic than white guys.

Finnegan was in the detectives' pen. He wore a checked sports coat so loud I had to look away. Between his stubby fingers, he held a slip of paper. I grabbed it. An address: 20 Suffolk Street. "Good work. I need to know about cars registered to this address. Get the makes and plate numbers," I said.

"Okey doke." He drank from a mug that read, "Feel Safe at Night. Sleep with a Cop." He peered around me. "Lady D. is on the hunt for you."

"I know. She tried to pin me when I got in. Any idea what bee is in her bonnet?"

"Nope." Finnegan enjoyed an odd relationship with Mrs. Dunsmore. She gave him hell for smoking, his filthy desk area, and his wardrobe. He bared his nicotine-stained teeth at her and offered to make her the fourth Mrs. Finnegan. "Hey, when you see her, tell her I took the call and recorded the number," he told me.

"Huh?"

He waved his hand. "She'll know."

I said, "We got a situation up at Sweet Dreams."

He cocked his head. "Someone knocked over the candy store?"

"Someone broke in and wrote hate speech on the wall."

"That's no way to show holiday spirit." He didn't ask what kind of hate speech. "You hear about the storm? Should be a fun day."

I wished I shared his enthusiasm. On my way back to my desk, Mrs. Dunsmore planted herself in front of me. "Chief, half the crew is out."

"Half?"

"They're really sick. Not taking pre-holiday days." I'd noticed the waste bins full of crumpled tissues and the coughs. I'd escaped contagion. Not being popular had perks. "This coming storm is a bad one," she said.

On a normal day, we could survive with a skeleton crew. Idyll, Connecticut, wasn't plagued by crime. The snow-shovel fistfight had been the most exciting event until Mr. Gallagher's call this morning. "Another thing. John wants you."

"John," I said.

"Miller." She saw my confusion and grimaced. "On dispatch." Mrs. Dunsmore was appalled that I didn't immediately recognize every name in the station. We had three Johns, and I hadn't lived here for a thousand years, unlike some people I could name.

"Finnegan says he took the call and recorded the number," I told her.

"Good." She walked away. So much for including me in their work.

John Miller wore a green sweatshirt and a Santa hat. He was one of those people who decorated everything, including themselves, for the holidays. It was a wonder we weren't best friends. "Chief." He kept one ear cocked toward his panel. "I heard back from Hopkins."

"Missing kid. Yeah. I heard the call."

"His name is Cody Forrand. He's six years old, and he's still missing. I sent Klein and Wilson to help search. That leaves us down one unit."

Half the shift was out sick. "How long has Cody been missing?"

He glanced at the big clock above his mounted phone. "Almost two hours. Oh, and another thing." His Santa hat listed toward his left ear. "He's got a medical condition. Something about not being able to handle cold weather."

I looked past him, out the window. The snow fell, the flakes like white bullets raining down. "Shit," I said.

John Miller nodded. His Santa hat tilted too far and slid onto the counter with a soft plop.

The weatherman was on the radio, even more excited. "We've heard from folks in New Haven. They've got two inches already, and there's plenty more to come. Expect decreased visibility and high winds. The governor is urging people to stay off the roads."

In a neighborhood of larger ranches, 176 Spring Street was a small home. Its door sported a faded wreath. No signs of our patrol cars. On the small lawn stood a plastic playhouse, its pitched roof covered in snow. I knuckled the front door. A man yanked it open. His anxiety rolled off him in waves, like heat.

"Good morning, Mr. Forrand. I'm Chief Lynch."

He glanced past me and asked, "Did they find him?"

"Not yet." I stepped into the entryway. Hats, mittens, and scarves in bright crayon colors hung from pegs. The adults' coats were visible only in small patches below.

"Sorry, I'm Pete." We shook hands. His fingers were cold. We walked inside. The living room floor was a minefield of action figures and half-dressed dolls. A bare fir tree was propped in the corner, no gift-wrapped boxes below. Christmas was two weeks away. Stockings were tacked to the wall, their flat, baggy forms cheerless. Smells assaulted me. Wet clothes. Burnt toast. Urine. Coffee. Above the TV, a family photo hung off-center. Dad posed behind son; and Mom, behind daughter, who was older than her brother. Cody had brown hair and eyes. He looked small for six, but the photo might be old.

"This way." He walked through the living room and into the kitchen. A petite woman stood near the wall-mounted phone. A girl, her hair in two dark braids, sat at the table, coloring. Breakfast remains cluttered the table and counters: loaf of bread, stick of butter, banana peel, cereal boxes, milk-filled bowls, and mugs.

"Mrs. Forrand, I'm Police Chief Lynch. I'm here about Cody."

"He's been gone over two hours! In this weather he . . ." She stopped, eyes on her daughter, unwilling to finish the sentence.

The girl put her crayon down. Looked up at me. "Cody has CIPA." Her eyes were light gray, her stare unblinking.

"CIPA?" I asked.

Mrs. Forrand tucked her hair behind her ear. "It's a nervous-system disorder. Very rare. He won the genetic lottery. He can't feel pain."

"He can't feel pain?" I asked.

She clucked her tongue. "It's worse than it sounds. He's broken four bones and burnt himself I don't know how many times. It's hard to teach him to be careful."

"Cody's like a superhero," the girl said. "He just doesn't know when to quit."

"Where are the other police?" Mrs. Forrand asked, looking out the window.

So they hadn't reported in to the parents. Well done, Hopkins.

"They're searching. I'm sorry, but what is Cody's problem with the cold?"

Mrs. Forrand said, "He can't regulate his temperature, and he doesn't feel the cold like you or I would, so we have to set time limits for him, to keep him safe."

"What time did he leave the house?"

"7:30. He was bouncing off the walls, excited by the snow day. He was supposed to be gone twenty minutes. When I called him inside, he wasn't in the yard."

Mr. Forrand said, "I checked his friends' houses. They hadn't seen him. I walked around, calling his name. When I got back, he hadn't shown, so Jane called the police. I went out again, ten minutes ago." He glanced at the wall clock. "Hell. I should call work. Tell them I'll be out all day." He cleared his throat. "I thought we'd find him by now."

"He's always had this condition?" I asked.

Mrs. Forrand walked to the table. Picked up a cereal bowl. "Since birth."

Her husband said, "He wasn't diagnosed until almost two years ago." He raked his hand through his hair. "We didn't understand why he didn't cry when he got hurt. We thought he was this super tough kid. None of the doctors knew what was wrong."

"They thought we abused him," his wife whispered. "Because of his injuries."

The girl piped up. "There's only thirty-two kids like Cody in the whole country."

Mrs. Forrand carried the bowl to the sink. Her blond hair needed washing. Her eyes had dark circles. She looked like she'd had more than a rough morning. Drugs?

"Has Cody gone missing before?" I asked.

"Why are you asking that?" She crossed her arms.

"I wondered if maybe he had a hiding place we should check," I said.

She bit her lip, worked it between her small teeth.

The girl stood up. "I can help look."

Her parents turned to her, ready to object.

"I'm eight," she said. "I'm not a baby. Besides, he'll come if he hears me calling."

Her mother swatted the idea away with her hand. "No, Anna. Stay inside. The police are looking for him. He'll be home soon." Anna bit her lip, a mirror gesture of her mother's.

"Anna," I said, "do you have any idea where Cody might've gone?"

"Doug's house, but Dad already checked there. Twice."

"Please," Mrs. Forrand said. Her hands shook. "Please find him."

"Maybe we should get the press involved," I suggested.

Mr. Forrand said, "Won't that slow us down? I think we should search first. He's out there, freezing, and he can't feel it!"

"Can you get neighbors to help?" I asked.

"Of course. I wanted to go before, when they arrived, but they wouldn't let me." *They* being my men. "His birthday's in six weeks," he said. "He'll be seven years old."

I snuck a look at my watch. Would he? Cody Forrand had been missing over two and a half hours.

CHAPTER TWO

I radioed Hopkins. Told him to meet me outside the Forrand house. He pulled his car in front of the house, got out, and waddled over to me, hitching his pants every five steps. Billy, the station rookie, came too.

"Status?" I aimed my remark at Hopkins.

"Lady across the street saw Cody when she walked her dog, around 7:45 a.m. Next-door neighbor saw him too. After that, nada. We've canvassed four blocks."

"Do you have a pic?" I asked. He pulled a glossy photo from his jacket. Cody had that too-wide smile kids give in school pictures. He wore a navy V-neck and had spit-flat hair. "We'll need copies. Billy, why don't you get on that? Get some flashlights, too."

Billy's gloved hands were tucked under his armpits. His lack of body fat was a liability. "Sure thing." He looked at Hopkins. "Keys?" Hopkins tossed him the set.

"What about the other team?" I asked. "Dispatch sent another car, yeah?"

"They went to the park, the one with the big playground," Hopkins said.

"Walker Park? Bring 'em back. We're getting neighbors and more men from the station. Then we'll start searching."

He muttered, "We've been searching." I let it go. It was cold, and he'd been outside over an hour. Assuming he hadn't made Billy do all the legwork.

The volunteers gave us trouble. Whole families appeared. Kids cried, "I'll help find him!" I told Officer Klein he should arrest the next parent who brought a child to help search. He wiped snowflakes from his cheeks and said, "Seriously?"

Mrs. Lutts, the dog walker who'd spotted Cody, told me, "You should talk to Angela May."

"Did she see Cody?" I asked.

"No, she's a psychic. She helped find my wedding ring last year, and she found the Peterson's lost cat, Marmalade."

"Uh-huh." *A psychic?* What was with these people?

Mrs. Forrand's sister, Jessica, showed up while I examined a map. She was younger and blonder than her sister. "Why haven't we started yet?" she demanded.

Time ticked away. We waited for Billy to return. Mr. Forrand stomped his boots and said, "Ready yet?"

We assembled the volunteers into two-person teams, one civvy and one cop. There were fewer cops, so two teams were composed of neighbors. I asked them if they had everything they needed. "Are we supposed to have walkie-talkies?" one asked.

Damn it. Of course. The civvies didn't have them. I told Klein to sort it out.

The snow fell sideways, blown by a wind that made everyone shiver. Even big guys like me felt the chill. How could Cody survive this? *He can't feel the cold.* No pain was a superpower. *One that could kill him.*

Yankowitz and Robinson showed up last. Yankowitz tugged on his earflaps. Made me wish I had some. My skullcap kept creeping up, exposing my ears. "Chief?" He seemed scared. I'd nearly fired him, after he wrecked a patrol car. I'd taken him off meter-maid duty and found something he could do: restart our town's abandoned K-9 program.

Mrs. Forrand tugged the front window curtain aside, watching people pace the snowy road. I moved out of her sight line.

"I was thinking, if it would help, I could bring Skylar." Yankowitz rocked on his heels. Made deep half-moons in the snow. He was a little heavy. A lot of my men were.

"She's my other dog, trained in search and rescue," he said.

Another dog? Jinx, his German shepherd, was trained to sniff out drugs and take down bad guys. "Skylar could find Cody?"

"The snow might make it tough, but she can show us where he headed."

A neighbor approached. Mr. Waterson, former Army. He'd told me when he arrived. "Um, Chief, where are the water bottles?" he asked.

"Water bottles," I repeated.

"You have to make sure searchers stay hydrated." He looked around. "Some of these folks need better gear, you included. In this weather, cotton kills."

"I'll get somebody to fetch water."

Yankowitz peered at my map. "You need to halve the area they're searching. He's a kid. He didn't walk six miles. Not in this," he said.

"Only have 'em search a quarter mile?" I asked. It sounded too small.

"Most searches done in good weather, you don't run a survey bigger than this." So Yankowitz knew about search and rescue. That made one of us.

"Go get the dog," I told him.

"Hey, everybody, change of plans," I called. The volunteers grumbled. Mr. Forrand said, "We need to get out there. Now!" I said we needed water, and a neighbor piped up, "I've got a case in my garage. If someone comes with me, we can grab 'em." Officer Dix said he'd help. I had Klein rezone the map, halve everyone's areas.

Mr. Forrand stomped over. "Why are you redoing the maps?"

I told him the search area was too ambitious.

"What if Cody got that far? We need to be out there, looking. Not waiting for water!"

I said, "If we don't find him, we'll widen the area. I need to consider everyone's safety." He muttered, "Idiot." I pretended not to hear.

After the maps were changed, we gathered everyone and went over protocol: Search the assigned areas for a boy wearing a red coat and blue snow pants. If they found Cody, radio for an ambulance. Return to the Forrands' house when they finished. Hopkins would stay at the house.

He'd alert us if Cody returned, and serve as our liaison for on-the-ground situations. The water bottles arrived. Each volunteer took one. Billy tested that everyone was tuned into the right radio channel. Mr. Forrand said, "Let's go already!" I sent them off and wished them luck.

Snow pelted every bit of bare skin. The back of my neck was half numb. I could've sat in my car, run the heater, or gone inside, like Hopkins. It felt wrong. I'd sent twenty-two men and women to search in this. I could wait until Yankowitz showed up. When he did, a furry golden dog jumped from his car to the snowy ground. It barked, once, the sound muffled by the snow.

"Golden retriever." I knew this breed. Mostly from TV commercials.

Yankowitz said, "Her name is Skylar. She's four years old." Skylar snapped at falling snowflakes.

"She's done searches before?" I asked.

"A few, and she's had lots of training."

Yankowitz gave Skylar an order. She stopped playing and followed us to the front door. Mrs. Forrand opened it after one knock. She started back when she saw the dog. "Oh!" Her hand flew to her mouth.

Yankowitz said, "It's okay. She's very gentle."

"Doggie!" Anna hurtled toward us, arms extended.

"Anna!" her mother warned. Too late. Anna had wrapped her arms around the dog's neck.

"This is Skylar. She's a trained search-and-rescue dog," Yankowitz said.

Hopkins came out of the kitchen, a muffin in his hand. "Where's Jinx?" he asked. All of us had met Yankowitz's other dog. He'd become the station mascot.

"Home," Yankowitz said. "We'll need a piece of Cody's clothing."

Mrs. Forrand nodded, though she looked uncertain. "Anna, honey, leave the dog alone." Anna got in one last, long pet, from Skylar's ears to her rump.

Yankowitz told Mrs. Forrand, "Something he wore recently is best."

"How about his pajamas?" she asked. "I'll go fetch them."

"We'll come," I said. A look around the house wasn't something I'd pass up. Maybe we'd find a clue to Cody's location. A few feet later, I found three deep holes puncturing the hallway's plaster at waist level. Smaller than a fist, but deep. I stopped to examine them. Hammer? The holes, ragged paint and plaster at the edges, spoke of rage.

"Where did these come from?" The plaster left white dust on my fingertips. She'd mentioned abuse accusations. What if there was something to them?

"Golf club," she said. "Cody made two holes before I heard him. He caught Anna on the shoulder with the third."

"Ouch," Yankowitz said.

"She was only bruised, thank God," Mrs. Forrand said. "It's hard for Cody to understand pain. How other people feel. It's totally foreign to him."

"Any trouble at school?" I asked. A kid like Cody might be a problem when a disagreement on the playground broke out. Might hit too hard or never stop hitting.

"That hasn't been the problem," she said.

Her comment made me ask, "What *has* been the problem?"

She rubbed her arms. "Kids at school, boys, mostly, dare Cody to do things. Jump off the top of the slide. Touch hot things. Cody loves attention. So he does it, every time. Last month he cut his arm with an X-Acto knife on a dare. Didn't tell us because he knew we'd be upset. He needed a tetanus shot and an overnight stay at the hospital."

She turned into the first room on the right. The smell of urine was strong here. I didn't figure Anna for a bed wetter, so it must be Cody. Maybe it was part of his condition. There were two bunk beds. "Cody's bed is on top," Mrs. Forrand said. The room's décor was a mishmash of glitter, robots, sports teams, and plush animals.

She picked up a pajama top from the floor. Yankowitz took it with a "thanks."

When we reached the living room, Hopkins was there. "We got an injury," he said. "Idiot got lashed in the eye by a tree branch. Had to reassign teams. Goddamn civvies."

"Hey," I said. "Language." I jerked my head toward Anna, who lay on her stomach on the floor, a blue crayon in hand.

She said, "I'm making Cody a picture of trucks." I gave it a glance. The truck was a rectangle on two circles with one square window.

We walked outside, back into the cold and blowing snow. Yankowitz held the pajama top in front of Skylar and gave her an order. Skylar lowered her head and moved, quickly. Yankowitz, attached by a long lead, followed at a distance. The dog went inside the child-sized playhouse, and then came back out. Moved toward the backyard. Across the white lawn was the back of a yellow ranch. A house where no one had answered during the first neighborhood sweep. Skylar trotted downhill. She stopped. Her muzzle nudged the snow. "Has she got something?" I asked.

"Give her time," he said.

Skylar led us to the yellow house. The lights were on. A car was covered in snow, and there were no tracks in the drive. Not driven since the snow began. Maybe the owner had seen Cody. "I'm going to knock," I told Yankowitz. I walked to the front of the house, where two shallow cement steps led me to the dark-brown front door. There were no holiday decorations. I wondered if the occupant was Jewish or Muslim. Then I remembered where I was: Idyll, Connecticut, in the year of our Lord, 1997. I rapped the rusted brass knocker against the door and waited. The door opened a few inches to reveal a strong-jawed young man.

"Help you?" he said.

"Hi there. A boy from the neighborhood is missing. Cody Forrand. He went outside to play and hasn't come home. We're asking folks if they've seen him."

"Nope." His answer cut short my next line.

"You haven't seen his picture." I held up the photo.

His eyes bounced off it. "No. Sorry."

"You are?" I asked.

"Mike." He tapped his foot. Jittery.

"Got a last name, Mike?"

"Calloway."

"Anyone else live with you?"

"Nah," he said.

"What were you up to this morning?"

"I was—" He stopped. Thought. "Sleeping in. Work was cancelled."

"Where's work?" This guy set off alarm bells. Maybe he didn't like cops. Maybe something else.

"Idyll Elementary." He didn't open the door wider.

"You're a teacher?" He seemed awful young.

"I teach computing. This is my second year."

"Maybe you had Cody in your class. Cody Forrand." I held the photo up.

This time he looked. "Don't think so. Sorry. Um, I've got breakfast nuking in the microwave. It's gonna explode if I don't get it."

"Okay," I said. "Thanks for your time."

He closed the door so hard it vibrated in its frame.

The dog had led Yankowitz four houses away. When I reached them, he said, "She's been back and forth here. Neighbor see anything?"

"Says no."

My voice must've betrayed my skepticism. "You don't believe him?" he asked.

"He was weird. I don't like weird."

Skylar whined. Yankowitz patted her. Snow fell from her coat. "She's reached the end." He pulled a bone from his pocket. "Good girl," he said.

"She go near any of the houses?" I asked.

"The house you checked and that one." He pointed to a white house. I checked my notes. Billy had rung the doorbell but got no response. "Whoever lives there sure has the holiday spirit." He wasn't kidding. The house had lights strung on the roof and electric candles in every window. Three wise men and a giant plywood Snoopy oversaw a nativity scene on the lawn. A dozen ceramic elves lined the walkway.

"I'm going to bring Skylar up." He pointed to the sloping lawn we'd descended.

"I'll check this house," I said. "Then meet you."

The doorbell played "Silent Night." The woman who opened the door wore a red sweater with white reindeer. "Oh!" She stepped back. "Come in! Come in. Don't fuss about your boots." I gave up trying to kick the snow off and stepped inside. I removed my hat. Its black wool was white with snow. She pushed up her glasses. "My, it's really blowing out there, isn't it?"

"Sure is. Ma'am, a boy has gone missing. I wonder if you've seen him?" I handed her the photo. The heat turned the snow into rain. I dripped fat drops onto her Santa mat.

She looked at the photo. "Cody," she said. "Forrand, isn't it?"

"Yes. He was playing outside this morning. Hasn't been seen since."

Her hand smacked her sweater reindeers. "I did see him, this morning. He was playing near the neighbor's house. Mr. Calloway's."

"The teacher?" The one who'd seemed shifty. Who'd denied seeing Cody.

"I thought Cody was looking for something. Kept peering at the ground. I was going to ask him, but the oven started beeping. I'm baking cookies for the church bake sale. Would you like one?"

My stomach rumbled. I hadn't had anything but coffee. Coffee that sat in my car, stone cold now. "No, thanks. What time did you see Cody?"

"It must've been about ten minutes before eight. That's when the cookies had to come out of the oven. You've got to be careful. Butter cookies burn so easy."

"Did you see him after that?"

"No. I put the next batch in, and I forgot about Cody. My sister called and I got to talking with her. Wait. The doorbell rang, later, but I didn't catch it in time. Phone cord doesn't stretch that long. Do you think it could've been Cody?"

"No. Probably a policeman. Mr. Calloway, next door, has he lived here long?"

"Almost two years. He teaches at Idyll Elementary."

"Okay. Thanks for your help, Mrs. . . . ?"

"Ms. Hart." She leaned on the "mizz" and added, "Never married. Not the type. From what I hear, neither are you." She winked. Dimples appeared.

Back outside. The storm felt worse after being indoors. I thought of what she'd told me. *She's a lesbian?* She belonged to a church? Did the neighbors know? My radio beeped. Billy reported that a Mr. Cullen on Dogwood Avenue had seen a boy like Cody around 8:15 a.m. The volunteers chattered. Two said they'd head to Dogwood. Others said they were closer. I got on the radio and said, "Stop talking." They didn't. I yelled it. They stopped. I walked uphill, against the wind. Yankowitz stood outside his car. Skylar lay on the back seat, eyes alert. "Dogwood Avenue?" I asked him.

"Small dead-end road five blocks from here," he said.

"Yankowitz will check out Dogwood," I said into the radio. "Everyone else, check your area. Return to base when you finish."

"You sure you'll be okay out here, Chief?" Yankowitz asked. "Your gloves aren't up to the job. Your boots either."

My leather gloves were wet, and my boots weren't keeping my toes dry or warm. I blinked a snowflake from my eyelash. "I'm fine. Head out."

He drove away. I looked up, into the falling snow. It was like looking into outer space. Stars zooming past. Where was Cody? *God, don't let the kid die. Just this once, don't be a complete fuck. Not this time. Okay?*

"Chief!"

I looked back at the Forrands' house, where Hopkins stood. Bastard wore only a shirt. Cozy as a bug in a rug. I should swap him out with a searcher. See how he liked it out here, with wet feet and a runny nose.

"Chief, they found him!"

All my animosity disappeared. I ran toward Hopkins, eager for the news.

For once, God had listened.

CHAPTER THREE

Anna jumped up and down. "They found him! They found him!"

"Where?" I asked.

"At the McManus house, on Beech Street," Hopkins said. Beech Street was two streets over. How had we missed him?

Anna stopped jumping. "Cody isn't allowed to play there," she said.

Mrs. Forrand said, "She's right. Those boys are always trying to get Cody to do stunts." Her eyebrows leapt a half inch. "Has he been there the *whole* time? Since this morning?"

We all checked the clock. Noon. Perhaps he'd never been cold at all, but sitting, warm, inside the McManus house.

Hopkins said, "Should we call an ambulance?"

Mrs. Forrand seemed dazed. She asked, "Can I see him first? I want to see him."

"Okay. Hopkins, who's with Cody?" I asked.

"Officer Dix and a neighbor volunteer, Mr. Phelps. You want me to send 'em back here?"

"We'll go to them. You stay here and recall all the volunteers."

Hopkins said, "Will do." He gave me a smile. It was hard not to feel good. We'd found the missing kid, safe and sound, two weeks before Christmas.

Anna zipped her quilted purple coat. "Should I bring Sammy?" she asked.

"Who's Sammy?" I asked.

Mrs. Forrand said, "Cody's favorite stuffed toy. It's a raccoon. His Uncle Greg gave it to him."

Anna said, "He's not really our uncle."

"He's Pete's best friend," Mrs. Forrand said. "Cody adores Greg.

Anna, let's leave Sammy here. Cody can play with him when he comes home."

Mrs. Forrand directed me to the McManus house. Inside, Dix stood with Mr. Phelps. They watched three boys, seated on sofas. Crumbs and juice boxes littered the coffee table. "Cody!" Anna called, bounding into the room ahead of us. She stopped short. "Where's Cody?"

"Right here." Mr. Phelps pointed to the youngest boy, who was drinking from a juice box. He had brown hair and eyes.

"That's not Cody," Anna said, outraged.

Mrs. Forrand stared at the boy. The expression in her eyes wasn't one of love.

"If that's not Cody, who is it?" Dix asked. He looked to me. I had nothing.

"It's Brian McManus," Mrs. Forrand said. Her voice was colder than the wind outside.

"*You* said it was Cody," Dix said to Mr. Phelps, who had gone goggle-eyed.

"He said he was." Mr. Phelps gestured at Brian McManus. "I don't know Cody that well. They look alike."

The two older boys erupted into laughter. The tallest, perhaps twelve, clutched his stomach. Mrs. Forrand walked over and seized his ear. She pulled upward; he yelped. "Ow! Let me go!" He stood.

"Not until you tell me what's going on. Where's Cody?" She twisted his ear.

He screamed. "Agh! I don't know. *I don't*. We heard people were looking for him, and we thought it would be funny to pretend Brian was Cody."

The middle boy scanned the room, searching for an escape route. There wasn't one. "We thought it would be funny," he said in a small voice.

She released the oldest's ear. He cradled his head. "I'm calling my dad," he said.

Dix said, "Oh, we'll speak to your parents, son. Where are they, anyway?"

"Dad works at Con Edison. Ma had to check on Aunt Cindy. She's supposed to be home soon."

"So they left you three alone here, huh?" Dix shook his head. "Wonderful."

"Where's Cody?" Anna asked.

"We don't know," Brian said. He slurped the last of his juice. "Really."

Neither did we. And I'd had Hopkins recall all the volunteers. Fuck.

"Did you finish searching your area?" I asked Dix.

"We had two more houses and yards. Plus one shed," he said.

"Mr. Phelps, report back at the Forrand house. Thanks for your help."

"You're stopping the search?" Mrs. Forrand yelled.

"No," I told her. "Dix, finish searching your area. Then come back here and tell Mrs. McManus what a *help* her boys have been."

"My pleasure," he said. "Boys, it looks like Christmas might be cancelled."

Over the complaints of the McManus clan, I said, "Mrs. Forrand, I'll take you and Anna home. We'll re-coordinate there."

"You boys are bad," Anna said. She stood before Brian. The boy they'd passed off as Cody. He couldn't meet her gaze. "I hope Santa skips your house."

The middle boy, eyes glued to the ground, snorted. "Santa's not—"

"Hey!" Dix yelled.

Anna stared at the boy. "I know Santa's not real. I've known it for years. I'm not stupid." She turned to walk away. Pivoted and said, "Not like you."

Chaos reigned outside the Forrands' house. Teams of volunteers hurled questions. We hadn't found Cody? But we'd called them in. Said we'd found him. They'd come back, and now we were going to send them out again? They had kids to watch, dogs to walk, driveways to clear. Underneath it all was a tidal shift. With the weather worsening and no sign of Cody, it was clear that they no longer bet on finding a live child. And of course none of them wanted to find a corpse. I paired Hopkins with Billy. Put them in charge of finding which zones had been left unexplored. We'd send the neighbor volunteers home. The police would search the remaining areas.

Mr. Forrand appeared beside my car, hat missing, hair wet. "I heard what happened with those McManus boys. I'm going to sue their parents!"

"I understand you're upset, sir."

"Upset! Those little shits cost us precious time. Half the volunteers are headed home. Cody's been gone over five hours. No one is looking for him. You don't have children, but if you did—"

"Sir, I need to reorganize the search."

"If you hadn't bungled this search to begin with, Cody might be home."

It was fear talking. His son might be dead. Yet his words rankled. Should I have dispatched teams faster? Not redrawn the maps? I should've made sure it was Cody at the Beech Street house before I recalled the volunteers. But who could've predicted those kids would pull such a prank?

"Excuse me, Mr. Forrand, I need to call in." I got in my car. He stood beside it, eyes scanning the whitewashed world. I picked up my handheld and asked to speak to Finnegan. He'd better be back from Sweet Dreams.

"Chief, you need a cell phone," Finnegan said when he came on line.

"Yeah, yeah." I'd been told this by the mayor and the selectmen. Were they willing to foot the bill? Nope. "Look. Cody Forrand is still missing. Some brats in the neighborhood pretended one of them was Cody, and we called off the search. Too soon. Now I've got the neighborhood searchers packing it in. How many men are at the station?"

"Four, but they're all out. There was an accident on Main. Three cars. Plus a medical emergency. Old guy shoveling. Probably heart attack."

"Can we get the staties? Maybe a helicopter? This kid won't survive out here."

"Have you considered that he isn't out there? Maybe someone took him?"

"I've got no evidence he was snatched. Ask more neighboring towns to keep an eye out, will you?"

"Sure. I'll try the staties too, but blizzards stretch 'em thin. They might not be able to assist." He sounded aggrieved. No one liked a missing-child case.

"If you can't reach me, call Hopkins. He's at the Forrands' house."

"Of course he is. While the rest of you get snowed on."

Finnegan's teeth weren't chattering either.

Mr. Forrand had moved away from my car. I got inside his house without attracting his attention. In the kitchen, Mrs. Forrand hovered by Hopkins, who tapped a map. "Here," he said. "They came back when we said he'd been found."

I looked over his shoulder. "Is that the only area left to explore?" It was nearly three miles away. Lots of houses. "That and here," Hopkins tapped the map with a pencil eraser. "I sent Klein to check them out. He's due back any minute."

I said, "Finnegan's going to call the staties. See if we can get a helicopter."

"In this weather?" Billy asked. Mrs. Forrand was on the verge of tears. I jerked my head toward her and gave him a death glare.

I said, "We've asked neighboring police to keep an eye out. Billy, head back. Give Finnegan a copy of Cody's picture for distribution. Help make calls."

"You don't need me to search?" He unfolded himself from the chair. His cheeks were still red, but he had energy reserves. Blessed are the young, for they are fit.

"I'll take the last area. Send the others back to the station. Hopkins, stay here and write up your notes."

Jessica, Mrs. Forrand's sister, entered the kitchen as Billy exited. "Hey, what's going on? You're leaving?" she asked. "Aren't you going to go back out and search?"

I took the map from Hopkins. "I'm checking the last unsearched area," I told her. "After that, we need to regroup and see if we can get more state resources."

"If he's out there and you leave . . ." she lowered her voice, "he could die."

"If we can get a helicopter, we can search a wider area."

She looked bedraggled. "Fine, but make sure you keep us updated. They're losing their minds." Mrs. Forrand wept quietly by the sink. Jessica rubbed her back and murmured, "Stay strong, Jane. Cody needs you."

Another two inches of snow had fallen. I had to clear the rear window and windshield of my car. I eased it onto the road using a combination of speed and prayer. *Hey, God. You listening? Take your finger out of your ear and let's do this.*

The area to be searched had plenty of houses. No one had seen Cody. I asked people with basement doors and outside access to look inside. They obliged but found nothing—except one woman who shouted, "Oh! He did buy the necklace!" She'd found her Christmas present early. I rubbed crusted snow from car windows and peered inside. My fingers throbbed. The snow was over my boots, soaking my pants. Cody would be in worse shape. Only he wouldn't feel it. *He's not feeling anything. Six hours. A healthy kid couldn't survive this. And Cody wasn't a healthy kid.*

"Shut up," I told myself.

I checked under porches and in garages. My nose dripped as I trudged through snow to check another shed. The door was ajar. Inside, I saw red. Cody was wearing red. I pushed the stiff door a few inches so I could squeeze inside. Two filthy windows failed to let in the dim light. I walked toward the red, avoiding a mower and a rake. Smacked my leg into a large table. I edged closer. It was a coat, hanging from a nail. I picked it up. Too much fabric. Too big. Hell. I stumbled outside. The snow had quieted the world.

What if he was somewhere out here, buried under a drift? We'd need the medical examiner. A cold flake attacked my temple. *As long as it wasn't Damien Saunders. Please let them send someone else.*

Four weeks ago, I'd have been happy to see Damien. Was happy, when he invited me to a restaurant just across the Massachusetts border. I'd thought he was being protective of my reputation. When I showed up, he sat at a table in the back with five others, three men and two women. One look at Kate, with her butch haircut and flannel shirt, and I knew this wasn't a date. It was an initiation, into a club I didn't want to join.

They called themselves GALP, Gay and Lesbian Police. Three, including Damien and me, were from Connecticut; three were from Massachusetts; and one was from Rhode Island. They sometimes met at each other's houses, but not often. They were paranoid their colleagues would see out-of-state cars in their driveways and ask questions. The Rhode Island officer, Sally, said she'd been given a polygraph and asked if she was gay during her hiring process. Damien listened to their fears and smiled gently. That smile made me want to tip the table, watch the silverware clash to the ground, the glasses spill foam onto the floor.

The cop from Hartford, Lou, asked what it was like for me, now, at work.

"Fine," I said. Damien pursed his lips. He knew about the magazine incident. "I mean, they're not throwing me a pride parade or anything. I don't want them to."

Then they spiraled off into what *they* wanted. To be able to attend events with their boyfriends and girlfriends; to be able to train officers on how to handle young gay offenders; to receive backup on dangerous calls. Because if your fellow officers knew you were gay, would they come? Some hadn't in the past. Everyone had horror stories.

I leaned back, drank my beer, and watched Damien. He wanted me to join the flock, to help other gay officers.

They were cops. They read my resistance, felt my anger and confusion. They all said, "Hope to see you next time." Only Sally had the fear, or courage, to ask, "You're not going to say anything, about us?"

"No. I would never do that." She didn't know me. I didn't blame her for asking.

In the parking lot, Damien approached me. His scar was white on his tanned face. How was he tan? I didn't care how or why. I didn't care at all. "Thomas," he said. I'd told him to call me Thomas because no one else did. I'd been stupid. "Thomas, I'm sorry. I thought you'd be happy to meet some fellow officers, but I get the impression—"

"Next time you want me to join a club, ask. Don't make me drive a hundred miles to listen to the gay version of the 'I Have a Dream' speech."

"I just thought listening to their stories might make you . . ."

"What?" I said.

"More sympathetic," he finished.

He was finding fault with me. Him. The guy who'd made me drive all the way out here, thinking it was a date. He'd lied, essentially. Fuck him. I didn't need his goddamn disappointment. I had plenty of my own.

Snow dripped down my neck. The cold made me shake. I'd have to return to the station. With no idea where Cody was. In the car, I drank the last of the water and wished for another bottle. I flexed my stiff fingers and exhaled a gust of frozen air. Time to pack it in. Head to the station and refocus the search. Should I head back and tell the Forrands? Or give Hopkins the honor? My toes stung. Fuck it. Let Hopkins break the news. He'd been warm all day.

CHAPTER FOUR

At my office desk, wearing dry socks, I'd hoped things would seem less bleak. And they might've, if a state police officer hadn't been cataloging all of my search errors over the phone. His complaints included that I hadn't contacted the state police soon enough and I hadn't contacted any news agencies. I'd assumed that Cody had gone off on his own. That he hadn't been snatched. I'd allowed these assumptions to drive the search. I'd gotten the dog involved too late. I'd asked for a helicopter when all available copters had been dispatched.

Instead of telling him I'd pitched the idea of contacting the press; instead of confessing that I hadn't known we'd had a search dog; and instead of asking how I could know the helicopters' availability, I asked, "What do you suggest we do now?"

"Get the parents on TV, pronto. Send men to any house where you got no response. Put that kid's face everywhere. Do it and do it big. Because if this goes bad, you don't want it to look like you didn't put in the effort." My fingers and toes throbbed from exposure, and this guy thought I hadn't put in the effort? "Chief, this is going to go one of two ways. You'll find the kid or you won't. If you don't, or if the kid is dead, people won't blame the parents for letting him play outside. They'll blame you."

I put Dix on flyer duty with Klein. Dix had kids. He knew what we needed. "My daughter, Cara, had a school report and she insisted on these plastic sleeve things. They'll protect the flyers from the snow." I sent Billy to check the houses where we'd failed to rouse anyone. Hopkins was in charge of telling the Forrands we wanted them to make a public appeal. I was in charge of getting TV coverage.

You'd have thought it would be easy. Missing kid in a blizzard. Networks live to cover that stuff, right? Except today some famous Hollywood couple had split. The actor had been cheating on his wife with his young co-star. The movie they'd starred in was about an extramarital affair. "Hollywood is three thousand miles away," I told the guy at Channel Four. "This boy is local, and he needs help."

He said, "I'm sorry, but people care about this gossip. They eat it up. Besides, we've got deadlines. Maybe if you'd come to us sooner." The news crew couldn't reach the Forrands in time. Not with the roads the way they were. I finally got someone at Channel 7 to agree to run it on the seven o'clock news. The others would pick it up for the ten o'clock report. When most folks would be in bed, exhausted from shoveling.

A copy of Cody's photo sat on my desk. I pinched the bridge of my nose. We had to keep looking. He might be somewhere we hadn't searched. Warm and safe, but scared.

You don't believe that.

All the men who should've left during shift change stayed. They called other stations. Put up flyers. Checked more houses and garages and sheds. Finnegan insisted he could help; that he could work the break-in and the Cody search. Mrs. Dunsmore had dinner delivered. She warned me the selectmen would grumble at the expense. "Which is why I classified it as a training," she said with a smile I'd come to fear most days.

"Thanks. You should go home." She'd gotten in earlier than I had.

She rubbed her crucifix and looked toward the window. The storm had died. A bitter cold had set in. "Do you think we'll find him alive?" she asked.

I rubbed my hair. It had dried stiff. "He's been gone ten and a half hours."

"Do you think someone grabbed him?" She'd worked at the Idyll Police Station for twenty-nine years. She knew what happened to kids who were snatched.

"I hope not." If you ask cops to rate their most hated criminals, pedophiles are number one. I was no exception. Four years ago, I'd had a case. A guy took his girlfriend's daughter to Central Park. Claimed the girl took off after her balloon floated away, and he lost her. A dog walker found her body three days later, off a path in the Ramble. Rick, my partner on the force, had said it was the boyfriend from the get-go. The boyfriend always dated women with young daughters. Was always such "a help" with babysitting. Never minded braiding the girls' hair or taking them to the movies. He almost got away with it. We had no forensics, no witnesses. Until Rick remembered the girl loved ponies. We went to the stables in Central Park. Found out the scumbag had brought the girl there the day she disappeared. A young woman working there recalled when she saw them. It was two hours after the guy said the girl ran off. We got a search warrant. Found the evidence we needed to prove he'd raped and killed her. Rick might not have ended on a high note, but he got justice for that girl. Sarah. Her name was Sarah.

"Chief, you okay?" Mrs. Dunsmore asked. She stood in front of my desk. "The boys have the TV set up," she said.

Most of the guys were gathered around the small set. "Hopkins, they didn't want your ugly mug on cam?" Finnegan called. Hopkins flipped him the bird.

On-screen, the smiling co-hosts bantered about the storm with the weatherman, who promised, "We haven't seen the last of this front. Expect more snow in the coming week." The men gathered around the TV groaned. The male co-host put on his somber face. "In urgent news, tonight we bring you the story of a child in danger." The screen was overlaid with the words "Child in Danger" in bright red letters. A loud siren sounded.

"Is this a segment?" Hopkins asked.

"Yup," Dix said. "Child in Danger. Last one was a runaway from New Haven."

"Jesus wept," Finnegan muttered.

Klein said, "I think they found that runaway." Dix shushed him.

"Tonight, we bring you news of a local boy who has gone missing." Cody's picture filled the screen. "Cody Forrand, age six, was last seen outside his parents' house this morning in Idyll." Cody's picture was whisked to the upper right corner of the screen. The co-host frowned. "Young Cody isn't just any boy. He has a rare medical condition. Congenital insensitivity to pain with anhidrosis, or CIPA. It makes him vulnerable to cold temperatures. We spoke to his parents, Peter and Jane Forrand." They aired footage of Mr. and Mrs. Forrand, who were sitting on their sofa. They'd slapped makeup on Mrs. Forrand and styled her hair. She looked better, but worried. No makeup could conceal that.

"If anyone has seen Cody," she said, "please call. He's our little boy, and we just want him home." Her face crumpled and she squeezed her husband's arm. He grimaced.

"Please," Mr. Forrand said. "Cody's six years old. He was wearing a red coat and blue snow pants. If you saw him, or," he swallowed, "if you have him. Please. Bring him back to us. We miss him. We love him."

The male co-host's face appeared on screen. He said, "Police looked for Cody this morning but called off the search due to today's blizzard."

"The fuck?" Dix said. "Did he say we stopped searching because of the snow?"

"Of all the made-up stories," Hopkins said.

"We sound like pussies."

The anchorman recited a telephone number for people to call if they'd spotted Cody. "What's that number?" I asked. "That's not ours!" I tapped the TV screen.

Klein said, "I think it's the TV station's number, Chief. Looks familiar."

"Why? Why didn't they give out *our* number?" I yelled.

No one knew. No one was happy about it. We had people experienced at taking tips calls. Who did they have answering their number? Probably a college intern.

"Why did they do that?" Billy asked. Even the rookie knew it was bad.

"I think maybe the Forrands are upset with us," Hopkins said.

"What? Why?" I asked.

"Well, first we took a while to get mobilized, and then we called off the search because we thought we found him."

I said, "And we went back and searched all the areas after we realized the McManus kid wasn't Cody. We had to come here and call out to the staties and news stations. He wouldn't be on the news if we were outside now!"

"It's their boy, Chief," Mrs. Dunsmore said. "They're beside themselves with fear. You can't take anything they say or do now to heart."

Yet I did. We all did. After the news report, I saw men crumpling pieces of paper, digging the toes of their boots into the carpet. Frowning at the phones. It was bad enough, not finding the kid. We'd all wanted to bring him safe to his parents. We'd failed, and now we'd been made to look like the bad guys on the seven o'clock news.

Phones rang. I clapped my hands. "Let's get to it, guys! I want an update on what we've heard from neighboring towns and any likely leads in fifteen."

"Chief," Mrs. Dunsmore said. "Mayor on line four."

"What's this about a missing boy? Why didn't I know of this?" On an outrage scale of one to ten, Mayor Mike Mitchell was at twenty.

"We were up to our necks searching."

"It's on the news! And what's this about you stopping the search because—"

"They got it wrong. Mrs. Dunsmore will see that they don't repeat it."

He harrumphed. "She'll get it sorted. I want to be updated, Chief. We had that murder, and now this. Doesn't look good for the town."

"Kids go missing, all the time." My phone beeped.

"Not kids with what he's got, that medical condition. We have to get ahead—"

"Excuse me, sir. I've got another call. Might be the staties."

"Oh, good. Maybe they can send help. Perhaps—"

I hit the button, cutting short his bright ideas. "Chief Lynch," I said.

"Chief, this is Hauser." My scoldy statie. "Saw the news. Christ. What'd you do to piss off the anchors?"

"No idea. The parents may be upset."

"Well, get them on your side. Quick. This kind of thing lives on in people's minds. People lose jobs over this." This guy's motivational speeches were awful.

"Any word on a helicopter?" I asked.

"Tied up. Besides, he'd have to be lying atop a pile of snow for us to find him. No. What I've done is run you a report of local pedophiles. Faxed it over."

I told him about the mixed-up phone numbers on the news.

"They gave the TV station's number? God almighty. You sure you didn't arrest one of the news anchor's kids or something? Well, good luck. I'm gonna go home and dig out my driveway. Unless my son did it." He laughed. "Not likely."

His report was in the fax tray. The papers smelled hot and inky. He'd defined "local" broadly. One name had an Idyll address: Andrew Trabucco. I took it to Finnegan. He handed me a paper. "Info about the person from this morning. Single guy. Here's his car info." Right, my prank caller. I'd forgotten. "Oh, and the Sweet Dreams break-in. Man, what a mess. Whoever did it was thorough. Smashed all the glass jars to bits. Tore down some of the shelves from the walls."

I'd forgotten about the break-in. My brain's focus was all Cody. "Any leads?"

He blew a smoke ring away from me. "We dusted for prints. Got a few. The graffiti wasn't friendly. 'Leave before we kill you.'"

"Whoa." This was serious.

I handed him half the faxed sheets. "Local kiddie diddlers. Let's check 'em out, starting with Andrew Trabucco." I sat across from him. Wright wouldn't be happy about my ass in his seat, but I didn't care.

He held the papers away and squinted. "You need glasses," I said.

"You sound like my ex," he said.

"Which one?" He collected ex-wives the way other people collect baseball cards.

"Linda. Number two. She works at an eyeglasses store. Probably wants to sell me a pair, get a commission." He shook the page. "Andrew Trabucco? Never heard of him."

"Probably the way he likes it. Oh, and we should check one more guy. Young computer teacher lives near the Forrands. Mike Calloway. He acted shifty when I spoke to him, and a neighbor saw Cody near his house this morning."

We checked databases and made some calls, following the life and times of pedophiles. After an hour, Finnegan said, "Imagine some rando snatches Cody Forrand. It's gonna get weird fast."

"Weirder than usual?" I asked.

"Well, yeah. Cody doesn't feel pain, right? So nothing this guy does will hurt him. That might freak the guy out."

"Maybe. It doesn't mean he'll let him go. He might get angry."

Finnegan laced his hands behind his head. "This isn't going to end pretty, is it?"

I wanted to believe it could. But I didn't see how. "Not likely." I set the papers down. He said, "Our boy Andrew Trabucco has quite the résumé. Indecent exposure, possessing child porn, and sexual assault of a male minor. All by age twenty-one."

"How old is he now?" I asked.

"Um." Finnegan did the math. "Thirty-three."

"Why didn't we know about him?" Guys like Trabucco were required to register when they moved so that police could keep tabs.

"He got out in '87, before the registry started."

I glanced at my watch—10:30 p.m. "I'll drive by his house. See what I see."

"If you don't see anything?" he asked.

"We'll drop by tomorrow, bright and early. Any other candidates?"

"Nope. Most of 'em are back inside."

"Mine too. One is dead." I stood and stretched. My arms ached. "You okay reviewing the others?"

He nodded. "See you in the morning?" His way of asking if I needed him.

I did. "If not sooner. Goodnight."

A fit of coughing broke out behind me. Billy stood, one hand on a desk, bent over, hacking. "Billy, you okay?" I reached out a hand.

He shrank back. "Fine. Probably nothing."

"The same nothing half the men have? Head home. Get some sleep."

He pushed himself up. "I'm good." Another coughing spasm tore through him.

"Go home. You're sick. We can't afford to lose you. Rest. Take medicine."

He wiped his nose like a little kid. "Okay. I'll be in tomorrow. I'm covering for Morris." Of course he was.

I wished the men good night and thanked them for staying. They shrugged off the praise. The outside air was single-digits cold. My boogers froze stiff and sharp. Trabucco lived at Haywood Court, four blocks from the Forrands. I turned the radio on. Bing Crosby sang "White Christmas." I wrenched the dial. "Not now, Bing." I'd had enough snow to last a lifetime.

One window was lit at Andrew Trabucco's house. In his driveway was a car with a frosting layer of snow on it. I popped my car door, the sound loud as a gunshot, then crept across the road, my boots wet within seconds. I wanted to peek in the side window, which meant wading through two feet of snow. I paused at the edge of the lawn. Fuck it. No guts, no glory. I hopped onto the snow. The top layer had iced over. It was like walking through crème brûlée. A body passed near the window. I ducked. God, it was cold. Through the window I saw, atop a table, a cage. Inside was a brown rabbit. Along the room's far side was another cage, with a hamster wheel. Kids loved pets. That could be how he lured them in. "Want to see my hamster? You can feed him."

From the edge of the room, he appeared, tall and heavy. He wore a flannel shirt and khaki pants. He came toward me. I ducked and heard metal screeching. I counted to forty. Trabucco sat on the couch, the rabbit on his lap. He stroked the animal. I scanned the room for signs of Cody. A small coat or mittens or boots. Nothing. A tray supported a microwave dinner. Every few moments, Trabucco would stop petting the rabbit, lean forward, and fork food into his mouth.

I waited. Watched. My wet pants stiffened. My eyes burned. No evidence of Cody. Besides, how would he have snatched Cody? Out for a walk in a blizzard and he sees Cody and invites him to his house? Seemed unlikely now that I had eyes on Trabucco.

I crunched a path back to the car.

My driveway was full of snow. A shovel was propped beside the porch, only its wooden handle visible. I parked along the road. Absolutely against the post-storm parking ban. We ticketed for such infractions. The thought of picking up the shovel and clearing the driveway was absurd. I needed hot water. I needed rest. I needed my brain to stop asking, "Where's Cody?"

CHAPTER FIVE

I blinked against the bathroom's lighting, its pink and black tiles too much to bear at 1:30 a.m. I'd gotten two and a half hours of sleep. My face, puffy and shadowed, confirmed it. I had hung my uniform on the bathroom hook, but the shower's steam had failed to remove its wrinkles. My other uniform was at Suds, which didn't open for another ten hours. I packed a thermos of coffee, precaution against the tarry sludge the station coffee had reduced to at this hour. My gloves and hat rested against the baseboard heaters. I scooped them up. Dry, thank God. And so day two of the search for Cody Forrand began.

Clouds were glued onto the night sky and the air felt hard, like glass. My car seat creaked beneath me, frozen rigid. The radio gave news instead of carols. A tanker carrying heating oil had flipped over on Route 84 outside Waterbury. Cleanup crews were on site. People were asked to be on the lookout for a missing boy. Cody Forrand. Age six. Brown hair and eyes. Wearing a red coat. Last seen on Spring Street in Idyll. Great. If any insomniacs were listening, maybe we'd get a call.

Darryl, the dispatcher, greeted me. John Miller, of the Santa hat, had gone home.

Finnegan had also gone home. I looked over his notes. Next to Andrew Trabucco's name he'd written "Two Wheels since June '95." Two Wheels, the local bicycle shop. Must be where he worked.

In my office, I found an eight-page equipment survey. State purpose of equipment: handcuffs. Really? I had to explain handcuffs? I pushed the survey aside and made notes. Ms. Hart saw Cody at 7:50 a.m. She thought he'd been looking for something. Had he left the house carrying something? A toy or stuffed animal? What about Mr. Calloway, the teacher? Had we turned up anything there? I wrote, my pen clenched so hard that my palm cramped and I had to stop. After a few minutes, I was back at it. While I worked, the sky outside lightened to the color of a new bruise. I rolled my shoulders and stood. Time to look around the station.

Yankowitz came through the front door, carrying a large brown paper bag. A yeasty smell traveled with it. I followed the bag to the coffee machine. "What's inside?" I asked.

He jumped. "Whoa, Chief. Didn't see you there. Want a bagel?" A New Yorker born and bred, I had strong opinions about bagels. This one was too fat. It would be too chewy. Ah well, beggars can't be choosers.

He asked about Cody.

"No word yet." I sawed at the bagel with a plastic knife. It was like trying to saw a tree with a licorice rope. "Would it be any use to try again with Skylar?" I asked.

"Nah. There's a crust of ice over the snow. Ruins scent work." He pinched his lower lip. "There's a thaw due in four days."

We stood, eating warm bagels, thinking of the thaw, of the melting snow revealing Cody Forrand's corpse. I took another bite. "There's a pedophile who lives four blocks from the Forrands."

"Jesus. Really?"

"Yeah."

"I heard they started reporting the correct phone number for tips."

"Thank God," I muttered.

"Chief, phone call," someone behind me yelled.

I snagged another bagel and thanked Yankowitz.

"Chief, we got good news," said Hauser, the statie who gave only bad news. "We got hold of a helicopter. It'll head out your way at eight o'clock. I'm not sure how much help it will be. If he was out there long..."

"I know. We're checking the list of local sex offenders you sent."

"Good luck. Oh, and good work getting the TV stations on board. The other recaps were better."

"Thanks." That was down to Mrs. Dunsmore, but I'd take the credit. This guy thought I was clueless. I needed the boost.

I sniffed my shirt's pits. Maybe I could send someone to Suds. Then again, maybe the Forrands would be impressed by my lack of sleep or clean clothes when we met. I dialed them. Mrs. Forrand answered on the first ring, her voice two degrees away from hysterical. I told her about the helicopter. Hoped the good news would calm her.

"A helicopter?" she said. "Now? Where are they looking?"

I told her they'd scout an area miles wide, keeping their house at the center.

"Will it help? Your men stopped searching. Now you're sending a helicopter when he's been gone over twenty-four hours."

He hadn't been gone twenty-two hours, but I didn't contradict her. "Mrs. Forrand, my men never stopped searching. They're still searching for Cody."

"You put a bunch of signs on telephone poles. When no one in their right mind was outside yesterday to see them." Yet she had. Or someone had, and told her. I took a breath. She railed on, her voice climbing. We hadn't started looking soon enough. The first twenty-four hours were crucial in these cases. Those hours were gone.

Again, I swallowed a comment that it hadn't been a whole day. "How's 8:30 a.m.?" I asked. "We can come by and review what we know with you and your husband."

"I think we'd rather liaise with another officer," she said.

"Another officer? Officer Hopkins?"

She huffed. "Not him. Don't you have any female police officers?"

"I'm sorry. No." Why did she want a woman?

"Well, what about the young one?"

"Officer Thompson?" Billy? Our rookie? I wasn't sending a newbie into this quagmire. "I'll send Detective Wright." Wright was well dressed and professional.

"I hope he doesn't expect us to feed him." She hung up. The food comment was a dig at Hopkins. He'd snacked his way through their home. I'd have a word, later.

The shift changed. I shouted at everybody to circle up. Half the men looked like death, pale faces, red eyes, Billy among them. I told them the news about the copter. That made them smile. Wright, our full-time detective, wore a gray suit. His red tie a nice choice. His grimace ruined the picture.

"We'll run checks on local sex offenders and work the tips line. If anything looks promising, we'll search. Don't talk to the press, especially if they ask about calling off the search early. That didn't happen. I know that. You know that. Now let's see if we can't work a Christmas miracle." One or two guys kissed their medallions. Saint Michael on a chain.

I stopped by the card table where Joanne Devon sat. Joanne had worked the tips line on the North murder. She was good at sorting attention seekers from possible witnesses. I mouthed, "Anything?" at her. She held her hand up. Spoke into the phone. "Thank you, sir." She hung up. Her fingernails were painted silver today. "We're getting lots of calls. Mostly from folks who want to help. Can they help search for him?" She tapped her nails against the tabletop.

"So much snow fell. He'd be nearly impossible to find outside."

She frowned. "I know. Poor kid. I don't know what to hope for: that he got snatched and might be alive, or that he's passed on and isn't in pain."

"He never was in pain," I said.

"That's right. So bizarre. I didn't even know that was a thing. That CIPA. My daughter, she's a nurse. She said there's very few cases. It used to be if you had it you didn't make it past childhood." She bit her knuckle. We both thought the same thing. Maybe Cody hadn't survived childhood.

She handed me pink sheets. "Two seem possible. First was a boy, spotted about a mile from Cody's house around 9:00 a.m. Second was seen at 10:00 a.m. in a parked car at a gas station outside Rocky Hill. Right hair color and size. No coat."

I walked the tips to the detectives' pen and left them on Finnegan's desk. Wright walked backward when he saw me approach. He bumped into a whiteboard. Tried to play it off. "Finny says you went by this guy Trabucco's house last night?"

Finny. He and Finnegan had nicknames for each other. Everyone had a nickname. Billy was Kid or Slim or Hoops. Hopkins was Babe. He resembled Babe Ruth. Me? I was Chief. Always Chief.

"Yeah. I scoped his place from outside. No sign of Cody."

"Warrant?" he asked.

What part of "no sign of Cody" had failed to register? "No. Hey, I need you to stop by the Forrands' house at 8:30 a.m. Update them. They want someone who won't eat them out of house and home."

"Hopkins?" he guessed. I nodded.

"I need them updated, reassured, and I need to know if Cody was carrying anything when he left the house."

Billy appeared behind Wright's desk. "What can I do?" he asked. Wright gave him a look that would've made most men back away. Billy didn't.

"Check the location of the tips and plot them on the map." I pointed. "Use the little red dots." We'd mark the sightings in case there was a pattern.

"Chief, phone!" a baritone shouted.

Back in my office, I got my first reporter looking for an angle. Tim Clinton from the *Hartford Courant*. "Chief, is it true you called off the search for Cody Forrand?"

"No."

"Have you investigated whether this could be a kidnapping?" Tim sounded young and hungry, a dangerous combo.

"Do us a favor and put Cody's picture on your front page," I said.

"What would the headline be?" As if he expected me to provide content.

"'Have You Seen This Boy?' It's a classic. Also, to the point."

"How are the parents holding up?" he asked.

"Why don't you ask them?" I regretted saying it. It sounded flippant, and I didn't want him calling the Forrands. Not before Wright had spoken to them. "We're searching for Cody. Neighboring police are on alert. A helicopter is looking for him now."

"Now? Isn't it late for that?" he asked.

"Are you suggesting we *stop* looking for Cody Forrand?" I asked.

"Chief Lynch," he said. Paused. "You're *the* Chief Lynch, right? I didn't put two and two together when I got handed this story, but you're the gay police chief."

Not now. Now was really not the time. Months ago I got a lot of calls from reporters looking to do a story on me. I'd turned them all down in strong-enough language to discourage further attempts.

"I'll guarantee you front-page coverage of Cody Forrand if you'll give me an exclusive about you."

"No."

"Nothing sensational. Just a day in the life of the state's only gay police chief."

"You're really going to bargain a child's life for an exclusive about me?" I asked.

"Kid's probably dead, and if he isn't, you'll want to do everything you can to ensure he gets home, huh?"

"I'd like to talk to *your* chief," I said.

"He'll just try the same deal."

I hung up the phone and stared at the receiver. Fuck. Had I just endangered Cody by not making the deal? Should I call back? No. I didn't have time to give interviews about my life. It was on the newspaper to do right by Cody.

Finnegan had returned. He sat, loafers propped on his desk. His hands shook on his pen though. I think we all felt it. Rattled. We wanted Cody Forrand home, safe. We doubted we could get it done. We'd slept a fraction of the night. We were exhausted and sick, and no good news was coming.

"Any joy?" I asked.

"Tip number one was a bust. I spoke to the caller, and the boy he saw was taller and older than Cody. Apparently he hadn't seen Cody's picture. He must've heard about a missing boy and thought 'Hey, I saw a boy yesterday.'"

I kneaded my forehead with my fist. "Do I even want to hear about number two?"

He swung his feet off the desk and onto the floor. "You betcha. Second caller saw a boy matching Cody's description at a gas station. He was inside a car, holding a box. She didn't see the driver."

"And?"

"And when I spoke to her, she told me she wasn't sure it was him. She was pretty sure it wasn't because his clothes didn't match the descriptions. She'd wanted to help. So she'd talked herself into thinking the boy she saw was Cody."

I picked up a telephone book and hurled it at Wright's desk. It clanked against the side. Fell to the floor. "God save me from witnesses!"

Finnegan nodded. "Amen."

A voice yelled, "We've got a chief call!"

Finnegan shouted, "I've got it." Then, "Which line?"

"Two," the voice yelled. Was it Johnson yelling?

"Isn't it for me?" I asked.

Finnegan snatched up the receiver. "Idyll Police Station. Yes?" He scribbled on paper. Was he transcribing the call? "Uh huh. Wow. Okay. When do you think that will be?" He wrote some more. Hung up the phone. Punched *69. *A chief call.* He wrote down the number.

"Was that what I think it was?" I asked.

"Hmmm?" He wouldn't look at me.

"Was someone calling to share opinions about me?"

"You're a busy man, Chief. This wasn't important." Something familiar about this. What? I scratched my neck. It clicked. Yesterday, Finny had me tell Mrs. Dunsmore he'd tracked the number and logged the call.

"How many of these have we been getting?" I asked.

"A few more than you have at home." So he knew why I'd had him track phone numbers recently. Of course. He was doing the same damn thing.

"How many?"

"About forty."

"Forty." I felt like a stone was stuck in my throat.

"Some are repeat callers though, so probably only twenty-five, really." Was that supposed to make me feel better?

Billy came around the corner, map in hand. The red dots went as far west as New York City and as far north as Portland, Maine. Most sightings were local. Six ranged outside Idyll, north and west. Rocky Hill. The gas station. The witness had recanted. I tried to pull the dot off. It clung. I pulled harder. The dot came off, and with it, a quarter inch of map. "Fuck!" My shout made Billy jump.

Wright said, "Problem?" He stood nearby, hands in the pockets of a long wool coat. Dove gray. His wife had good taste.

"All I've got is problems. Billy, fetch me some aspirin. My head's in a vice."

"Maybe I got something to cheer you up," Wright said, unwinding his scarf. Billy stopped, wanting to hear news.

"Did you convince the Forrands we aren't sabotaging the search for their son?"

"Nope."

"Thanks," I said.

He set his coat carefully on his chair. "Not that it matters much."

Finnegan frowned. "Why's that?"

Wright smiled. "They found him. They found Cody Forrand."

CHAPTER SIX

We threw questions at Wright like darts at a board. "Where was he?" and "Is he okay?" and "Who found him?" He clasped his hands together. Ready to tell us a story.

"Call came in," he checked his watch, "twenty-five minutes ago. Grocery employee in Canton found him outside the store. Alone. They took him to a hospital."

"Are we sure it's him?" I asked. I wouldn't fall for a second false identification.

"Cops seemed sure," Wright said.

"Did he say how he got there? Who took him?" Finnegan asked.

Wright said, "Don't know. I didn't take the call. The father did."

"Why didn't you go with them?" I asked.

"I offered. They declined. Said Cody was found and they didn't need the police."

"What about who took him?" Billy asked. "We have to find him, right?"

"Which hospital?" I asked.

"Children's in Hartford. Cody's specialists are there."

"Wright, why don't you share the news," I said. He hadn't earned the announcement. He hadn't searched yesterday, and he'd only gone to the Forrands because I'd made him. On the other hand, it might grease our wheels. Our relationship required a lot of grease.

Wright's update was met with cheers and whoops and mutters of "Thank God." More kissed medallions. I stopped by Joanne's desk. "Guess I can head home, huh?" She'd driven on icy roads to get here early, only to leave two hours later.

"Thanks," I said.

"No problem, Chief." It hit me then. Joanne's attitude hadn't changed, not since my big reveal at Suds, when I informed the station I was gay. She treated me as she had before. Maybe she had a gay cousin.

Billy handed me a bottle of aspirin. My headache had receded. I set the bottle down. "Where's our map?" I asked. Billy fetched it.

"Why's there a hole in it?" Wright asked.

Finnegan looked at me. He said, "Witness problem."

Canton, where Cody was found, was southwest of us. "How far to drive here?" I tapped Canton on the map. Wright said, "Forty, forty-five minutes, in good weather." I traced the most direct route with my index finger. We had two dots that matched the route. One in Wallingford and one where the hole was. The gas stop in Rocky Hill.

Finnegan got there first. "Maybe that gas station sighting was legit."

"What sighting?" Wright asked. Finnegan explained.

"He wasn't wearing the right clothes," Billy said.

"Maybe the kidnapper made him change. We should check the description against what he's wearing today," Wright said.

I said, "I'm going to the hospital. We need to ask Cody who took him."

"Can't the Canton cops do that?" Billy asked. Wright snorted. Finnegan laughed.

Wright said, "They've got a part-time force supplemented by state police, and they've won the Big Fish Award twice, back-to-back years."

"Big Fish Award?" I asked.

"The Big Fish is awarded each year, for falling for the most outrageous story. Waterbury won for sending a team to check out reports of a shark in Hop Brook Lake."

"You're kidding me," I said.

"Nope," Finnegan said. "Apparently none of 'em knew sharks prefer salt water."

"Why did the Canton cops win?" Billy asked.

Finnegan said, "They believed the president needed an escort through town, on Halloween."

Wright said, "A neighboring station pranked them. But honestly, they fell for it. If the president were coming to visit your Podunk town, you'd hear about it before the day of. The story was he was bringing his grandkids trick-or-treating."

"Reagan?" I guessed.

"Bush," Finnegan said.

Wright said, "We're dealing with cops who fell for that story." He gave that a second's thought. "I'll go with you."

"Fine. Finnegan, check out the bike shop. See about Mr. Trabucco's schedule yesterday."

We walked outside. I flexed my gloved fingers. Looked ahead. Stopped. Wright collided against me. "Whoa. What's up?" He stepped off of me as if I was on fire.

The driver's side of my car had been tagged with Day-Glo orange spray paint. Sprayed over the police emblem and the words *Police Chief* were three letters that took up the six feet of the door of my Crown Victoria:

FAG!

I removed my glove and touched the paint. Dry. I walked to the other side. Unmarked. The spine of the *F* was a trembling line. Done in a hurry. I knelt to look under the car. "Do you see a can?"

"What?" Wright said.

"A spray can. Do you see one?" I wanted evidence. Wright crunched around the lot. My knee was on the cold wet ground. My eyes searched the snowy lot. Footprints. I'd stomped all over the place. Damn it.

"No can," he said.

I didn't want to get up, to see pity in Wright's eyes. Bad enough with Finny and the phone calls. I stood and brushed the snow from my knee.

Wright said, "Some asshole comes onto police property and tags our car? Oh, no, no. This won't stand." Wright might be homophobic, but he was a cop. The golden rule of not fucking with cops trumped any feelings he had about me.

"Let's go," I said. "We'll deal with this when we get back."

"You sure?" he asked. I nodded. Cody Forrand's kidnapping was more important than my graffiti. Besides, I wanted to put time and distance between my car and me.

Wright drove like it was second nature. Probably was. I'd not owned a car until I came to Idyll. Oh, hell. The mayor. He'd acted like giving me a car was a big favor. Was there any way to keep the graffiti news from reaching him? No. Billy was his nephew. Besides, everyone in Idyll talked. He'd know soon enough.

"Your kids are at Idyll Elementary," I said. "They have a computer teacher? Mr. Calloway."

"Maybe. Joshua has a class in computers. Why?"

"He acted weird when I asked about Cody. Wouldn't look at the photo."

Wright changed lanes. "Great. Not enough I have to worry my kids might get snatched off the streets. Now I have to worry about pervy teachers?" He exhaled loudly. "Idyll was supposed to be better for them." Better schools, less crime, and a lot whiter than his old neighborhood. When he'd first joined the Idyll force, locals reported that a black man had stolen a cop car. I was surprised he'd moved here, better schools or no.

The Connecticut Children's Medical Center was an odd building. A half circle of brick and glass jutted out front. We hurried through automatic doors, into a large reception area. Holiday decorations hung on the walls. We waited behind a father who held a sleeping girl. Her chubby face rested on his shoulder. She snored softly. "I've paged Dr. Cansalitz," the brassy-haired receptionist said to him. "He should be here soon." The father edged away, his steps careful and slow.

Wright showed his badge and asked for Cody Forrand. The receptionist tapped at a computer. Frowned at the boxy monitor. "Room 372."

Inside the elevator, I asked, "So what do you think happened? Did the kidnapper panic?"

Wright said, "Maybe the press coverage freaked him out. He decided to dump Cody before he got caught."

"Makes him about a thousand times smarter than most kidnappers," I said.

We got off on floor three and took a left.

He said, "No doubt. What I don't get is why yesterday? Everyone knew about the blizzard. Must've been hard, driving out there. And why dump him at a grocery store? That's dangerous. People around. Not like some empty lot."

We reached room 372 and scanned the hallway. "Where's the cop?" Wright said. We stepped into the room. It had one bed. I hadn't pegged the Forrands as able to afford a single. Despite its privacy, it was crowded with family and staff. On the bed reclined a small boy. His left hand had an IV line tube snaking from it. His hair looked dirty. No obvious injuries. He wore a hospital gown and was tucked under a thin white blanket.

"You must be Cody." I stepped to the foot of his bed.

"Who are you?" he asked.

"I'm the chief of police in Idyll. This is Detective Wright." Wright waved.

Cody said, "He doesn't look like a policeman."

I hoped he meant Wright's uniform, not his skin color. "Wright gets to wear whatever he wants because he's a detective," I said.

"And because I want to look good, unlike him," Wright said, jerking his thumb toward my dirty, wrinkled uniform. Cody giggled.

"How are you feeling?" I asked.

"Hungry," he said.

"Do you want some food, baby?" Mrs. Forrand asked. She brushed his hair back. He squirmed. Mrs. Forrand asked if he could have lunch. A doctor looked up. "Sure. We'll get you a menu." He told the nurse to fetch it. "We" was apparently a royal term.

"Cody, can you tell us about yesterday?" I asked.

Mr. Forrand said, "He's spoken to the police. He doesn't recall much. He was drugged."

"Drugged?" Wright asked.

One of the doctors said, "We'll know more when the tests come back."

"Cody, do you know how you got here?" Wright asked, notebook out.

"In an ambulance."

"And before that?"

"On the boat."

Mrs. Forrand said, "He means the boat outside the grocery. The kind you feed quarters into and ride. That's where they found him." She took a shaky breath.

"And before that?" Wright asked. "Before the boat?"

"A car," Cody said. "Do you have a gun?"

"Sure do," Wright said. "Do you know what kind of car?"

Cody picked at the tube in his hand. His father said, "Careful, Cody."

A nurse checked the IV. "It's fine," she said. "Just leave it in, okay, honey?" She patted his arm.

"What color was the car you were in?" Wright asked.

"Silver."

His mother broke in. "He said it was white, before you came."

Cody tilted his head. "Where's my Lego truck?"

Mrs. Forrand said, "Honey, I'm sure Santa hasn't forgotten."

"Cody, buddy, who was driving the car you were in?" Wright asked.

"I want the Lego truck!" he yelled.

Wright looked at me. I gave a half shrug. No one seemed surprised by his outburst. Maybe they'd heard it before? "Did you have a Lego truck before?" I asked.

"Where is it? Why'd they take it away?" He looked around the room.

"I think Cody needs food," his mother said. A menu was produced. Mrs. Forrand leaned against his bed's railing and held it for him. "What looks good, sweetie?"

"French fries," he said.

"How about something to go with those, huh?" she suggested. Cody pouted. "How about chicken nuggets?"

"No." He whipped his head back and forth. My neck hurt just watching. His didn't, I realized. It couldn't.

"Honey, stop." His mother put her hand against his head. "Macaroni and cheese?"

Every suggestion was met with, "No," until they'd exhausted the entrées. Anna said, "I had chicken nuggets today." I'd forgotten she was present. She sat in a chair, a giant book on her lap. *Grimm's Fairy Tales*.

Cody said, "I want chicken nuggets."

Her mother gave Anna a weary smile.

The food order was placed. Chicken nuggets, French fries, and chocolate milk. With that squared, Wright began again. "Cody, what's your favorite TV show?"

"*Mighty Morphin Power Rangers*." He answered immediately.

"He likes the Red Ranger best," Anna added.

"Did the person who drove you in the car look like anyone you've seen on TV?" Smart. I wouldn't have thought to ask that.

Cody said, "It was a Mighty Morphin Power Ranger."

"The person looked like a Power Ranger?" Wright asked, his skepticism evident.

"He's still loopy," Mrs. Forrand said. "He kept talking about elves earlier."

Great. We'd have to re-interview him, once the drugs were out of his system.

"I want my Lego truck!" Cody wailed. He beat his hands against his legs.

"Baby, Christmas isn't for twelve days." Mrs. Forrand said. "Remember? We're going to make cookies for Santa and treats for the reindeers."

"Cody, how many people were in the car with you?" Wright asked.

Cody ignored the question and looked at his sister. "Read me a story," he said.

"Cody, buddy, can you tell me who was in the car?" Wright kept his voice even.

"My leg hurts!" Cody shrieked. Everyone's head snapped up at this.

"I thought he couldn't feel pain," I said.

"He can't," a balding doctor said. He stepped forward and asked, "Which leg?"

Cody hesitated. "That one." He pointed to his right leg.

"Cody, remember what we said about telling the truth?" the doctor asked. "About how important it is for us to know what's going on?"

"Yeeeees."

"Does your leg hurt?"

Cody shook his head. "No." He kicked his legs. "I'm hungry."

The doctor said, "Okay. We'll go check on your food." He turned to the nurse and jerked his head toward the door. Man, I needed a nurse.

"I think he's done here," Mr. Forrand said. He rubbed Cody's arm. "He needs rest."

"One more question," Wright said. "Cody, did you know the person in the car?"

"I think so," he said. "Yes."

"Who was it?" Wright's question was fast, urgent. Cody smiled, a weird Mona Lisa smile. Then he shook his head.

"I'm sorry," Mr. Forrand said, shoulders slumped. "Maybe later, when he's rested." He sounded tired. Probably hadn't slept. I looked at Wright. We withdrew.

In the hall there was still no cop or guard. "What do you think?" I asked.

"We know as much as we did before we came here," Wright said. "I'm not sure what Cody knows and what he doesn't."

"Nice call on the TV thing. Too bad he's still fuzzy on what's real."

"Yeah," he said. "I just worry . . . what if he forgets details? I wanted to get to him while he still remembered things."

"I forgot to ask if he remembered stopping for gas," I said.

"Later," Wright said. "We can't afford to upset the parents now."

I knew he was right, and that Cody was still recovering, but I wanted to go inside and ask just that one question. Only I knew I wouldn't stop at one, so I kept my mouth shut.

CHAPTER SEVEN

Wright went to find the Canton cop who'd accompanied Cody to the hospital. I paced a strip of flooring outside room 372 until the medical staff exited Cody's room. "Doctor?" I asked. Two men turned. The balding guy and a guy with a small panda attached to his stethoscope. "Does one of you usually treat Cody Forrand?" The younger one walked away, leaving bald guy to stare at me.

"I'm Doctor Frazier. I treat Cody," he said.

"Chief Lynch. I'd like to ask you a few questions."

"Mind following me? I've got twenty minutes and a lunch I haven't eaten." I followed him to a break room. People in scrubs and lab coats sat at small tables, eating or reading. Dr. Frazier grabbed a foil-wrapped tube and a soda from the fridge. He unwrapped the foil to reveal a sub. He sat and took a large bite. I took the opposite chair.

"How long have you treated Cody?" I asked.

He chewed. Put a finger in the air. Swallowed and said, "Two years. My colleague saw him in the ER and flagged him for me. I specialize in nervous-system disorders." He took another hungry bite.

"Must be one-of-a-kind. I hear his disease is quite rare."

He drank from his can. "Used to have another patient with CIPA. Aaron Donner. Same age as Cody. He died. Almost six months ago. They knew each other, were in and out of here, sometimes at the same time."

"How did he die?" I asked.

"Hyperthermia. People with CIPA don't produce sweat, so they don't cool down like you or me. They get high fevers that can lead to seizures."

"They told me Cody can't deal with cold."

"True. I didn't see any signs of hypothermia when he came in, though. No damage to his extremities that would indicate he'd been outside long."

"You think someone took him?"

"I'll leave that to you. He had a sedative in his system, but I didn't see signs of abuse besides one or two bruises, and those are typical for Cody."

"His mother said she and her husband were accused of abuse before his diagnosis."

"Not uncommon. Nurses and doctors keep seeing the same kid come into the ER; they start asking questions."

"Is there anything you can tell me from when he arrived that might help?"

He thought about it. "Not really. When we figure out what type of drug he had in his system, we'll let you know."

"Do you think Cody knew who took him?"

He checked his watch. "I have no idea, but Cody will lie, especially if he thinks it'll benefit him. You saw what he said about his leg? He's been pitching that for a few months. Always gets a reaction. When it doesn't, he'll come up with something new."

"Doesn't sound like you like him much."

"My job is to treat Cody, to keep him alive. Liking patients isn't in my job description."

"Do you have any idea who might've taken Cody?" It was a shot in the dark.

He stood and tossed his can and foil into the trash. "No." He dusted his hands and straightened his lab coat. "However, I'm not surprised the person didn't keep him."

Wright stood outside Cody's room. He unwrapped a piece of gum and folded it into his mouth. "You find the Canton cop?" I asked.

"In the cafeteria. He's headed back to his station now. Says he's needed there. Also says since Cody was taken on our patch, the case is all ours."

"How thoughtful," I said.

"Yup." He chewed his gum. "Seems the kid who gathers shopping carts from the parking lot saw Cody near the rides outside the store. Saw him again when he came out fifteen minutes later. When he asked

Cody where his parents were, Cody seemed confused. Kid got his manager. Manager phoned the cops."

"Why did the cops call the Forrands? Why not call our station?" I asked.

"Probably wanted to be heroes. They don't often get the chance."

"What about Cody's clothes?" I asked.

"Cody was wearing jeans and a blue sweater with a truck on it when they picked him up. And guess what? The cops called an ambo right away. Didn't interview the manager or the grocery worker. No one else has either."

"Guess I know how you'll be spending your afternoon," I said.

"Guess I do."

"The hospital gonna get a security guard on this door?" I asked.

"They said it's a secure facility. Lots of cameras and key cards." He looked at Cody's room. "You think whoever snatched him will try again?"

"No, but I'd feel better if they watched this room. I'm headed back to . . . hell. We have one car." Mine had "FAG!" written on the side. "Guess I'll call for a ride. Did you see a pay phone?"

"It's 1997. You need to get a mobile, Chief." He pointed. "Down the hall."

I found the phone. Told dispatch I needed someone to pick me up. Darryl said, "Uh, Chief, I don't know how to tell you this, but, um, someone spray-painted your car."

"I know. Send someone for me. I'll meet them outside Emergency."

The lobby was busier than when we'd arrived. More kids holding their arms or bleeding. A few were bald. Cancer kids. I looked away.

When my ride arrived, Dix was at the wheel. "How was Cody?" he asked.

"He'd been given a sedative. Otherwise, he looked good."

"Did he tell you who took him?" he asked.

"Nope."

"Say how he got there?"

"By car, but he didn't provide details."

"Hey, Chief, about cars. Your car—"

"Got tagged. I saw it."

"Oh." He blushed so that his face nearly matched his hair. "I, we're looking into who did it."

"How's that going?" I asked.

"No one saw anything."

I turned on the radio. The weatherman said we'd get two more inches by ten o'clock. I groaned. "My driveway."

Dix picked up on my complaint. "You need your drive cleared? My cousin, Dave, has a plow. I'll call him when I get in. He can clear your drive in two minutes." He seemed delighted to solve this problem.

"Thanks." Now that my car had "FAG!" on its door I couldn't park it on the street.

"So, I saw that Ellen DeGeneres was named Entertainer of the Year," he said.

Ellen DeGeneres. The tiny blond actress. She'd announced she was gay this spring. Oh, God. Dix was trying to talk gay with me. And he was choosing lesbians as his topic. "Dix, I don't care about Ellen DeGeneres. I care about sports. You want to talk about sports?"

We managed to stay on hockey and basketball for the rest of the ride home.

Inside the station, the men looked at me, and then away, fast. Their paperwork became fascinating. It was worse than the day after I came out. Okay, maybe not. A close second. Finnegan, bless his hide, said, "Saw your car. I'm on it. You're gonna have to talk to her ladyship about getting it repaired." Finnegan had a box full of nicknames for Mrs. Dunsmore. So did I. I couldn't repeat mine in polite company.

"Hey, I've got Cody's clothing description. Let's check it against the tips," I said.

"Any other leads?" he asked.

"He had a sedative in his system, so we didn't get much from him. The car that took him might've been silver or white. Wright is scoping out the grocery parking lot. No one interviewed the kid who saw Cody or the manager who called the cops."

Finnegan whistled. "Glad I don't live in Canton."

"I'm going to drop by Suds." No. Dix had told me they'd had a burst pipe. Hell. "Scratch that. I guess I'm going to see Lady Du."

"She's out today. You'll have to call her at home," he said.

I imagined her home. It probably had Catholic artifacts: a painting of Jesus, a photo of the Pope, and maybe a saint card. One of those cross-stitch things about happy homes. Bookcase full of cookbooks so she could keep one step ahead of the bake sale ladies. And cats. If ever a person was a cat lady, it was Mrs. Dunsmore. Her information was in the Rolodex I'd inherited from my predecessor, Chief Stoughton. Her card read Grace Dunsmore. Address and telephone neatly typed on a card yellowed with age. She probably made it herself back in the 1960s.

She answered on the third ring. "Hello."

"Mrs. Dunsmore, it's Thomas Lynch. I'm sorry to disturb you at home."

"Thomas," she said, trying it on for size. "How can I help you, Chief?"

"My car was vandalized in the parking lot."

"I heard." I should've known. She heard everything.

"Where do I take it to get it fixed?"

"Jerry has our contract. I taught him years ago at CCC. He was not an apt pupil."

"Do I need to fill out twelve forms?" She'd probably say yes. Maybe give me a hint as to where the forms lived. No offer to help fill them out, though. She had her limits.

"You're the police chief. Tell him to fix it." She coughed. "And tell those boys they better find who defaced your vehicle. Next thing you know, we'll have drug addicts asking us to open the evidence storeroom so they can get high."

I didn't comment. My mind traveled a different path. "There's no front-facing camera at our station. I usually park out back. There's a camera there." I couldn't remember why. Some ancient tale of a hit-and-run. "I parked out front today."

She got it. "You think whoever did it knew about the cameras. Chief, it's not just people at the station who know. Fire Department knows. DPW knows."

Sure, but how many of them had been at the station today?

Jerry's repair shop was known as Carl's Cars. It sat on the eastern edge of town, bordered by high chain-link fencing. Signs warned me not to trespass and to beware of dog. The lot was full of cars in various states of wreckage. Nearby was an ambulance with no bumpers. The office was in a building the size of my tool shed. Grease-stained papers were stacked atop a waist-high divider. Behind it stood a guy in denim overalls, smoking. He said, "You need a tow? All my guys are out right now."

"My car needs work."

He exhaled a stream of smoke. "You look outside? We got lots of cars need work. Not enough damn people to fix 'em. Goddamn cousin ran off with a skank he met at a bar. I'm down a man. Now I got Phil calling, telling me he fell off his fucking roof, trying to clear icicles."

"The driver's side got tagged," I said. "Orange spray paint."

He stubbed his cigarette out. "Your car?" He looked at my uniform. "Bet it was a dare. High school kids. What did they write? Pig? Donut lover?"

"When do you think you can fix it?" I asked.

"Without Phil and that rat, Ronnie? I'm a full week behind, I tell ya, and this snow's not helping."

"A week?" No way I was driving my car for a week.

"That's how far *behind* I am. Can't do better than two weeks, maybe three."

"I'm the chief of police."

"Yup," he said.

"I can't take it to another garage because yours is contracted to service our vehicles."

"True. Unless you want to pay out of pocket."

"When do we negotiate that contract? Yearly?" He'd never get our business again.

He grinned. "Hardly. Try every four."

"I'm gonna have a chat with Dunsmore," I muttered.

"Mrs. Dunsmore?" He straightened reflectively. Swallowed. "Oh, hell, man. Don't bring her into this. Let me take a look." He followed me outside. Walked to the driver's side and surveyed the damage. *FAG!* The letters seemed to glow.

"Huh," he said.

"You'll fix it by Friday?" I wanted a guarantee.

He bent to look at the letters. Tapped the *F*. "I'll have to redo the seal."

"Skip the seal. Get the graffiti off. You can do the seal later."

He took his eyes off the door. Looked me over. All six feet four inches. "Must've been one hell of a dare," he said.

I couldn't be without a ride, and we didn't have a spare patrol car. He led me to the loaner, a battered wood-paneled station wagon. "You kidding me?" I asked. The car was half my age.

"It's this one or the ambulance, and that's not legal, cuz of the bumpers."

"Fine." I popped the back. Retrieved everything from my car and put it in the roomy rear of the station wagon.

"Heat's a little iffy," he warned.

He wasn't kidding. Lukewarm air coughed on and off. The shocks on the wagon were shot. I felt every pebble as I drove. Across from me, a big SUV rolled past a stop sign and struck a mailbox half buried in snow. The mailbox teetered on its post before falling. The driver sped by like nothing happened. I cut the wheel and followed. License plate started 853. Why did I know that? 853. Shit! My prank caller. I fumbled my notepad and flipped the page. This was his car. Oh man. Maybe today wasn't a waste.

Getting him to stop was a problem. My car had no siren. I honked my horn. Stuck my head out my window. The driver checked his rear-view and accelerated. I sped up and held the horn. He tapped his brakes. I waved my arm and kept honking. He slowed and pulled to the right. Hopped out of his car.

"What the fuck, dude?" he yelled.

When I got out of my car, he reassessed the situation. I gave him a

good look at my badge. "Sir, license and registration." He paused. "Now."
As he fumbled with the glove-compartment latch, I peered in the car.

"Here." He extended the documents.

"What's in the box?" I asked.

"What box?"

"The one behind your seat."

"Just stuff to drop off at the church donation bin." Ah, a Christian.

"Sir, you're aware you hit a mailbox back there?" I gave him my
best cop stare.

He blinked. Shifted his weight. "Um. I . . . thought I heard something. I didn't realize it was a mailbox. Geez."

"After you rolled through a stop sign."

"I stopped."

Normally I'd run his plates. I couldn't. However, I did have my
ticket forms handy. I wasn't expected to write tickets. For folks like
him, I made an exception. I thought for a moment. Scribbled on a
ticket. Handed it to him.

"A hundred twenty-five!" A vein by his temple pulsed.

"Failure to stop. Wanton destruction of public property. Failure to
pull over."

"You're not in a police car!"

I crossed my arms. Stared. Waited.

"I know the mayor," he said.

"So do I. My name's Thomas Lynch. In case you want to call later
and complain. Maybe I should also give you my home phone. No, wait.
You already have it."

The dawning comprehension on his face was beautiful to witness.
He knew what he'd done. Made that phone call to my house. How did
I know? I couldn't know, could I? The path of his thoughts was as easy
to follow as flares on a dark road.

"Have a nice day," I said. Lord knew mine was looking up.

He stood outside his car, frozen in place. Ah, karma. You beautiful
bitch.

CHAPTER EIGHT

Three pink memos were laid atop my desk. *Mayor called. Call from mayor (Again). Call the mayor back, ASAP.* He must've heard about my car. Damn it. I dialed the phone.

"Why are you harassing the Forrand boy?" the mayor said. No "Hello" or "How are you?"

"Harassing?" I repeated, sure I'd misheard.

"Mrs. Forrand complained that you interrogated her son in the hospital."

"We interviewed him, to see if he could ID who took him."

"Leave him be."

"We shouldn't continue to investigate his kidnapping?" This question would bring him back to Earth.

"He's been found. He'll be home soon, in time for Christmas. Everyone's happy."

I pinched my forearm. Had I fallen asleep? Was this a nightmare? "You know who'll be happy? The bastard who grabbed Cody. You want that guy around? Maybe give him time to pick up another kid?"

"Of course not. Continue investigating, but leave the boy alone while he's in the hospital. He's been through enough."

"We have no idea what he's been through," I pointed out.

He let that sit a moment. "I heard the flu is sweeping through the station. Hope you've got enough men for the caroling detail. Also, I haven't heard about the tree-lighting ceremony."

Hell. I knew there was some holiday event I'd forgotten to staff. "Really? I'm sure we called over earlier. I'll see you get the details." Watching Mrs. Dunsmore work had taught me a trick or two. I didn't mention my patrol car. I was surprised he hadn't.

I found Finnegan chugging a Dixie Cup of water. He crumpled

the cup and tossed it at the trash can. "Your eyes need checking," I said. He'd missed by a foot.

"My eyes are fine. It's my aim that sucks."

I recapped my call with the mayor for him.

"She complained? What for?" In his Boston accent, the word was "fo-wah." "If it were my kid, I'd want the cops to nail the perv and lock him up for life. Jesus. What if he does it again? How's she gonna feel?"

"Lucky it's not her kid? Hey, what's with our boy Andrew Trabucco?" I asked.

He bent to pick up his cup. Groaned and put it in the trash bin. "He went to work the day of the storm. Called his boss to ask why the shop wasn't open. Boss told him to haul ass back to his place before the blizzard hit. Boss said that call was at 9:00 a.m."

"Any proof he went home?"

"Nope. I haven't spoken to Trabucco. His phone is shut off, and he's not home." He held up a finger. "However, your weirdo computer teacher is in the clear. He was at work today, so there's no way he dumped Cody in Canton. Oh, and you're gonna love this. Our doubting witness? Definitely saw Cody at the gas station. Her description matches what Cody was wearing when they found him."

"Have they got video at the gas station?" I asked.

"Checking on it. One other sighting seems possible. Someone saw a boy in a silver car parked at the Wallingford public library. The library was closed, and the caller was about to tell the driver, but the car sped off before he could."

"Silver car?" I asked.

"Silver or gray. Four doors. No plate number. No other details." He looked past me. "Look what the cat dragged in."

It must've started snowing again. Wright's hat was covered with it. He took it off and considered the flakes. "Why do I live here? Why don't I move to an island with palm trees? And no snow, ever." He tossed his gloves onto his desk. "You want to learn how to screw up a case, take lessons from the Canton cops. Not only did they fail to interview *anyone* on scene, but they also failed to take any pictures or video.

The kidnapper's car could have been in the lot." Not likely. Once he'd dumped Cody, he most likely drove away, fast. Wright wasn't wrong to be angry, though. The cops should have taken video. We could've reviewed it with Cody.

"Grocery employees give you anything?" I asked.

"The manager says the lot was less than a quarter full when they found him. He looked for cars with an adult, but the ones he spoke to claimed Cody wasn't with them. He talked to as many people as he saw, and then he called the police." He picked up his damp gloves and smacked them against the desktop. "One other thing. There was no boat ride outside the grocery. A car ride and a carousel, but no boat."

"Cody must've been loopier than we thought," I said. "Maybe it's just as well the interview got cut short. Might be chasing our tails right now, looking for elves."

"Least we'd be chasing something," Wright said. "Wait. There *were* elves, painted on the grocery windows facing out, near the rides. Maybe Cody wasn't totally wackaloo."

Finnegan updated Wright on the sightings we thought were legit. Wright looked at the map. "So here." He tapped his finger at the hole where Rocky Hill should've been. "And here." Wallingford. "And here." The last was Canton. "Huh." We all stared at the map. "He headed south."

"But then dumped Cody back north," I said.

Wright asked, "Any of our predators from south of here?" Finnegan picked up a greasy paper plate, an overfull ashtray, and several folders before he found the fax sheets. He flipped pages and said, "No. None that aren't locked up."

I said, "Okay. See you. I've got to go work on the Christmas-carol detail."

"Lucky you," Wright said. I almost told him to fuck off, but we weren't friends.

Billy stood outside my office. "Chief, can I, uh, talk to you?"

"Sure." Billy followed me inside, eyes on his boots.

"You okay?" I asked.

"Yeah. It's about your car. I didn't have anything to do with that. I know I said bad things, and I don't want you to think I had anything to do with the graffiti."

"Billy, I didn't think you had." Billy was dumb in the way young men are. He'd made stupid remarks in the past. He wasn't the type to tag a car with a slur, though. He looked at me, pleased. God, he'd be great to play poker with. Kid couldn't mask a single emotion. "I don't suppose you have any idea who did it?"

He closed my door. "I was in Evidence this morning. I had to make room for the golf clubs." Right. The clubs that had been used to smash the windows of an unused commercial building. "So I moved some of the old stuff back there. You remember those kids who tagged bridges a while back? We had their spray cans. I thought we had more, but I didn't think about it until I heard about your car."

"Billy, are you telling me a spray-paint can is missing from Evidence?"

"The log says five cans. There are three now."

"We didn't use any for, say, road emergencies?" It wasn't like the cans were going to be used in a criminal case. The kids had been let off with trash-picking duty.

"Don't think so," he said.

"Did the log say anything about colors?"

"Pink and orange," he said.

Oh, God. "Did you mention this to anyone?" He shook his head. "Don't. This stays between you and me." I'd need to check the names of everyone on duty.

He nodded, opened the door, and walked out.

My hand reached for the phone. I dialed a number I'd learned recently. Ring, ring. No answer. Before his message came on, I hung up. Why bother Damien Saunders about this? Not as if he'd know who trashed my car. I'd wanted sympathy, plain and simple. But sympathy wasn't answering.

I exited my office and made a show of checking the roster. "Christmas-carol duty calls. Hope you guys like 'Jingle Bells.'" My announcement prompted groans and one shout of, "It's cold as balls! Why do they have to sing *outside*?"

I wrote down the names on the board. Brought it to my office. This assumed that whoever had tagged the car had been on duty. It made sense. See the car out front, where no cameras were. Grab a can, tuck it in your coat, wander outside. Kneel down and spray. Whole thing could've taken two minutes. What about his clothes? Would he be clean? Or would some paint have made it onto his coat? A few specks of Day-Glo orange.

Was my tagger the same wise guy who'd snuck a copy of *Playgirl* into my mail five weeks ago? Imagine my surprise at finding six naked college hunks grinning at me from under my *In-Service Training Courses Spring/Summer 1998*. Three of the hunks held their college pennants in strategic positions. I'd laughed. Held the magazine up and said, "Very funny. I'll put this out so you all can borrow it." Several of the men had approached, curious. When they saw the magazine, they paled. Stumbled. Walked backward. They didn't grin or offer up jokes. They looked appalled. As if I was holding kiddie porn.

I'd have to check the roster for the day of the *Playgirl* incident. October 22nd. It was seared into my memory. The work-detail files were arranged in the steel-gray cabinets by Mrs. Dunsmore every Thursday afternoon. I opened the drawer. It squealed. I checked the tabs for last week of October. Brought the file to my desk. Opened it up. I checked the list of names. Checked today's list.

Thirteen names in common:

Burns
Dix
Dunsmore
Edgars
Finnegan
Hopkins
Johnson
Klein

Miller
Thompson
Wilson
Wright
Yankowitz

Weird. Finnegan and Wright rarely worked the same day. Maybe it had something to do with the North murder. Cases like that take time to wrap up. I didn't want to believe someone I'd worked a murder with would write "FAG!" on my car. Therein lay the problem. Someone I worked with had likely done that. Billy? He'd been truly anxious just now, and he'd brought me the paint cans evidence. I ran a line through his surname, Thompson. Mrs. Dunsmore? I should be so lucky. The only way I'd lose her as secretary was through death. Mine or hers. Probably mine. I ran a line through her name.

I looked outside. It was dark. White light streamed past. No, not light. Snow. Flakes falling past the panes. I just couldn't catch a break.

CHAPTER NINE

Sunday. Cody Forrand was still in the hospital, untouchable. Finnegan and Wright would call if they found the kidnapper. While they'd huddled over papers last night, I'd said, "Call me if you find the guy, yeah?" Wright's frown bisected his forehead. "Of course," he said. Only there was no "of course." Not with me driving a wood-paneled station wagon. Not with that copy of *Playgirl* I'd thrown into the trash so that everyone saw me do it. Not with my list of graffiti suspects, which included Finnegan and Wright.

Wannerman's was having a holiday sale. Cardboard snowflakes hung from the ceiling. Bing Crosby crooned carols. I stared at rows of gloves marked with 40% off tags. I needed size XL, so that halved the selection. Some were cloth, some rubbery. Others had little clips on the side.

"Help you?" asked a young man in a Wannerman's polo. His khakis had creases sharp enough to cut bread.

"I need gloves," I said.

"A gift? Or are they for you?"

"For me."

He glanced at my hands. "Skiing or general use?"

"General," I said.

"I like these." He grabbed a pair of black gloves with orange webbing between the fingers. "Try them." I slid my right hand inside. The bottom inched up, to my wrist bone.

"Too short," he said. "How about these?"

The pair he handed me were thicker. They covered my wrists. I flexed my fingers. "These are good. Warm."

"Waterproof too. I mean, don't stick your hand in a pond while ice fishing."

"I don't plan to. Thanks." Bing Crosby gave way to some breathy singer claiming all she wanted for Christmas was me. I walked to the registers. Damn. The line was ten people long. I looked toward the doors. No. I needed the gloves. Shoppers had carts filled with long johns, mittens, and ski poles. A couple bickered about whether Mary needed another jacket. A child wailed, the only understandable word "Santa." Ah, the holidays.

I looked at the hats display, two feet away. Mr. Neilly, a town selectman, examined a purple kid's hat. "I didn't say he wasn't capable, Joe, but what kind of example does it set?" I didn't hear his friend's answer, but I heard Mr. Neilly's reply. "He told everyone! Stood in the middle of Suds and gave a speech. That's not seemly." I turned away. Settled my eyes on the cashiers. "He's the chief of police. He should be above reproach."

"His personal life isn't your concern," Joe said.

"Next!" a cashier called. Everyone took a step forward. Could I sneak past? Put the gloves down and walk out?

"If he kept it private, it wouldn't be a problem. He announced he was gay in a bar!"

The woman in front of me looked Mr. Neilly's way, a frown on her face. My hands gripped the gloves. Screw this. I wasn't going to let an octogenarian run me out of a store. I rotated my torso and looked toward the hats. I stared until Mr. Neilly turned and saw me. His face got paler than the store's cardboard snowflakes.

"Hi, Mr. Neilly!" I called. Everyone heard me. "Holiday shopping?"

He nodded like a marionette. "For my grandchildren." He came closer. Mustn't appear rude.

"I'm Joe," his friend said. Joe was much younger.

"My son," Mr. Neilly said.

That explained the same nose on their faces. Joe shook my hand. "Pleased to meet you. I've heard *so* much about you." His father looked like he'd have a heart attack.

"The pleasure's all mine," I said. "Happy Holidays."

The line shifted forward. I hurried to close the gap. Joe and his father went back to the hats. Bing Crosby returned. I got my gloves.

The air outdoors had warmed above freezing. Sunshine bounced off the snow, blinding me. I put my sunglasses on and scanned the street out of habit.

"Chief!" Charles Gallagher shouted. He stood outside the gift shop that sold crystal, jewelry, and ceramic angels. I could live here for twenty years and never go inside. He hurried over, a lavender bag in hand. "Glad I caught you."

I wished I could say the same. "Shopping?"

He looked at the bag. "Display items for the store. I've ordered from our usual place, but they won't arrive for another week, and we don't have that kind of time. So I bought some from Marie's shop, even though she charges an arm and a leg for them." He kicked a piece of ice with his boot. "I heard about your car."

"Suppose everyone has by now."

"So that's the second attack this week? Or have there been more?" he asked.

"No," I said. "Just your shop and my car."

"Dave's so upset he's sick." He squinted against the sun's glare. "Why now? We've lived here twenty-two years."

"Maybe some idiots got it in their heads to get drunk and stupid."

"Has there been any word on our report? For the insurance company."

"Ask Detective Finnegan," I said. "He's handling the case."

"He's back on it now that the boy's been found, right?" he asked.

"He's still helping with that. We need to find who took Cody."

"Look, I don't want to be a bother, but we need that report before we can file the claim. We can repaint and restock, but we want to upgrade the back door and we need the insurance money for that. This is our biggest sales season, bigger than Valentine's."

"I understand, and—"

"I'm not sure you do. You've been here, what, a year? We've made Idyll our home for over two decades. We expected more, from the community, and our police."

Across the street, a huge man caught my eye. Andrew Trabucco, coming out of the toy store. Holy shit. "Mr. Gallagher, I've got to go."

"Wait, Chief—"

I hurried across the street, in front of oncoming cars. Horns honked. Andrew Trabucco had a bag in his hand from Treasure Chest. It was like seeing a serial killer with a length of rope, duct tape, and a hacksaw. He turned left, down the alley between the bank and post office. "Hey!" I said. He stopped.

"I'm Police Chief Lynch. What's in the bag?" I asked.

"A present." *Wrong answer.*

"For who?"

His lower lip stuck out. "My nephew, George."

"Your nephew."

He looked to the right of my face. "Yeah, for Christmas. He's four."

"What did you get him?"

I wasn't in uniform. He didn't have to answer my questions. He reached into the bag and pulled up a rectangular box. On the box was a Lego plane and a tiny pilot.

"Come on," I said.

"Where?"

"To the police station."

"I don't want to. I've got to go home and feed my fish," he said.

"Later." I hoped he wouldn't run. He was big. It would take work to subdue him, and my utility belt was at home. There were spare cuffs in the back of the station wagon, several hundred yards away.

"The sooner you cooperate, the sooner you can get home and feed the fish."

The fight went out of him like air out of a balloon. "They have to be fed by two o'clock," he said.

I glanced at my watch. 12:00 p.m.

☀

I held the toy-store bag in one hand and Mr. Trabucco's meaty upper arm with my other. "Fight at the toy store?" Klein asked as we marched past.

"No," I said.

He called, "It'll happen. Does every year around this time. Wait and see."

I hustled Trabucco back to the interview room. Settled him into a chair.

"What's this?" Finnegan asked, when I got to his desk. "I haven't tracked him down, so you go looking on your day off?" He wasn't as territorial as Wright, but Trabucco was his lead.

"Saw him coming out of Treasure Chest with this." I showed him the Lego kit.

He eyed the box as if it might explode. "Didn't Cody say he had the truck kit?"

"Maybe he's upgraded to planes. I figured it was enough to bring him in."

"Yeah." He stuck a pen in his mouth. Spoke around it. "If he took Cody, he drove him south, then returned home where you saw him, and later got him, drove north, and dumped him at the Canton parking lot."

"Maybe he left him somewhere? A motel room? Cody was drugged. Maybe he slept while Trabucco came home and played with his pets." I chewed on the idea. Spat it out. "Scratch that. His car had snow on it. He hadn't driven it that far."

"Besides, his car is blue," Finnegan said. "Maybe he borrowed one? Rented one?"

"Stole one?" I suggested.

"What did he claim the Legos were for?" he asked.

"His nephew, George."

"He's got an older sister. She's got a son. So . . ."

"So he might've been buying a goddamn Christmas present." It had looked so good, when I first saw him with the Legos. Damn it.

"Or not. It's a good cover," he said.

Wright showed up with two cups of Dunkin' Donuts coffee. I wondered what bet he'd lost. "What are you doing here?" he asked.

"Dropping off Andrew Trabucco. I saw him with this." I pointed to the Lego box.

Finnegan told Wright our worries: the driving, the wrong car, and the nephew.

Wright said, "Doesn't mean he didn't do it. Why don't we show Cody his pic?"

"We're banned from interviewing him while he's in the hospital," Finnegan said.

"Since when do we take orders from the mayor?" Wright asked. "We can call the Forrands. Tell them we think we've got the guy, and ask to show Cody some pictures. They won't object. It's a chance to put the guy behind bars."

I wasn't as confident. "If he lied about the Legos, you can call the Forrands."

"Who's gonna talk to our friend?" Wright pointed to the interview room.

"Finnegan," I said. "It's his guy."

Finnegan spat out the pen he'd chewed. "Great. Chatting with a pedophile. My idea of a nice, relaxing Sunday."

"Better make it quick," I said. "He's got to be home by two to feed his fish."

Forty minutes later, Finnegan walked into my office. "You weren't kidding about the fish. Every five seconds it's 'I need to go home and feed my fish.' They're *fish*, for fuck's sake."

"So, is he our guy?" I asked.

"He says he went out twice the day of the storm. Once to work, which we know about, and then to the pet store. Should be easy to check. Can't have been a lot of shoppers that day. I asked about the Legos. He said it's what his sister told him to buy."

"You ask about Cody?"

"No. I was waiting to see if he'd fall into it. So far . . ." he shrugged. "I'll have Wright check the sister and pet store."

"Sounds good."

He whistled a carol as he walked away, hands in his pockets.

After he left, I uncovered the rosters I'd been studying. Yankowitz was off the list. He'd been at dog training the day of the *Playgirl* incident. Three down. Ten to go. Assuming it was a cop. Maybe whoever trashed Sweet Dreams had gotten the balls to tag a cop car, or maybe one of my pranksters had graduated beyond nuisance calls.

Annoyed, I decided to work on the world's stupidest assignment, the holiday events work details. Mrs. Dunsmore was out sick. There was the caroling and the lighting of Main Street, and the Winter Festival with its sleigh rides. Some days I felt like I'd stepped into a goddamn Norman Rockwell painting. There was also the interfaith celebration. "Interfaith" in Idyll meant Protestant *and* Catholic. I checked and rechecked vacation schedules. Crossed out names. "Done!" I said.

"Figured out where they put Hoffa's body, have you?" Wright asked from my door.

"What have you got?" I asked.

He loosened his already-loose tie. "Trabucco's sister said she told him to buy the plane kit. He was at the pet store, like he said. Made an impression on the pair working the registers."

I exhaled a slow hiss of breath. "It was too good to hope the local pedo would be our guy. I'll get someone to take Mr. Trabucco to his car. Let Finnegan know."

I left my office and scouted the station. "Hey, Dix. Got an errand for you."

He squinted. "Yeah?"

"Finnegan's bringing Mr. Trabucco out of interview. Take him to his car. It's somewhere near Treasure Chest."

A middle-aged man came by. "Excuse me? I'm here to talk to Officer Klein."

Dix pointed. "Second desk."

"Thank you." The man nodded.

"Aw, Chief, isn't that the pedophile? I don't wanna drive him," Dix said.

"Don't worry, Dix. You're not his type."

The middle-aged man stood too close. I gave him a look, and he moved to Klein's desk, where Klein typed a report.

Ten seconds later, Mr. Trabucco hurried past Finnegan. "I need to

feed my fish! It's a half hour past their feeding time!" Finnegan followed, rolling his eyes.

Dix said, "Come on, Mr. Trabucco, I'll take you to your car."

Finnegan watched Trabucco hustle away. "I wish he'd been our guy."

"Delivery for you, Finny," Billy said. He handed over an envelope.

Finnegan opened it. "Ah, the pictures from the break-in."

"Can I see?" I asked.

He handed them over. The floor looked as though it was covered
in crystals. Broken glass. I wouldn't have recognized it if not for the
candy scattered amongst the shards. Red licorice ropes and flattened
chocolate discs. The words "YOU COCKSUCKER!" dripped in two-
foot-tall green letters. The word *you*, as if addressing a specific person.
Charles Gallagher? David Evans? "This feels angry. Personal. Not like
a hate crime," I said.

"Looks pretty hateful to me," Finnegan said.

"Did they mention any recent problems? Grudges? Fights?" I
asked.

"Said Mrs. Gerwitz gave him grief about a box of chocolates she
complained was stale. I haven't talked to Mr. Evans. He's sick."

"This is more than a stale-candy complaint." The red spray-paint
message, "Leave Before We Kill You." Hasty and messy and ominous.

"Before I grabbed Mr. Trabucco, I ran into Mr. Gallagher. He
needs your report," I said.

"Right, right. Been a bit busy," he said.

"Could you get to it today? Now that Trabucco's out of the
picture?"

"You think the same people who did this tagged your car?"

"Can't rule it out."

"Why is Mr. Gallagher bugging you about this? Is it because you're
gay?"

"Pardon?"

"Seems like a raw deal for you. Someone tags your car, and now
you've got Mr. Gallagher on your jock, wanting help. You sure it's
worth it?"

I let that sit. "Being gay?" I finally asked. Klein was nearby, eavesdropping, his visitor gone. I sighed. "You know, Finnegan, now that you mention it, I'm sold. Sign me up for hetero training. What's first? Catcalling women on the street?"

He scratched his scalp. "Not bad, not bad. Look, if you follow up with the library witness, I'll get the report done for Mr. Gallagher."

"Thanks, Finny."

He looked at my face, like I was a puzzle. "You know, you could just bust my chops. Tell me to fucking do it."

"Suppose I could, but then I'd lose my trophy for Most Beloved Police Chief."

He laughed so hard he coughed up half a lung. It wasn't that funny. I returned to my office. The phone rang. I picked up. "Chief Lynch."

"Chief." Mayor Mike Mitchell said. "I'm calling about Sweet Dreams. How's the investigation coming? We've gotten several calls about it from the press."

"Really?" Cody's kidnapping and return had dominated the local news, once everyone stopped losing their damn minds over that Hollywood couple's breakup. "What's so newsworthy?"

"Apparently they've heard about your car, and they're drawing conclusions that Idyll isn't a welcoming community. That's balderdash, Chief."

Was it? What about my prank calls?

He continued, "Now, look, your men are investigating both incidents. Taking them seriously, as they should. I don't see any reason to talk to the press."

"Right," I said.

"I knew you'd see reason. I told Mr. Neilly you weren't the sort to air dirty laundry." I inhaled hard. He wanted to silence me? He heard it. Tried to backpedal. "Mr. Neilly and I were talking, saying what a fine job you did, getting the Forrand boy home."

"That wasn't down to me," I said. "We haven't found the guy who grabbed him."

"You will. I have every confidence in you, Chief." He was one step away from waving pom-poms and shouting my name through a mega-phone. "If any reporters bother you, you can just send them my way."

"Uh-huh. Bye now." I hung up.

Keeping your mouth shut was a necessary skill for a small-town cop. You run into the same people you arrest, regularly. Thursday night you're putting Mr. Lehigh in a cell to sleep it off, and Saturday morning you're both at the gas station. You pretend nothing is different, that you haven't smelled his vomit or seen him sob like a child. Now the mayor was warning me not to talk. He didn't know me. If he had, he'd know the last thing I wanted was a reporter turning my life into a human-interest piece. So why did it burn under my collarbone? Why did I want to punch something? I didn't want to talk, didn't want to discuss the graffiti on my patrol car. I also didn't want to be told not to talk. Life was just fucking hilarious that way.

CHAPTER TEN

I blinked against the dark and the cold. My limbs moved before my brain caught up. Before I thought to wonder, "Who's calling so late?" I stumbled to the phone. "Lynch."

"Chief. There's a fire," John Miller said, in his dispatch voice. He might've been reciting the date and temperature, given his calm.

"Fire? Where?"

"Andrew Trabucco's house. It's burning now."

"He inside?"

"No. They got him out."

"Too bad," I said, my voice low.

"What's that?"

"I said I'll head over."

I hung up the phone and rubbed my eyes. 2:42 a.m. I'd be warmer in street clothes. I grabbed my new gloves and old hat. Zipped my jacket up to my neck and stepped outside. The porch creaked. I shivered my way to the station wagon. Inside, I cranked the heat. It coughed cold air. Fuck. When could I get my patrol car back? Today was Sunday. No. Technically, it was Monday. Four more days.

The fire engine's flashing lights were angry and bright. Two patrol cars were parked nearby. A small crowd, huddled in pajamas and winter gear, watched the firemen aim water at the smoldering house. One of the onlookers sat in a wheelchair, a blanket tucked up to his chin. Soot and water droplets fell from the sky.

The left half of the house was a mess. The front windows had burst. The roof had a hole punched in it. The firefighters aimed their hose at the roof. A smaller group doused bushes and trees near another house. Officer Wilson told a teenager to back up a few more feet. Why were people out? It was freezing.

I approached Wilson. He nodded when he saw me. "Word?" I asked.

"Trabucco got out. Some of his pets didn't. He was having a goddamn meltdown when I got here."

"Where is he?"

"The ambo. EMTs were worried he was gonna have a heart attack."

"He won't be coming back soon," I heard someone say.

"Good riddance."

I turned. Looked at the couple speaking. He wore half-specs and was in a tatty blue bathrobe. She wore a bright ski jacket over reindeer-print pajamas.

"What did you say?" I asked.

They took a sudden interest in their footwear. "Nothing," she said.

"No. You said, 'Good riddance.' You said it about Mr. Trabucco. Why?"

She huffed a cloud of vapor at me. "We know he likes to touch little kids. He lives near us! We have a daughter."

"She's away at college," her husband said.

"She wasn't always!"

I didn't point out that their daughter had been too old for Mr. Trabucco when he'd moved in, or that he preferred boys. I asked, "Who told you?"

"Mr. Ellington," the man said.

"Joel!" His wife elbowed him.

He rubbed his side. "What, Gretchen? You think they won't find out? He's been telling everyone on the block since he got back from the station."

"He was at the police station?"

"This afternoon. His car was broken into. Presents stolen."

"And?" I said.

"He said a cop called Mr. Trabucco a pedophile."

Dix. Dix had said it in front of the guy who was there to see Klein. Shit.

"Thanks for your time. You should go inside now." They sidestepped icy patches and crossed the street to the house directly across from Trabucco's.

The firemen had stopped spraying. The air was wet; the char smell, terrible. I walked toward the first engine. Chief Hirsch's posture gave him away. He was forever leaning against things. Maintaining a casual vibe. Even in the midst of a house fire.

"Chief Lynch!" He didn't straighten. Kept one shoulder glued to the engine.

"Quite a scene," I said.

His face was sooty, his nose nearly black. "Think we've got it extinguished."

"Any idea what caused it?"

He lifted his chin and used it as a pointer. "Smelled gasoline near where it started. We found an empty can tossed in the backyard. Lucky we got here quick. Wind was strong. Could've spread to the neighbors." I wondered if the burnt smell bothered Hirsch. Or if he was used to it. "Heard the occupant was a pervert." I nodded. "Aren't you supposed to notify us when these types move into the neighborhood?" I liked his emphasis on the word "you." Cute.

"He moved here before alerts were mandatory."

"Wonderful. Any other men like him we should know about?"

"I assume you'll be looking the house over soon?" He frowned. Wondered where I was headed. "You find anything inside that's *criminal* in nature, let me know." Porn. Kiddie porn. If we found anything in Trabucco's house racier than a Sears catalog, we could charge him.

He smiled. "Of course." We were on the same side, for once.

I walked toward the ambo. Mr. Trabucco sat on a cot, a blanket over his shoulders. His feet were bare. He had a blood pressure cuff on and wore an oxygen mask. One of the EMTs looked me over. I was out of uniform, but she must've sensed cop.

"What's his status?" I asked.

"Blood pressure's high. He inhaled some smoke before he got out of there. We wanted to bring him in, but he kept refusing, babbling about his animals." I thought of the cages. The small furry bodies.

"He got some out. Firefighters rescued some too. But he," she jerked a thumb toward Trabucco, "keeps saying he's got more inside."

"Is he okay to talk?"

She glanced at him. "Keep it brief."

I nodded. Put my hands on the side of the ambulance and hoisted myself up. The vehicle rocked. Another EMT, a young man, shifted so I could sit opposite the patient. Trabucco was wide-eyed, his face grimy. His breaths were loud under the mask.

"Mr. Trabucco. Can you tell me what happened tonight?"

He heaved a breath. Removed his mask and said, "Fire. They burnt my . . . They . . ." A tear cut a path through the soot on his face.

"When did it start?"

"Bugs woke me. Thumping in his cage. The clock said 1:49 a.m. I smelled something burning and got out of bed. The living room was on fire. I picked up Mario's cage and ran outside. Put it by the street. Then I ran back in and got Yoyo. I heard sirens. It was hard to breathe. I could hear Fiona, my cat, meowing. The firemen made me leave. They dragged me out." He coughed.

The EMT gestured to him. "Mask on," he said. Trabucco settled the mask back on and breathed.

"Did you see anyone? When you first saw the fire?" I asked. He shook his head. "Did you hear any voices? People talking?" Another shake of his head.

He took the mask off. "Why would someone burn my house? My animals? I didn't do nothing." He knew why. Had to know why. But men like him lived in denial.

"Somebody found out about your past," I said.

His eyes got wider. His breathing harsh. Ragged. It reminded me of Rick dying. After he'd been shot. No. This asshole, he was nothing like Rick. Rick had been good. This man was a piece of human waste. I stood up.

"Wait!" Trabucco pulled the mask down. "You'll find who did this, right? They'll go to jail? They killed, they killed my sweet babies."

I hopped out of the ambulance and came face-to-face with Wright. "What're you wearing?" I asked.

He looked down at his yellow, striped pants. "Snow pants. It's colder than a witch's tit." He looked at the smoking house. Firemen had entered. "So someone lit his house on fire."

"Dix said something in front of a neighbor, Mr. Ellington, about Trabucco being a pedophile. Seems Mr. Ellington's been telling the neighbors about it all day."

"So one or more of them decided to clean up the neighborhood?" he asked.

"Looks that way."

"Fanfuckingtastic. We don't have enough men for the kidnapping, plus we have the break-in. Now we gotta investigate this." He tugged on his hat. "I'll take pictures."

"You brought a camera?" I asked.

He nodded.

"I'll take statements," I said. A gust of icy air made me hunch into my coat, turtle-like. It was going to be a long day.

CHAPTER ELEVEN

Nate had let me into Suds hours before opening so I could retrieve my clean uniform and a week's worth of laundry. Inside the station, I took my uniform to the locker room. The locker room had one semifunctional shower, two toilets, and sixteen tiny lockers. The men stored deodorant and fresh t-shirts inside. The shower was running. Surprising. Last time anyone used it was when a skunk sprayed Billy. I stuck the hanger's hook into one of the locker slats and peeled off clothes. In winter, it was like peeling an onion. I was down to my skivvies when the water shut off. I tore the plastic from the uniform. Damn stuff clung to itself. Before I could get the shirt off its hanger, Hopkins came around the corner, naked and dripping.

"Whoa!" he yelled.

"Hey!" I shouted.

He looked about, panicked. I looked away. God, now I'd have that image in my head. I unbuttoned the shirt. His bare feet slip-slapped as he ran away. "Where's my towel?" he said. I got my shirt on. "What did you do with my towel?"

"I haven't seen your towel. I got here two seconds ago. I need to change. Give me a moment and I'll have a look."

"No! No. I . . . I'm fine."

"You're wet and naked. How's that fine?" I pulled on my pants.

"I'll be okay. Are you done yet?"

"No." I shoved my feet into my boots. Smoothed my shirt. If anyone else were here, Hopkins would be laughing, making comments about the size of his sausage. Because it was me, he was acting like a goddamn girl. "I'm done." I grabbed my stuff and exited the room. Dix stood by the door, a towel in hand. He saw me and lost his smirk. "Give it to him," I said. "He's about to have a heart attack."

In my office, I said some bad words. I shadowboxed for two minutes. Threw jabs, hooks, and uppercuts until my heart raced from exertion, not rage.

Three raps at the door. "Come in, Mrs. Dunsmore." Her face was paler than usual.

"There's something wrong with the plant." She'd given it to me when I came on board. Before we got to know each other.

She lifted one droopy strand. Then she moved the pot a few inches to the left. "Have you been watering it? Looks overwatered to me." She poked the soil with her long index finger. "I saw your holiday work detail. Bad news. Clyde and Quint called in sick." She inhaled. Her breath rattled. "Normally I'd tell them to drag their sorry selves in here, but Clyde has walking pneumonia. Quint has got that flu."

"Does everyone get sick here?" I asked.

She managed a crooked smile. "Thankfully you've got a city-bred immune system." I waited. She never complimented me unless . . .

I groaned. "I have to work the interfaith event tomorrow night?" We had three criminal investigations underway. Three actual cases, and I had to babysit churchgoers?

"There'll be hot cocoa." She rubbed one of the plant's limp leaves.

Swell. Cocoa. That changed everything. I left the office to see if any actual work was being done.

"Hey!" Finnegan waved his hand. He was happy to see me or he'd had too much coffee. "Heard about the fire. Late night?"

"Yeah, and damn cold too."

"Who you think did it?"

"Neighbor. One of 'em found out about Mr. Trabucco's past and told everybody who lived nearby."

"Sounds like a neighborhood cleanup project."

"Yeah, except the fucker who lit it could have taken out a neighbor's house. High winds, lots of trees."

"In happier news, I've narrowed the time window on your patrol car getting tagged. It happened between 9:45 a.m. and about half past ten, when you and Wright discovered it."

"Does that tell us anything?" I asked.

"It wasn't Captain Hirsch. He was at a fire-training seminar."

"Did you really consider him?" If so, he wasn't trying.

"Naw, not really. I whittled some names off my long list though." His intonation made it clear that he wouldn't tell me whom he'd cleared. "I'll find him. My momma didn't raise any fools. Well, except my brother, Dave. He's almost simple, Dave is."

He wanted me to laugh. I wished I could. But the idea of a list, longer than mine, bothered me. I returned to my office and my Selectric typewriter. I had two evidence vouchers to fill in for the fire. My aggression went into pounding the keys.

"Chief!" My fingers stilled.

Wright stood in the doorway. "You didn't hear me knock. You, um, type."

"Yes."

"No, but you really type, like Mrs. Dunsmore types."

I took a swig of coffee and said, "Don't do that."

"What?"

"Compare me to Mrs. Dunsmore."

He fought a smile. "I can only hunt and peck." I'd seen. It was painful to watch. Took Wright half an hour to type what took me five minutes. "Update on the fire. It started around 1:30 a.m. I sifted through our reports, and we can eliminate a few people. Mr. Carson, the spectator in the wheelchair, has advanced Parkinson's."

"Okay. Who else?"

"Miss Folks is out. She got home from her hospital shift just before 2:00 a.m. Officer Wilson had to help guide her car down the street."

"So who do you like for it?" I asked.

"Neighborhood parent," he said, without hesitation. "I can't see a regular Joe getting worked up enough. But someone with young kids? They'd want him gone."

"How many people on our list have kids?"

"Five, and four of them make up two couples, so . . ."

"Focus on them first. Let me know if you need more manpower."

I'd spoken on autopilot. ". . . Except we don't have any. Everyone's sick. I've got to patrol the interfaith celebration tomorrow night."

"They recruit a Buddhist? Or are they counting the UU guy?"

"UU guy?"

"Unitarian Universalist, the religion for people who hate their childhood religions. They have this long-haired dude who holds up peace signs along Main Street."

"Ah, him." I'd seen him, holding a rainbow-colored peace sign. Waving at cars. I'd assumed he was an old hippie who lacked the funds or energy to go west.

Finnegan appeared. "Could you both come take a look at something?" He led us to the VCR/TV combo set up by his desk. We looked at it expectantly. "Footage from the gas station where Cody was spotted. There's one camera, inside, behind the cashier." Damn. That meant we wouldn't see Cody in the car. Couldn't hope to get the car's license plate or make and model. "It gets worse. You can pay at the pump using a credit card," he said.

"Really?" There were one or two gas stations where I'd seen this. "Oh, hell. So it's possible our kidnapper isn't on camera."

"Bingo. I ran the tape twice. Expanded the time our caller gave us. Problem is our kidnapper could've paid at the pump, and getting credit card information will take—"

"Forever?" Wright said.

"Near enough. Only five people appear between 10:00 a.m. and 2:00 p.m. Not surprising, given the storm. Two are women. Three men. One of them, this guy." He pointed the remote and hit a button. A small man stood at the counter, credit card in hand. He looked up, saw the camera, and turned so that his face wasn't visible.

"He turned from the camera," Wright said. "Did he buy gas?"

"Yes, and a pack of gum."

"None of the others seemed good?" I had to ask.

Finnegan said, "Nope."

"Good luck," I said, glad it wasn't on me to hunt gas-station guy down. "I'm going to stop by Sweet Dreams later."

"Why?" Finnegan asked. "Have there been more problems?"

"No. I just want to see the damage for myself."

Finnegan shook his head. "Gay community service."

Wright's head snapped up. "Is that a thing?"

Finnegan laughed. I walked away.

Sweet Dreams's front windows were covered with butcher paper. A note on the door promised the store would reopen in two days. Someone had scrawled, "Looking forward to it!" I tried the front door. Locked. But there was music playing, loudly, inside. The back door, pried open by the vandals, was still damaged. I pushed past it into the back office/storage space and then walked out onto the store's floor. Heavy bass thumped through the soles of my boots. AC/DC. "You Shook Me All Night Long." By the wall, Nate, the owner of Suds, hammered wooden shelves. Another man taped baseboards with blue tape. No sign of Mr. Gallagher or his partner, Mr. Evans.

The broken glass was gone and the floors cleared of candy debris. The graffiti remained. "YOU COCKSUCKER!" took up half of the biggest wall. There was no dick art. Unusual. People who enjoy destroying private property are often the same people who enjoy drawing pictures of dicks. The death threat was near the front door, squished into a small area, like an afterthought. The paint colors were different. Death threat in green. Insult in red. Death threat not capitalized. Looked like two different graffiti artists.

The music stopped, abruptly. "Hi, Chief!" Nate said. "Come to help?"

"You're fixing up the place?" I asked.

"I offered to help. Didn't want them to be closed during their busiest season."

I peered at the scratched-up floorboards.

"Careful," Nate warned. "We've been over the surfaces with a Shop-Vac, but there may still be stray glass."

"I keep finding pieces with my fingers," the other guy said.

"Lincoln, this is Chief Lynch."

Lincoln looked like Nate. Same Native cheekbones, but he was heavier and his hair curled, unlike Nate's long, straight curtain of hair. "Nice to meet you, Chief Lynch," Lincoln said.

"Call me Tom." I looked at the tools and drop cloths. "What can I do?" I didn't have other plans, and it would be rude to leave. They needed help. Finny's voice whispered, "Gay community service" in my head.

Lincoln said, "Once I finish taping, you can start painting."

Nate unlocked the front door, promising more volunteers would arrive.

The wall paint color was "Sparkle." Even for a gay couple, it seemed a bit much. I pried open the lid with the flat end of a screwdriver. A gust of cold air swept the corner of the drop cloth upward. Two men entered, barely visible behind stacked pizza boxes.

"Just set those there," Nate said, gesturing to where the candy scale and register usually stood. Were the machines damaged? "Tom and Lincoln, here are Fred and Randy, if they ever emerge from those amazing-smelling pies."

"Harry's Pizza?" Lincoln said. He sniffed the steam rising from the boxes. "I've died and gone to heaven."

"Where's Harry's?" I asked.

"Hartford," Randy said. He wore a leather jacket and had mutton-chops. "Best pizza ever."

"Don't start," Fred said. They were a couple. It was obvious from his tone and their body language.

"Hey there, anybody home?" a woman called from outside.

"It's Sharleen," Nate said to Lincoln. "Open the front door for her, will you?"

Sharleen entered, dressed in heels and a suit. Nate explained that she was a lawyer.

"I'm also the owner's daughter. Charles's daughter," she said. Interpreting my expression, she said, "From when he was married to my mom, before he came out."

"Nice to meet you. I'm Tom."

"What do you do, Tom?" She set her briefcase down by the pizza table and grabbed a paper plate.

"I'm the police chief."

She put two veggie slices on her plate. "You gonna catch the bastards who trashed my dad's shop?"

"Better hope you do," Fred said. "You don't want Sharleen on your case."

We ate the pizza before it got cold. More people came. Ms. Hart, the Christmas décor goddess who lived near the Forrands came over and said, "Nice to see you again." People swapped stories about Sweet Dreams and its owners. The time Charles and David helped raise money for the Girl Scouts so they could travel to Washington DC. The summer they'd hosted a wedding in the store between two customers who'd first met there. The time they'd sold alcoholic chocolates unwittingly to children. "Dad made a point to try all the candy *before* selling it after that incident," Sharleen said.

The front door opened to reveal Damien Saunders. A breeze set paper plates spinning to the floor. I hadn't known he'd be here. Should've expected it. He greeted everyone in the room. Laid his hand on my shoulder when he said hello.

"Did you bring the plans?" Nate asked Sharleen.

"Yup." She withdrew a folder from her briefcase. "I had to make copies so Dad wouldn't notice they were missing."

Nate said, "Should be able to do most of this. The stenciling, though, we can't. Need to let the walls dry first."

In the plans, the large defaced wall had the store's name painted, in gold, along with a handful of candy-shaped decorations.

Sharleen told me, "My dad has wanted to redesign the shop for years, but it's never the right time. They were going to take two weeks in January to do it, and then this happened. I want to surprise him. He thinks we're slapping basic white on the walls."

He wanted to redecorate and then this happened? How fortuitous. Then again, Charles Gallagher had been truly upset when he'd called me. And I couldn't see him writing those words on his store walls.

"Let's get to work!" Sharleen said.

I taped the crown molding above the wall with the cocksucker graffiti. Lincoln taped the baseboards. Nate played music. By the time I had roller in hand, coated with Sparkle paint, a shiny white, the music was late Beatles.

Lincoln's section looked better than mine, more even. "Hey, Chief," Nate called. "Mind giving us a hand?" He and Fred held a wooden shelf above their heads. "We need height." I set my roller in the tray. Took the shelf from them and held it where they told me. Sharleen said, "Higher." I extended my arms. "Is that level?" she asked. Nate gave me a level. I laid it atop the wood.

"A bit up on the right. Nope, just a fraction down."

"Let me take the other side," Damien said. He was nearly as tall as me.

"Up again to the right. Perfect! Hold it," Sharleen said. We held the shelf while Nate marked the edges for brackets. Damien smelled nice. I hated that I noticed.

We gave the shelf to Fred, and I returned to my roller. I'd nearly finished the wall when I realized no one was speaking, it was just the radio and me singing "Ob-La-Di, Ob-La-Da." My mouth closed faster than a Venus flytrap's. How hadn't I noticed the quiet?

Ms. Hart called, "That's a beautiful voice you have." Lincoln grinned at me.

"Would someone please shoot me?" I asked. "I can provide the gun." I peeked over my shoulder. They were watching. "Really. You just point and shoot. It's not hard."

"Did you ever sing choir?" Jerry asked.

"No." Not my scene.

"Too bad," he said, as if I'd missed my calling.

"Okay, let's leave him alone. If it makes you feel better, Tom, you're crap at painting," Nate said.

"Thanks." I scowled, but I was grateful.

"Come help me. Lincoln will finish the wall."

Glass jars were unpacked. Shelves were hung. The graffiti had disappeared beneath two coats of paint. The scale and register were in place. "Let's wrap it up, folks," Sharleen said. "It's late. Thanks, everyone. Dad and Dave will be so pleased."

I headed out. Damien followed, whistling "Ob-La-Di, Ob-La-Da." He caught my look and said, "You do have a nice voice. I couldn't carry a tune if it had a handle."

He exhaled hard. "Grapevine tells me your car had 'fag' spray-painted on it."

"That explains why I'm driving this." I pointed to the station wagon.

His jaw unhinged. "Oh my god. Do they still make those?"

"No. This is an original," I said, tapping the hood. I'm working on finding out who did it."

He shivered. "You think it has anything to do with what happened to the store?"

"No, but I've got no evidence." Except the paint colors, and a feeling.

"Hope you find who did it."

"Thanks."

He looked as if he'd say something more. I waited. "Have a good night, Thomas, and if I don't see you, Happy Holidays." He left. I stayed in the cold air, watching the exhaust from his tailpipe, wondering what I should've said in return. Because I hadn't said anything. Just stayed mute, like a puppet without a handler.

CHAPTER TWELVE

Sixty-four people had bundled up and come out for the interfaith celebration Tuesday evening. They carried lit tapers, drank cocoa, and discussed holiday plans. The gazebo loomed before me in its dull white glory. Town lore said it had burnt to ashes, twice, and been rebuilt. Maybe that was why the candles had Dixie Cups around them. A surprised cry made me hustle forward. I found the Forrands: Mom, Dad, Anna, and Cody, standing nearby. The family was surrounded by people three deep.

"He's okay?" someone asked.

"What a brave boy!" another said.

"I'll drop off some cookies tomorrow. Oh, no, it's no trouble," a woman insisted.

"We've made an extra pan of lasagna. Please. You're probably dead on your feet. Have you had time to shop?" another asked.

Mrs. Forrand said, "I'm behind." The group made sympathetic noises. Much arm patting and offers of babysitting, shopping, and baking ensued. Mr. Forrand, extraneous in this talk of gingerbread, looked up and saw me. He threaded his way through the people. Stopped and said, "Cody got home this morning."

"He's okay in the cold?" The celebration was scheduled to last seventy minutes.

"We'll swap off bringing him to the car and running the heater."

"I'd like to talk to Cody," I said. When *had* they planned to tell us he was home from the hospital? My guess was never.

His face tightened. "We heard about that man, the pedophile."

"He didn't take Cody."

"He lived four blocks away!" People looked over. He lowered his voice. "Why weren't we told?"

"He wasn't on the registry. We interviewed him. He didn't do it. Couldn't have." I pressed on. "We need to talk to Cody, to find the person who took him."

"*If* you find the guy."

"Did you have a bad experience with the police?" He tensed up at my question. "You claimed we stopped searching for Cody when we didn't, and you don't think we'll catch who did this."

"We've seen things go badly before. The town Jane is from, Chaplin. They had a missing-kid case and the cops bungled it." He looked over his shoulder. His wife had picked up Cody. "I don't want Cody upset. He had nightmares, in the hospital."

"Understood."

Mrs. Forrand called, "Pete."

He waved at her. "I've got to take Cody to the car. You can talk to him inside." He left and took his son from his wife. Cody wrapped his arms around his father's neck. They walked across the snow, toward the church. I followed them to the minivan parked in the church's lot. He fumbled the keys and dropped them to the pavement.

"Allow me." I scooped the keys up and unlocked the driver's door. Mr. Forrand settled Cody in the back and turned on the heat.

"Hi there," I said to Cody as I sat beside him.

"You're that policeman," Cody said.

"Chief Lynch. You remembered."

He grabbed a box of animal crackers from the seat pocket in front of him. "Want one?"

I didn't, but I wanted him to talk so I said, "I'd love one. Thanks." Cody rummaged in the box and withdrew a cookie. Handed it to me. I said, "Gorilla, looks like. Missing a foot. Must've tangled with a tougher animal."

"Elephant!" Cody said, waving his cookie at mine.

"Cody, the car you got in the day of the snowstorm. What did the driver look like?"

"A Mighty Morphin Power Ranger!" He spewed crumbs as he spoke.

"Talk *after* you finish chewing, Cody," Mr. Forrand said from the front seat.

"So it was a man?" Billy had shown me pictures of the Power Rangers. There were five, but only two were female. The Red Ranger was male.

"It was a Power Ranger." He explained it as if I was trying his patience.

"So he was dressed all in red?"

"No, just the mask."

Mr. Forrand's hand stopped adjusting the heat dial. "Mask?" he asked.

"The Mighty Morphin Power Ranger mask." Cody kicked his legs against his father's seat. "Didn't have the whole suit." He sighed. "That would have been awesome."

"What was the person wearing?" I kept my tone light. *The kidnapper had worn a fucking mask?*

Cody shrugged. "A coat. I dunno. Ooh! The tiger. Rowr." He dangled the tiger cookie before my face before shoving it into his mouth.

"Cody, was the car you got into parked on your street?"

"Nope!" He kicked his legs.

"Was it on Weymouth Avenue?" The street where Ms. Hart and Mr. Connelly lived, and where Skylar had lost Cody's scent.

"Yup!"

"Why did you get inside, buddy?" I asked.

"Yes, why, Cody?" His father's voice shook.

"Because it was a Power Ranger!" Cody smiled. "And he had a present!"

Mr. Forrand shook all over. "Oh, God. Buddy, remember how we talked about not getting in strangers' cars?"

I gave him a "Not now" look and asked, "Was the present the Lego truck kit?"

"Yup!" He laughed. Then, like a tap turned off, his laughter stopped. "Where is it?"

"I'll help you find it if you can tell me where you went."

"We drove," he said. "It was boring, but I had my truck kit and the Power Ranger said we could build it when we got to the Power Ranger base."

"Did you stop for gas?" I asked.

"No." He rooted through his cracker box. "Wait. The Power Ranger said we needed some before we could get to base."

"When you got to the Power Ranger base, what did it look like?"

"Home," he said.

I met Mr. Forrand's puzzled look with one of my own. "Home," I repeated.

"The bed wasn't a bunk bed, but it had my robot sheets, and a stuffed animal like Sammy; but it wasn't Sammy, because real Sammy's tail is cut in half. He had surgery. Uncle Greg says Sammy's almost as tough as me." Whoa. The room had Cody's sheets and favorite stuffed animal? The kidnapper had attempted to replicate his bedroom.

"Cody, buddy, do you know who drove you there? Who wore the mask?"

He shook his head. "The Power Ranger said it was a secret. If I became a Power Ranger, I could find out. I didn't get to."

"Cody, for God's sake! That Power Ranger wasn't a good person!" his father shouted.

Mrs. Forrand jerked the side passenger door open, letting in a gust of cold air. "What's going on?"

"Why's Daddy yelling?" Anna asked, poking her head out from behind her mother.

Cody yelled, "My leg hurts!"

Mr. Forrand said, "Cody's kidnapper had his sheets and a stuffed animal like Sammy. He told him he'd become a Power Ranger." His hands trembled. He was envisioning everything that could've happened to Cody.

"What?" Mrs. Forrand's face was puckered in confusion. "Sammy?"

Mrs. Forrand and Anna climbed inside the minivan, taking the front passenger seat. I explained that it seemed that whoever had taken

Cody had been inside his bedroom. Mrs. Forrand's hysteria matched her husband's. "He was *inside* our house? When?" She clutched Anna tightly to her chest.

"The bad man came to our house?" Anna asked, looking from her father to her mother.

"Oh, honey, come here." Her mother hauled Anna to her chest. "Don't worry. The bad man can't come near you."

"Or Cody?" Anna's eyes went to her brother, who tipped the animal cracker box upside down, spilling crumbs onto the seat.

"Or Cody," I said. "Stay calm; we'll do everything we can to keep you all safe. I'll assign a patrolman to your house. In the meantime, I need you to make a list of anyone who's been in your home since Cody got Sammy or his sheets."

"I don't know when—" Mrs. Forrand began.

"June!" Anna interrupted. "He cut up the old sheets, remember, Mom?"

Mrs. Forrand nodded, a fist to her mouth. "Yes, June. Right. What a memory you have, lovebug." She kissed her daughter's head.

"Since June then," I said.

"What about the plumber?" Mrs. Forrand said.

"What plumber?" Mr. Forrand asked.

"A few weeks, maybe a month ago, while you were at work, we had a leak in the basement. I tried to reach you, but you were in a meeting, so I called a plumber." She was defensive. As if plumbing expenses required a two-spouse vote. "A guy came. He said it had to do with the washing-machine hookup. He fixed it."

"I don't remember getting a plumbing bill," Mr. Forrand said.

"He did it for free. Said it was such a tiny thing. He poked around upstairs, asking if we needed any other work done, and I think he went in the kids' room."

"Why?" he demanded.

"I don't remember. Something about their beds and how he'd had bunk beds as a kid. He had a twin brother, he said. He must've seen the sheets."

"What company did he work for? Do you remember his name?"
I asked.

Her arms were tight around Anna, and her eyes were glued to
Cody. "I don't remember. I think I got the name from a circular, but I
threw it away."

"You let a plumber look at our child's bedroom?" Mr. Forrand's
voice was angry.

"I didn't think—" she began.

"After Chaplin? After Vicky?" he asked. What were they talking
about?

She said, "The kids weren't home! They were with Jessica."

"Jessica, your sister?" I asked Mrs. Forrand.

She said, "Yes. She has horses. The kids love to help feed and groom
them."

"Okay. Well, I think you should go home now. Skip the rest of the
event here," I said. "I'll have a policeman meet you at your place. Please
work on that list."

"Cody," his father said. "Can't you tell us who took you for a drive
the other day? We won't be angry. We just need to know."

"No," Cody said, his voice lower and softer. His pale face was a
moon in the window's reflection. "I didn't get to stay at base. I didn't
get to find out, *or* meet the Green Ranger." His body slumped. He
leaned his head against the window and said, "I want to go home."

After exiting the minivan, I crossed the street to the park. A man
was speaking; he wore a coat open at the neck to show his clerical collar.
He asked the crowd to remember those less fortunate and urged us to
donate to the food pantry and to pray for those in distress. The priest
beside him grimaced. Catholics like prayers to serve specific purposes.
You don't go chucking them out willy-nilly.

"Let us find forgiveness for everyone, even those whose choices
we might not approve of. Do not fall prey to intolerance or hate.
Remember God's grace touches us when we are selfless, when compassion is our compass."

I edged past the crowd, aiming for the beat-up station wagon.

A woman peeled away from the group. She held her candle up. "Chief Lynch?"

She stepped aside so as not to interrupt the minister. Her stiletto-heeled boots left tiny divots in the snow. Close up, she was stunning. "I'm Sandra Patterson. I work at the high school, as a guidance counselor." She extended a red-leather-gloved hand. "I chair the local LGBT chapter. I'd love it if you'd come and give a talk at the school."

"A talk."

"On how you became a police officer."

"I passed the tests."

She smiled. "And about what it's like, as a gay man, being a community leader."

"No thanks. Public speaking isn't my thing," I said.

"I've seen you do it. Press conferences and the school talk about drunk driving."

I'd been roped into the drunk-driving gig by the selectmen. Next year, I'd find a sacrificial goat, like Billy. "That's my job," I said.

"Exactly! You have a position of influence. Many of our gay youths feel powerless. It would be inspiring for them to hear from someone like you."

"Ms. Patterson, thank you for the offer, but what I want is a world in which I'm not approached to speak just because I'm gay."

She tilted her head. "You *are* gay," she said.

"Yes. I'm also Irish, and I don't like anchovies. No one cares. And I don't mind being gay. I do get tired of everybody else honing in on it." I took a breath, then said, "You have a beautiful face." She'd opened her mouth for a rebuttal, but my compliment disarmed her. "You ever get tired about hearing how pretty you are?"

"Well, sometimes I wish—"

"Imagine that's the only thing anyone ever talks about when they discuss you. In your company. Outside it. The *only* thing."

"I take your point, but these kids, they aren't living your reality. Many aren't out, not even to their families."

"And the day they 'come out' as everyone calls it, that's the day they'll know how I feel. I'm sorry, but I can't brag about that. Most days it's a pain in my ass."

"I see."

"I'm not sure you do. I don't see how you could."

She lifted the candle. "You're very handsome. Ever get tired of hearing that?"

"Never," I said.

She laughed. "Well, I can't say I'm not disappointed, but it's been a pleasure, Chief. Maybe I should have you come talk to the Debate Team instead."

On the way to the station, my car's engine sputtered. I thought of what the minister had said, about compassion. I laughed. I drove this wreck because someone had written "FAG!" on my car. A store was destroyed because someone hated that the owners loved each other. I was racing toward the station because some sicko thought it was fun to kidnap a child and bring him to a bedroom with a stuffed animal like his favorite. Compassion seemed like a fairy-tale notion, something Santa might bring if we were all very good.

CHAPTER THIRTEEN

I grabbed Klein off patrol. Told him to go to the Forrand house and note any suspicious activity. "Suspicious activity?" he asked. He ran his hand through his hair. Tried to anyway. Guy had so much gel in there, a hurricane-force wind couldn't shift it.

"Cars driving by frequently. Anyone paying a lot of attention to the house."

"Should I take down license plates?" He looked excited.

"Sure." That should occupy about six minutes of his five-hour shift. "Don't leave until your relief comes." He bounded out of the station, eager to protect and serve.

Wright was in his wool coat, ready to leave. Go home. Kiss his wife. Maybe watch his kids sleep. That's what he thought. "I've got news," I said.

"Why do I suspect that your news means I'm not getting out this door?"

"Cody Forrand and his family were at the interfaith event."

"Cody got out of the hospital?" He was surprised, and annoyed.

"I questioned him. The person who took him wore a Mighty Morphin Power Ranger mask."

"What? Oh, hell."

"Gets better. Sounds like the guy gave Cody the Lego truck kit he wanted so badly, and when he drove him to his place, he had a bed outfitted with the same sheets Cody has at home. And a stuffed animal just like his favorite."

"Not a stranger," Wright said.

"At the very least, it's someone who's been inside their house and his room. I've got the Forrands making a list of people who've been in the room since June, when Cody got those sheets."

"Is anybody with them?" he asked.

"Just sent Klein."

He rubbed his nose. "You want to call my wife and explain why I won't be home?"

"Nope. Finny here?"

"He left to meet Mr. Evans. Guess he's finally well enough to talk about the break-in." He took off his coat. "Why couldn't it have been the local pedo?"

I got Mr. Forrand on the phone and asked him to give me the details on Cody's truck sheets. Manufacturer, style, and the store where they were purchased. "How's the list coming?" I asked.

"Most of the people are friends or family." He was glum.

"We need *all* the names. Anyone who had no part in this should be eager to help. We'll clear them quickly."

"I'll call you back." He hung up.

A knock brought my head up. Finnegan stood in the doorway, in the windbreaker he wore whether it was ten degrees or a hundred degrees outside. "You talk to Wright?" I asked.

He nodded. "Crazy. Hey, I finally interviewed Mr. Evans about the break-in. He saw a red pickup truck idling near the shop a few days before the incident." Idyll had two apple orchards, and rural areas, but pickup trucks weren't common in town.

"He give you anything else?" I asked.

"Just that he locked up the night of the break-in around 10:00 p.m."

"Kind of late, isn't it?" The store usually closed at 7:30 p.m.

"Holiday inventory and shipping, he said."

"Okay, so the break-in happened after 10:00 p.m. and before, what, 8:30 a.m. when Mr. Gallagher reported it?"

He said, "Yup. Of course, that part of town isn't exactly hopping after ten." I didn't point out that there was no part of Idyll hopping after 10:00 p.m.

"What about the restaurant nearby?" I asked. "The Tavern House?"

"They close at 11:00," he said.

"I'll see if anyone there saw the truck. You need to shift your focus back on the Forrand case."

"You think Cody knows who took him?" he asked.

"No. He was upset about it, too. Because he hadn't discovered the secret of the Power Rangers."

An hour later, Mrs. Forrand appeared at the station with Cody in tow. She gave us two sheets of paper: one was a list of people who'd been in their house since June, and the other had details from Cody's sheets. "Some of it wasn't readable," she said. "The tag's been through the wash so many times."

Cody did a quiet 360, his mouth open. A few of the men, recognizing him, stopped by and said hello. Answered his questions about chasing criminals (as if they had) and using their guns (ditto). While they distracted him, the detectives and I asked Jane Forrand follow-up questions about the plumber and about Cody's toy raccoon, "Sammy." Was the toy always in his room? Would everyone on her list have seen it? Unfortunately, it seemed Sammy was beloved, and Cody took it everywhere. Jane said they'd had to turn around mid-trip more than once because Sammy had been left at a gas station or rest stop. So it was likely that anyone who knew them or had been in their house longer than five minutes would know about Sammy.

"His Uncle Greg bought it," she said. "After Cody burnt his hand on the stove. I'd taught him 'hot' and 'danger,' but the second I turned my back, he laid his palm on it."

Wright shuddered.

"I smelled his skin burning." She winced at the memory.

Finnegan looked green in the gills. "What about babysitters?" he asked, eager to change the subject.

"Babysitters?" she repeated, as if learning a new word. "My sister, Jess, watches them sometimes, but with Cody, I can't just leave him with some teen from the block."

"I was on TV!" Cody said.

"Were you now?" Dix asked, humoring him. "When?"

"Cody," his mother said, "what did we say about telling the truth?"

"I was *almost* on TV," Cody said.

"Better," she said. "Can we get back, now? Pete's half out of his mind with worry, but I wanted him to stay with Anna. Calm her down. She's obsessed with locking all the doors and windows now."

"When was Cody on TV?" Wright asked.

"Oh." She looked at Cody. "Five months ago, we went to New York. We'd been asked to be on the *Sally Jesse Raphael* show, for a program on children with rare medical conditions. There was Cody and Beau, a boy who can't be exposed to sunlight, and Jennifer, who has progeria, which makes her age at an accelerated rate."

"I think my wife saw that show," Dix said. "Cody was *on* it?"

"No," she said. "He got fidgety and wouldn't sit still long enough for them to include him in the show." She turned her grimace to a smile. "But we saw the Statue of Liberty, didn't we, hon?"

"Yup!" Cody said. "And a mouse!"

"It was a rat," she whispered. "The things kids think are cool." She shook her head. "Come on, bud. Dad and Anna will be wondering where we got to."

"Bye, policemen!" Cody said. He held up his hand for a high five. We all smacked his palm, lightly, forgetting, again, that we wouldn't hurt him if we exerted too much pressure.

"It's too bad about the TV thing," Wright said, after they'd left. "Almost seemed like a lead. Sicko sees Cody on TV. Decides to grab him."

Finnegan grabbed a bag of Swedish Fish from his desk drawer. He showed me the sixteen names the Forrands had listed. Wright critiqued them. "A third are family, a third are friends, and the last third are acquaintances or laborers, like the nameless plumber. Sixteen isn't a lot of names."

"Isn't it?" I calculated who'd been inside my house since June. Five people, one of them Damien Saunders.

"You'd think they'd be friendly with other parents. I can't tell you how many people Janice has paraded through our house in the past two weeks."

"Your wife is social," Finnegan said. "And none of her kids has a terrible disease. Maybe that kept the Forrands from getting out much."

"Maybe," Wright said. He sounded envious.

"Did we hear anything about the drug Cody had in his system?" I asked.

Finnegan moved his candy aside and said, "Yeah. It's a barbiturate used by people who suffer insomnia, but it's in other things like migraine medicine."

"Maybe someone on that list can't sleep or has headaches," I said.

"So the person grabs a kid with a disease that requires constant watching? Talk about a recipe for insomnia *and* headaches," Wright said. "I don't get it. Why take *him*?"

I said, "Maybe whoever grabbed him didn't plan to keep him long. Most don't."

"Then why re-create the bedroom?" Wright asked.

"Who knows?" Finnegan said. "We'll start on the vehicles. See if any of these folks drives a silver or white car."

"You can't do much more now. Go home, get some sleep. Come back bright and early with your shiny thinking caps on."

"Listen to Chief Cheerful." Wright yawned. "He doesn't have to assemble an air-hockey table before Christmas."

"Don't worry," Finny told him. "You've still got eight days."

"Damn it," I said. "I haven't bought gifts yet." They both looked at me. "I didn't hatch from an egg. I have a family." I swiped a candy fish from Finnegan's desk. "I'd better send somebody to relieve Klein."

"Has he stopped calling?" Wright asked.

Klein had misunderstood my remark about reporting suspicious activity. He'd telephoned me about every car that drove by the Forrands' house.

"Yes, though I suspect I'll get a twelve-page report with all of his findings. I'll be sure to share it."

"Thanks," Wright drawled.

"Nighty-night, detectives." I wandered toward the front of the station. There was a poster of Cody Forrand on a bulletin board we'd failed to take down. Thank God his mother hadn't seen it. I stared into his brown eyes and wondered who'd taken him. Who would steal a broken boy? Why? I unpinned the poster and crumpled it, tossing it into the nearest bin.

CHAPTER FOURTEEN

Being a cop, you get used to a fragmented life. One minute you're analyzing bloodstain spatters, and six hours later you're holding up spaghetti-sauce jars, picking the one you want. You'd assume your mind would reject red sauce after seeing a kitchen soaked in blood. But you'd be surprised at the brain's ability to compartmentalize. Bloodstains go here; spaghetti sauces go there. So though part of my brain was focused on who had taken Cody Forrand, the other parts were dealing with mundane nonsense, such as the fact that it was eight days until Christmas. I hadn't bought a thing. And I didn't have eight days. I had five. I visited my family on the 22nd. I wrote "Shopping" and put the note front and center on my desk. I'd leave early. Hell, technically, I was off today.

A German shepherd trotted toward me. "Hi, Jinx." Jinx sat by my knees and looked at me with dark liquid eyes. I wasn't fooled. I'd seen him take down a man in training. He'd seized the cop's padded arm with his big teeth. Refused to let go until Yankowitz shouted the magic word. Even then, you could see Jinx debate whether to obey.

"Tough guy." I ruffled the fur at his collar. Worked my fingers into his nape and massaged the skin below. The dog relaxed, its legs splayed in pleasure. "Or maybe not so tough after all, huh?" I whispered, putting my face near his. His breath was hot and rank. I pulled back. "You need to brush your teeth."

"I do brush his teeth."

I looked up. Yankowitz held a cup of coffee between his hands. He smiled. "Jinx likes you." He made it sound like an achievement.

"Thought dogs liked everyone."

"Hardly," he said, "and not Jinx. You should see him around Hopkins."

Jinx didn't like Hopkins. I rubbed behind his ears. "Good dog," I said. "Do you need me?" I asked Yankowitz.

"No. Jinx gets bored. I was making sure he wasn't getting into anything he shouldn't."

"Such as?" I asked.

"Mouse traps."

We had them at the station. Some of the men acted skittish around them. My city breeding paid off here. Mice? Roaches? No problem. Those damn raccoons, though. Nearly gave me a heart attack four months ago, sneaking out from under my porch.

A knock at the door. Wright. He was late. Maybe he'd gotten some real information from the Forrands. He stilled when he saw the dog. "I can come back," he said. His eyes never left Jinx.

"It's fine. We can talk now," I said.

He didn't enter the room.

"Jinx won't bite," Yankowitz said. "Unless I tell him to."

Wright glanced his way, then back to the dog. Yankowitz was enjoying this. Small wonder. Before I'd put him in charge of our K-9 crew, he'd been a meter maid. Bottom of the food chain. Wright, as detective, was at the top. I let Yankowitz have it, for another minute. Then I said, "Later, Jinx."

Yankowitz said, "*Herkommen.*" Wright slid into my office and hugged the opposite wall as the dog walked past and out.

"Don't like dogs?" I asked. We'd sent a survey when we'd begun the K-9 unit. No one had objected. I hadn't expected them to. Macho posturing is what cops do best.

"Got mauled when I was six," he said. "German shepherd. Don't mention it to the guys."

"Ouch. How'd your talk with the Forrands go?" I asked.

He sat in a chair opposite me, the one with sturdy legs. "They had a visitor. Friend of the family, Mrs. Donner."

"Didn't she have a kid with CIPA that died? What was she doing there?"

"Brought them food. Their kitchen was overflowing with casseroles and cookies." His stomach rumbled. "Anyway, she was there, along with the family." He slapped his notepad against his knee. "I wish I could've talked to Cody alone. Every time I asked a question, they'd talk over him or clarify."

"What did he say?" I asked.

"Same old, same old. Silver car picked him up near the Christmas house."

"Ms. Hart's."

Wright nodded. "Cody says the driver said they were going to go to the Power Ranger base. Looks like he ate a snack. Pretzels. Then he had cocoa, which was likely drugged, so his memory after that is pretty spotty."

"Did he say anything about where he was taken?"

"He thought he was asleep in his room. Then he realized Anna wasn't there and the bed he was in wasn't a bunk bed, so..." he shrugged. "I asked about windows, doors, anything, but he didn't remember. I asked if he ever saw the person without the mask on. He said no. He said he thinks that maybe the person wore a black coat. Then his mother weighed in, saying that before he said it was brown. Mrs. Donner said kids with CIPA couldn't distinguish colors as well as other kids because they often develop eye infections at a young age. Mr. Forrand said Cody hadn't had eye infections."

"So not much new information."

"No, although there was one thing. I asked him what the car smelled like, and he said, 'old lady.'"

"The car smelled like old lady? What does that mean?" I asked.

Wright said, "Mothballs?"

"Lavender perfume?" Like Mrs. Dunmore wore.

Wright said, "I'm going to put Dix and Klein on tracking down sellers of the Power Rangers mask and the sheets. Oh, and we should pull photos of everyone on the Forrands' list."

"Okay." I rubbed my eyes. We needed more men. I knew what the selectmen would say if I broached the topic. They were still grumbling about the overtime paid out during the North murder investigation.

He walked to the doorway and looked both ways, for Jinx, before stepping out.

What next? "Shopping" stared at me. No time like the present. I dialed my brother, John. Marie picked up. "Hi, Marie. How are you?"

"Tom! I'm up to my elbows in flour. Baking. Some stupid PTA thing. If they don't turn out right, I'm buying cookies from Madonia Brothers."

"Can't go wrong with Madonia Brothers." The thought of their prosciutto bread made me homesick.

"John's at school." My brother taught at NYU. "Or did you call to speak to me?"

"I need to do Christmas shopping. What are the boys into this year?" I asked.

"Moody silences, backtalk, and a lack of hygiene. I swear, Tom, you think you know how bad teenagers are and then your child turns into one. Like raising a werewolf. Gabe is almost as bad as Tyler." Gabe was twelve; Tyler fourteen.

"How does that translate into gifts?" I asked.

"Can I have a Taser?" she asked. "For when they get out of line?"

"Sure. And for them?"

"Gabe's into music, that mumbling crap that was always on the radio. He's begun to play guitar. You could get him picks and some sheet music. Tyler's into sports."

"Sports?" Tyler was built like John. Average height and lean. "Which ones?"

"All of them, in video game form. He's big into this fantasy league nonsense. I'll figure out who his best player is. Maybe you can get him an overpriced jersey."

"Sure. Let me know."

"I'll talk to them tonight."

"Hey, Marie, the boys don't play with Legos anymore, do they?" There'd been a time when colorful plastic cities littered their floors. John once told me I didn't know pain until I'd stepped on Legos, barefooted. I didn't mention that he'd never been shot on the job.

"No. Oh, I miss those days. They used to hug me, and tell me they loved me. Why do you ask?"

"I've got this case. Kid had a Lego truck kit and I wondered—"

"*The* truck kit?"

"Huh?"

"The truck kit is one of those die-for toys. You know, the stupid toy that gets crazy popular and grown-ass adults wrestle in stores over it? That's the truck kit. It's a special edition. It was on the news the other day. A fight broke out in FAO Schwarz over the last one."

"Thanks. That's helpful. Might be easier to track it."

"I'll give you a ring later. Let you know what I learn from *los sobrinos*." Marie spoke better Spanish than me. I'd picked it up in school and on the job. I'd probably forgotten most of it. Idyll didn't have a large Hispanic population.

"*Hasta luego*," I said.

I found Finnegan. "Just spoke to my sister-in-law, and she tells me people are fighting to get that truck kit Cody had. Might be an easier lead to follow than the sheets."

"Thanks." He glanced at my gloves. "You headed out?"

"Off to the Tavern House. See if anybody saw something the night of the Sweet Dreams break-in."

The Tavern House had a wooden sign hung above its door on short chains that creaked in the wind. Inside, bricks emerged from plaster walls. Big wooden beams crisscrossed overhead. At the edge of the dining room was a fireplace big enough to roast a pig. The waitstaff wore costumes that included lederhosen. Odd, since the cuisine was American. "Table for one?" the hostess asked. She'd been spared the costume and wore a sweater with black pants.

"I'm here on police business. Was the restaurant open the night of the 11th?"

"Day before the snowstorm? Sure."

"Were you working?"

"Yes."

"Sweet Dreams was vandalized that night, sometime after 10:00 p.m. Did you notice any vehicles parked down that way?"

"No. I had to pick up my sister, and it was a slow night, so I got out at 10:15. I don't remember seeing anything."

"Anyone else here work that night?" I asked.

She looked into the dining room. Pointed to a woman with her hair in Heidi braids. "Helen was in the dining room with Jodi. Jodi's not in tonight. The chef, Francis, and I think, Jason." She grimaced. "Yes. Jason was on because he kept making remarks to Jodi about her size. As if he's anything to write home about."

"Think I could talk to them?"

"Let me ask the manager." She disappeared. I perused the menu. Butternut-squash soup, salad with beets and goat cheese, rack of lamb, and duck breast. The prices made me blink. The hostess returned and said to the couple behind me, "I'll be right with you." She twitched her shoulder, indicating I should follow. Through the kitchen doors the temperature rose along with the noise level. Pots banging, shouts of "two salmon!" and underneath it all, a tinny radio playing country music. A man in a dress shirt and tie greeted me. "Hello, I'm Jeremy Rivers, the manager. Won't you come into my office?"

The office was a cramped room filled with menus, bills, checks, and orders. "Pardon the mess." He cleared a chair by removing a milk carton filled with wine glasses. "You want to hear from people who worked Thursday night?" He licked his thumb and pushed it through papers. "Charles and Dave are great people. I hope you find whoever wrecked their shop." He snatched up a sheet. "Here it is. Okay, you've spoken to Rachel, our hostess. Helen was here. Jodi, but she's out today. Patrick and Jason, and the chef, Francis. We're just wrapping up lunch. I can send people in as they become free."

I spoke to Patrick, the dishwasher, first. On the night in question, he'd gone out back for a smoke around 9:30 p.m. He'd clocked out at 11:30. He couldn't recall seeing anyone parked near the store or seeing or hearing anything suspicious.

Helen came next. She'd left work at 11:15 that night. "Oh, gosh, I *wish* I could help." Her braids flopped as she shook her head. "I was on the phone the second I got out. New boyfriend—I wasn't paying attention. I'm *so* sorry. My mother's always telling me I'll be murdered cuz I keep my phone to my ear and don't watch my surroundings."

The chef, Francis, smelled of garlic and cigarettes. "You wish to know what I saw? I saw snow and ice and the same little businesses, dark and closed, I see every night. I should've taken that job in Las Vegas when I was twenty, but *c'est la vie*, yes?" His vague French accent was a put on. His ignorance was not.

I'd given up hope when Jason appeared. His haircut teetered on mullet. He stood, arms crossed, near the door. "Have a seat," I said.

"I'm fine here."

Not worth arguing.

Before I asked a question, he said, "I don't know why someone hasn't trashed the place before now. They sell candy to kids. What sort of idiots let their kids shop there? They probably have a 'special room' where the kids get 'special' candy."

Was Jason a former victim of abuse, or did he just have a filthy mind?

"The shop was vandalized after ten o'clock on the night of the 11th. Did you see something?" I asked.

"Something like two men making out?" he asked.

"Did you see that on the 11th?" Dave had worked alone that night, according to Finnegan, and Charles hadn't picked him up. He'd been at home.

"No, but I saw it before. They think they're so hidden in their car. Like people don't have eyes." A car? Charles and Dave didn't strike me as the PDA type.

"You're sure it was the owners?" I asked.

"I saw him, both times, the little fairy." Dave was the smaller of them. "Always wearing those fucking bow ties and prancing around." Definitely Dave. "The candy probably has AIDS. I bet people get sick from it."

What kept me in my seat was the knowledge that once I started hitting him, I'd be unable to stop. "When did you see them?" I asked.

"Last week and the week before that. It's not right," he said.

"But you saw nothing the night of the 11th?"

"Naw."

"You sure?" He said nothing. "What car do you drive, Jason?"

"Why do you want to know?" he asked.

I stared and counted slowly in my head. Got to eight before he said, "A VW bug." Not a red pickup truck. Ah, well.

"The other man you saw, with Mr. Evans. What did he look like?"

"It was his 'business partner,' duh."

"So you saw Mr. Gallagher?" I pressed.

"Who else would it be?" It almost made me laugh. This guy hated gays, but he was ready to believe in their absolute fidelity. "He wore a Bruins jacket." I'd never seen Mr. Gallagher wear sports gear. "So are they gonna leave town or what? I saw a sign saying they'd reopen today."

"Why should that concern you?"

"We shouldn't have gays selling kids candy!"

Mr. Rivers pushed the door open, forcing Jason further into the room. "Is there a problem?" He glared at Jason.

"No," Jason said. He didn't look Mr. Rivers in the eye.

"Chief Lynch?" Mr. Rivers asked.

"I'm good. Thanks for the loan of your office."

Jason crept out the open door and Mr. Rivers shook his head. "I'm sorry. Jason isn't . . . I gave him the job because I was short-staffed. His parents are lovely people. I don't know how they ended up with him."

I shook hands with the manager and headed back out into the cold. The wind tried to take my hat, with no success. So David Evans was seen canoodling with a man other than Charles Gallagher. I thought about the graffiti and what had bothered me about it. The tone of the comments was different. One was a cold death threat; the other was angry and personal. Jason, in all his hateful spite, may have cracked the case. I hunched against the cold air and walked up the street.

Sweet Dreams looked amazing. Nate and crew had brought the plans to life. The gold-stenciled name, the glass jars, and new shelving, it all looked great. Mr. Evans stood behind the counter, ringing up a customer. He wore a bow tie and a maroon sweater-vest. His gray hair was freshly cut. He looked like he'd lost weight. He did not look as though he'd been ill recently.

"Good afternoon," I said, once he was free from customers.

"Chief Lynch, welcome. Place looks great, doesn't it?"

"It does. Do you have a moment? I need to discuss the break-in."

His lips pursed and his eyes swept down. "It breaks my heart to think about it."

I suspected there was more truth in that statement than he'd intended. "I just need a few minutes."

"Sure." He walked to the door and flipped the sign to "Back in Ten Minutes!" Honestly, this town. If you tried that in New York, you'd be out of business in a week.

He waved me through to the back office, where the new rear door kept the winter cold outside. Boxes marked "Suckers" and "Licorice" stood alongside gift-wrap rolls. He sat at the desk. I leaned against a shelving unit. "So, about the break-in," I said. "Who do you think is responsible?"

"Me? I've no idea. I just can't fathom it."

"It's not nice, being made to feel different," I said. "Hated."

He swallowed. "You understand. I heard about your patrol car."

"Hazard of the job," I said. "But your store? That must have felt personal."

"Of course," he said. "Charles and I both felt attacked."

"I just have one more question."

"Yes?"

"What time did you return to the store to write 'Leave Before We Kill You' on the wall beside the door?"

"What do you mean?"

"Please don't lie. I know it was you. You saw the damage to the store and tried to divert attention from the graffiti with your death threat."

"Why would I do that?" His voice cracked like a pubescent boy's. He winced.

"Because you didn't want Charles to find out about your affair? Because you figured this way you could fill out a police report and get the insurance money. Redo the store like you've wanted to for years."

"No," he whispered.

I stepped forward. "We had a child abduction to pursue and you let us process your store as if a hate crime had been committed. Would you like to talk to the Forrands? Apologize for wasting our time and resources while their son was kidnapped?"

He lowered his face to his hands. "No. Please, no. I didn't *know* that would happen. How could I?" His words came in a mumbled rush. "I'm sorry, but this store is my life. Charles is my life! If he found out . . ." He looked up, tears on his cheeks. "Please, you can't tell him. If he finds out, he'll leave. I cheated, once before. I swore I never would again. I didn't—"

"You need to come to the station and make a statement. Tell us who did it. And don't lie. I've a pretty good idea who it is." Utter lie.

"I didn't mean for any of this to happen. I didn't know Zack would go nuts when I told him we needed to break it off. I came back to the store because I'd forgotten a DVD Charles wanted to watch. The door was broken in. Glass everywhere. And that graffiti. He meant it for me." You cocksucker. "If I make the statement, will you tell Charles?" He still wanted a way out.

"So you got some spray paint and wrote the death threat to obscure who did it."

"I had some in my car, from an old art project. I thought if I wrote the death threat, Charles wouldn't find out about Zachary."

"Come by the station," I said.

"We had a nice life," he said wistfully. As if it was all over, just like that.

I walked out the front door. The bell jangled. Coming up the street was Charles Gallagher. He waved to me. I waved back and hurried to my car. I didn't want to witness what happened next.

CHAPTER FIFTEEN

Wright looked worse than I'd ever seen him. His suit was wrinkled and his bloodshot eyes watered. His body curled over as he hacked into a handkerchief. "God, you sound like Finnegan," I said. Even Wright's glare lacked heat.

"Kids are sick, my wife is getting sick, and now I'm sick." He sipped from his mug and grimaced. "I know I'm bad off when coffee tastes gross." He put the mug down. "You think the staties, if we asked . . ." If he'd put on a clown nose and began juggling, I couldn't have been more surprised. We'd had a state detective in to help with our murder, and Wright had been a complete jackass to him. "I don't want this kidnapper to disappear."

"He won't." I had no business making this claim, but I didn't want us calling for help every time we had something tougher than a DUI. I'd gotten the break-in cleared up. Now we just had the kidnapping and arson. Oh, and my graffiti.

"Finnegan checked the cars. There are four people on the Forrands' list with gray, silver, or white cars. One belongs to the sister, one to their former minister." He raised a brow.

"Eh, men of God are still men," I said.

"Right. Then we've got a family friend, Camille, who Finnegan is talking to."

"Who's the fourth?" I asked.

"Greg Baker." He sneezed.

"Greg Baker. Uncle Greg? The same guy who gave Cody the original Sammy raccoon?" I asked.

"Guess he's next." He coughed. "I need to go talk to him."

"Why don't I go check on Uncle Greg and the others? You stay here and chug cough medicine. Give me the names and addresses you need checked."

On the road to interview "Uncle" Greg, my gloved hands gripped the steering wheel. Cold air blasted my face. "Two more days with you," I told the car. I turned the heater off and the radio on. "Frosty the Snowman" assaulted my ears. Good god, was that children singing? I snapped the radio knob fast, and it came off, landing in the footwell. The children sang on. "Fuck!" I tried to manipulate the little metal stub, but my gloved hand wasn't up to the task. The children chorused "thumpity thump thump"s. I tore off my right glove and used my bare hand. The volume could be lowered but not silenced.

"Silent Night" came next. Sung by children more out of tune than the last group. I sped up, reaching Chaplin right after the shepherds quaked. Chaplin was where the Forrands had lived before moving to Idyll. It was Jane Forrand's birthplace and where she and Pete had met, at the local gas station. He'd had a blowout a mile away, and she worked the register. I learned this from Uncle Greg, who lived near the center of town, in an old Victorian painted purple.

From the outside, the place looked like it belonged to an eighty-year-old lady. Inside, it was another story. Greg Baker's living room contained a large TV, a massive leather couch, and more than one gaming system. An electric guitar was propped in a corner. Movie posters hung on the walls: *The Godfather*, *Goodfellas*. The place screamed single straight man. Greg settled me on the sofa and offered me a drink. I declined. He stood, cracking his knuckles. "How can I help?" he asked.

"I'm trying to figure out who could've grabbed Cody. You've known the Forrands a long time."

"Since before the kids were born. Me and Pete went to college together. We took jobs at the same insurance firm, though I came out here a year earlier."

"You still work there?" I asked.

"Yup. Can you believe it? 1989. God, time flies."

"Pete isn't there anymore though, right? He switched jobs?"

"He took a job closer to Idyll, once they moved. The commute was a bitch."

"Right. Plus, Cody's illness must've been tough to manage. All those hospital visits."

"Yeah." He sat in a lounge chair, his butt perched on the edge. "Poor Pete. At first it seemed like he had this really chill kid who, like, never cried. And then it turned out it was because of the disease. Pete and Jane felt awful, like they should've known earlier."

I fast-forwarded to the present. "Cody says he got into the car that took him away. Does that strike you as odd?"

"Cody does stuff without thinking through the consequences, you know?" he said.

"So you're not surprised?" I asked.

"I am, actually. I know he got the stranger-danger talk from Pete and Jane." He lowered his voice, though we were alone. "By the way, I hope Pete hasn't been weird around you. He told me, about your being gay."

He had what? Why?

"You gotta understand, Pete comes from a conservative Christian family. Very big on sin and punishment. So if he isn't always the most tolerant, maybe try to understand why he's that way." Did this explain why Pete didn't want me to interview Cody? Why his wife complained I'd "harassed" them in the hospital?

"I don't remember seeing you during the search for Cody. Were you at work?"

"Yeah. I didn't hear about it until that night. I wanted to help, but Pete told me to wait until the roads got better. Then Cody was found. Guess prayers work."

"You're a religious man?"

"Lapsed Catholic."

"You drive a silver Impala?" I asked. He nodded. "How does it handle in the snow?"

"It does all right."

"Do you have any idea who might've taken Cody?"

"No. None."

"I imagine you don't see as much of the Forrands since they moved."

"Pete and I still get together for an occasional beer. Sometimes I watch the kids."

"That's nice of you."

"I'm Cody's godfather. Besides, they're great kids."

The doorbell's chimes sounded. "Excuse me." He bounded from his seat and clomped downstairs. A minute later, he returned, followed by a boy with green eyes.

"This is Nathan," Greg said, ruffling the kid's hair. "His mom, Lisa, lives next door. She had to run to the vet's. I'd promised I'd babysit. Is it okay?" he asked.

"Sure, I'm almost finished," I said.

Nathan went for the video-game controller. He sat cross-legged on the floor. "Keep the volume down, huh buddy?" Greg said. "I need to talk to this policeman."

"Cool," Nathan said, his eyes never turning from the screen. A giant dragon swooped across the screen. "I'm going to beat that orc today!"

"Great, buddy," Greg said. So he had video games for the kids to play. How thoughtful.

"You babysit a lot for the neighbors?" I asked.

He shrugged. "I help out." He watched my face. "Not often."

"Cody sure seems into the Power Rangers," I said.

"Oh, man, that show. I've watched it with him. It's crazy bad."

"So you know his favorite Power Ranger?" I asked.

His eyes went wide of my face. "Of course, the Green Ranger."
Gotcha.

"Thanks for your time. If you think of anything, call the station?" I handed him a card.

"Sure. Absolutely. If there's anything I can do, let me know. It's just terrifying, thinking about it. I'm so glad he's safe."

Nathan pushed buttons on the controller. Explosions sounded. "Take that!"

"Aren't you fierce?" Greg told him. "Hey, Nathan, you want some cocoa?" He clicked the door closed behind me. My hands tingled. Cocoa.

I regretted the loaner's lack of police radio. I wanted someone to check Greg's background, now. I'd have to wait until I got back. Maybe I *should* look into buying a mobile phone.

The next person on my list was Jane Forrand's younger sister, Jessica, who still lived in Chaplin, on a poorly paved road with a horse barn out back. Jessica had a scattering of freckles that seemed out of place in winter. She led me to a living room with a worn quilt on the sofa and a blazing fire. "Cold out there," she said.

When I asked how many people lived in Chaplin, she laughed. "A little over two thousand. Everybody knows everybody's business. Jane hated it. She couldn't wait to move to New York."

"New York?"

"She wanted to be an actress. Figured if she could get a lead on a soap opera, she'd be set for life. She was in all our school plays. Got all the leads. She was so pretty and outgoing."

I wouldn't have described Jane Forrand as pretty.

"This is Jane, her senior year in high school. Prom queen." She handed me a photograph she'd fetched from a side table. In it, a younger Jane had a tiara in her blond hair. She wore a billowing turquoise gown. "Jane won all the queens: prom, May, and homecoming. Everybody thought she'd go to New York after college, but then she met Pete and," she shrugged, "things changed."

"She finished college?" I asked.

"Oh, yes. Theater major at Quinnipiac College. She met Pete when she was a junior. He was already out of college. They got married after she graduated. He worked for a big insurance company. She got pregnant with Anna. They bought a house, on Cypress Boulevard. Beautiful place."

"So they lived in town?"

"Yes. They moved two years ago, when things got difficult."

"Difficult."

She scrunched her nose as if something smelled bad. "It was Cody, all his bruises. People noticed. He hadn't been diagnosed yet. It was nonsense, of course, but it took a toll. Then Pete lost his job."

"Layoffs?" I asked.

"I think so. So they sold the house and moved to be closer to his new job." Interesting. Greg hadn't said Pete had lost his job. Someone was wrong, or lying.

"Who accused them of child abuse?" I asked.

She bit her lip, like Jane. They could've been twins in that moment. "Their neighbor, Mrs. Kimble, started the rumors. She's a retired teacher. She thought Cody got injured too often."

"Does she still live in town?"

"Yes, at 15 Cypress Boulevard, next door to their old house."

"About the kidnapping . . ."

"Jane says you think it's someone who knows them, who knows Cody."

"It looks that way. Can you think of anyone who'd do that?"

"No. Unless it was one of those people who likes to have sex with kids." She knotted her hands together. "Wasn't there one in your town? Jane said—"

"It wasn't him."

"We had a girl go missing here, in Chaplin. Vicky Fitzgerald. Five years ago. She was taken by a pedophile. Found in the woods. Everyone turned out to search for her. It was awful." This was the case Mr. Forrand had mentioned, the one that had soured him on the police, and sparked that argument with his wife.

"How well do you know Greg Baker?" I asked.

"Greg? He and Pete go way back. They met in college out in Colorado."

"He's still single?"

She picked at the sleeve of her sweater. "Greg's a big kid. I can't imagine him settling down. He's got a, what do they call it? Peter Pan complex. He'll never grow up. Why do you want to know about Greg? You don't think he had anything to do with Cody, do you? Greg loves Cody. He's his godfather."

"I'm just asking questions. Trying to piece together who knows what. That's all."

She harrumphed at me. "You'd do better to look at that plumber Jane hired."

"She told you about him?"

"Yesterday. She's been trying to remember his name. It's driving her bonkers."

"Thanks. If you think of anything, please, give me a call."

"I will. I promised to come down soon to babysit so Jane can go shopping. She wants to make this Christmas special, after everything Cody has been through."

I got into my car and checked the list of names Wright had laboriously typed. He'd put on the silver car owners and folks who were on the Forrands' list but who didn't own a silver car. There were friends, and the minister. I added a name to the bottom. Mrs. Kimble, 15 Cypress Boulevard.

The friends were a motley collection with one thing in common: they'd known Jane all their lives. They confirmed much of Jessica's narrative. Jane was talented, destined to leave Chaplin and do big things. Soap operas, movies, whatever she wanted. Then she'd met Pete. He'd been from Colorado, exotic by Chaplin standards, with enough money to buy a house on the second-nicest street in town. They'd hosted dinner parties, helped at local charity events. Everything roses. Until a few years ago. Everyone brushed aside the rumors. "Of course they didn't hurt Cody. It was the CIPA. Only no one knew what that was. Poor Cody. Always at the hospital, but never crying. Such a trooper." They seemed to forget Cody didn't cry because he didn't feel pain.

The minister said the Forrands were at church every Saturday morning. "Until they moved." I asked if he'd heard the rumors of child abuse. "I didn't credit them. Anna was fine, and if Cody got hurt, it was because he played hard."

When I asked if he'd heard of Cody's kidnapping, he said, "Everyone in Chaplin has. It's that kind of place. People in each other's back pockets. I'm glad he's home, safe." He moved a hymnal. "Some people don't believe in evil. I'm not one of them. I'm sure you understand, in your line of work. We had a child go missing five years back. Killed." Everyone I'd spoken to had mentioned Vicky Fitzgerald.

He had no idea who might bear the Forrands ill will. "Certainly there were some happy to see them knocked off their perches. The golden couple no more, but that was idle envy. Nothing more. Nothing *active*."

When I asked about the snowstorm, he told me he'd been in church during the worst of it. "Discovered some drafts. We need to get that window fixed." He pointed to a tall stained-glass window with a hole near St. Peter's right foot. The service schedule confirmed his account, though I wondered if anyone had attended during the blizzard. Still, he wasn't a spring chicken and it was difficult to imagine him in a Power Ranger mask. Plus, his car, a gray Escort, was a rundown vehicle that didn't look like it could survive a blizzard.

It was just into the supper hour. I hesitated to make another visit. I could return tomorrow. Even as I decided, I turned the steering wheel toward Cypress Boulevard. The mailboxes had house numbers on them. Mrs. Kimball's was a simple gray box. That meant that the mailbox shaped like a miniature house, down to its tiny shingles, had belonged to the Forrands. The real house behind it was huge, with a wraparound porch. Its windows were framed by white holiday lights. A mini turret at the top. Mrs. Kimble's house was modest compared to the castle next door. Lights gleamed through her drawn curtains. The doorbell chimed the standard high-low note. The inner door swung open, and a woman peered at me through bifocals.

I introduced myself. She tilted her head like a robin, opened the outer glass door, and said, "Mind if I see your identification?"

I showed my badge and opened my wallet. Idyll didn't have police identification cards, so I flashed her my license. "If you like, I can give you the number for the police station. You can call and give them my description."

She reached for the phone. "What's the number?" I recited it and she dialed. I heard someone answer, "Idyll Police Station." She hung up. "Good enough for me." She waved me inside. "What did you want to ask me about?"

"The Forrands, they used to be your neighbors."

"I remember." She led me into a living room with a burning fire. Fireplaces were big in Chaplin. She sat in a rocking chair. I took a seat in the overstuffed chair opposite. The chair felt like it was pushing me out of it.

"You heard about the kidnapping?" I asked.

"Of course. It knocked poor Suzy Longford's engagement news down several notches. Poor Suzy." She tsked and rocked. The floor-boards creaked.

"Can you think of anyone who didn't like the Forrands?"

"Enough to kidnap their child? No. And why take Cody? Anna, maybe. She's a sweet girl. Bright." She caught my look of surprise. "I'm not advocating kidnapping. I'm saying that of the two, you'd want Anna. Cody is a tornado."

"I heard you suspected abuse?"

She laughed, mid-rock. The chair's legs pointed upward as she cackled. "Dear me." She came back down, the rockers creaking. "People made such a fuss. Yes, I worried about him. He was always being whisked to the doctor's with some truly worrisome injuries. I taught first and second grades; I've seen abused children. His parents didn't seem the type, but Cody did run them ragged, and they were having difficulties. Money problems. First the landscapers stopped coming, and then pieces of furniture went missing. Jane smiled and said she'd decided that they didn't fit the rooms. She was selling them. Trying to keep their heads above water. Then he lost his job, and there was no way they could keep up the mortgage payments."

"Why did he lose his job?"

She laced her fingers together over her middle and said, "I don't know." True? I thought not, but I didn't push.

"I've heard they were quite the couple. Maybe others were envious?"

She smiled. "Of course they were. We haven't seen much of them since they moved, but word is they've come down in the world." I thought of the Forrands' small house, with its holes in the hall, and its reek of urine. They certainly had.

"I'm guessing the abuse allegations didn't make their lives easier," I said.

She fixed me a look. "I never filed a report. I may have asked more questions than others did, but I realized his injuries were self-inflicted the day I saw Cody hitting his arm against a tree. He kept yelling, "Hi-ya!" and hitting it, over and over. Jane had to pull him away. She rolled up his sleeve and his arm, it was swollen and blue with a massive bruise. I remember she asked him, 'Why didn't you stop?' and he said, 'Because I wasn't finished.' He was only three and a half years old."

The fire popped. We both looked to it, the flames eating the wood.

"I can't imagine who would take Cody Forrand," she said. "It must have been a stranger. We had a little girl go missing. Back in '92, Vicky Fitzgerald. Some man grabbed her, raped her, and killed her." She looked at the flames, lost in thought.

"It seems likely that whoever took Cody knew him."

She stared at the fire. "Why? He's a very sick boy."

"Can you think of anyone who might've taken him? Someone who—"

"No," she said, cutting me off. "It must've been a stranger who took Cody. Someone with no idea of his condition. Maybe that's why he let him go."

"The kidnapper?"

She nodded. "Maybe he realized Cody was broken. Decided to return him."

"Like an unwanted gift."

Her lips flattened into a thin, hard line. "Something like that."

CHAPTER SIXTEEN

Friday afternoon. Billy delivered me a stack of newspaper articles. He'd really done his homework on the Chaplin kidnapping. The first article was from the *Hartford Courant*. On September 25, 1992, it was the front-page story.

Six-Year-Old Girl Missing

Connecticut State Police are searching for six-year-old Victoria Fitzgerald, who went missing from her Chaplin home's front yard yesterday afternoon. Her mother reported her missing. Victoria has blond hair, brown eyes, is 42 inches tall, and weighs 48 pounds, according to reports. State Police search-and-rescue crews, K-9 teams, and volunteers are looking for the girl.

A photo of a smiling Vicky accompanied the story. She had a dimple in her right cheek. On the third day after her disappearance, the *Courant* ran the following story:

Search Continues for Missing Chaplin Girl

Victoria Fitzgerald's disappearance has stunned the 1,950 residents of Chaplin. Since she went missing Thursday, 100 volunteers have assisted the police, Fire Department, and sheriff's deputies to search the woods and fields near her Laurel Street home. Many neighbors have assisted in the search for Victoria. Mr. Peter Forrand, a Chaplin resident, donated food to searchers and had co-workers from as far as Boston post flyers of the missing girl. Dogs and helicopters have also been deployed in the search for the six-year-old. The trees of Chaplin are wrapped with flyers featuring Victoria's picture. A special mass will be said this afternoon at Our Lady of Lourdes Church.

Victoria was last seen playing in her front yard. She'd returned from school, eaten a snack, and gone outside. Mrs. Woods, Victoria's first-grade teacher, described her as "sunny and smiling, a joy to teach." Victoria's parents are divorced, and her mother has primary custody. Both parents appeared on TV, pleading for her safety. Each has agreed to take a polygraph test. Police will not report the test results, because they are an investigative tool.

So they were eyeing the parents, hard enough to ask them to take a poly. Not that the test proved a damn thing. Polygraphs can be beaten, or wrong. That's why they're inadmissible in many states.

As the days dragged, it seemed clear from the articles that suspicions had focused on the father. He'd divorced Vicky's mom a year earlier. The custody battle had been contentious. She had primary custody, and he could only see his daughter one weekend a month on supervised visits. That was damning. Was he a hitter? A drunk?

The next article was darker but not surprising.

Body of Child Discovered in Chaplin Woods

The body of a child found in Chaplin Woods appears to be that of missing six-year-old Victoria Fitzgerald. Investigators have not positively identified the body as that of the missing girl yet, but they state that it was found two miles from where she was last seen on September 25. The corpse was found in an area not included during the searches for the missing child. Chaplin Police, when asked about this omission, said the case was still active and that they were unable to comment.

State police have indicated that, pending a coroner's determination, it appears the child was murdered. There have been no arrests at this time. Fitzgerald's family has been notified of the discovery.

State officer Stephen Whittaker insists the parents were cooperating with investigators and federal agents by opening their homes to searches and by taking polygraph tests. The results of those tests are not being released at this time.

Most of the reporters backed off the parents as suspects once it was released that Vicky had been sexually assaulted, strangled to death, and dumped in the woods. The police began looking at people with criminal records of sexual misconduct. A week later, they hauled in Gerald Biggs, a thirty-six-year-old plumber from Hampton. He had a record for public indecency. He admitted, while in custody, that he fantasized about young girls and had followed some home from school in his truck. Cops got a warrant. Searched his home. In his living room they found blond hairs and a rope. The weave of the rope matched the abrasion patterns on Vicky's neck.

On October 4, 1992, the *Hartford Courant* ran this:

Alleged Killer of Local Girl Commits Suicide in Cell.

Gerald Biggs hanged himself.

Gerald Biggs was a plumber. Mrs. Forrand said she'd let a plumber in their house, and he'd looked at the kids' twin beds. If Sammy, the raccoon, had been in the room, he'd have seen enough to restage it. What were the odds on two pedophile plumbers being the bad guys here?

Billy peeked around my door. "Any help?" he asked.

"How did you get so much so fast?" I asked.

He colored. "I think the librarian has a crush on me." Billy attracted women like sugar did ants. "She remembered the case. So did I, once I looked at the articles. Poor girl."

"Peter Forrand's name appeared in some articles."

"Small world, huh?" Billy said. That right there was why Billy would never be a detective. He saw that coincidence and thought "huh," whereas a guy like Wright would see it and think, "How likely is that?"

I decided to run it by Wright, but he disappointed me.

"Mr. Forrand mentioned the case, more than once. He had young kids at the time. Probably scared him. He obviously hasn't forgotten it."

"You don't think it's hinky?"

"Hinky?" He barked a laugh. "How? Everyone in Chaplin knew about it, and half our suspects are from there. Besides, he searched with you. How could he have had a hand in Cody's kidnapping?"

"What if he arranged it?" I asked. "You've seen their place. They're living close to the bone. Maybe he thought if they got rid of Cody, things would get better."

"Well, if he hired someone, he didn't get his money's worth. Cody was returned."

"It might explain why he's been less than willing for us to interview Cody."

"I'd say reluctant, not unwilling." He appraised me. "You really are a suspicious bastard, aren't you?"

"Yes. Have we heard any word on the plumber?"

"Nah. We had Mrs. Forrand go through the yellow pages, see if any of the business names seemed familiar. She picked half a dozen but admitted she wasn't sure if any of them were the right one."

Finnegan walked past, Mr. Evans behind him. Mr. Evans's right eye was swollen nearly shut. Uh-oh. Looks like Mr. Gallagher hadn't taken the news of the affair well. An hour and a half later, Finnegan found me working on the stupid inventory form Mrs. Dunsmore insisted I finish before I left for "vacation" on Monday. One day, with my family, in lieu of Christmas. Some vacation.

"What's got you trying to out cuss Dix?" Finnegan asked.

"Inventory form. I have to explain the purpose of each piece of equipment."

"Seriously?" he asked. I growled. "Okay, point taken. I've got good news. The Sweet Dreams break-in is all but closed. I've got Klein and Billy looking for one Zachary Gabriel, former lover of our David Evans."

"Fantastic. Do I have to explain how a Taser works on this fucking sheet?"

"Easy, Chief. You know you could just crib from last year's form?"

"What?" I looked up so fast my head nearly snapped off my neck.

"The form. Why not just pull last year's? Lady Du must have it filed somewhere."

Unsavory words erupted from my mouth. Why hadn't she told me I could just copy last year's answers? Why wasn't she filling out this damned form? I threw a pen at my plant. It missed by several inches.

"Maybe now you've solved the break-in, you can find who tagged my car," I said.

Finnegan flinched. "We're working on it."

"Uh-huh."

"We are." Defensive? He ought to be. It had been a goddamn week. I bet if Chief Stoughton's car had been vandalized, these asses would've solved the case by now. I stalked to the file cabinet to see if I could find last year's form. Finnegan exited my office without another word. Finally using his brain. Sure enough, there was a copy of last year's inventory report and the year before that and the year before that. I slapped all three down on my desk. Kneaded my brow, and got to work. After an hour, I decided to call it a night. I gathered my coat, hat, and gloves. The station was lively, given the hour.

"Did you hear about Sweet Dreams? It was one of the gay guy's boyfriends that destroyed the place. I thought when gay men raged out they *redecorated*." Snickers and laughter.

Two men's relationship had just exploded. Hilarious.

At the front, Officer Burns spoke to the dispatcher, his elbows on the counter. "Did you see his shiner? Guess someone wasn't happy about being the *other* man." He chuckled.

"What's so funny?" I asked.

Burns straightened and said, "Oh, nothing, Chief."

"That's what I thought. You want to gossip about active cases, do it at another station." The dispatcher inhaled a sharp breath. I shot him a look and stormed out the door. Then recalled I'd parked in the back. Damn it.

At home, I ate leftover Indian that wasn't better the second day. One of the kitchen cabinet handles had come loose. The shallow brass

handles often scraped my knuckles. My eyes drifted to the peeling linoleum floor. The house needed a makeover. Badly. I'd begun repairs.
Taken down wallpaper. Painted the guest bedroom. I hadn't made
more progress. Why?

Because you were thinking about leaving.

"No, I wasn't." I shook my head. "I wasn't."

Because everyone knew I was gay? I wouldn't cut and run. Couldn't
cut and run. Hadn't been in the job a year yet. And who'd have me?
The news would follow me to whatever new town I settled in. The gay
police chief.

"I wasn't," I whispered. The peeling linoleum told another story.

CHAPTER SEVENTEEN

Jerry looked like he'd sucked a lemon. "I can't believe you called her about your car," he said.

I set the keys to the station wagon on his cluttered counter. "Who?"

"Mrs. Dunsmore." He rubbed his chin. It made a raspy sound against his calloused hand.

"What? I didn't."

"Yeah, well, she must like you."

"Like me? She can't stand me."

"Could've fooled me. C'mon." He snatched my keys from the small board behind him. Around the corner, half hidden by an ice cream truck, was my car. The driver's door glinted in the sun. Graffiti gone. Seal restored. "I thought—"

"Thought what?" He was spoiling for a fight.

He'd told me he couldn't do the seal. That had been before Mrs. Dunsmore had called. No wonder he was grumpy.

"It looks great."

"Damn well better. I also topped up your oil and replaced a frayed fan belt."

"Thanks. Oh, the radio knob on the wagon is broken. It's on the dash."

He gave me an invoice. "Fine. Whatever."

I unlocked my vehicle. Transferred my gear from the station wagon's trunk back to my car. Racked the seat back. Closed the door. Inhaled. Gripped the steering wheel. I'd always thought that people who named their cars were weird. That people who formed attachments to vehicles were one bullet short of a round. Driving back to the station in my car felt good, right. Add me to the car weirdo ranks.

Finnegan and Wright were huddled over the coffeemaker. Finnegan added enough cream and sugar to qualify his drink as dessert. Wright stirred his, over and over. He didn't add anything. Simply liked to stir. I'd learned their habits. It jolted me. When I'd arrived, I'd stayed apart. Done little to interact. I'd recently lost my former New York Homicide partner and best friend, Rick. So I did my damnedest not to learn this lot's names. I tried not to know their marital status or who their favorite athlete was, but it had begun to accumulate. You can't blind yourself, day after day. Information trickles in. Before you know it, you realize you could order your men's coffee for them.

A pile of folders and a fresh batch of mail was on my desk. Mrs. Dunsmore was back. I walked to the window and peered at my plant. It looked less anemic. She came in while I touched a leaf. I dropped my hand. Her parrot broach was pinned to the upper right of her dress. Bingo night then. See? Details. They creep in, even when unwanted.

"Picked up my car. Heard you had a word with Jerry," I said.

"Him. Did he take care of it?"

"He did. He said you must like me." Why had I said that?

"I told you he wasn't bright," she said. Well, what had I expected?

"Thanks for calling him." I saw the shopping note on my desk. "Damn it."

"Problem?" She checked the plant. Adjusted its spot on the windowsill.

"There may be no gifts at Christmas. By the time I've got a minute, the shops are closed." In Idyll, shops that stayed open late closed at seven or eight o'clock. "Not that it matters. I haven't any idea what to get my parents."

"The professors?" As if she didn't know. Mrs. Dunsmore gathered intel like squirrels gathered nuts.

"Yes, the professors."

"What do they teach?" Was she humoring me?

"My mother teaches eighteenth- and nineteenth-century literature, and my father teaches philosophy."

She turned from the plant and searched me for academic tendencies. Found none. "What did you give them last year?"

I told her about the t-shirts. "They didn't like them. Only thing they ever seemed to like were the day planners I bought. Maybe I'll do that again. If I can get myself inside a store before closing."

"Why don't you let me do it?" she asked.

"Do what?" On my desk was a message from Wright. His crabbed script was hard on the eyes. Something about Cody's raccoon?

"Buy your parents' gifts."

"What?" My head popped up like a jack-in-the-box's.

"I've got time, and I have to buy presents for the Toys for Tots drive." We had a program where people could donate wrapped children's toys and have minimal traffic tickets waived.

"I thought people dropped off toys."

"I always buy extra. Don't worry. It doesn't come out of the budget." That meant she bought them herself. "Believe it or not, I used to be a personal shopper years ago at a department store in Hartford."

"I'd believe it if you told me you were a Cold War spy," I said under my breath.

"A few questions." She grabbed a piece of paper from my desk. "What's your mother's favorite color?"

"Red. Or red-purple. She's got this scarf thing she loves because of the color."

"Father's favorite TV show?"

"Um." I thought. "*Gunsmoke*?"

Within five minutes she'd extracted strange and various pieces of information from me. "Leave it to me," she said. I felt as stunned as a hit-and-run victim. Why was she being nice? Was it left over from when she served the prior chief, Stoughton? He'd struck me as the sort who loved having others do favors for him.

At their desks, Finnegan and Wright swapped papers. "Any news?" I called.

They looked up, squinting. "Is it possible to go blind from paperwork?" Finnegan asked. "That's good for a disability claim, yeah?"

"We've begun to check out Dix's list of toy stores," Wright said. He blew his nose into a handkerchief. Uh-oh.

Finnegan said, "Most of the stores didn't stock the Lego truck kit. Said they wish they had. Thing sells like hotcakes."

"What about the raccoon?" I asked Wright. "You left me a note."

He coughed. "Right. The raccoon. Made by some local company, so there can't be a ton of them. Wonder of wonders, the woman I spoke to at the company saw the news about Cody on TV. She's going to check into recent area sales."

I said, "Good. Hey, do you know if there's something up with Mrs. Dunsmore?"

"What do you mean?" Finnegan asked. His head was down again. Scanning papers.

"She's acting odd."

"Well, her niece is back in the hospital. Breast cancer." He scratched his eyebrow. "Chemo is a nightmare."

"Her niece has breast cancer?" I asked.

"Yeah. She got diagnosed back in October." How did he know? Why didn't I? I'd been paying attention, hadn't I?

"Is the niece gonna make it?" I asked.

Finnegan shrugged. "She's got stage three, but she's young. Thirty-two. Has two kids. Tough to say."

Wright said, "Mrs. Dunsmore's been spending a lot of time with her, but she can't if she's sick." Her cough. She'd stayed home. Probably trying to avoid our germs.

"Huh," I said. Because I had no idea what else to say.

I grabbed Billy. Told him to find out where Peter Forrand had worked prior to his current job, and to pass the information to Finny.

"Sure thing," he said. "Any, um word, on the other thing?"

My brain was blank until he looked away and I realized he meant my car. "No, nothing yet." Finnegan didn't seem to be exerting himself. Then again, neither was I.

CHAPTER EIGHTEEN

Ella Fitzgerald sang about the joys of sleighing. The house smelled of eggnog and cinnamon. Before Marie brought Christmas eggnog into our lives, I thought I didn't like it. I drank that first cup, years ago, to be polite. Pretty sure Dad did too. Now we crowd the bowl until she gives us dispensation to ladle it into tall glasses. I sat in a large armchair, sipping the nog, watching my nephews play an involved game called Magic. They sprawled on the floor. Gabriel's limbs made me think he might surpass his older brother, Tyler, in size. Tyler was a dark blond and resembled John. Gabriel was darker and looked like Marie and me, which led to many jokes.

"Attacking," Gabriel said. He moved cards forward, aligning them sideways.

"Blocking," Tyler said.

"Boys, you ready for presents?" Marie called. She carried a plate of cookies into the room. How could anyone eat cookies after the brunch we'd just had? John leapt up to help her. "I've got it," she said. He insisted on taking it from her. She wiped a curl from her face. "Tom needs to be on the road before it gets too late."

"I'm fine," I said.

Gabriel said, "I told Marc at school that we were celebrating Christmas five days early, and he said it was sacrilegious."

"Sacrilegious?" I looked at John. He was parceling out gifts. "What kind of crowd are you letting your kids run with?" John laughed and handed me a rectangular package wrapped in green paper:

To TOMMY,
Love MOM and DAD.

143

It was shirt-weight heavy. Probably a button-down I'd never wear. I got my game face on.

"So many!" My mother clapped her hands as the boxes rose to meet her knees.

"You're getting ours now," Marie said. She, John, and the kids were spending Christmas Day with her family upstate. My mother pouted, but only a little. I suspected it was more for show. She'd enjoy a quiet holiday at home.

"It's going to be a quiet Christmas," Mom said, making me reconsider my assessment.

"I'm going to sleep in," my father said. He sipped his eggnog and peered through his bifocals at the package before him. The silver-and-gold wrapped box was Mrs. Dunsmore's handiwork. I had no idea what was inside. She wouldn't tell me. I'd contemplated unwrapping the gifts. Making sure she hadn't given my parents whoopee cushions, but then I'd have had to rewrap them, and they'd never look as good.

"Can I go first?" Gabe asked. He held up a tube wrapped in reindeer print.

My mother smiled. "Of course."

Gabe tore the wrapping paper and cast it aside, near his brother's foot. Tyler said, "A poster?" Gabe looked inside the packaging and withdrew a rolled-up tube of thick paper. He unrolled it. "Pearl Jam!" he said. A black-and-white photo of five dudes on a beach. One avoiding the camera's gaze. The "mumble rock" guys, as Marie had said.

"Thanks, Grandma and Grandpa," Gabe said.

Tyler went next. He opened my gift, a large jersey with Faulk on the back. "Awesome!" He held it up. The jersey would swallow him. Marie had assured me he'd wanted a large. That it was how the kids wore them these days. "Thanks!"

"You go next, Tom," Marie said.

"John's younger than me," I said. "And you're younger than John."

"I'm the hostess, and I'm telling you to open your gift."

I picked up the gift from my parents. Everyone watching, I tore a swath of wrapping paper, "right down the middle!" John called. I did it every year and he called it, like a sportscaster. It was a childhood game, a silly brother thing we kept at. We didn't have many such rituals. Unpicking the tape from the box's sides took time.

"Nonna used half the roll," Tyler said.

"Did not. I only used a quarter of it," she countered.

The boys laughed, high on sugar and gifts.

When the box was wrestled open, there was tissue paper to plow through, and then I found a hat. A fur-lined hat with earflaps. Like Yankowitz had, only nicer. I'd have laughed at such a hat two years ago. Would've asked why they were casting me as an extra in *Fargo*. I pulled the hat on. "How do I look?"

"Like you're in Fargo!" John called.

"Hush," Marie said. "Tom is so handsome, he makes it work."

"Handsomer than me?" John asked.

"Much," she said.

"Do you like it?" my mother asked.

"It's great." I meant it. "This winter has been brutal."

"I check the weather sometimes, where you are. So much snow."

I didn't know she did that.

"Now for me!" Dad said. He went for my gift. I watched him easily separate the box top from bottom. Mrs. Dunsmore wasn't as big a fan of tape as my mother. He rustled inside. Dear God, there was something inside, right? She hadn't wrapped empty boxes? That would be too cruel. "Aha!" He pulled his hand out. Dangling from his fingers was a gold gun that looked like it came from a science-fiction film.

"Now where did you find this?" Wonder in his voice.

As if I knew.

"What is it?" Marie asked.

"It's a Buck Rogers Rocket Pistol, and," he turned it over, "A bottle opener! Hah! This must be a new one. I had one of these when I was a boy. The gun. I loved it." He looked up and smiled.

"I'm glad you like it." Damn. I was going to have to give Mrs. Dunsmore a raise. I hadn't even mentioned Buck Rogers in our conversation.

Never one to be outdone, Mom said, "Ooh, I want to open mine."

She went right for my gift. It had a cardinal ornament attached to the package. Mom complimented me on my wrapping. John snorted. He knew I couldn't wrap a book without botching the job.

"Oh!" she said. She pulled out a pair of red slippers. Slippers? She kicked off a shoe and slid her foot inside. "It's lined! And warm. Oh, these are *very* nice. Thank you, Tommy." She kicked off her other shoe and put the second slipper on. "I might not ever take these off." Shoot. I'd have to give Mrs. Dunsmore a raise *and* two weeks' extra vacation.

Marie looked at me, eyebrows raised. I gave her a smug smile. She narrowed her eyes. I drank the last of my nog. "Anyone else need a refill?" I asked.

"I'll take one," Dad said, handing me his cup.

In the kitchen, Marie grabbed more napkins. "Okay, 'fess up. Who bought those gifts?" she whispered.

I put my hand to my chest. "I'm insulted. What makes you think I didn't?"

"Last I heard, you had no time for shopping. Are you seeing someone?" She smiled, ready to be let in on the secret.

"God, no. You think I'm dating a secret shopper?"

"Sounds good to me."

"Trust me. The person who bought those gifts is the last person in the world I'd date."

"So, a woman."

I nudged her ribs with my elbow. "C'mon, Miss Nosy. We've got gifts to open."

She sighed. "Fine. Whoever she is, she's a keeper."

"You've no idea what you're saying." I pictured Mrs. Dunsmore, rubbing her crucifix.

We returned to the business of opening gifts. Gabe seemed to like the sheet music and guitar picks I'd gotten him. The boys gave my mother a pair of leather gloves I'm sure Marie chose. They'd picked out *Life of Brian* for my Dad. "I know what I'm watching on Christmas!" he said.

"So much for a quiet day at home," Mom said. "I'll be listening to him sing all afternoon." She didn't care for musicals. She found them ridiculous.

The phone rang, interrupting my father's version of "Always Look on the Bright Side of Life." I wore my hat. It made my ears hot, but my mother smiled whenever she looked my way.

John answered it. A moment later he yelled, "Tommy!"

"What?" I shouted from my chair.

"Phone call."

My neck hairs stood on end. The only people with this number were at the Idyll Police Station. I hustled to the phone. "Lynch here," I said.

"Chief," Wright said. "Cody Forrand is gone."

"Gone?"

My father swung into verse three. My mother begged him to stop.

"His mom went Christmas shopping. Dad was at work. The aunt, Jessica, was watching the kids. Cody went to his room to play. A while later, the aunt peered in. He's gone. They can't find him."

"How long?" I checked my watch.

"She called it in about thirty minutes ago. He could've been gone at least a half hour before that."

"The parents are home?" I asked.

"Yeah, and hysterical. They can't believe he was taken from the house."

"Was the room's window locked?"

"Mr. Forrand swears up and down it was. Says he's been locking everything up tight. Anna insists on it. Follows him through the house as he does it."

"I guess the aunt is out of the picture."

"Yeah, she was making cookies with Anna while Cody played in his room."

"You call the staties?"

"Yup, and we've got calls out to other area stations to keep an eye out for him."

"Put Mrs. Dunsmore on the press. The faster we get his picture on

TV, the better." I stared at the pictures on my brother's fridge. Holiday at Disney World. One from last year's Christmas. The kids' smiles bright. "I'll leave now. It'll take me two hours, maybe a little less."

"Safe driving."

Safety wasn't first on my mind. Speed was.

CHAPTER NINETEEN

Wright stood by a huge map pinned across two boards. At its center was Cody Forrand's street. Red circles radiated outward. One, two, three, four. "We're calculating how far he might've gotten if he was taken by car. We figured sixty miles per hour, every hour," Wright said.

"He's only been gone three and a half hours max, right?" I asked.

"Hedging our bets." A frown pulled the left side of his mouth down.

He told me they had calls out to neighboring towns. The local news stations had run an alert an hour ago, flashing Cody's picture. That explained the ringing phones. "We've got two calls that look like maybes. One from Ellington, one from Woodstock."

Ellington was west. Woodstock was northeast.

He said, "The sooner we can figure which one is right, the sooner we might have a direction to pursue." He coughed, hard. Grabbed a lozenge and popped it in his mouth.

"Feeling any better?" I asked.

"Fever is gone. If I could just breathe without coughing, I'd feel human again." He looked at the map and said, "I also called the FBI."

"What did they say?"

"They asked if he was some politician's kid or from a rich family. When I told them no, they said to update them in two hours."

"Will they send someone?" I asked.

"Guy I spoke to sounded intrigued. Who knows?" He waited. Probably expected me to rail at him for involving the feds. He'd wait forever. It was a good call. Feds had plenty of resources and experience. We had a tiny department and a missing, sick kid I worried wouldn't survive this second grab.

149

"I'm wishing we'd kept patrol at the house," Wright said. He'd decided yesterday to pull the detail. The Forrands hadn't complained. They were tired of having a "guest" at the house. "Yankowitz is agitating. Wants us to use his dog."

"We should."

"It didn't find Cody last time," he said.

"Last time the trail was cold and we had iced over snow on the ground." So much for Wright being on point. "Yankowitz!"

He came around the corner, short of breath. "Can Skylar track Cody now?" I asked him.

"Sure. I've been *trying* to get her there for hours." He shot Wright a look.

"I'll come with you. Who's at the house?" I asked Wright.

"Finnegan was, but we needed him back here, so Klein is there now."

We left, and got in Yankowitz's K-9 vehicle. Jinx sat in the back. "I need to drop Jinx at home and get Skylar," Yankowitz said. He drove, at exactly the speed limit.

"You can put your foot down," I told him.

"We're coming up on the center of town," he said.

"Yankowitz, we're trying to find a missing kid. Time is critical. Put your foot on the gas and drive like a cop."

We sped through town, Yankowitz constantly checking his mirrors. He pulled up in front of a single-story house and let Jinx out of the vehicle.

Cody had been taken, again. In the afternoon, from his house. Ballsy. What was Cody worth? I stared at the bright sky and tried to imagine a motive. I was impatient and annoyed by the time Yankowitz appeared at his front door, leash attached to Skylar. Behind him stood a blond holding a large bag. I got out of the car. Met her halfway.

"Chief, this is my girlfriend, Lindsay."

"Pleasure to meet you. May I take the bag?" I asked.

She handed it over. "There's water in there. Protein bars, and a few treats for Skylar." She smiled. A dimple appeared in her left cheek.

Yankowitz was punching above his weight in the romance department. "Good luck. I hope you find him soon."

We got in the car. I set the bag in a rear foot well. Yankowitz peeled onto the road. We reached the Forrand house in four minutes. "Good driving," I told him.

"Completely unsafe," he muttered.

The driveway was full of cars. More were parked along the street. Klein's car was there, alongside a news van. Jessica opened the front door, Anna behind her in a dress covered with floury handprints. Right. They'd been baking cookies when Cody went missing. We walked inside. Mr. and Mrs. Forrand sat on the living room sofa, talking to a newscaster. She leaned in, jotting down notes. Then she looked up; saw our uniforms and the dog. "Are you tracking Cody?" she asked.

I didn't answer her. I walked to the kitchen. Inside, people gathered around the table and leaned against counters. Klein was wedged in the corner by the cupboard. The smell of coffee was strong. Pizza slices lay on plates of congealed grease, teeth marks visible in the abandoned pieces. Amidst the family members were friends, several from Chaplin.

I'd wanted to escape the reporter, but the Forrands had followed me and now we had a big audience. "Okay. We're going to use the dog to track Cody. Jessica, when was the last time you saw Cody?"

She wrung her hands. "About 2:15? Anna and I were starting to make cookies. Cody asked if he could play trucks instead. I said sure and he went to his room. I walked past him on my way to the bathroom. Around 2:00."

"And then?"

"We put a batch of cookies in. I went to see if Cody wanted to help decorate them once they'd cooled. I went to ask, and he was gone."

"How'd he get out? The front door?" I asked.

She shook her head. "We would've heard or seen him walk by."

"So how was he removed from the house?"

"I don't know." Tears ran down her face. "I'm so sorry. Jane, I thought he was safe. I didn't—"

Jane's face was stony, but she said, "It wasn't your fault, Jess."

The reporter appeared at the edge of the room, eager for more story.

I said, "I'd like to see his bedroom." The Forrands moved as if to follow. "Just me and Officers Klein and Yankowitz." Klein looked surprised at my statement, but he eased his way through the crowd, apologizing as he passed the parents.

Outside the kids' bedroom, I asked, "Klein, do you have a list of everyone here?"

"No."

"Make one. Next to their names, write when they arrived." I looked in the kids' room. "The both of you stay here for a minute." I stepped into the room. Toy trucks were arranged on the carpet, in two lines. I stepped over them to reach the window. Its sash was waist-high. I slipped on gloves. Tugged upward. Grunted. Pulled harder. The window came up. No way Cody had the strength to open this.

I stepped out of the room. "Yankowitz, get started with Skylar."

A woman blocked my passage down the hall. She had graying hair and wore a long prairie skirt and a vile yellow sweater. Her pale lipstick made her look older, not younger. "You shouldn't be here," she said.

"Pardon me?" Was there a crazy aunt someone had neglected to mention?

"You," she pointed a bony finger at my chest, "shouldn't be here." Klein and Yankowitz watched, unsure what to do.

"Ma'am, I need you to go back to the Forrands and leave us to our work."

"I know what you are," she said. "They told me. Everyone knows. You're a sinner. You're an abomination against God."

"The only abomination here is that droopy outfit. Now, are you going to leave or shall I have one of my men escort you outside?"

"The wrath of God is coming," she said before leaving.

"Who the hell was that?" I asked.

"Mrs. Donner," Klein said. "She had a son who was friends with Cody."

"Yeah, her son died of the same disease Cody has," I said. So she was a grieving mother. The thought did little to cool me down.

I stomped down the hall and examined the master bedroom. It was big enough to accommodate a queen bed and a matching set of furniture. This room had two windows. I tested the sashes. Looser, able to be lifted. If either had been opened, the aunt would've told us. So how had he gotten out? Two doors opened into closets. One was filled with bedding, towels, and board games. The other, with clothes.

Two bedrooms. One bathroom. Two closets. Back door off the kitchen, where Anna and Jessica would've seen him. Front door? Maybe, maybe if they were busy with the cookies. Wouldn't they have felt the chill air? Heard the door open and close? "Basement," I said. "Where's the basement?" I walked to the hall where Skylar pawed at a door between the bathroom and the kids' room.

"I think the cellar is here," Yankowitz said.

"Let me." I opened the door and flicked the light switch to the right. A musty smell rose from below. Yankowitz and Skylar went down the steps. I followed. At the bottom was a large white laundry basket, half full of towels. Beside it, a toy truck. To the right were a washer and dryer. Skylar sniffed as she walked. Big plastic bins labeled "Thanksgiving" were set beside unlabeled cardboard boxes succumbing to damp, their edges rotting. Past them was a grouping of end tables and lamps. Around the back of the stairs was a pool table with scarred and torn felt. Probably a centerpiece for a big room back in the Chaplin house. Atop the worn felt, more boxes were stacked. Beyond the pool table, shallow stairs led upward to double doors. Skylar was at the doors, barking.

Yankowitz pushed them open. We walked up into the backyard. I looked down. The snow was trampled. I grabbed my flashlight and illuminated the crushed snow at our feet. Was that a small set of prints, near where I stood? Had Cody come outside this way, under where his aunt and sister baked cookies, oblivious to his absence?

Skylar mazed a path through the backyard, down toward the yellow house of the young computer teacher, Mike Calloway. My gut got tight. I grabbed my radio from my belt. Told Klein to keep everybody indoors. I didn't want helpers mucking up the scene. Skylar trotted past Calloway's house, continuing down the street. Ms. Hart's house lit up the block with its Christmas lights. The Santa cutout on her roof looked like a burglar. I stomped my feet to keep the blood flowing. The temperature had plummeted. Bad news for Cody, if he was outside. I doubted that, though, just as I doubted he was safe, wherever he was.

A sharp bark. A second one. I hurried forward. The street ended in a cul-de-sac. Shy of the turnabout, Skylar barked at a car. Yankowitz aimed his flashlight at the license plate. Connecticut. He swept the beam. It was a silver Toyota Camry. Yankowitz peered through the windows. I jogged to him. Was Cody inside?

"I don't see him," Yankowitz said. A folded plaid blanket was on the back seat.

"Trunk?" I sketched the sign of the cross. I didn't want to find Cody dead in that trunk.

Skylar sniffed the passenger door. Barked again.

"Can we get it open?" he asked.

Oh, I'd get it open. First things first. Whose car was it?

I sent Yankowitz to inquire at the closest house, the one at the end of the cul-de-sac. He and Skylar got to the front steps and rang the bell. Yankowitz spoke to a woman. She pointed at the car. A minute later, he returned to me.

"Not their car," he said. "She said it doesn't belong to the neighbors. She noticed it a half hour ago but can't say for sure how long it's been there."

"We can't wait to see who this belongs to," I said.

"You gonna smash the window?"

"No. I'm going to break in like a car thief. I need a shoelace."

He knelt and began to unlace his boot. "Too thick," I said. "I need a sneaker lace."

"Okay." He walked back to the house he'd left. Spoke to the woman again. After a minute Yankowitz came to me, sneaker lace in hand.

"Keep the flashlight on the window for me."

I tied a loop in the middle of the shoelace. Knotted it. Then I fed the loop behind the passenger door window and, using either end of the shoelace, flossed it back and forth so that the loop hovered above the door lock. I pulled on the lace end to the right. Got the loop over the lock. Pulled either end tight and yanked upward. The lock popped up.

"Holy crap," Yankowitz said. I opened the door handle, and then reached over and lifted the driver's side lock. It smelled of mothballs and the soap my grandmother wore. This was the car. The car that took Cody.

"Put on gloves and search the glove box." He did. I hurried to the car's rear. In the trunk was a spare tire, a jack, a lug wrench. No Cody.

I came around to Yankowitz. "Anything?" I asked.

"Nope. No registration. No maps. No owner's manual. Nothing except a pack of tissues." He got up. Crunch. He stopped. Lifted his boot. Rummaged in the foot well and lifted up a bright-yellow plastic brick. "A Lego," he said. Was it a piece of the truck set Cody kept going on about? I grabbed a bag from my inside coat pocket and held it out. He dropped the piece inside.

"I'll get Wright out here. Can you call in the plate number? I want to know who owns this car."

He gave Skylar a command, and the two of them hurried away.

If this was the car that had taken Cody, where was he? I radioed Klein. Ordered him to babysit the car. He came, trailed by Mr. Forrand, who was so close on Klein's heels he was going to give him blisters.

"What did you find?" Mr. Forrand called. His breath came out in visible white puffs. Lord, it was cold.

I put up both hands. "Stay there, please. The fewer prints, the better." Mr. Forrand held up his gloved hands. "Boot prints," I said, pointing at my feet. He lowered his hands. Came no further. Klein remained where he was too.

"The dog tracked Cody's scent to this car. We're investigating whom it belongs to. A crime team will process the car. Klein, I need you to keep an eye on it until they show up. Mr. Forrand, do you recognize this car?"

"It's dark out," he said. I shone my flashlight. He peered, bending forward. "No, I don't think so."

"Why don't you go back up to your house? Ask Jessica if she saw a gray or silver Toyota near the house today." Normally, I wouldn't involve him. I'd prefer cops did the interviews. However, I had few men and this would keep him from complaining about us to the TV reporter.

He turned and trudged up the hill. When he was out of earshot I said, "Klein you can come closer. I'm going to check the nearby houses. See if anyone saw who parked this car."

I interrupted families preparing dinner or wrapping presents. None complained. People's first thought at finding a policeman on their doorstep is that someone has been hurt or killed. Once you've established that's not true, relief floods over them. They happily answered my questions. No one had seen the driver of the car. A few people had noticed it parked, and a few said it had been there two hours or more. Yankowitz and Skylar found me while I crossed the street.

"I'm going to let Skylar search more," he said. "I might have called her off too quickly." He gave her another sniff of Cody's pants. She trotted down the street. I watched her recede. An Idyll patrol car came toward me. I waved at it to pull over. Wright got out, followed by Billy.

"This it?" Wright pointed to the Toyota.

"Yes, and it smells like old lady, like Cody said."

He said, "The owner is one Arlene Pearl. Lives in Barkhamsted. That's about fifteen minutes from Canton."

"Where Cody was found, in the parking lot," I said. "Where's Arlene Pearl now?"

"At home. She had no idea her car was missing. Lady's eighty-four years old. Doesn't drive much. Said she didn't think she'd taken the car out in at least two weeks."

"Crime-scene team coming?" I asked.

"Yup. They actually seemed interested."

"Great." Maybe they'd hustle. "Anybody on our list live near Barkhamsted?"

"Finnegan is checking," Wright said. "I don't get it." He peered at the car. "Kid goes out the basement, and then what?"

"I wish I knew. Klein, head back up to the house. Billy, why don't you help me on the door-to-doors?" I told him we wanted to know if anyone had seen the car's driver or had seen the car being parked or driven.

"Sure thing, Chief. Where should I start?" I pointed and he jogged away.

Yankowitz and Skylar were out of sight now, lost to the dark. Why couldn't Cody have gone missing during summer? The sun would still be blazing away at this hour, and my toes would be warm.

"I'm going to finish checking the street," I said.

Wright said, "I'll keep the looky-loos away from the car." A few neighbors had already appeared outside their homes, coming to see what the fuss was about.

Ms. Hart was at home. The scented air that hit me when she opened the door told me she was still baking. "Chief Lynch," she said. "Come in out of the cold. Oh, dear. What's wrong?"

"Cody Forrand is missing."

"Again?" She brushed her hands on her mistletoe apron. "His poor parents. Come into the kitchen where it's warm." I hesitated, and she said, "I'm not going to devour you like some fairy-tale witch."

I followed her into the kitchen. Small bowls of icing stood on the table alongside candy and chopped chocolate. "You've got all the fixings of a fairy-tale witch."

"Suppose I do. Give me one second." She slid a red oven mitt on her hand and withdrew a baking tray from the oven. Gingerbread men, ten of them. She set the tray onto a cooling rack and removed the mitt. "How can I help?"

"There's a silver Toyota Camry parked outside, a few houses down. I don't suppose you saw it today?" She'd probably been in her kitchen the whole afternoon.

"Silver, you say? I did see a car when I ran out to pick up Snoopy from the lawn. He'd toppled over. There was a gray, or silver, car parked near the Hendersons' house. I wondered who it belonged to because the Hendersons are away. They left yesterday for Minnesota, to visit their grandkids."

"What time did you see the car parked there?"

"It was 1:30 p.m. I'm fairly certain of the time, because I had dough chilling in the fridge, and I had to take it out in fifteen minutes."

"And later, did you happen to see it?"

"No." She used a spatula to free the gingerbread men from their tray. "Wait. I ran outside to give Janice a tin of cookies. That was at, oh, three o'clock or so."

"And the car?"

"You know, I couldn't swear to it, but I don't think it was there."

"Thank you."

"Wait. Before you go, take a cookie." She handed me a gingerbread man. It was still warm. The spicy scent recalled Marie's eggnog, and how, hours earlier, I'd been happily drinking it. So much could change in an hour, in a minute. Cody inside. Cody outside. Here. Gone. Safe. In danger.

She put two cookies in a bag and gave it to me. "In case you need a boost later. Are you sure there's nothing else I can do to help?"

"Pray," I said.

She nodded. "Of course."

Before I reached the door, I'd beheaded the gingerbread man. It was delicious, tender and spicy. I stepped outside, moaned my appreciation, and found myself face-to-face with Billy. Who looked startled. Probably because I was making sex sounds.

"Good cookie." I held the headless gingerbread man up.

He said, "I think you ought to come next door."

"What's up?"

He shifted his weight. "Mr. Calloway's acting strange. Didn't want to let me in at first, and then tried like hell to get me out of there fast."

"You think he's hiding something?"

"Yeah, and I think I know what it is."

"Cody?"

"Not that."

We walked over. I finished my cookie. Mr. Calloway answered our knock. "What now?" he asked Billy. His eyes slid off me like eggs off a greasy pan.

"We thought of another question," Billy said.

"Ask it."

"Mind if we come indoors?" I huffed a breath. It turned into icy vapor. "It's awful cold out here and we've been hoofing it for a half hour."

He waved us inside and kept us trapped in the foyer. His house was warm. Really warm. No wonder he was wearing a t-shirt. "What's the question?" he asked.

The foyer smelt funny, like gym socks. No, not gym socks. I looked at Billy. He tilted his chin upward. "Mind if I use your bathroom?" I asked.

"What? I—" He looked behind him.

"I've really got to go," I said. "Something about this winter chill."

"I, fine. Fine. Here. I'll show you." Upstairs the smell was stronger. Skunk-like.

He led me upstairs, past the den area, to a hallway. "Here," he said, flipping the light switch. I stepped inside a baby-blue bathroom decorated with a floral-print border. Not that I had any cause for judgment. Not with my starlet bathroom styled in black and pink. I leaned against the sink and breathed in deeply. The smell was undeniable up here. I leaned over the tub and set my hand to the tiled shower wall. Heat radiated through. I flushed the toilet and ran the sink. Waited a few moments and exited the bathroom.

"Thanks," I said.

"You're welcome." He stood in the hallway, blocking my path. "What was your question?" he asked as I turned away, to the den.

"Did you happen to see another car parked behind the silver Toyota earlier?"

"No, I told him, I didn't see the car." He pointed to Billy.

"Okay, then. Thanks." I walked down the steps and outside, Billy behind me. The door slammed shut behind us.

"Was that—?" he asked.

"A grow lab in his house? Definitely. The heat? The smell? No wonder he acted so anxious the first time I knocked on his door."

"So what should we do?"

"Do?" I turned to face Billy's eager face. "Nothing. We don't have time to bust a small-time pot grower while we try to find Cody Forrand."

"But—"

"Tomorrow, if we've found Cody, we'll get a warrant. Search his place. Assuming he doesn't trash it all tonight."

"You think he knew we knew?" Billy asked.

"He'd have to be a Grade A idiot not to. C'mon. I see the crime-scene guys."

A van was parked ten yards behind the Toyota. The techs had arrived. Suited up and gloved, they looked like men in a space movie. One lifted his gloved hand in greeting. Mike Shannon. Wright watched. Billy hurried to tell him all about the grow lab.

Mike came over. "Hello," he said.

"Hi."

We'd had an encounter a few months ago. Mike was fun, casual.

"This the kidnap vehicle?" he asked.

"Search dog thinks so." Were Yankowitz and Skylar still tracking? They'd been gone nearly twenty minutes. Maybe I ought to send someone after them.

"Can't believe the kid got taken *twice*. Is he like the Lindbergh baby?"

"Hardly," I said.

"Shannon!" one of his colleagues yelled.

"Coming!" He said, "I'll keep you posted."

"You got my number?" I asked.

"I'm sure I can find it." He winked and set off for the car.

Wright spoke from behind me. "You know him?"

I jumped. God damn it. How long had he been standing so close? "He worked the North case."

We watched the techs. Yankowitz came, Skylar at his side. "Looks like Cody was headed toward Gray Street. We walked it half a mile. Then Skylar turned right."

"Toward Route 74," Wright said.

"The car is right there." Billy pointed.

Yankowitz drank from a water bottle. Swallowed and sighed. "I know. What if the kidnapper took him, stashed Cody somewhere, and then dropped the car back here?"

"Why?" Wright's question echoed my own thought.

"So we fixate on the car instead of searching for Cody?" Yankowitz said.

"We're doing both," Wright said.

"I've got to get Skylar back in the K-9 unit for a break. You need me for anything else?" Yankowitz asked.

"No." I leaned over and pet Skylar's rump. "Good dog."

"Wright, come with me to the house. Billy, stay by the car. Let us know if the techs give us anything," I said.

Wright and I got in his car and drove around the corner. More cars were parked outside the Forrands' house. Great. More people to get in our way. Inside, I sidestepped people, saying, "Pardon me" and ignoring their questions until I found Klein, seated at the kitchen table, poring over a skinny notebook. I cleared my throat. He didn't move. "Klein." That startled him.

"Oh, Chief. Got your list." He held up the notebook as if it was a homework assignment. "I asked everyone when they arrived and—"

"You asked them?"

His bright eyes dimmed a little. "Yeah. I wasn't here when half of 'em arrived, so I asked them when they got here."

"O-kay." He knew he'd done something wrong. Clearly, he didn't know what. "Klein, it's likely someone close to the family took Cody. We can't take their statements at face value." He looked at his notebook, as if it had betrayed him. "What about Jessica?" I asked.

"What about her?"

"Ask her when the people on your list arrived. If she isn't sure, check with Finnegan. He was here first. When you finish, you'll ride with me to the station. Billy will stay here."

Mr. Forrand found me. We walked to his bedroom to talk. Mrs.

Forrand stayed in the living room, clutching Anna like a life preserver and talking to her Chaplin minister, who'd appeared minutes ago. "What's happening?" he asked.

"The techs are examining the car. All area police are on the lookout for Cody."

"Are you going to search the neighborhood?" His voice rose.

"I don't think he's in the neighborhood, Mr. Forrand."

"What if he is? What if this has nothing to do with the other attempt?" he asked. Did he believe that? Or was it that imagining his son holed up in a tree fort was a whole lot better than contemplating other options?

"We've got to pursue the strongest lead, the Toyota."

He ran his hand through his hair. "I don't understand." His voice broke. "I—" He shook his head. Tears were on his cheeks.

"We'll do everything we can. Your friend, Greg Baker. Has he stopped by?"

"No. He's probably still at work." He chewed a thumbnail.

"Could you call him and check?"

"Why? You don't think Greg..." His eyes grew wide. "Greg is Cody's godfather! He'd never hurt him."

"We can place the call," I said.

"You're wasting time. Greg is a good guy. He loves Cody."

"He spends a lot of time with children for a single guy his age," I said.

Mr. Forrand paced away from me. "We're going to hold a press conference."

"When?" I asked. "Where?"

"Soon. The newscaster, she recommended we do it, and Jane has been saying we should talk to more press. Get his picture out there."

"It's a good idea. We can have it at the station." I didn't trust them, not after the last appeal. "We'll release those details we want made public."

He stuffed his hands under his armpits. "Okay. When?"

"We need to wrap things up here. How about in an hour, at the station?"

"Okay." He looked around the room. "God, I wish I had a cigarette. I quit, eight years ago. When Anna was born. I could use one now."

In the house, people were moving about, picking up things and setting them down. Too much energy and not enough outlets for it. Klein spoke to Mrs. Forrand. Anna was no longer in her arms. When he'd finished, I jerked my head toward the front door.

"You get what you need?" I asked.

"Yes."

"Let's go." We stepped outside. It was even colder. I breathed onto my hands.

"You think it's someone in there?" He jerked his thumb toward the house.

"Maybe. Maybe not. We need to get the Forrands to come in, make a statement."

"You don't think they had anything to do with this?" Disbelief made his voice climb.

"Cody's a thorn in their side. Sick kid. Needs constant watching. They wouldn't be the first parents to explore an alternative path."

Klein's jaw unhinged. "But, but that's awful."

"It's life," I said.

Klein drove to the station with his hands at ten and two. He checked his mirrors but kept his foot low on the gas pedal. So I skipped my Yankowitz lecture.

"Did you like living in New York?" he asked.

The question brought me out of a thought I'd had about whether there were multiple people involved in Cody's kidnapping.

"I grew up there." It was hard to be objective. All of my firsts were in New York: first day of school, first kiss, first arrest.

"People there seem more . . . worldly."

Oh boy. Was this conversation headed to Gay Town? Population: Klein and me. I'd suspected he was gay; got confirmation from the local nutter, Elmore Fenworth, this summer. Klein was still living where I'd been a few months ago: in the closet.

"People there definitely see a lot more different types than folks here. That doesn't necessarily make them more tolerant," I said.

"Oh. Must've been tough, being a cop there."

"It's not exactly a cake walk here at the moment."

"Oh, right. I mean here it's usually drunks and maybe a drug bust. Not exactly *Law & Order* stuff."

"Uh-huh." I almost told him nothing was like TV made it out to be. That city policing involved as much paperwork and drudgery as a small town. It wasn't entirely true. There were fewer periods of no activity in cities. You had more big crimes. But, I didn't think he was interested in the difference in police stats between the two places.

"You thinking of moving?" I asked.

His gloved fingers gripped the wheel harder. "Me? No, not really. Just curious."

I snuck a look at Klein. He was okay. A little small and shy for me, but he'd do fine in a city where there was something for everyone. He had nice teeth. That was a plus.

"Let me know if you change your mind." Now why had I said that? I wasn't looking to become Klein's gay mentor. I wasn't anyone's mentor.

"Thanks." He smiled. His grin belonged in a dentist's ad.

CHAPTER TWENTY

Finnegan was hard at work on his second or third pack of the day.
"Anything?" we asked each other, at the same time. He set his cigarette atop a pyramid stack of stubs and shook his head. "So far no one friendly with the Forrands lives near Barkhamsted. Greg Baker left work early today. Personal time. He's not answering his phone."

"Could we get someone to drive by? Check his place?"

"I'll call," he said. "What's up with the car you found?"

"Techs are on it, but you know how long those tests can take. I had a thought on the way over. What if there's more than one kidnapper?"

"Risky, but maybe. Cody never said anything about two people, did he?"

"No. There could've been one driver, and then Cody was drugged so if there was someone else, I don't know, I'm spit-balling. The Forrands want to have a press conference. I've urged them to have it here."

He looked around the station. "Where you gonna put everyone?" Men hustled, waving papers, shouting. It looked like the floor of the Stock Exchange. There wasn't room for the Forrands and a bunch of reporters and camera people.

"Outside," I said.

"Outside? It's fifteen degrees." He exaggerated, but not by much.

"People watching at home will see it's cold. They'll pay even more attention when they think about a kid out in these conditions. Tell Wright he's our rep."

"Tell him yourself." He pointed.

Wright walked our way; a glower set so deep in his face a crowbar couldn't pull it free. I said, "Hey, we're having a press conference in," I checked my watch, "thirty minutes. You've been elected Mr. TV."

"Why?" he asked.

Because I didn't need more press. "You're most photogenic," I said.

"Where will we have it?" He gave the station the same skeptical eye exam Finnegan had.

"Outside, so hold on to your hat."

He clenched his hands. "I was just beginning to feel my fingers."

Mrs. Dunsmore appeared, wearing pumps and a nice dress. Church clothes. Interesting. She unwrapped her scarf. "How was your holiday?" she asked me.

"Interrupted," I said. "Thank you for the gifts. My parents loved them."

She smiled. "Good. I've left the receipts on your desk." She looked at our map. "All the TV networks are covering the abduction. They want to know where to set up."

"Chief thinks the good viewers at home will work harder to find Cody if they see his family and Wright freezing their asses off," Finnegan said. "So it'll be outside the station."

The Forrands arrived four minutes later. *Frantic* was one word to describe them. *Pale*, *shaken*, *upset*, and *on the verge*, were others. They'd brought Anna with them.

Jane Forrand said, "She wanted to be with us." Maybe Anna didn't feel safe at home.

Mrs. Dunsmore went into action. "Hello, there. I'm Mrs. Dunsmore. We've met, once before, at the church last Thanksgiving, I think it was."

"Oh, yes," Jane Forrand said, attempting a smile.

"Why don't we see if we have some hot cocoa?" Mrs. Dunsmore said to Anna. She looked at Mrs. Forrand. A nod from Jane indicated this would be acceptable. "Come this way, and I'll tell you what we have planned." They all walked toward the coffee area.

Wright said, "What should I omit during our dance with the press?"

"The Legos," said Finnegan.

"And the sheets. I'd mention the mask and the stuffed raccoon. Maybe that will get us something," I said.

"Like a lot of whack jobs calling," Finnegan cautioned.

"We need to give something more, and that mask stands out. Maybe someone will recall seeing it."

Mrs. Dunsmore returned to park Anna in her office. She put Wright in charge of the Forrands, so he could tell them what we were willing to reveal and what they should keep their mouths closed about. She left to coordinate the press, who were less than enthusiastic they'd be working out of doors.

Everyone was busy, except me. I visited Mrs. Dunsmore's office. On Anna's lap was a giant book of fairy tales. "Yours?" I asked, pointing to the book.

She squirmed and said, "Yes."

"Big book." I picked it up. Size of a cereal box. Weighed six pounds. "You read this?" I made it sound like I couldn't believe it.

"Some of it's too young for me." Too young for an eight-year-old? "I read it to Cody, sometimes."

"Does he have a favorite story?"

"He likes the story about the boy who left home to learn about fear."

"I don't think I know that one," I said. "What's your favorite?"

"'Hansel and Gretel.'"

"I know that one. Kids get lost in the forest and end up at a house made of candy. Then a witch kidnaps them." Ouch. Not the plot point to emphasize.

"Gretel saves the day." She pointed to the book. "Hansel helps, in the beginning, with the crumbs and stones, but it's Gretel who saves them from the witch."

"So she does." As I recalled, Gretel pushed the witch into a hot oven and locked the witch inside. A gruesome rescue.

"What's your favorite story?" Anna asked.

"Mine?" I should say something. Anything. I'd liked stories when I was young, hadn't I? "I used to like 'The Three Little Pigs.'"

"Why?" Her question came hard on the heels of my answer.

Why? "Because the good pig is rewarded."

"But his brothers die." She was fixated on brothers, those saved and those lost.

"I'm not sure he could've saved them."

"He didn't try!" Her face puckered.

"How's the cocoa?" I asked.

She sipped from the mug. "Good." Her face told another story. So she was capable of lying.

"Did Cody ever tell you about any special friend he had?" I asked.

"A friend like from school?"

"No. An older friend, maybe."

"A big kid?"

"Older, an adult, like me or your parents."

"No. Why would he be friends with someone like that? We know about bad adults. We're not stupid." Okay. Scratch that.

"Did he mention being scared recently?" I asked.

"Cody doesn't get scared, or hardly ever. We watched *Jurassic Park*, and he didn't hide his face once behind his hands. I did, five times."

"Do you have any idea where he is?"

"No, and it's not good for him to be gone. He needs me. He gets hurt and he doesn't know it, and I have to tell him and make him show Mom. He tries to take his goggles off when he plays with the boys, and he could lose an eye, you know. Like that." She snapped her fingers.

"You take good care of him," I said.

"I have to." She pushed her hair back, another gesture of her mother's. "It's like he's made of glass, but he thinks he's made of—"

"Steel?" I suggested.

"Titanium."

"What happens when you grow up and go to college?" No way a kid this bright wasn't headed for college.

She frowned. "Maybe he'll be better then. Know to not roughhouse. Dad says all boys are like Cody at his age. I don't think that's true, though. Jimmy Saunders isn't like that. He likes art and animals, and he always washes his hands before lunch."

When I was young, boys like Jimmy were considered "light in the loafers." We alienated those boys, put them in their place.

"Do you think they'll find Cody at the grocery again?" she asked.

"I don't know," I said. "That stuffed animal Cody loves. Sammy. Uncle Greg gave it to him?"

"Cody got Sammy when he was four. Uncle Greg told Cody raccoons are nature's fiercest creatures and that Cody was like one." Fiercest creature? Sounded like someone couldn't find a tiger in the gift shop.

"Did he give him any Lego kits or toys?"

"For his birthday, Uncle Greg got him a remote-control helicopter."

"What did he get you for your birthday?" I asked.

"A doll," she said. "I would've preferred books."

Maybe Uncle Greg preferred boys?

"Anna, do you have any idea who took Cody?"

"No," she said. "I asked him, a hundred times. He said it was a Power Ranger, but Power Rangers are on TV. They're not real. He doesn't get that."

"Do you think he'd have left again, if the Power Ranger asked?"

Her eyes got glossy with tears. "Yes," she whispered.

"What about babysitters? Who watches you when your parents are out?"

"Aunt Jess mostly, and Cara." She smacked her palm to her mouth, eyes wide.

"Who's Cara?" I asked.

Her cheeks were red, and she shook her head. "I'm not supposed to say."

"I'm a policeman, Anna. You have to tell me the truth."

"Cara lives on our street. She's in high school. She's watched us if Aunt Jess couldn't, but Mom told us not to tell Dad, because he thinks Cara is flighty." Interesting.

"It's go time," Finnegan said, peering around the doorframe.

I looked up. "Be there in a second." I stood and said, "Thanks, Anna. Now you stay here until your parents finish talking to some reporters. It shouldn't take long."

"Okay." She opened her giant book and leafed through the pages. As if I'd disappeared already. Or like she was used to stepping out of the spotlight and into the shadows. With a brother like Cody, she probably was.

Bright lights were trained on the middle of the stairs leading to the police station entrance. Wright stood beside Jane Forrand, who was flanked on the other side by her husband. A microphone stood, its mesh black stump angled toward them. Reporters bitched about the falling temperatures while checking their teeth in small mirrors.

"Are we ready yet?" one reporter asked. Her voice filled the parking lot. Everyone turned. Mrs. Forrand squinted into the crowd. A woman in a tan coat took a step backward. "Jake, is this mic live?" It most certainly was. The reporter swore while holding the mic well away from her.

Wright put a cough drop in his mouth. He cleared his throat. "We're ready," he called. He gave the press one last chance to jockey for position. Then he stepped to the microphone and began. "At approximately two thirty this afternoon, Cody Forrand went missing from his house on Spring Street. Cody is six years old. He was wearing jeans, a blue-and-white striped shirt, and green socks. He is forty-four inches tall and fifty-two pounds, with brown eyes and hair. A week ago, an unidentified driver took him from his home in a silver Toyota Camry. If anyone has seen Cody today, please call the Idyll Police. Cody has a medical condition that makes him vulnerable to the cold. It's not clear that his abductor knows this." In all likelihood, his abductor knew just that, but we hoped this bit would appeal to viewers.

Wright said, "When Cody was taken on the 12th, the kidnapper may have worn a mask. It was of a red Mighty Morphin Power Ranger. If you saw anyone wearing this mask and driving a silver car, please call." Cue the nut jobs. Finny was right. That request would generate a lot of nonsense, but what could we do? Withholding it wasn't an option. "We're also interested in anyone who may have sold a stuffed animal like this one, in the area recently." He held up Sammy. Photo flashes went off, creating a strobe effect. "Cody's parents, Jane and Peter, would now like to make a statement."

Wright stepped back, and Jane moved to the microphone. Her face, spot-lit by TV cameras, looked ghostly pale. "Cody is our baby boy. He's sick, and needs care. Please, if you've taken him, return him to us. He needs us. We just want him home." She clutched the scarf at her throat, her voice raspy with tears. "Please." Her husband wrapped his arm around her and angled toward the mic to say, "We're offering a $10,000 reward for anyone who can help us bring Cody home." He squeezed his wife's shoulder and kissed her hair.

Ten thousand dollars? How would they get $10,000?

The reporters shuffled their boots, excited by this news.

Wright said, "We'll now take questions."

Pale hands shot into the sky like human fireworks, glowing in the darkness.

Wright pointed. "You."

"Cody has been abducted twice within two weeks. Why has he been targeted?"

Wright's exhale was loud. "We don't know. We're hoping everyone can help us bring him home safely, soon."

"Was there a ransom note found, either time?"

"No comment," Wright said. He could've said no, but then we might be flooded with fake ransom notes. "Yes, you." He pointed to a reporter from the local paper.

"The Mighty Morphin Power Ranger mask. Was that seen today, or during the first attempt?"

"The first attempt." He looked to his left. "Yes?"

A younger reporter, minus a camera crew, asked, "Mrs. Forrand, where were you when Cody was taken?"

Wright put up a blocking arm, but she leaned past it, toward the mic, and said, "Shopping for Christmas presents."

"And you, Mr. Forrand?"

Wright said, "We're not here to interrogate Cody's parents. It's cold and getting late. Do you have any questions for me?" He'd let annoyance color his tone. Not great, but at least he'd shut down the questioning of the Forrands.

A movement behind him caused reporters to look up. Klein came through the station. He stopped, a deer in headlights. "Go back inside!" Mrs. Dunsmore told him.

"I've got a car accident," he said, his voice carrying.

"Use the *rear* exit!"

Laughter rippled through the crowd. Wright's jaw moved. Grinding his teeth, no doubt. "You have a question?" He pointed to a male reporter bundled in a Patriots scarf, repping Channel Four. The man asked, "Has the FBI been involved?"

"They've been contacted. I can't say more about their involvement. Next?" He selected a woman from Channel Five.

"What about the pedophile who lives near Cody Forrand's house? Has he been questioned in relation to this case?"

"We've questioned several people, including a neighbor with past criminal charges of sexual misconduct," Wright said.

"What about the arson of that man's home? Are the Forrands suspects in that case?"

"No," Wright said, with force and venom.

"Please," Mrs. Forrand said. Her voice shook slightly. Everyone's eyes went to her. "Help us find our son. We want Cody home." She inhaled, hiccupped, and then turned, sobbing, into her husband's arms.

"We're done," Wright said. "Thank you for your time." He ushered the Forrands inside while a few reporters tossed out last questions. Wright ignored them.

Mrs. Dunsmore said to me, "I hope you didn't say we'd pay out $10,000."

"Hardly. They'll have to sell their house for that money."

We walked up the steps. Someone called, "Chief Lynch!" I pivoted. The Channel Five woman stood two steps below. Her made-up face was clownish off camera. "Is it true your police car was vandalized recently with a gay slur?" she asked.

I said, "No comment," and half pushed Mrs. Dunsmore into the station before anyone could get us on film.

Inside, I told Finnegan I wanted him and Wright to split up the parents and question each separately.

"Anything you want me to ask?" he said.

"You might ask where the 10k reward is coming from. Also, see if the missus has anything to say about Uncle Greg."

He said, "Speak of the devil—Chaplin cops did a drive-by for us, and he's not home. No lights on. Neighbors haven't seen him since he left for work this morning."

"You got an APB on his vehicle?" The very new Impala he purchased. We'd discovered that he had bought it three weeks ago, and that Cody hadn't seen it before his abduction. Of course, now we had the Camry. None of this made sense.

My stomach rumbled. It was well past dinnertime. "I'm gonna send out for pizza. You want any?"

"Sure. I'll have a pineapple and pepperoni with olives."

"Like hell," I said. Finnegan liked to order disgusting combos that assured he'd have a whole pie to himself. Not today.

Officers came through the front door. More than were on shift. "What are you doing here?" I asked Dix. He'd been on duty earlier. Had gone home in the afternoon.

He said, "I want to help. Some of the other guys do too."

"I'm not sure the selectmen are gonna be happy about paying overtime," I said.

"I've got a boy, Charlie, in Cody's class." He rubbed his mustache. "Charlie asked if I could find Cody. I told him I'd try. I don't really give a damn about the overtime."

"Great."

"That only applies to this instance," he said, holding up his finger.

"Got it."

More officers came in as I checked on the tips. When the Forrands emerged from their interviews with Wright and Finnegan, I made a point of introducing Dix. Dix told them about his boy, Charlie.

"Oh yes, Charlie," Jane Forrand said. "He came to Cody's party last year, didn't he? He has red hair?"

Dix nodded. "He's our red devil."

Jane looked about the space, full of men, and asked, "Where's Anna? Anna?" Her voice was pitched high. "Anna!"

"She's there," I said, pointing to Mrs. Dunsmore's office.

She knelt by Anna's chair and kissed her forehead. "I got worried when I couldn't find you." She hugged her daughter.

"Mom, you're squeezing too hard!"

"Oh, sorry." Jane stepped back. Swept a loose strand of hair behind her ear. I tried to see the high school beauty in the woman before me.

"Anna was telling me about her favorite story," Mrs. Dunsmore said.

"Rapunzel," Mrs. Forrand said, a smile on her lips. Anna didn't correct her. Mrs. Dunsmore frowned. She'd caught the error.

"It's time to go, Anna." Mrs. Forrand struggled, her arm stuck in her coat sleeve.

"Allow me," I said. I held the coat's arm steady.

"Thank you."

Mrs. Dunsmore watched as she slotted her arm into the sleeve.

Jane grabbed Anna's hand and said, "Call us the moment you hear *anything.*"

She pulled Anna in her wake. Anna called, "Bye!" over her shoulder.

Mrs. Dunsmore said, "Poor thing probably doesn't get much attention with her sick brother." She rooted in a desk drawer. Withdrew an oval tin. "Mint?"

"No, thank you."

She took one and considered the small round mint on her palm. "What I don't understand," she said, "is why none of you mentioned that Mrs. Forrand is pregnant."

"Pregnant?" I said.

She smiled and popped the mint in her mouth.

CHAPTER TWENTY-ONE

"**P**regnant?" Wright said. He chewed his pizza like it might make a run for it.

"You sure?" Finnegan asked. He eyed his plain cheese slice with mistrust. God, did he really *like* those gross combos he ordered?

Mrs. Dunsmore gave Finnegan a look that would wither stronger men. "You have three ex-wives and four children, and you can't spot a pregnant woman?" she asked him.

"I guess not," he said.

"What about you?" she asked Wright.

He said, "She's not really showing." He traced a bump before his belly.

"She is, a little. If you look closely," she said.

"Why isn't he getting a lecture?" Wright asked, looking at me. Then he dropped his gaze. Realizing.

"Gay," I said. "Remember?" I turned to Mrs. Dunsmore. "Don't suppose you know how pregnant she is?"

"I'm guessing first trimester," she said.

"Does it mean anything?" Wright asked.

"It means they didn't tell us," I said.

"My wives waited until three months passed before they told anyone," Finnegan said. "Just in case something happened." He reached for another pizza slice. The detectives had commandeered two pies.

"Can they test for CIPA?" Wright asked. "Before the baby is born?"

"You think they'd abort if the baby had CIPA?" Mrs. Dunsmore asked.

"I can't imagine them caring for two kids with that disease," Finnegan said. "Think of the expense."

"And the time," Mrs. Dunsmore said.

I repeated what Anna had told me about her secret neighborhood babysitter, Cara. "Jane Forrand lied to us about that," I said. "Now, with this pregnancy . . ."

"You think the mom grabbed Cody?" Finnegan asked. "How? She was out shopping. She came back with gifts. I saw them. Besides, you saw how freaked she got when she didn't see Anna here. Naw. She feels guilty as hell for leaving him this afternoon."

Dix came over, sheet in hand. "Tip just came through about the mask."

I grabbed the memo before Wright could. "Thanks."

"Hey, you guys got more pizza? We ran out." Dix leaned forward, hand extended. Finnegan slapped his hand with a ruler and said, "That's for detectives."

"Dix, don't listen to him." Mrs. Dunsmore said. "Take the box." Finny grabbed another slice before Dix could take it away. "You act like children," she said.

"So what's the scoop?" Wright couldn't read over my shoulder. Not tall enough.

"Woman says she sold a Mighty Morphin Power Ranger mask back in November. Says she remembers because it was after Halloween," I said.

"Where?" Finny asked.

"Treasure Chest," I said.

Wright snatched the paper from my hand. "I want to go talk to," he peered at the note, "Barbara McCabe. Maybe the kidnapper paid with a card."

"See you," I said, trying not to get excited. It was one tip. It might not be our guy. Could be that someone was just taking advantage of post-Halloween sales.

"What are the chances?" Finnegan said. He was running the same calculations I was. Possibility plus location plus hope minus probability.

"You think the parents are involved?" Mrs. Dunsmore asked. "I assume you interviewed them for a reason."

"Given her pregnancy, we have to consider it," I said.

"You insisted on the interviews *before* you knew that." She didn't miss a beat.

"We have to look at who stands to gain. There's no ransom. They don't seem to have enemies. So far, we've got Uncle Greg, and he could be our man, but if not . . ."

Finnegan said, "Mr. Forrand could've hired someone. He strikes me as a capable guy. He and his wife had a nice life in Chaplin. Cody comes along, and it falls to pieces. He was something of a hero in that Vicky Fitzgerald kidnapping, directing volunteers and resources. Why didn't he do that in the search for his own son? And, if his wife is pregnant, he knows they can't afford another child."

Wright's plate of pizza crusts was unattended. He didn't eat the crusts. I loved them. Rick used to call them "pizza bones." He'd ask, "You want my pizza bones, Tommy?" Offering me a greasy paper plate heaped with uneaten crusts. I grabbed Wright's plate.

"He might have thought it was the best decision in the long run," Finnegan said. "I looked into that job he lost, back when they lived in Chaplin. There were rumors he was skimming funds. Nothing proven, but lots of gossip. Maybe he thought slamming us on TV could throw us off our game."

"If he had a hand in it, it explains the sheets, fake Sammy, and mask," I said.

"If he paid someone," Mrs. Dunsmore said, "there'd be evidence. Check his accounts." It was a testament to Finny's relationship with her that he didn't blink at being told what to do by a secretary.

"Good idea," Finnegan said. "I'll put Klein on it. He used to work at a bank."

"Really?" I asked.

"Yeah, back when he was a kid, he used to deposit my checks. Then one day the place gets hit. A man in a balaclava carrying a water pistol tries to hold the place up."

Mrs. Dunsmore said, "The water pistol looked real, or so I heard."

Finnegan snorted. "Klein saw it wasn't a real gun, but he hit the panic button. Got the cops there. Decided he liked being a hero and applied to be a cop a week later."

"Here?" I said. "Not a lot of opportunities for heroism."

"If he helps find Cody, it would be something."

True. If he helped find Cody, it would be something. The hours were ticking away. The chances of finding Cody *alive* decreased with each sweep of the clock's hand. It was hard to be a hero when what you found was a dead child. Look at Victoria Fitzgerald's case. There were no heroes there.

Mrs. Dunsmore reminded us to unplug the coffeepot when we left, because the cord was frayed and we were going to burn the place to the ground one of these days.

"When we leave," Finnegan said. "When's that again?"

"When you find Cody Forrand," she said.

"Chief, call!" Darryl yelled.

Finnegan, Mrs. Dunsmore, and I exchanged glances. Did he mean a chief call or a call for me?

"Chief, line four! It's Andrew Trabucco's sister." Someone booed, low and loud. "And she's pissed."

"Thanks, Darryl!" I snatched up the phone. "Chief Lynch."

"Chief Lynch, this is Wanda Trabucco. I just saw the news report, about that missing boy, Cody Forrand. Is it true his parents burnt my brother's house down?"

"No. I believe my detective was clear that the Forrands aren't suspects."

"Who then? Have you even looked into it? Four of his pets died, and he could've been killed. I know you don't think he's worth the air he breathes, but he's not a monster. He was abused by our uncle, when we were little. He's tried to get help, to get better. He hasn't been in trouble once since he got out of jail, and now someone tried to kill him in his sleep. What are you doing about it?"

"We're investigating the arson, Miss Trabucco. I can't comment on an open case."

"But you can have a press conference for that boy. Pull out all the stops there. Because he's worth something and my brother, well, you've just written him off, haven't you?"

I had nothing to say to that, because if we were comparing worth, than yes, I counted Cody Forrand, an innocent boy, worth more than a thirty-three-year-old pedophile who'd never be rehabilitated. "Good night, Miss Trabucco," I said.

Finnegan looked up at me. "I'm guessing she wasn't calling for your Christmas-cookie recipe?"

"Not exactly," I said.

What was Cody's doctor's name? Fray-something. Frazier. I found his number and called. Though it was 11:02 p.m., he answered.

"Is it possible to test an unborn baby for CIPA?" I asked.

"Yes. Most people wouldn't get the test, because the condition is so rare. You'd need two parents with a defective *NTRK1* gene, and even then not all such couples produce a baby with CIPA."

"A couple like the Forrands, if they got pregnant, they could test the fetus?"

"Theoretically, yes. We'd test the amniotic fluid. It carries risks, but a couple like the Forrands would want such a test done. Not that they'd need to. Why?"

"Why wouldn't the Forrands need the test?" I asked.

"Mr. Forrand had a vasectomy, shortly after we diagnosed his son. They asked me what the odds were of having another child with CIPA. I couldn't be sure. No one can. They decided not to risk it." He hesitated, and then asked, "Why are you asking? Did you find another couple with a CIPA child?" He sounded excited. Probably the way a hunter felt after spotting his second white elephant.

I didn't answer, and he said, "There is no other couple. It's them, the Forrands, isn't it. I suppose the vasectomy could've failed." His flat voice belied his own statement.

"Or not," I said, knowing he considered the same possibility. That Mr. Forrand's vasectomy hadn't malfunctioned. That he hadn't impregnated his wife.

"I'm sorry," he said. "I shouldn't have said anything. I spoke before I thought."

"Thanks for your time." I didn't promise to keep what he said between us. How could I? I was a cop. And my kidnapping vic's mom was having an affair. I looked at my office plant and asked it, "Where did she find the time?"

CHAPTER TWENTY-TWO

Wright went home around 2:00 a.m. when his cough worsened and I'd told him for the eleventh time to get some damn sleep. Finny stayed, chain-smoking, lost in the tip reports that said Cody had been spotted in Waterbury and Boston and New York and Colorado. Colorado? Had he been smuggled onto a plane?

At 2:45 a.m., my brain was fuzzy. Rather than go home, I showered in the locker room after I'd barred the door with a chair. The hot water woke me, though the stream was a pressureless trickle. When I exited the locker room, dressed in a fresh t-shirt and sweatshirt, Finnegan said, "Violating dress code." I tossed a balled-up memo at his head. He didn't evade it. It smacked his temple and fell to the floor.

"Uncle Greg is still MIA," he said.

Maybe he was our guy. His car hadn't been spotted since he'd left for work. But why would he use the Camry, only to abandon it on the street behind Cody's?

Finnegan's phone rang. "Please don't be a nutter," he said. "Detective Finnegan, Idyll Police. Who?" He straightened. "Yes. Okay. Now? You know how—. Okay. See you soon." He swiveled his chair and said, "I'll be damned. The FBI is coming."

The station looked as though a hurricane had hit. We'd dumped stuff on desks to make room for maps and paperwork. There was snow gear under and near radiators. Fuck it. The FBI wasn't coming to do a house-cleaning inspection. Still. We'd need to give them space. I walked to the front. Dix was at a desk, at work on the Camry timeline.

"Dix." His head was tilted, eyes down on the sheets. I said, "Dix" louder. He snorted and jerked his head. "Dix, the FBI is coming. Can you clear some desks for them? Toss what we don't need in the evidence area."

He rubbed his eyes. "Okay. Sorry. I didn't mean to—"

"It's fine. Go home after. You're wiped. We'll need you back here later."

He looked ready to fight, but he stood and said, "A few hours would be good."

I asked Finnegan to get status reports on all inquiries. He grunted and shuffled off to talk to Klein. I thought of the bank holdup story while I watched them talk. Had becoming a cop been anything like Klein thought it would? Or did he miss the bank? The regular hours, the holidays, the interactions with people who were, on average, pleasant?

The front door opened thirty-five minutes later. A Latina woman led the group. She extended her hand. "I'm Agent Teresa Waters. You must be Chief Thomas Lynch." I assumed she'd noticed my uniform. Realized I had a sweatshirt on. Damn. We shook hands. Her palm was cool and dry.

"Thanks for coming," I said.

She indicated the men behind her. "Agents Dennis Mulberry and Matthew Cisco." They waved their hellos. Mulberry was white and older than Cisco, who was Latino and looked like a bodybuilder. When did the FBI start hiring muscle? He maintained the ramrod posture of a fed. That, plus his hyper-vigilant gaze were a dead giveaway.

"Come on in. Detective Finnegan will bring you up to speed," I said.

"We'd like to ask some questions first," she said. They approached the big map, peering at the X that marked the Forrand house. We'd run out of space for the ever-widening circles. Cody had been gone too long. Agent Waters looked at the piles of cigarette butts and coughed. "You guys still smoke indoors."

"I do." Finnegan waved his lit butt in one hand. "Detective Michael Finnegan."

Agent Waters stared at the cigarette like it was a deadly snake. "I'm going to have to ask you to extinguish that. I have asthma." She strode to the nearest window and opened it. "I can't be around secondhand smoke." Cisco lifted another window frame six inches. Cold air rushed in. Papers rustled.

"Okaaaaay." Finnegan extinguished his butt and slid a pile of ash and filters into the nearest trash can. "Work must be hard. I thought feds smoked nonstop."

"President Clinton passed an executive order in August prohibiting smoking in federal buildings that report to the executive branch. Maybe you heard?" she asked.

Things were off to a great start.

"When was Cody taken?" she asked.

"Approximately 2:30 p.m.," Finnegan said. "It appears he exited via the basement doors to the backyard. Whomever took him must've opened the doors. They'd be too heavy for Cody." Mulberry took notes.

"So the kidnapper was outside the house?" she asked.

"Looks that way," Finnegan said.

"You dusted the door for prints?" she asked.

Finnegan and I looked at each other. "No," I said.

"No." She didn't ask why. She waited us out. I'd have respected that move if it didn't make me so damn angry. We'd fucked up. She'd caught us.

"We assumed the person wore gloves. It's cold out," I said.

"Get a unit to dust the doors," she told Cisco. "We'll need exclusion prints from you or whoever was there."

"I wore gloves," I said. Had Yankowitz? Fuck.

"From the basement door, Cody went where?" she asked.

I kept my mouth shut and looked at Finnegan. He said, "Our dog tracked his scent to a car parked on Weymouth Avenue. Cody wasn't in it. Techs processed the car. The dog followed the scent down the road toward Route 74."

"Could've hopped from there to Route 84 easy," Mulberry said as he scribbled in his notepad.

"When did you find the car?" Agent Waters asked.

"6:50 p.m.," I said. "We interviewed neighbors. It appears to have been parked there, disappeared, and then reappeared, but the reports conflict."

"Cisco will take a look," she said. "There's been no ransom? No demand?"

"None," Finnegan said.

"Detective Finnegan, please give Agent Mulberry everything you have. I'm going to speak with the family." I thought of the Forrands, at home, waiting. They'd be happy they got the FBI's attention, and a female agent to boot.

"There's something you might want to know." I told her about Mrs. Forrand's pregnancy and her husband's vasectomy.

She pursed her lips. "Interesting. They know you know?"

"Nope," I said.

"Any idea who the father is?" she asked.

"No."

She cocked one brow. "Anything else I should know before I meet the family?"

Finnegan shared his hypothesis that the father might be in the frame. She asked questions. "It's a theory," he said, one step from angry. She left to confer with her men.

Maybe they'd lift prints from the basement doors. Maybe they'd find who took Cody. I didn't care if they got the glory. If they found Cody, they could have it all. I didn't want a dead kid on my conscience. A flash of Cody's smile and his hand dangling an animal cracker before my face came to me. I tried to blink it away. Not now.

I hoped Finnegan was doing better with Mulberry than he had with Waters. She could've gone easier on him about the smoking. Ah, well. She probably had to be aggressive to get to where she was. Some poky small-town detective wasn't going to get in her way.

Timelines, photos, and Captain Hirsch's arson report got moved aside. Under them, I spotted a list of names. My graffiti suspects. I'd been too busy with Cody. Looking at the names, I almost wished the feds hadn't come. I would have to devote time and attention to this list. My spine ached, a reminder of the time I was pushed down the stairs by some scumbag back in New York. Sometimes I swore it predicted trouble. And yet it hadn't hurt earlier, when I'd been sipping nog and opening presents and someone had put Cody Forrand into a silver Toyota Camry.

I looked at the list of names again.

Fuck.

Even my pain was unreliable.

CHAPTER TWENTY-THREE

I drove through the snow, the flakes like feathers. The radio reminded me that there were only two days until Christmas. Not that it mattered. I'd had my Christmas, yesterday at Marie and Johnny's. It had been one of our better family holidays. It would've been nice to see what they'd got Mom and Dad. To tease Johnny if, for once, his gifts fell short of mine. I cracked my driver's window. The chill air kept my eyes open. I'd snatched three hours sleep at home. I could've slept longer, but wondering what the feds were up to and if any leads had broken had tortured me until I threw my blanket aside.

Instead of cigarette smoke and burnt wool, the station smelled like the air after summer rain had fallen hard. Then I noticed the machines. Two hip-height gray-and-white columns that hummed in the detectives' pen. A third stood in the hall outside my office. Klein gave me a good morning. When he saw my frown and followed my finger, he said, "Oh, those are air purifiers. Agent Waters said they'll get rid of the stink and the secondhand smoke."

"Did she?" I wondered how the machines had gone over with Finnegan. He wasn't around to ask. He'd gone home to sleep and maybe to smoke and say out loud exactly what he thought of Agent Waters and her air purifiers.

"Where are the feds?" I asked.

"Out," he said. "They brought donuts and bagels this morning. You want one?"

The feds were playing nice. Sort of. They disapproved of our housekeeping, but they brought us baked goods. Hell, I liked the smell here. If they wanted to leave the purifiers behind when they wrapped up the case, I wouldn't complain.

"Is Wright in?" I asked.

"He left with Agent Waters, to meet with the Forrands."

"Again?" Agent Waters had gone there last night.

Klein said, "Something about fingerprints."

They'd brought bagels from New Haven. I took an onion bagel to my office. Sat and wondered what to do next. I could call stores about Cody's bedsheets, but maybe that had been completed. I needed a status update before I wasted time redoubling efforts. The bagel was tough and a little eggy. I liked it. I was contemplating a second one when Finnegan knocked on my door. His eyes had pouches that could double as bookbags.

"Can we talk?"

"Sure." Was he going to complain about the feds and their air purifiers? I hoped not.

He closed the door. "I contacted a handwriting expert about the graffiti on your car."

"A handwriting expert? It was spray paint."

"He said it didn't matter. Writing is writing. With one word to go on, he couldn't be positive, but he thought it likely the person was left-handed."

I saw Wright, scratching out a note with his right hand. Right-handed Wright.

"Why left-handed?" I asked.

"Something to do with the way the letters were formed and the spray-paint droplets. The concentration of the paint splatter at certain points. I can give you his number if you want to talk to him."

"No, it's okay." I exhaled. It wasn't Wright. "Good thinking," I said. "I wouldn't have thought to ask a handwriting expert."

"It'll still take time to whittle down the list. We'll have to come up with some pretense to visit people and see which hand they write with."

"Visit people?" I asked. Why would we need to visit our men at home?

"Yeah. It's not like they hang out here," he said.

We stared at each other, trying to figure out what the other was thinking.

"Who's on your list?" I asked.

"Mostly callers to the station, but I included people who called you at home. Why are you giving me that look?"

"Is Burns left-handed?" I asked. His name had moved to the top.

He scratched the corner of his right eye. "I don't know. Wait. You think it was one of *us*?"

"Did you exclude everyone here?" I asked.

"No," he said. "But I didn't put them at the top of my list. Why do you assume it was us?" He was on high defense now. Arms crossed, brows low.

He needed convincing? Fine. "Two cans of spray paint went missing from Evidence before my car got tagged. One of 'em was orange."

He blinked. "That's not proof."

"No, it isn't, but neither is making a call to the station," I said.

He lowered his arms. "Might've been nice to tell me what you were thinking."

"Ditto."

"You're gonna feel bad when you're wrong," he said.

I wished that were true.

He said, "I'm still gonna work my list."

"Fine." He left. I felt sure that whether he believed me or not, he'd be watching Burns's hands today.

Only half the men on my list were on duty. I walked around, checking which hand they used to answer the phone, to write notes, to grab their radios. Burns, left hand. Dix, left hand. I watched Klein for fifteen minutes without seeing him use his damn hands. He talked to other guys, waiting for a call to go pull someone from a snowbank. When I did see him use his hands he held a magazine with both. I was about to intervene, but John Miller called to him. He set down his magazine with his right hand, and then picked up his radio with his left. Fucker. Was he ambidextrous? He picked up his coat with his left hand and his hat, a second later, with his right hand. I'd get him to write something down for me later. That ought to determine what was what. Agent Waters and Wright came in as Klein walked out. My handedness survey could wait.

"Good morning, Chief," Agent Waters said. She looked tired.

"Updates?" I asked.

"Plenty," she said. "Let me grab coffee first."

She left and I hissed, "Everything okay?" to Wright.

"Yeah," he said. Offered nothing more. Sometimes, I longed to shake him.

Waters returned, sipping coffee from a navy-blue mug with the FBI seal on it. She said, "I never use other people's mugs. I've seen too much stuff." She pointed to a mug on Finnegan's desk, half full of coffee, with a suspicious bloom on top of the gray-brown liquid. "Like that." She took another sip of coffee and glanced at the map.

"I hope you don't mind, but we've got more people coming in to help. They won't all be in your space here, but some will."

"You need anything? Gear, radios?" I asked, predicting she'd say no.

"No."

I could hardly object to more manpower. More brains, more bodies, meant a better chance of finding Cody. Though as long as he'd been gone, the chances of finding him alive were slim. She set her mug on the corner of Wright's desk and said, "The prints on the basement doors were smudged partials."

Wright said, "Mr. Forrand said he'd been down there a few days ago, hiding Christmas presents."

"He used the outside doors?" I asked.

"Didn't want the kids to see him with bags of gifts, so he parked on Weymouth Avenue, walked up to his backyard and opened the basement doors."

"Which were unlocked?" I shouldn't have been surprised. People in Idyll didn't lock their front doors, much less their basement doors. They lived in an imaginary world where burglaries never happened to people like them.

"If he had bags of presents, why did his wife go shopping yesterday?" I asked.

"They still had shopping to do for the kids. Some of his gifts were for his wife." Entirely plausible. I wondered if anyone had checked the hidden stash.

Agent Waters said, "There were gifts for her in the pile. We checked. A cashmere sweater and some lingerie."

"I'm guessing he doesn't suspect she's cheating, then," I said.

"Seems that way," she said.

"Does he know she's pregnant?" I asked.

Wright said, "He'd have to be dense not to, unless she doesn't get sick. My wife got sick, a lot. Like having food poisoning for four months."

"Weaker sex, my foot," Agent Waters murmured. "Cisco called in from Sturbridge. We'd had a call that a young boy was crying in a car parked outside a drugstore in Sturbridge, Massachusetts. The age and description fit. The drugstore manager says that kid and his mom come in regularly. Cisco stopped by the house. Think it'll be a while before *that* kid pitches a fit in public."

"I didn't realize we were aiming Scared Straight at the youngins," Wright said.

Agent Waters smiled. "Get 'em while they're young," she said. He chuckled. Well, these two seemed to be enjoying each other's company. Terrific.

"Any other leads?" I asked.

"More spottings, though none looked as good as the Sturbridge one. I've got someone checking on Uncle Greg."

"Still not home?" I asked. He was looking better and better for it. "Maybe we should throw more men at him?"

"He doesn't have a record of diddling kids," she said.

"Doesn't mean he's clean," I said. "He certainly had access to the house."

She sipped her coffee. "We'll see."

"What about the plumber?" I asked. The one Jane Forrand had mentioned.

"There are an awful lot of plumbers out there," Waters said. "And a lot of them are medium build with dark hair and eyes. She thinks maybe he drove a white van, maybe."

"It's better than nothing," I said.

"Just," she said.

"Hey, Detective!" Johnson yelled. He poked his head around the corner.

"What?" Wright barked.

"Just picked this up for you, from Treasure Chest. Lady said it was important." He held out a bag. Looked like it was empty.

Wright pulled a red mask from the bag and settled it on his face. "How do I look?" he asked.

"Stupid." I said. And worse than that. The mask didn't cover his face. The eyeholes didn't align. I could see his chin and forehead. Not much of a disguise.

"Is that an adult-sized mask?" Waters asked.

Wright took it off and handed it to her. She looked at the back. Frowned. "Doesn't say anything about size." She slipped it over her face.

"She's hidden behind that," I said, before turning to Wright. "A lot of your face showed. So if that's the real size of the mask, Cody got grabbed by a woman or a man with a small face."

"Ugh, it smells," Waters complained, unsnapping the elastic that held the mask in place. "Let's check if the mask came in multiple sizes. See what type the store owner sold. If this is the only one, then we're looking for someone with a small face."

"Any progress on the Lego kit or the sheets?" I asked.

"Mulberry's leading that effort. That man loves a list. Hey, there's a guy in the Forrands' neighborhood. Some teacher. Mr. . . ."

"Calloway," I said.

"Right. He has a camera set up on his house."

"Surveillance? Where?" I asked.

"Outside, near the eaves. If he has footage, we need it."

"I can get that for you," I said.

"Yeah?" she asked.

"Leave it to me. Mr. Calloway and I are old friends."

My fist hammered Mr. Calloway's door, the wood yielding to my assault. "Coming!" I heard, followed by the hammering of feet on stairs. The door opened. He was in sweatpants and t-shirt, his feet in thick socks with a red band on top. His hair stuck up every which way like a child's. "You again?" he asked, blinking. I'd woken him.

"Me again." I pushed the door open and stepped inside.

"Don't I have to invite you in?" he asked.

"Why? I'm not a vampire." I trod upstairs. Four large, lumpy black trash bags, cinched shut, awaited disposal. "Going out of business?" I asked, toeing one of the bags with my boot.

"Hey! Leave that alone. Don't you need a warrant?"

"You have a surveillance camera mounted on your house." The camera was aimed at the street. The street where the silver Camry had been parked.

"Is that a crime?" His attempt at tough-guy was pathetic.

"I want the camera footage," I said.

"I don't record video. It's just to deter burglars."

"Too bad. If you had video footage, it might help with our kidnapping inquiries. You remember, right? We came by, asking questions about a missing child? You not only didn't help, you didn't mention your camera. Oh, well. I guess it's time to see how much marijuana you have. It's like a game show, only in reverse. The more you have, the more you lose. I'm really hoping it's in excess of four ounces."

"Wait!" He stepped in front of the trash bags. "Okay. I'll check the footage."

"You'll give me the footage," I said.

"If I give you the footage, you'll leave?"

"Once I watch you dispose of those bags."

"I'm getting rid of them."

"I'd like to make sure," I said. "They're collecting over on Main Street today."

"You want me to illegally dump my trash in someone else's bins?" His outrage was adorable.

"I don't think that's the most serious offense you've committed recently."

"I'll grab the feed." He walked down the hall, to a room at the end. I thought about following him but decided against it. What if the idiot had something else illegal in there and I had no choice but to bust him? I only wanted the footage.

He handed me a heavy square disk minutes later. "It's a zip drive. With DVR files on it." He might have been speaking Swahili. "Have one of your young guys figure it out."

"Okay. Grab the bags. Let's go," I said.

"What? Now?" he asked.

"Yes, now."

"Are you gonna grab one?" He huffed under the weight of three bags.

"Hell no," I said. "See you outside."

Twenty minutes later, I watched him add his garbage bags to the waste bins lining Main Street. I prayed none of the bags split while being taken away, or the DPW workers would be in for a surprise.

It turned out that Agent Cisco knew more than how to lift weights. He knew a thing or two about DVR files. He took the disk, smiled, and said, "I need a laptop."

"You've got more laptops?" I'd already seen two in use. Our station had three old desktop computers that weighed as much as Billy, and a lot of typewriters.

"Your tax dollars at work." He winked and walked away. I admired the view until Agent Waters said, "Did you get anything?"

I told her Cisco was prepping the footage. "He's good with computers and gadgets," she said.

"Mulberry loves lists and Cisco's into gadgets. What's your specialty?" I asked.

"I'm a human lie detector," she said.

"Really?"

She smiled wide. "Really."

Cisco watched the footage in the interview room, where no one would disturb him. I sent Billy to check if he needed food or drink. He came back to tell me Agent Cisco was drinking something called Red Bull from a can.

"Red Bull?"

"He says it's got caffeine and drinking it's the only way he'll be able to watch hours of mind-numbing camera footage of one of the quietest streets in America." Billy paused. "It's hardly the quietest street. I mean, we had a drug dealer on it."

"We don't know that he was dealing," I said.

"Are we really gonna let him off?" he asked.

"We've got bigger fish to fry."

Wright knocked on my doorframe. "You'll never guess who we found!" he said.

"Cody? Where is he? How—"

"No." He coughed. "Greg Baker." He seemed annoyed by my leap.

"Where?" I asked.

"Drunk tank over in Sprague."

"Drunk tank? How long?" I asked.

"Since 6:00 p.m. yesterday."

"Hell." He could've snatched Cody. Stashed him somewhere and then gotten drunk enough to get tossed in jail. It was a tight timeline, though, unless Uncle Greg was the easiest of drunks.

Waters babysat him at Wright's desk. Greg sat, head in his hands. When he lifted his face, it was not a good color. "I told you, I'd never hurt Cody." He said it like a robot, without inflection and as if he'd repeated it a dozen times before. When he noticed Wright and me, he groaned. "I've been locked up all damn night. I just want to go home."

Waters said, her tone friendly, "You left work at—"

"Two o'clock" I raised a brow. She shook her head. He'd have had to speed to Idyll to snatch Cody.

"Do you usually leave work that early?" she asked.

"No."

"Did you have an appointment?" She picked up a snow globe Wright had on his desk. Some crappy souvenir his kids had given him.

"No." He crossed his arms, sullen.

"Then why leave early?" She turned the snow globe over and watched the plastic white snowfall.

"Because you'd just sent a guy to my job to ask people about me. Because people were talking. I overheard Cary Anne Shaw wonder aloud if I was a pedophile." He spat the word, as if it was poison.

"So you decided to leave. Where did you go?"

"The bar," he said. "In Franklin. Even though I just got my two-year chip. I flushed that all away yesterday on Jaeger and beer." He clutched his skull.

"Can anyone verify you were at the bar?" Waters set the snow globe down.

"The bartender," he said. "I didn't get up until I left to drive home."

"And got picked up by the Sprague police."

"Yup. Over the limit. It's my second violation, which means I can't drive my car. Just another piece of my life you've destroyed." Greg's eyes settled on me. "Are you happy?"

"No," I said. "Cody's been missing since yesterday. We want to find him."

"I have told you and told you. I didn't take him!" His shout filled the space. He buried his head in his hands again.

"You lied to me, more than once," I said. "You told me Peter Forrand chose another job, but he didn't."

"He got fired, okay? He got fired and I never told anyone cuz he's my best friend, and it really didn't seem pertinent to Cody's kidnapping."

"Why was he fired?" Agent Waters asked.

He sighed. "He'd missed a lot of work, and there were questions about expense reports he'd submitted."

"Stealing?" she asked.

"They never charged him. They just asked him to go."

"You also lied about Cody's favorite Power Ranger. Why's that?" I asked.

He winced. "I could tell where your line of questioning was leading. You thought I liked kids. I thought if I made it seem I didn't know Cody so well, you'd drop it. Got that wrong, didn't I?"

"You're in luck," Agent Waters said.

Greg Baker chuckled, a laugh of bleak despair. "Oh, really? How's that?"

"I believe you." She tapped her lips. "So, who do you think kidnapped Cody?"

He smelled like stale booze and sweat. "I don't know."

"C'mon Greg, you've known the family since before Cody was born. You must know their family and friends. Who among them might be clever enough to kidnap Cody?" She waited and added, "Stupid enough to try twice?"

"I don't know," he said.

"Anyone like him more than he or she should?" She'd lowered her voice to a near whisper.

Her words brought his head up fast. "That's what you said about me! That's what everyone thinks now, that I like kids. Jesus. I just like kids because they're not fucking sneaky and awful the way adults are. Kids don't drive you to drink."

"Some do," Wright said under his breath.

"Maybe someone didn't like Cody, or thought his family would be better off without him," I suggested.

"That's messed up," he said. He stood, one hand on the desk for support. "I don't know who took him. I can't imagine who would, okay? I want to go home, to shower. To see if I still have a job."

I thought Waters would stop him. Clearly, he thought the same. As he walked toward the exit, he kept casting looks over his shoulder, checking to see if we'd pursue him. We didn't.

"So," Wright said to Waters. "You believed him?"

"He has a former DUI. And we did send a guy to his office to make inquiries. An innocent man would drink. Yeah, I believe him."

"Think we just ruined his life?" I asked. For weeks they'd look at him funny at work. I doubted anyone would ask him to babysit soon.

"I want to find Cody Forrand," Agent Waters said. "If someone ends up without his sobriety chip because of it, so be it."

Cisco came over as I digested Waters's statement. "Who wants to watch some grainy camera footage?" he asked.

In the interview room, Cisco sat at his laptop, two empty cans of Red Bull at his elbow. Agent Waters was behind his right shoulder. Wright stood to the left, which put me directly behind Cisco. His haircut looked recent, no stubble below the sharp edge of closely cut hair.

"Watch this," Cisco said. We looked at the screen's low-quality picture of Weymouth Avenue. You could see a slice of Mr. Calloway's yard and much of the sidewalk and street. "There." He stopped the film. A car was caught, mid-street.

"Is that the Camry?" Waters asked, quicker than Wright or me.

"Yup."

"What's the time?" Wright asked.

"1:50 p.m."

He hit a button and the car drove past. "It moves out of frame. Stays that way until 2:18 p.m." He hit buttons and sped the film. Then he slowed it. A dog and a man appeared and disappeared, then a car, driving in the opposite direction. "The Camry," he said.

"Let me see it again," Waters said.

He obliged, stopping the car mid-drive. The resolution wasn't great. We could see a driver, but no facial details. "Not wearing a mask," Wright said. That much was true.

"Can we enhance it?" Waters asked.

"I'll ask the lab boys," Cisco said. He punched some buttons. Made time speed by. "A few people walk by, and I'll try to get higher-res on their faces, but at 4:15 p.m., this happens." We watched as the Camry drove past, again.

"Why return?" Agent Waters said. The question on everyone's mind.

"Unless the driver was expected someplace nearby," I said.

"Like the Forrands' house?" Wright asked.

"If Cody got in that car, how did no one see him?" Cisco asked.

"Why doesn't he appear on camera?" Agent Waters asked.

"The car was parked out of the camera's frame when we found it," I said. "Assuming the driver parked in roughly the same place earlier, Cody wouldn't have come within view."

"You think the driver knew about the camera?" Cisco asked.

"If he knew, I doubt he'd have chosen that street," Waters said. She tugged at the ends of her hair. "Let's look at that timeline you guys made of the Forrands' guests; and, Cisco, get the lab boys these files now. I want a better picture of the driver's face."

"Gotcha," he said.

"You need a ride?" I asked. I could send Klein.

He turned from the screen. "Nah. I can send it via e-mail." He typed on his keyboard for a minute and said, "They've got it now."

"Like magic," I said.

"Something like that." He rolled his neck. "It'll take time before we hear anything. I got time for a sammie, boss?" He asked Waters.

She said, "Grab me one too. Oh, hell, get lunch for the whole crew. I don't want Mulberry bitching about being forgotten."

Cisco said, "Mulberry never forgives and never forgets." He paused in the doorway. "Where am I going?" he asked.

Wright said, "There's Idyll Sub Shop or Papano's."

I groaned. "Papano's is overrated."

"Papano's has a better meatball sub," Wright said.

"I suppose you want one," I asked him.

He half bowed. "That would be lovely. Thanks for asking."

Waters laughed. I shook my head and muttered, "No respect."

"Chief!" Billy called. "You got a call, from the mayor."

"Why don't I take you to Papano's?" I said to Cisco. "Home of the world's most overrated sandwiches."

"What should I tell him?" Billy asked.

I thought of several things Billy could tell his uncle. "Tell him I'm out." I walked to the front door, Cisco following, whistling a tune I recognized as, "Wake Me Up Before You Go-Go."

CHAPTER TWENTY-FOUR

Cisco adjusted the passenger seat. "So, you're avoiding your mayor?" he said.

"Always." The car before us wove slightly. Drunk driver?

"Is it true he tried to quash press about possible hate crimes?" How had he heard about that?

The car wove again. I couldn't see the driver's head. "One second," I said. I checked for oncoming traffic, and then passed the vehicle, slowly. White hair, short, wearing eyeglasses. I got in front of her and checked the rearview. I could pull her over, but she hadn't hit anything, and I didn't have time to spare.

"God save me from the elderly," Cisco said.

"It's the teens who are more likely to kill you on the road."

"So, about the mayor?"

"He tries to squash any bad press. He doesn't want to scare tourist dollars away."

"Is that the sort of intrigue and dark secrets they talk about small towns having?"

"No," I said, turning onto Main Street. "By dark secrets, they mean the sudden, forced retirement of Mrs. Horowitz, beloved high school history teacher, who had a heroin addiction that would've killed lesser mortals."

He whistled.

Papano's had white flocking on its windows. Instead of festive, the windows looked dirty. Inside, it smelled of hot cheese and bread. Cisco read the giant blackboard behind the counter, with its list of sandwiches. Thirty of them. Never trust a menu with more than twelve items, my father told me. No one can make more than twelve items well. It's the one piece of advice he's given me that I follow.

"What do you recommend?" Cisco asked.

"Leaving," I said. "Since we're here, the cheesesteak is okay and the chicken cutlet is probably the best thing they've got."

"Okay." He stepped to the counter.

Matt, the owner, carried in two bags of groceries. "Hey, Chief," he said.

"Hi, Matt." Despite my preference for the sub shop, I was inside Papano's often enough that the owner knew me to say hi and bitch about the weather.

He pushed through the back doors and reappeared a minute later, while Cisco was handing the counter kid a credit card. Matt said, "Any word on Cody Forrand?"

"Nope," I said.

"Poor parents. Must be out of their heads." He brightened. "You think they need food? I could send some platters over."

"They don't need food." Their house was filled with platters. People looking to help decided food was what was needed.

"Ah, okay. Well, I hope you find him soon." He began to refill the salt-shakers from a big box of salt. He looked up from pouring a steady stream of white crystals. "This guy FBI?" He jerked his head toward Cisco.

Cisco said, "This guy is FBI."

"Ah, good. About time. No offense intended, Chief, but with a kidnapping you want the FBI, right? Those guys probably handle them all the time."

"Except Sundays and holidays," I said. Cisco fought a smile and lost. "Kidding," I said to Matt.

"Ah, I gotcha. I gotcha. Probably better go help with your order. You guys have big appetites." He swung back through the doors.

Something buzzed. Cisco fished a small phone from his jacket. "Agent Cisco," he said. "Yeah? They're sure? Great. No, we're getting the food. Right. I don't know." He covered the bottom half of the phone and asked, "How long?"

"For the order? Fifteen, twenty minutes." We'd ordered a lot of hot subs.

"Twenty," he said into the phone. "Yeah." He folded his phone shut and stuffed it into his pocket. Rocked forward onto the balls of his feet.

"What's up?" I asked.

"Tech boys called Waters about the driver video."

"They made an ID?" Wow, that was fast.

"No, but we've got a gender. The driver was female."

"They're sure?"

"Yup. Waters wants us back as fast as possible. Faster, probably. Patience isn't her strong suit."

I yelled at Matt that we needed to get back to the station fast. He yelled back to hold my horses. In the end, we got four bags' worth of lunch in sixteen minutes.

Driving with my foot as close to the floor as I dared, I said, "It's gonna break."

"What's gonna break?" Cisco asked.

"The case. It has that feel, you know? Like when something you're trying to tear apart weakens and it's on the verge of giving?"

"If you love investigating so much, how come you're a police chief?" he asked.

"Long story."

"But you love it."

"It's the best feeling there is, when a case like this is about to go down." It was. Everything tingled, from my scalp to my toes. It felt like it did before a big thunderstorm.

"The best feeling?" Cisco said. He gave me a look that made me wonder, about more than one thing.

"Second-best, then."

He laughed. I joined him.

There were eight of us. Me, Waters, Cisco, Wright, Mulberry, Klein, and two agents who'd been chasing tips and had been recalled now that we knew the kidnapper was a woman. The map had been removed from the boards. One now served as a who's who of all the women attached to the Forrands. Mrs. Forrand, Jane, was front and center. To the right was Jessica, her sister. Above her, Cody's grandmother, Jane's mother. Then Mrs. Donner, mother of Cody's dead CIPA friend, Aaron, was to the left. Under her were Camille Forrester and Kristine Leonard, friends from the Forrands' Chaplin days.

"Jessica is out," Wright said.

"What if she helped whoever took him?" Waters asked.

"Anna would've seen. They were in the kitchen together the whole time," he said.

"Anna's bright," I said. "She would've noticed if her aunt was acting oddly."

"Okay. What about the grandmother?" Waters suggested.

"She was with her husband," Klein said. He'd taken her statement at the house yesterday. Had tracked the comings and goings.

"She might be lying. Could be in it together," Waters said. "But the Camry was stolen while they were on a shopping trip to New York with some folks from their church."

"Doesn't seem likely," Mulberry said. It was the first time I'd heard him venture an opinion.

"That leaves these three." Wright gestured, pointing to the two Chaplin friends and Mrs. Donner.

"What do we know about her?" Waters asked, tapping Mrs. Donner's photo.

"She had a son, Aaron, same age as Cody," I said. "He had the same disease. He died earlier this year."

"So, she's, what, looking for a replacement kid?" Waters asked.

"You think she'd snatch a healthy one," Cisco said. "Less work."

"Did she think the Forrands weren't looking after him properly?" Waters said. "Start checking her whereabouts on both attempts and see if she could've stolen the car."

"Mrs. Donner's crazy," Klein said. All eyes went to him. "She kept calling Chief Lynch a sinner and telling him he shouldn't be part of the search."

So much for keeping that to ourselves.

"Sinner?" Waters asked. "She religious?"

"It appears so," I said.

"Huh. What about this one?" she tapped Camille Forrester's photo.

Klein said, "She was at the house yesterday. She's friends with Jessica. They were in the same class together in Chaplin. She's engaged, due to be married next summer."

"A bit busy to be adding a child to the mix," said the fed who'd just arrived. Hartman? Harmon?

"That leaves Kristine Leonard," Waters said. Kristine was a stunner. The one woman whose picture made the guys linger.

"She was a friend of Peter, the husband," Klein said.

"My wife wouldn't let me have a friend like that," Wright said.

"How'd she feel about Cody?" Waters asked.

Klein shrugged. "She seemed upset, but no more than you'd expect. She kept checking her phone while she was at the house."

"Check her out," Waters said. "The rest of you, focus on Mrs. Donner. She's been in the house before?"

Wright said, "Yes. She'd visited before, with Aaron, when he was alive."

Klein said, "She had a child with that disease die. Why take another? What kind of person wants that?"

"A sicko," Waters said, staring at the pictures, her tone bored.

"Chief! Telephone!"

I said, "Let me know what you need," and walked to my office to pick up my phone. "Chief Lynch."

"Chief. I tried calling earlier." The mayor liked to tell you he'd called and missed you. Lots of our conversations started this way. "That arson on Haywood Court. How's the investigation coming?"

"It's in progress."

"Now, I'm sure you and the fire captain are doing your jobs." He was lumping me in with Hirsch? Must be cold in hell today. "But it seems to me that whoever set that fire did the neighborhood a favor. I mean, let's not kid ourselves, right? No one wants a pedophile across the street, watching their kids playing on their lawn."

"I don't suppose they do."

"I knew you'd understand. I mean, it's not as though anyone was harmed. The guy got out unhurt."

"His pets didn't, not all of them."

"That's a shame, a real shame. But no loss of human life, right? And I'm sure the house was insured. He was renting. The owners will get insurance money and clean it up, and they can get someone suitable in there."

"Uh-huh."

"So we understand each other?"

"I believe we do. Thanks for calling, Mayor." He thought he'd won me over. That I'd roll on my back like a puppy wanting a belly scratch.

He'd said: *No one wants a pedophile across the street, watching their kids playing on their lawn.* Could have just been talk, but it was awfully specific. Across the street. I checked the names Wright had given me. Trabucco lived on the even side of the street. The Flynns and the Van-Wycks, both families with children, lived on the odd-numbered side, across the street.

Mrs. Dunsmore was in her office, her back to me. She wrapped her scarf about her neck.

"Are the Flynns or the VanWycks on Haywood Court friendly with the mayor?" I asked.

She snorted as she turned. Tucked the end of her scarf further into her coat. "That's an understatement. Frank VanWyck was best man at the mayor's wedding. He and the mayor went to school together. Played hockey together. Practically Siamese twins, those two."

"Thanks."

"Why are you asking?"

My instinct was to tell her nothing. However, if this shook out the way I thought it would, she'd find out soon enough. "The VanWycks might've been involved in that fire."

She crossed her arms. Let the idea settle. "If I were you, I'd send one of your detectives to investigate."

"They're working the Forrand kidnapping. They've caught a break."

She set her purse down on her desk. "Chief, this isn't going to make you any friends. You'd do better to let Wright or Finnegan talk to the VanWycks."

Maybe she was right, but I wasn't going to make them handle

something sticky so I could remain clean. "I'm not looking to win a popularity contest."

"No kidding." She fingered her scarf. Something below. The cross. Damn it.

In its neighborhood of well-kept homes bedecked with wreaths and holiday lights, the Trabucco house looked awful with its punctured roof and char marks. Glass littered the lawn. The house's front door hung ajar. It smelled—of burning, of gasoline, and of hatred. The trees that had caught fire nearby were skeletal and charred. The VanWycks' house, by contrast, looked photo-shoot ready. Candles in the windows. Fir wreath with a red bow on the door.

Mr. and Mrs. VanWyck were home. They greeted me as if they'd expected my boots to dirty their white carpet. Their living room was cluttered with photos of family and friends. A giant Christmas tree held court, decorated with colored lights. Masses of gifts were gathered below its branches. Santa liked these people very much.

"Good morning, Chief," Mrs. VanWyck said. "May I offer you coffee?"

"No, thank you."

We sat down. I looked at the pictures within reach. One showed the mayor and Mr. VanWyck on the Nipmuc Golf Course. The same course where Cecilia North had been killed months earlier. Next to it was a photo of two kids at the beach. Elementary-school age. They'd had their children late. The VanWycks were my age or older.

"Mike mentioned you might drop by," Mr. VanWyck said.

His wife leaned forward. "He's such a dear friend."

The mayor had told them I'd stop by. Well.

"When we heard about that man," Mrs. VanWyck said, "we couldn't believe it. Of course, we weren't happy when we heard that the house had been *rented*. It's never good for the neighborhood when non-owners live nearby. They just don't invest the same care into the home."

"Then to find out he was a pedophile!" Mr. VanWyck said. "We bought a bicycle for our daughter from him. He helped her choose it. When I think of him helping her test the bikes . . ." He clenched his jaw. "We had to do something."

"So you set fire to his house."

"No one got hurt," he said.

"Animals died, and the fire almost spread to a neighbor's house. Would've, if the firemen hadn't come so quickly."

"I'm sorry about the animals. I love them. As for the danger, you said yourself, our firemen are top-notch."

"Why didn't you ask Mr. Trabucco to move?" I asked.

He reared back as if I'd slapped him. "What? I'm supposed to ask him to leave the neighborhood? Talk to him like he's a reasonable human being? He was going to say, 'Sure. I'll just pack my things and go'? Really, Chief, I thought you understood about these things."

I did understand. Better than him. But I also understood that he'd taken the law into his own hands. Set fire on a windy night when neighbors could've lost their houses or lives if the fire had spread. And his arrogance. In assuming I'd stop by, have a chat, and sweep it under the rug. That was what gnawed me.

I stood. "Would you like to grab your coat?"

"Coat?" They looked at each other.

"It's cold outside." They stared at me, confused. "We're going to the station."

"Why?" he asked.

"I'm arresting you, on suspicion of arson."

"But you talked with Mike. He told us."

"Mrs. VanWyck, you may stay here."

"This is absurd!" She stood. "That man was going to harm our children!"

They shouted a bit more. I waited them out. Mr. VanWyck saw I wouldn't be moved. "You're making a mistake," he said.

I didn't handcuff him, but I seated him in the back of my car. When he was settled, I asked, "You friends with the district attorney?"

"Why?"

"Because he's the one who decides whether to prosecute. I thought the mayor might've mentioned that."

He didn't respond.

The Santa-hatted dispatcher, John Miller, greeted Mr. VanWyck when we came through the door. "Hi!" I knew he aimed his greeting at Mr. VanWyck, because he'd never smiled at me like that.

Mr. VanWyck said, "Hello, John."

"Here for the Toys for Tots drive?" John asked.

"Already contributed," Mr. VanWyck said. "Perhaps not next year," he said, his voice low. A threat.

Fine. "Let's get you into an interview room." I didn't lower my voice. I could play games too.

Every cop inside watched as I walked in lockstep with him to the back of the station. Agent Waters called out, "Forrand case?" Her tone implying I'd best not be leaving her out of the loop.

"Arson investigation. Unrelated."

She turned her attention back to whatever I'd interrupted.

I took Mr. VanWyck to the room we used for interviews. It had a scarred table, two plastic chairs, and an ashtray. It smelled of stale cigarettes, sweat, and disinfectant.

"I'll send a detective in to take your statement."

He looked toward the window, set high in the wall. "I think I'd like to speak to my attorney first."

"Sure thing. You have a cell phone?"

He withdrew one from the breast pocket of his camel-hair coat. Flipped it open and peered at the tiny keypad. "Do you mind?" He looked at me and then at the door.

"There's no expectation of privacy here. I could insist you use the pay phone in the hallway." That phone didn't work. We let the rare perps who had an attorney use our desk phones. He didn't know that. Why would he?

He punched a button. I heard the phone ring once, twice before a calm voice answered. He said, "Douglas, I need you. I'm at the Idyll Police Station. No. Nothing like that. Can you come now? Yes. Thanks." He flexed his hand, snapping the phone closed.

"Would you care for a beverage?" I asked. "We have water and very bad coffee."

He smiled, but it didn't extend past his mouth. "No."

"Very well. Have a seat. I'll show your attorney in once he arrives."

"What's with that?" Finnegan asked when I reached the pen. Waters pinned a picture of Aaron Donner on the board beside the photo of his mother. Looked like we had a target in view.

"Meet our arsonist, Mr. VanWyck," I said.

Wright groaned. Finnegan laughed, but it wasn't happy. "You know he and the mayor are blood brothers?" Finnegan asked.

"He confessed, in front of me. What should I have done? Left him at home?"

"He confessed?" Wright said.

Cisco grinned. "Wow. You small-town cops have it easy. You show up and people just confess?"

Waters smacked his shoulder and said, "Play nice."

"He seemed to think he had nothing to hide," I said.

"He lawyer up?" Finny asked.

"Just did."

Wright massaged his brow. "You want to explain to my kids that Santa couldn't afford gifts this year after I get fired?"

"Why would you get fired?" Cisco asked.

"Because it's my case and I have to go in there and grill the man who donated the money we used to start the anti-drug program in our schools. The same man who cuts a $2,500 check to the Toys for Tots program each year."

"Maybe not next year," I said.

"Let me do it," Finnegan said. He adjusted his awful tie. "I'm part-time." Waters looked at him with admiration. He didn't notice.

"It's my case," Wright said. "My bullet."

I liked him better in that moment than I ever had.

He shook his head. "Let's just hope he has the good sense to keep his mouth shut. And let's hope he wore gloves when he set the damn fire."

CHAPTER TWENTY-FIVE

Mr. VanWyck kept his mouth shut with his lawyer by his side. Wright let him go after forty-five minutes of fruitless questions. When he returned to his desk, he cracked his knuckles and muttered, "Lawyers." Then he said, "What now?" to Waters. Finnegan handed him a gold pen. Wright stared at it in confusion.

"Early going-away present," Finnegan said, deadpan.

Wright tossed it at him. "Fuck you, Finny."

Finnegan laughed. Waters snickered.

My office had a stack of messages with the mayor's name on them. I wasn't naive—I'd worked long enough to know a thing or two about politics. The mayor would go nuclear when he found out I'd dragged his buddy in the station. I was in the right, but right yields to might, and I wasn't winning popularity contests with my rainbow flag. So, to save Wright and myself, I walked my fingers through my Rolodex. Found the name. Dialed the phone.

"Hello?" His voice sounded old. But then, he was.

"Hello, Mr. Neilly. It's Chief Lynch."

"Chief Lynch?" He sounded as though he thought I might be playing a prank. Given our last encounter, at Wannerman's, I wasn't surprised.

"Mr. Neilly, I have a delicate matter that's come up, and I'm not sure how to proceed. It involves the mayor."

"Mike." He didn't say his name so much as drop it. There was no love lost between the two. My forced attendance at town meetings had brought this to my attention.

"I don't want to dance around the topic." I cringed. Did that sound *very* gay? "Earlier today, the mayor warned someone that I would be coming to see them, on a criminal matter."

"Warned them?" His voice rose.

"Moreover, it seems he implied that no investigation would be forthcoming."

"What crime? Not that kidnapping, is it? By God, we can't—"

"No. Not that. The arson on Haywood Court."

"My, your department is certainly busy these days. You know, we never had this much crime before. Not ever." Meaning, not since I joined the department. As if the criminals had followed me from New York to Idyll.

I said, "The mayor knows who committed the arson, and he tried to influence me not to pursue it. Mr. Neilly, you were a volunteer firefighter, weren't you?" I knew he was. I'd seen him yakking it up with Captain Hirsch, talking about the "old days" when they had an honest-to-God bucket brigade.

"I served from 1945 to 1951." Jesus. The way he said it, you'd have thought he'd won World War II, single-handedly.

"I'm sure you can appreciate how that fire might have quickly gotten out of control. Captain Hirsch said it was a very near thing. Neighbor's house nearly caught fire."

"It *was* windy." Mr. Neilly's other passion? The weather.

"So, you see, I can't condone someone setting a deliberate fire, endangering lives."

"Of course not! That would be, er, dereliction of duty."

I cleared my throat. "Indeed. So I find myself in an awkward position. I don't want to bring a formal complaint against the mayor, but he can't interfere in police business this way. It smacks of cronyism."

"Yes, very awkward. Have you pursued the suspect?"

"Yes, he's been questioned and released."

"I see. I see. Who was it?"

"I'm not sure I can discuss that, sir. Seeing as how it's ongoing."

"Quite right. Not, I gather, a family member?" He was fishing now. Rod and bait out, for all to see. I didn't mind.

"Well, I think I can tell you, no. Not family, but a friend, a very good friend."

"Rest assured, Chief. I will look into this. I don't think you have to worry about the mayor hampering your investigation."

"Thank you, Mr. Neilly. Your dedication to your job, and to justice, does you credit." Was that laying it on too thick? It had sounded better, more reasonable, in my head.

"Don't mention it, don't mention it. Just doing my duty."

I pictured the mayor's face when good old Neilly paid him a visit. God, I'd pay good money to see that go down. I crumpled the mayor's phone messages and tossed them in the trash. Who would appreciate this story? I reached for the phone. Damien Saunders would eat this up. Maybe I'd been too harsh on him. Maybe he'd like to grab a drink, without his GALP pals. Maybe he'd know how things were between the owners of Sweet Dreams. I hadn't heard a peep from them since we'd booked Zachary Gabriel.

A knock at my door. I set the phone down and looked up. "Sorry to bother you," Cisco said.

"Not at all. Come in." I waved him in.

He stepped inside, gave the room a thorough stare, and said, "Waters wants me to check out the doctor who treated Aaron Donner."

"Dr. Frazier. I've got his number."

"No. I've got to ride down. Do interviews."

"You need directions?" I asked.

"I need a partner. The guy who was supposed to be assigned got pulled to assist on some drug bust in New Haven."

"You want me to lend you someone?" He could have his pick, but he might find the selection less than stellar.

"I was hoping you'd tag along."

"Me?"

"You were a homicide detective in New York, yeah?"

"Back in the day." It had only been eighteen months. Some days it felt like eighteen years.

"I'm guessing you know your way around an interview. Though if you need to stay here . . ." He nodded at the phone.

"Give me a sec."

"Sure thing." He stepped backward, out of my office.

I grabbed a pen and stuffed a notepad into my coat pocket. "Ready," I said.

I saw Klein on my way out. I told him I'd be at the hospital if anyone needed to reach me. "You don't have a mobile," Klein said.

Cisco paused. Said, "Really?"

"Really. I'm sure the hospital could page me," I said to Klein.

Cisco insisted on driving. He had a shiny black SUV. He turned on the radio. Christmas pop. Shut it off. "So, what's it like being a gay cop in a town like Idyll?" he asked, eyes scanning the road. Not what I'd expected him to lead with.

"About what you'd expect." Assuming he had an active imagination.

He unwrapped a stick of gum. Popped it into his mouth and chewed hard. "The feds are a little better to work for," he said. "They've gotten good at looking the other way." So he was gay. I'd suspected as much.

"Is this the part where we compare gym routines?" I asked.

"You couldn't handle mine, old man."

I mimicked typing a report. "Federal agent insulted police chief with inappropriate comments related to his body."

He grinned. Flipped on his turn signal. "Who do you think took the kid?"

"Mrs. Donner looks as good as anyone, but it still seems off. When we thought it was a random snatch-and-grab, it made more sense."

"Crazy people do crazy things," he said.

"That's great. That belongs on a pillow. 'Crazy people do crazy things.'" I framed my hands.

He laughed. The car was warm, the ride smooth. Today was shaping up.

Dr. Frazier wasn't at the hospital. He was in New York City, seeing the sights with his wife. We settled for his colleague, Dr. Larson, and a pediatric nurse, Annie Burr, who had treated both Cody Forrand and Aaron Donner.

Cisco interviewed the young doctor. I took the nurse.

"Aaron was a sweetie," Annie said. "Always said 'please' and 'thank you.' He loved the sherbet from the caf."

"What about Cody?" I asked.

"Cody was a handful. He'd climb out of bed if you turned your back. He was the kid you worry won't make it to age ten, because his rambunctiousness combined with his disease is a deadly combo. But he can be a charmer when he wants."

"Were you surprised by Aaron's death?"

"Kids with CIPA are more likely to die young. Still, given his inclination to stay indoors and take it easy, he seemed likely to beat the odds. But he didn't die of an injury."

"Hyperthermia, right?"

"Yup. It was early September. One of those Indian summer days. I guess Aaron wanted to wear his new school clothes, even though they were too hot. His mother said she told him to change when he got home. He went upstairs. She assumed he was in his room, playing. She found him an hour and a half later, collapsed on his floor. He hadn't changed and the air-conditioning was off on the second floor. A busted fuse. The downstairs units were working, so Mrs. Donner hadn't noticed. She called an ambulance. He had multiple seizures on the way in. When he arrived, he was unresponsive. We tried cooling him, but he stopped breathing. Every time we got him back, his body shut down."

"How was his mother?" I asked.

"Frantic. She wanted to be in the room with him."

"So, normal."

"Yes," she paused. "And no."

"No?"

"I've worked here eight years. Seen a lot of parents. You get all kinds. Negligent assholes who shouldn't be allowed to breathe, and the grateful ones who send you presents year after year for saving their child."

"What type was Mrs. Donner?" I asked.

"Demanding. Religious. You never forgot she was in the room. Half the time Aaron was here, I felt we were taking care of her, not him. There's a condition called Munchausen syndrome by proxy. It's when a caretaker, usually a parent, abuses a child in order to gain sympathy or attention."

"She had that?" I asked.

"No. Aaron definitely had CIPA. She couldn't have faked that. She behaved as if we ought to treat her specially, though. Don't get me wrong. Having a kid with CIPA is a nightmare. Still, you don't get a damn medal for it. I mean, parents of kids with terminal cancer don't expect awards." Doctors and nurses judged how parents behaved. It was no different than how cops evaluated parents. Five seconds, and we've decided whether they're deadbeats, saints, or simply unlucky.

"Any doubt about Aaron's cause of death." I asked.

"No. Why?"

"Did you ever see her, after Aaron died?"

"She volunteered at the hospital. Two weeks after Aaron died, she showed up, wanting to help. She said the hospital felt like home, and she felt closer to him here."

"Does she still volunteer?" Was it possible our kidnapper was in the building?

"No. She stopped, four months ago. Said her church work was keeping her busy."

"Does someone supervise the volunteers?" I asked. "Could I speak to him or her?"

"Mrs. Potts. She's on afternoons. I'll ask her to call you," she said.

"That would be great. Thanks." I stood. A small bump in the floor made me stumble. She didn't notice. She sighed and said, "Poor Cody."

Cisco said Dr. Larson hadn't been as forthcoming as Annie about Mrs. Donner's personality. Though he did refer to her as "the poor widowed woman" more than once.

"How was she widowed?" Cisco asked.

"Wright said her husband had a massive heart attack when Aaron was a baby."

"Who's checking Mrs. Donner's house?" I asked.

"Mulberry, assuming we can get in. The video footage isn't a slam dunk." It wasn't. Cody wasn't visible in any of the car's images. Tough to exchange what we had for a search warrant. "We'll put eyes on the house, warrant or no," he said. Surveillance duty in this weather. I didn't envy the sucker who drew that short straw.

"What now?" I asked.

"We report back. Waters may have some more leads."

In the car, Cisco turned on the radio. Commercials frantically urged shoppers to get their last-minute shopping done. "You celebrate yet?" he asked.

"Yesterday, in the city with my family."

"New York?"

"Yeah."

"I was supposed to have Christmas off this year, but unless we find Cody on our return drive, I doubt that's gonna happen," he said.

"You have to travel?" I looked out my passenger window. The night was dark as tar, the highway lights ugly and yellow.

"North Carolina. It's nice this time of year. No snow." He silenced the radio. "God, I could use an hour of sleep."

"Don't you have any of those caffeinated drinks with the bull on the can?"

"Not in the car. Mind if we stop for coffee?"

"Fine by me."

He zoomed off the next exit. Pulled into a McDonald's. I stepped onto the slushy lot, walking around the worst of the puddles. Only one other car, with Florida plates, in the place. We tromped inside and ordered two large coffees. The glare of the place: bright colors and fluorescence, made me blink. The pimply teen in the brown-and-yellow polyester uniform fumbled our change. Cisco told her to keep it, winning a giant smile from her. She wore braces. The elastics on them were blue.

Back outside, we stomped our boots on the pavement to clear them of slush and salt. Cisco said, "I hate to ask, but would you mind driving? I've barely slept for three days. We'd come off an abduction case before being called onto this one. I haven't been in my own bed in over a week."

"Sure." Might be fun to drive an almost-new SUV. He held the keys out. I grabbed them as I walked past. Cobra fast, he spun and grabbed the back of my neck. Pulled me in and kissed me. I stood, shocked still, the scent of him, musk and coffee, invading my space. His face was bristly. His hard arms reeled me in closer. His heat came at me. So close, I could practically feel his pulse. He stepped back, as fast as he'd grabbed me. "Sorry."

I looked around the lot. No witnesses. I should've been grateful, but part of me wanted an observer nearby, so I knew I hadn't imagined the whole thing.

"I act badly when I'm sleep-deprived," he said.

"You assault cops?" He stood a foot away, but I could still smell him.

"Not usually," he said. "Only the handsome ones."

Flattery. There's a reason they say it will get you everywhere.

"Next time, a warning would be nice," I said. "Sudden grabs could get you punched."

"I'll keep it in mind." He opened the passenger door and slung himself inside. I got in and started the engine. The view was different; I was a foot higher than the seat in my car. The car purred, a low rumble of power. I circled out of the lot and checked the road before pulling onto it. The car leapt when I depressed the gas. Power. "I could get used to this," I said, but Cisco's eyes were closed, his face slack. I looked longer than necessary before setting my sights on the road back to Idyll.

CHAPTER TWENTY-SIX

Mrs. Forrand was hysterical. Mascara ran in parallel streaks on her face. She kept pacing past the windows in my office. The stress couldn't be good for her baby.

"Mrs. Forrand," Agent Waters said. Her voice was cool and calm, but under it I sensed a frayed thread. Annoyance? "We need information. The sooner we have it; the sooner we find your son. Did Mrs. Donner ever mention another property besides the house in West Hartford? Was there a place she vacationed?"

"My baby. She took my baby." Mrs. Forrand looked almost feral now. "If I get my hands on her, I'll—"

"Honey," her husband said, reaching for her arm, and missing as she stalked past, muttering what she'd do if she got her hands on Mrs. Donner. He sighed and said, "She went on vacation with Aaron to Disney World, two years ago. Other than that, I don't know." He chafed his hands. "Her house was nice. I think her husband's death left her with some money. I don't think she had another home or anything like that." He picked up the mug of coffee we'd given him. "You're *sure* she took him?"

The feds had gotten a warrant to search Mrs. Donner's home. Waters let Wright tag along. What he'd told me had creeped me out. Aaron's bedroom had been remade. The same sheets Cody had at home were on the single twin bed. Pictures of Power Rangers hung on the walls. Lego pieces were stacked in a plastic tub on the floor. A family photo of the Forrands was on the night table. Sammy, the stuffed raccoon, was missing. Just like Cody.

"They wouldn't be asking us these questions if they weren't sure!" Jane yelled. She stopped mid-pace. "Would you?" She addressed Agent Waters.

"The evidence indicates it's her." While Cisco and I had been at the hospital, the tech boys had gotten a better image of the stolen car's driver. Mrs. Donner, without a doubt. Unless she had a twin. "Had she been spending more time with you recently?"

Peter frowned. "I suppose. After Aaron died, we saw less of her. Made sense. We didn't run into her like we used to, but about four months ago she began stopping by."

"She offered to help with the kids," Jane said. She wiped at her face with a tissue, smearing mascara across her cheek. "She'd watch them while I ran errands, or she'd come with us to the doctor's and keep Anna entertained while Cody had tests run."

"I always thought she liked Anna more," Peter said.

"So you're surprised she took Cody," Wright said.

"Of course we're surprised!" Jane said. "If we had any inkling she would take him, we wouldn't have let her inside. We've known her for, what, two years?"

"Almost two years," Peter said.

"She was nice. A little preachy, but other than that . . ." she took a shuddery breath and blinked back tears.

"What about her family?" Waters asked. "You said she has a sister in Vermont. Do you know where?"

"Middlebury or Burlington. I don't think they were close. Sharon mentioned her living in sin with some guy."

"How quaint," Cisco said.

"Do you know her sister's first name?" Waters asked.

"Lizzy or Lily or, no, Lilith. Lilith." Jane rubbed her hair. "I don't know her last name."

"We can get that," Waters said. In fact, we already knew it. Pitts. Lilith Pitts, sister to Sharon Pitts before she became Sharon Donner, widow, bereaved mother, and kidnapper. I wondered why Waters had withheld that information.

"How did Cody feel about Mrs. Donner?" Waters asked.

Peter thought, his brow crinkled. "He called her 'No Fun Franny' once," he said. He smiled at the memory. "No idea where he picked up that phrase."

"Do you find it curious that Cody would go with her?" Waters asked.

"She took him! He didn't go with her. She grabbed him!" Jane resumed pacing. She was going to wear a trench into the floor.

"No one reported yelling. Your sister didn't hear Cody cry out. It appears he went with her willingly."

"Maybe she drugged him, like the first time," she said.

"Maybe she lied to him," Peter said. "Told her we'd sent her to get him."

"Twice?" Waters asked. "After the first time, you'd think he'd be more suspicious."

"She stole our child and you're, you're criticizing him for not being, what? Skeptical enough? What the fuck is wrong with you?" Jane yelled. Peter reached for his wife, but she evaded him. "Cody is the victim here! Why the hell are you blaming him! What's wrong with you? With all of you?"

"I'm sorry," Waters said. "I'm not blaming Cody. I'm trying to understand what happened. Why he might've got in the car with her. Was it the Legos, or did she use some other persuasion?"

"The Legos?" Peter asked.

"The truck kit," Wright said. "The one Cody wanted."

"Yeah, but we hadn't given it to him yet. We almost did the day after he was released from the hospital. Then we couldn't find where we'd hidden it—"

"Why does it matter?" Jane broke in. "If she gave him toys or threatened him, what's the difference? We want him back. Now!"

"When Sharon was at your house, after Cody had been reported missing, did you notice anything odd? Anything off about her demeanor?" Waters asked.

"She brought us cookies," Peter said, as if he couldn't fathom it. "Store-bought. She apologized for not having time to bake any."

"How could she come to our house after she'd taken our son, and talk about cookies?" Jane asked. She looked at us as if we'd have answers. We didn't.

"What time did she leave your house?" Waters asked.

"I don't remember. Sometime before the press conference."

According to Klein and Wright's reports, Sharon Donner came to the house around 4:30 p.m. and left around 7:00 p.m. So Cody had been somewhere, alone, during those two and a half hours. Unless she had help?

"You never knew of any boyfriends?" Waters asked. "Close girlfriends?"

"She had her church group, but Sharon didn't *date*. She believed men and women should be together for one reason: to be married and have kids. In today's world, that's a tough sell for most men," Jane said. "Plus, she's mousy as hell. I begged her to let me give her a make-over. She could've been much more attractive if she'd let me tweeze her brows." She put her fist to her brow and started laughing. "Oh, God, the woman I wanted to make pretty took my child! What's going on?" She crumpled then, like aluminum foil being squeezed.

Peter wrapped his arms around her. "We've got to be brave for Cody, remember? He needs us to be strong, for him."

We waited for her to stop crying, or subside to sniffles, before we had another go.

"Were Cody and Aaron on all the same medications?" Waters asked.

Jane pulled away from her husband. "Cody doesn't take medications. Aaron did, for his eyes. Cody didn't need to."

Peter grabbed his wife's hand. Held it like a life preserver. "What if she hurts him?" he whispered.

"No." Jane shook her head. "No, she wouldn't."

He said, "Cody's not like Aaron. He doesn't listen as well, and he's energetic. She used to complain that he couldn't sit still."

"She wouldn't hurt him." Was Jane trying to convince her husband or herself?

"Peter," Agent Waters said. "Is there a reason you fear Mrs. Donner might hurt Cody?"

He looked at his hand, joined with his wife's. "I wondered sometimes about her."

"What do you mean?" she asked.

"Aaron had bruises, but he mostly played indoors, read books. So why so many bruises?"

"You think she abused her son?" Waters asked.

"No," Jane said. "Aaron wasn't into sports, but he was still a boy. He still played, and had accidents. Sharon wouldn't hurt him. She's too religious."

"'Spare the rod and spoil the child,'" Wright quoted.

"I wondered, but then people thought the same thing of us," Peter said. "Maybe Aaron did run into things."

Jane bit her lower lip.

"I think that's all for now. If you think of anything else about Sharon—a mention of a place she liked to visit especially, or any other close friends . . ."

"We'll call," Peter said.

"You'll find him," Jane said. "You have to find him."

We watched them gather their coats and go, back to their house, where they would walk past his empty bunk bed. Where they would wonder why their friend had taken their son. Where they would hope that she wasn't hurting him. Where they would pray to be reunited with Cody.

The second their coats cleared the doorway, the questions started.

"They *had* the Lego truck kit?" Wright asked. "I don't recall that."

"Me neither," I said. "Maybe Sharon knew where it was and grabbed it?" And yet, it niggled. Why hadn't they mentioned that they had the kit? "Did you notice Jane cut him off when he mentioned the kit?"

"Jane was quite worked up," Waters said.

"She does it, though. Interrupts. Wright, you complained about it when you interviewed Cody. How she kept talking over Cody's answers," I said.

"They all did," he said. "You don't think she had a hand in it?"

"She studied acting," I said. "She's already proven to be a good liar. She's pregnant with a baby that doesn't belong to her husband."

"There is something off about her," Waters said.

"Seriously?" Cisco said. "She's crazy with worry."

"That's what everyone keeps saying," I said. Wright and Cisco looked at me as though I was crazy myself. Waters didn't.

"Cody will end up in a hospital, sooner or later," Mulberry said. "When he does, the staff will call it in."

"Before or after she's abused him?" Waters asked.

"We don't know she abused Aaron. Did the hospital staff say anything about that?" Wright asked.

I repeated what the nurse had told me, the speculation about Munchausen by proxy. That Sharon Donner enjoyed the attention her son's illness brought. That she thrived on the sympathy it won her.

"Is that why she took Cody?" Waters asked. "She missed the attention? That could be lucky. Mulberry's right. We've got a report out to all hospitals. If a child with CIPA shows up, the staff will check the kid against pictures of Cody. She wouldn't get outside the gift shop before a dozen federal agents were on her."

"So we hope she takes him to an ER, looking for tea and sympathy? That's it?" I asked.

"No," Waters said. "We hope that, but we keep searching. She had to take him somewhere, and she doesn't have her stolen car. We've got cops looking for her vehicle."

"What if she flew?" I asked.

"Airports have been alerted. We haven't found her name on passenger lists out of Logan, Bradley, La Guardia, JFK, or Newark."

"What about TF Green?" Wright asked. The small Rhode Island airport.

"No joy," Mulberry said.

"Look, this woman may be smart. She may be crazy. Who knows? She isn't a career criminal. She's going to mess up. She'll use her credit card or try to board a plane or bring Cody to a hospital, and then we'll nail her," Waters said.

Wright eyed Waters like he wanted to believe. It reminded me of that silly TV show about the aliens, *The X-Files*. One of the agents had a poster with a UFO that said "I Want to Believe." Come to think of it, those were FBI agents on the show.

Waters straightened, then winced and held her hand to her lower back. "Let's catch her," she said. "And let's do it before Christmas, huh? I've still got a Barbie Dreamhouse that needs assembly."

"Aw, did Santa finally answer your letter?" Cisco asked.

Waters flipped him the bird and told him to check some video they'd been sent recently.

"What day is it?" Wright asked.

I checked my watch. "It's officially Christmas Eve."

CHAPTER TWENTY-SEVEN

Christmas Eve at the Idyll Police Station was more festive than I'd expected. A light snow fell outside, the pretty, postcard kind. Tinsel was strung along poles and desks. Mrs. Dunsmore wore tree earrings and a reindeer headband with fake antlers. At lunchtime, there was a Yankee swap. Even our FBI friends played along. Those with high numbers could choose to steal presents from those with lower numbers. Most gifts were bad. A bag of black-licorice coal. Superhero bandages. An FBI t-shirt that read "Female Body Inspector." Waters stole it from Finnegan. "You want to inspect female bodies?" Finnegan asked.

"I want to burn this," she said.

Cisco stole it from her and gave it to Finnegan. Waters said she'd have him sacked for it. Cisco toasted her with a dosed mug of "coffee."

Some of the gifts were okay. Lottery tickets. Bottles of booze. Movie passes. I stole the passes from the dispatcher, John. He wound up getting a mug that said "Bowlers Do It in Alleys," so he was happy. Someone "donated" a 1998 calendar of bikini-clad women. Mrs. Dunsmore and I rolled our eyes at it, then caught the other doing it, and stopped.

While Bing Crosby sang "Jingle Bells," the phones rang. Men left, yelling at us not to steal their swap gifts while they tended to accidents and calls of stolen Christmas gifts left in unlocked cars. Waters's cell phone rang. She left the party. When she returned, she said that there'd been a sighting of Cody outside New Haven. Local feds were on it and would call if it had legs. A half hour later, the call came. It wasn't Cody. Our hopes weren't dashed. We'd stopped raising them.

After the swap, I went to my office and reviewed paperwork, looking outside every now and again to see how much snow fell. Hours passed. Only two inches of fresh powder on the ground. Bing stopped

singing. The laughter got quieter, the buzzes and rings louder. Mrs.
Dunsmore stepped into my office, her tree earrings hidden by her hat-
squashed hair. "I'm off for the holidays. I'll be back on the thirtieth."

"Merry Christmas," I said.

"You too." She turned on her sensible heels to leave.

"Wait!" It came out louder than I'd intended. My stupid drawer
was stuck. I had to tug three times before it opened. "I got you something." I'd spoken on the phone to Marie. She wanted to know if I'd
found the missing boy. Only Marie and the boys ever seemed interested
in my work. After I'd told her we knew who took him, but not where,
she interrogated me on my parents' gifts. She should've worn a badge.
The woman was relentless. I finally confessed all, and she asked me,
"What are you getting her?" I told Marie I had no idea what to get Mrs.
Dunsmore. She asked me what she was like, and I said, "Terrifying."
After more prying questions, I admitted Mrs. Dunsmore had a parrot
pin she liked and that she wore lavender perfume and had a sick niece.

"You notice things, Tommy," Marie said. "Your brother didn't
notice his admin was pregnant until she was in her fifth month." She
sighed, and suggested I buy Mrs. Dunsmore a necklace like the pin.
"She may not want another pin," she said.

"Who says she'll want a necklace?" I asked.

"No one, you potato head, but in this case the thought *does* count.
And don't cheap out. Go to the jewelry counter and talk to someone."

"Here." I withdrew the box. Its silver ribbon got caught and
mangled in my ham-fisted extraction. It was shredded at the ends.
"Sorry."

She took it from me and stared. "Thank you," she said.

Oh, God, would she open it now? She didn't need to. I hoped she
didn't. We didn't need to draw this out. Make it a thing. It wasn't a
thing.

"Chief?" Billy stood in my doorway. "Waters wants you."

"Okay, thanks."

Mrs. Dunsmore tucked the flat box into her large purse and said
good-bye.

Waters stood outside the interview room, peering at her phone. "You wanted me?" I asked.

She looked up. Her hair was down today, and it made her look younger. She was thirty-five, tops. Must've worked her ass off to get where she was. "I need to visit the Forrands. Update them. Will you come?"

We had no news to report. Nothing but negatives. We knew Sharon Donner wasn't hiding out at her sister's home in Vermont. We knew she hadn't left the country. We didn't know where she'd taken Cody.

"Sure," I said. It was a crap job, but it would look best if we gave the update. Sending junior agents or patrolmen was cowardly.

The Forrands' house was lit up. We left boot prints in the fresh snow on our way to the door. On it was a large hand-painted sign that said, "We Miss You, Cody." Dozens of signatures, many children's, adorned the sign, along with one green handprint. We knocked and waited. Peter Forrand opened the door. A blast of warm air and the sounds of *A Charlie Brown Christmas* came at us.

"Did you find him?" Peter asked.

Waters said no, quickly, forestalling any false hope. "May we come in?"

He held the door, and we filed past. I noticed that the jumble of winter gear had winnowed down to carefully hung coats and scarves. The boots were filed by size. Three pairs: Dad, Mom, and Anna. Cody's were missing. Inside, the Christmas tree was lit with colored lights. Anna stood near it, a candy-cane ornament in hand.

"We were waiting for Cody to decorate the tree, but Jane said we should let Anna start," he said.

"Hi, Anna," I said.

She carefully hung the beaded candy cane on a branch near her shoulder. "Hi." She didn't ask if we'd found her brother. Of all the disappointments, false tips, and dead ends, the fact that Anna didn't ask if we'd found Cody made me saddest.

Wrapped presents were gathered under the tree. Jane came from the hallway, carrying a cardboard box. "I found them!" She stopped when she saw us. "What is it?"

"Not much," Waters said. "Can we talk?"

Mrs. Forrand said, "Okay. Anna, honey, wait until we're done, okay? The glass balls are really fragile. We'll put them on together." She set the box atop a coffee table. "I found some of my family's old decorations. We thought we'd lost them in the move, but they were in the cellar." She wiped a cobweb from her hair.

The four of us gathered around the kitchen table. Again, there was less chaos and more order. Neatly stacked containers of food were arranged near holiday cards. Agent Waters sat, and the rest of us followed.

"We're devoting considerable resources to finding your son," she said, "but thus far we have no new leads. There's been no activity on Sharon Donner's bank card or credit cards. We checked out her sister's home, but she hasn't been there."

"Could she have left the country?" Peter asked.

"It's doubtful. We're watching the airports. No one with her papers has passed through, and no woman with a child matching Cody's description has left the US."

"What about boats?" Jane asked. "Or trains?"

"We've got eyes on those too."

"Where do you think she is?" Jane's clenched hands were white at the knuckles.

A cobweb clung to the hairs by her temple.

"I don't know," Agent Water said. "Was there any place Cody wanted to visit? Disney World or the Grand Canyon? Any place she might have taken him?"

Peter said, "He loves big trucks. Not exactly a landmark is it?" He leaned back in his chair. "Do you think he's still alive?" His voice low, barely audible.

"Peter!" Jane said.

"Mommy?" Anna called.

"It's fine, honey. You start on the tinsel, okay?" Jane yelled, her voice high and tight. She turned to her husband and hissed, "Why would you say that?"

Her husband set his hand atop hers. "Honey, all the stuff we've read, it says that the longer the child is missing, the slimmer the chances the kid will be found alive."

"You know Sharon! She wouldn't . . . do *that*," Jane said.

Waters watched the exchange like an umpire. Only she wasn't making any calls.

"Do you think he's alive?" Peter asked me.

"I hope so. I don't know. You're right about the odds. However, he was taken by someone who lost her son, and she knows what a child with CIPA requires," I said.

"Yes, see," Jane said. "She knows to watch him. She knows."

Peter didn't seem convinced. He stroked Jane's fingers and asked us, "You'll be working during the holidays?"

"Of course," Waters said. "If you need to reach me, you have my number."

"And mine," I added.

"Mommy, I can't reach the top!" Anna called.

Jane said, "She's been so good. She didn't want to do anything without him. I insisted. I don't want her to suffer more than she has. I thought, maybe, decorating the tree, wrapping presents, it would help." She wiped under her eyes. "As if anything could help." She squeezed her husband's hand.

In the living room, Anna stood, tinsel in hand. The low branches were covered with the silvery threads. The top half was bare, too high for her to reach. "Help?" she asked. Her father took the remaining tinsel from her. "You point, and I'll toss," he said.

She pointed to the top, and he tossed a bunch of the tinsel at the tree. Most of the tinsel fell to the floor, only a few strands gripping the green needles.

"Dad!" Anna laughed. She had a belly laugh, and I realized I hadn't heard it. I'd never heard her laugh until now.

"Good night," Agent Waters said.

When we were in her car, she turned on the heat and lights. She stared out the windshield. "Do you think he's alive?" she asked.

"Do you?"

"No," she said. "I've been looking at Aaron Donner's medical files. I'm not sure he died like everyone thinks he did. The power outage that affected only the upstairs A/C unit? Never properly investigated. He was wearing long sleeves and pants. Why?"

"You think his mother was responsible?" If so, Cody's chances had just dropped.

"I think it wouldn't be hard to kill a boy like Aaron and make it look like it was his disease at fault."

"So that's why you think Cody's dead."

"It's one reason," she said. "One of many."

"You know, that's the happiest I've seen them," I said. "Their place was downright tidy."

"You think they're involved?" she asked.

"Yes. You?" If Waters didn't buy my theory, I'd have a much harder time. We needed the FBI's support.

She nodded. "Jane Forrand is lying."

"About what?" I asked, curious as to what made her sound so certain.

"Not sure yet," she said. "But she is. I'm a human lie detector, remember?" She flashed me a feral grin that made me glad we were on the same side.

My house was cold. Was it worth adjusting the thermostat dial? I left it alone and opened the fridge. Half a second later, I closed it. I didn't want anything cold. I opened the cabinet to the right of the fridge and found the half-empty bottle of Laphroaig that Rick had given me two birthdays ago. "Cheers, Tommy," he'd said.

"Booze?" I'd said. "How fucking Irish can you get?"

"Piss off, old-timer. This cost me fifty bucks. I'll take it if you don't want it."

"No." I'd hugged the bottle to my chest. "I'm keeping it, but you overpaid dearly, dumbass."

He'd punched my arm, and I'd put him in a headlock, and we'd drunk a glass each. God, I missed him.

I poured myself two fingers and replaced the bottle in the cabinet. A promise I wouldn't drink more. The force was full of cops with red-veined noses, beer bellies, and pasts full of golden days. I wasn't in a hurry to join their ranks. I took my drink to the living room and sat in my ten-year-old recliner. My fingers rubbed its worn nap.

I kept my eyes on my drink, away from the peeling kitchen floor and the thousand other items that needed updating or replacing. It was late and I was cold. In two hours, it would be Christmas. And Cody, alive or dead, wouldn't be home.

Time for bed. My sheets were cold. Another person would help warm them, but what other person would I bring back here? Someone I never planned to see again, that's for sure. I thumped my pillow, trying to work out the lumps. Someone I never planned to see again. My specialty.

CHAPTER TWENTY-EIGHT

Christmas Day dawned bright and warm, forty degrees in the sun. For the first time this month, I left my coat unzipped and my head bare as I drove to the station. It was early, people still inside their homes, unwrapping gifts and plundering stockings. At the station, the crew seemed healthier. Of our federal friends, only Cisco was present. He said, "Waters is home, probably assembling that Barbie house. I swapped, so I could have New Year's Eve in North Carolina. I hate New Year's here. It's always freezing, and you can't get a cab."

"Waters has kids?" I asked.

"Just one, a girl, age six." Cody's age. "She's cute. Named Jasmine. Over-the-top girly. Can't understand how she came out of Waters."

"Waters told me she thinks Cody's dead," I said.

"Yeah?" Cisco didn't seem surprised. "Stands to reason. He's been gone three days. Besides, she thinks—" he stopped.

"That Mrs. Donner may have killed Aaron? She told me."

His bunched muscles relaxed. "Yeah. Seems like a bitch to prove, though. Judging from what I've seen, no one floated the idea back then."

"Grieving mother of a sick kid. Why would they?" I asked.

"Now that she's a kidnapper, the shine's off," he said.

"True."

"What are your plans for the holiday?" he asked.

"Me? This." I swept my hand around. "Then probably home to watch my favorite Christmas special."

"*It's a Wonderful Life*?" Cisco guessed.

"*Rudolph the Red-Nosed Reindeer*. Groundbreaking stuff. The gay elf who wants to be a dentist? Moving."

He shook his head. "I hate musicals. Anything where people or cartoons start singing their feelings and then dancing, perfectly timed? Nah."

"Thus speaks a man who cannot dance," I said solemnly.

"Ha! I'm a hit on the dance floor."

"I'll bet you are." Cisco, in a muscle tee on a dance floor, would be a sight. I swallowed. The air felt thick. I recalled his kiss. "Time to check equipment inventory," I said. "See you later."

"Watch out for paper cuts," he said.

Back in my office, time passed slowly. I read two newspapers at my desk. The *New York Times* and the *Idyll Register*. The most interesting story in the *Times* was about the woman who'd been injured by the Cat in the Hat balloon during the Macy's Thanksgiving Day parade. The balloon struck a lamppost that rained metal onto the spectators' heads. Ms. Caronna had sustained a head injury and been in a coma, waking on Sunday. She'd probably sue Macy's or the city, or both. The *Idyll Register* carried two articles on Cody. One, a wrap-up of the case to date, stressing the involvement of the Federal Bureau of Investigation. The other was a collection of thoughts from Cody's first-grade classmates. "We miss you" and "Come home soon!" dominated the list. One boy, Joe Borden, wrote, "Come play Super Nintendo with me." I wondered if the kids understood why Cody was missing. Surely teachers and parents had explained to them. Then again, maybe they'd tread lightly on the abduction, since their own kids weren't at risk. A random stranger hadn't grabbed Cody; a woman who'd known him for years had. The parents might take comfort from this. They didn't have to worry about lurking pedophiles, not today.

I checked with the patrol and was hearing about the nudist runner who'd been spotted in the woods, when Cisco found me and said, "Cody sighting near New London, looks like it might be legit. We haven't got anyone close."

"You going?"

"I could use another pair of eyes," he said.

Klein, nearby, perked up, as if it was an open offer.

"Gimme a minute." I fetched my things from my office. I likely wouldn't come back but would head home after we checked out this tip.

"Merry Christmas," I shouted as I left. "Stay safe." *Stay safe* was a phrase my super used when I was a rookie. Back when I was community-policing in neighborhoods rife with bad guys with guns, it meant something. I still used it. Idiots with guns, addicts with knives, or plain bad drivers killed cops every day. So I guess it still meant something. It meant *be careful. Take nothing for granted.*

"You mind if we take mine?" Cisco said, twirling his car keys.

"Not at all." I was half in love with his ride. "So, what's the deal?"

"We got a sighting near New London. Kid fitting Cody's description, with a single woman. Caller saw them at a Hilton Inn during her two-day stay. She spotted them at the pool. Said the kid was cannonballing, into the shallow end."

"Sounds like Cody."

"Later, she's watching the news. Sees an item about Cody, and she says pool boy looks just like him."

"Anyone check with the hotel?" I asked.

"We called. No one registered under Donner, but there is a woman with a child registered under the name Pitts."

"Pitts," I said. "Like her maiden name?"

"Yeah. Maybe she's using IDs from back then. Who knows? Front desk says the woman and kid are due to check out tomorrow."

"A Hilton in New London? They didn't get far."

"She may have needed a spot to lay low, regroup."

"How's she paying for the room?"

"Cash. Front desk remembered. It's not as common as it used to be."

This was looking good. Real good. If they were staying at a hotel an hour away, we could have Cody back on Christmas Day.

"Who knows if it's them," Cisco said, attempting to pour water on my dreams.

"It sounds good."

He looked over at me, his dark eyes narrowed. "Yeah, it does." He looked back at the road. "Waters will be surprised as fuck if we find him."

"I'd like to see that."

Cisco made the hour drive in forty-five minutes, despite congestion around Willimantic. "Okay," he said. "Plan is we sniff around. Get eyes on the kid. If we confirm it's him, we call in the troops."

I checked my gun, buttoned my coat, and walked with Cisco into the lobby. A massive tree decorated in gold and silver dominated one side. We walked to the large front desk, where a young woman stood, frowning. She scrubbed the blank look from her face when she noticed us. "Merry Christmas," she said. "Welcome. Are you checking in with us tonight?" Her name tag read Pamela. She wore a blouse with a lace collar.

"Hello. I'm Agent Cisco, and this is Police Chief Lynch. We're here because you have a woman and child staying here. The child matches the description of a boy we're looking for who was abducted three days ago." He said all of it the same way he'd have said, "Yes, we're checking in. Two nights. Registered under Cisco."

Pamela's eyes got round. She made a soft, "oh?" sound.

"We need to know the room number of Ms. Pitts."

"Ms. Pitts, right." She started tapping on her keyboard.

"Is the pool open?" A man yelled across the lobby. He carried a towel and a paperback.

"Yes, until 10 p.m. tonight. That way." She pointed. "Sorry," she said.

"No problem," Cisco said. "Room number?"

"Room 311. At the end of the hall."

"That's great," Cisco said. "Do you have her car information?"

"We ask for the guest's license-plate numbers when they check in."

Cisco gave her a smile like she'd invented sliced bread. "Great. I need you to call Ms. Pitts and tell her that her car alarm is going off. If she says she doesn't have one, say it's the car with her license plate. Gently insist she come down and take a look. Don't place the call until we get upstairs, okay?"

"How will I know you're up there?" she asked.

He held up his phone. "With this. What's your number?" She

recited it for him and he typed it into his phone. "When I call you, you call her about the car. Okay?"

"Okay," she said.

"Great," Cisco said.

We stalked toward the elevators. "Flirt," I muttered.

"Me?" Cisco put his hand to his chest.

I shook my head and stabbed the Up button. "What's the plan?"

"Stake out the hallway, call Pamela, and wait."

We got in the elevator and ascended to the third floor. The doors pinged and opened. We faced a large glass mirror, under which a small desk with a tiny potted Christmas tree stood beside a squat black phone. We turned right. Signs showed us room 311 was to the left at the end of the hall. We stood outside, ears cocked for crying or conversation. Nothing. Cisco walked to 315 and made the call. Then he walked back. We heard the phone ring inside 311. It rang four times before someone picked up. We heard a female voice talking, and then silence. Was she coming or not? More murmurs, and then the door opened a crack. We stood out of sight until she stepped out, past the doorway.

"FBI!" Cisco yelled. He stepped in front and backed her inside the room.

"Mommy?" a small boy cried out. We looked. He was small, with dark hair and dark eyes and a runny nose. He wasn't Cody Forrand. His right eye sported a shiner turning green-yellow.

"Did he send you?" the woman asked. She was a good fifteen years younger than Sharon Donner. Thin and worn at the edges, with a split lip.

"Who?" Cisco said.

"Alex," she said.

"Who's Alex?" he asked.

She looked behind Cisco. "My husband." Her eyes welled with tears.

"Alex hits you?" Cisco said.

The boy came forward. He wrapped his arms about his mother's left leg and said, "Go away!" I admired his loyalty. I doubted his piece-of-shit father had.

"It's okay, pal," Cisco said, bending to squat so he was eye level with the kid. "We're here to help you and your Mom."

"Why did you come here?" she asked.

"We're looking for a boy who was abducted. Your son looks a lot like him. You, however, are much younger and more attractive than his kidnapper." She brushed aside his compliment, but she was pleased all the same. "What happened?" Cisco asked. "Why are you hiding?"

Ms. Pitts, whose real name was Amanda Molton, told him all about her abusive husband. She'd called the cops on him more than once. He'd be out of jail a day or a week later. Two days ago, he'd come home, drunk, annoyed that dinner wasn't waiting. He'd expressed his displeasure by hitting her with a drinking glass. Jacob, her son, had run into the room to defend her, and Mr. Molton punched him. Jacob was out cold. Amanda was frantic. Her husband restrained her from taking him to the doctor. She had to wait until her husband fell asleep. Then she gathered clothes and her son, and she drove five hours south until she reached the hotel.

"I should've stayed somewhere cheaper, but it's Christmas, and he loves the pool, and it's near the aquarium."

"They have beluga whales at the aquarium," Jacob said.

Cisco found out where she lived and left to make some calls. He was gone long enough for us to become uncomfortable and then pass through it. When he returned, Jacob sat beside me, explaining the differences between dolphins and porpoises.

Cisco asked Amanda if she had family she could stay with for a while. Amanda looked at her son, who was busy explaining to me *again* why whales aren't fish. Her mouth got tight. "My sister, but Alex looked for me there. She called me, yesterday."

"Okay. Stay here for the night. Tomorrow, someone from your town's police station will be in touch. If they're not, call me." He handed her a card. "You'll get a restraining order." He held up his hand. "*Another* restraining order. The old one expired. Does your husband have any bad habits besides drunken violence?"

"You mean like drugs?" she asked.

Jacob looked up from the book he'd been using to illustrate several of his points. "Hey, what's that?" I asked, pointing to an illustration of a hammerhead shark.

He rolled his eyes so far back I thought they'd disappear into his skull. "It's a shark. A hammerhead."

"He smokes weed, but not often. He had some pills a while back," she said, keeping her voice low. She'd noticed her son's interest in the conversation.

"Hammerhead," I said. "Do you think you could use his head to put a nail in the wall?" I mimed hammering. "Bang, bang. Thanks for your help, Mr. Shark."

"You're ridiculous," Jacob said.

"Jacob!" his mom chided.

"It's okay." I leaned toward him. He smelled of cereal and milk. "I am ridiculous. Everyone says so."

"Are the drugs in the house?" Cisco asked.

She shook her head. "His car."

"Good," he said. "Make sure you tell tomorrow's cop that."

They chatted while Jacob told me about the breeding habits of sea turtles. It was a grim story. Mother turtles crawled out of the ocean at night to dig a sand pit and lay up to 120 eggs in that nest. They covered the hole and swam away. Sixty days later, the baby turtles dug themselves out of the nest, a process that could take days. The hatchlings then made a run for the sea. Sharks, fish, and birds picked them off as they tried to scramble into open water and swim to safety. Only one in one thousand baby turtles survived to adulthood.

"That's terrifying," I told Jacob. "I'm going to have nightmares about that."

"That's nature," he said.

"Are you going to the aquarium tomorrow?" I asked.

"Maybe!" He turned to his mother. "Mom, can we go again?"

"We'll see," she said. She mouthed "expensive" to me.

"Well, we need to go, but if you have any trouble, call me," Cisco said.

"Thank you," she said. "And good luck, with your case."

"Hey, Jacob, Merry Christmas." I handed Jacob a wad of cash I'd taken from my wallet. "Maybe you can buy something from the aquarium gift shop tomorrow."

"Oh boy!" Jacob waved the bills.

"Oh, you don't have to—" she said.

"Merry Christmas," I said, pulling the door closed behind me. The lock clicked.

"That was nice," Cisco said.

"Not as nice as what you did. You think the cops will follow up?"

"They'd better," he said. "Or there'll be hell to pay."

"Good thing Wright wasn't here," I said.

"Why's that?" he pushed the elevator button.

"He has a thing about men who hit women and children."

"Doesn't everyone?" Cisco asked.

"Wright has it more than others."

The elevator pinged and the doors opened. We stepped inside. Cisco rolled his shoulders. "So much for being heroes on Christmas Day," he said.

"I think we did okay back there."

"We didn't find Cody."

"Did you think we would?" I asked.

"Yeah, I did."

"Makes two of us," I said.

CHAPTER TWENTY-NINE

Once we'd called in our failure to find Cody, we agreed we could murder a hamburger. We ate at a pub a few miles up the road from the hotel. It had a roaring fireplace and wreaths on the walls. The burger was good, as was the beer. The company was good, too. Cisco told me funny stories from his days at Quantico. I told him about the more entertaining nutters I'd met on the job, back in the city.

When the waiter came with the bill, he said, "I wish I got along with my brother as well as you two." We didn't contradict him, but the guy's eyes needed checking. Cisco was clearly Puerto Rican. I was half a foot taller and Irish white. Besides, I liked Cisco, and not as a brother.

In the car, Cisco half hummed a song I didn't recognize. The streets were quiet. He pulled off the highway and turned down a stretch of unfamiliar road. Then he pulled into the Red Roof Inn's parking lot.

"Where are we?" I asked.

"Home sweet home." He nodded toward the long, two-story building. "For now."

"They couldn't put you somewhere nicer?"

He smiled quickly. "Los federales are tight with the wallet."

We sat, the heater providing the only sound. "So, are you going to invite me in?" I asked.

He looked at me, his eyes a little sleepy. "I thought about fucking you in the car and then driving you home." The words went straight to my groin. "But you seem like the kind of guy who likes to be courted."

I laughed. Courted? I was the kind of guy who fucked in cars. Today, though, now, I preferred the idea of a bedroom. More space. More options. I unsnapped my seat belt and leaned toward him. So close I could see his stubble. His nose was twisted, fractionally, to the right. "So give me my roses and let's go," I whispered.

He pulled me in, his hand at the back of my neck. His mouth tasted of dinner and beer. His long lashes tickled my face. He pulled back, as fast as he'd pulled me in. Unsnapped his seat belt and opened his door. "Come on," he said. The rough edge to his voice, the impatience, made me grin.

We hurried across the lot, inside the hotel, up a flight of stairs, and three doors down the beige hallway. He inserted his key card into the door's slot. The light flashed red. He cursed and tried again. The light turned green, and a whirring noise preceded a click. The door opened. He pushed in. Then he tossed the key card like a Frisbee. It landed on the desk by the far left wall. Neat trick. The door swung closed behind us. I put the hinge lock on. He cocked a brow. "In case," I said.

He didn't ask in case of what. He removed my coat, too slowly for my liking. I half ripped his off, showing him how it was done. "In a hurry?" he asked, unbuttoning my shirt one slow button at a time. I shoved his hands away and ripped it off, buttons popping onto the floor. "Always," I said, shucking my t-shirt.

He ran his hands over my torso. When he reached my nipples, he pinched them gently. Then he removed his sweater and shirt almost as fast as I had. I took a breath. Damn, he was glorious. His torso belonged on a magazine. No, on a billboard. He had a true six-pack, and the little muscle cutout from his hips that made your eyes go down, down, down. I'd slept with good-looking men, athletic men, handsome men. Cisco put them all to shame. My hands shook as I reached out to put my palm against his abs. They convulsed.

"Ticklish," he said, between his teeth.

"Ticklish?" I used more pressure, sweeping my hands up, leaving a trail of goose-bumped flesh in my wake.

His head dropped and he exhaled in a slow hiss. My hands were at his shoulders and I tugged his face to mine. My lips were at his forehead. I bent my neck and bumped my nose to his cheek, urging him to turn. He did and I caught his lips with my teeth. Nipped at them until he opened them and my tongue swept inside. We gripped each other and kissed. I felt light-headed and powerful. I pulled at his pants. He

swatted my hand away and undid them. Then stepped out of his boxer
briefs. He stood, wearing only black dress socks. He must've kicked off
his shoes when he came inside.

"You," he said. His voice was husky.

My boots gave me trouble. The laces stuck. "Fuck," I said. Pulling at
the knot only made it tighter.

"Let me," Cisco said. He knelt and carefully worked at the knot.
It came apart at last and I kicked the boot off. The other yielded more
easily. The pants and boxers were a blur of tan and white fabric moving
through the room, thrown toward the first of two beds. Cisco was still
at my feet. He looked up. God, he was beautiful. He reached out and
put his hand on my cock. It jumped. He smiled and moved forward,
excruciatingly slowly, and kissed the tip.

His hand still on it, he worked the tip with his lips. Kisses, soft
licks. He moved his hand down, toward the base, and slid most of my
cock in his mouth. He was warm and wet and working his tongue in
ways that threatened my ability to hold on. He pulled back, and my
cock came free from his mouth. He worked his hand up and down me.
My head fell back. My thighs tightened. His hand came away. It felt like
a loss. I looked down.

He stood and grabbed for my hand. Led it to his cock, jutting
forward at me. I squeezed his thickness. Felt the immediate flex of
muscle. Then I pulled my hand back, spat into it, and began working
him in long, smooth pulls.

"Yeah," he said. His eyes shut, he breathed harder. I rubbed my
palm over his cock's head, in slow circles, and then faster, until he was
half panting. Then I knelt on the carpet, its fibers rough against my
knees. I took him into my mouth. He tasted like Irish Spring soap. He
moaned, the sound far away as I concentrated on swallowing him as
deep as I could. He thrust his hips forward, little lurches. His hand
fisted my hair, and a sharp starburst of pain pulled me out of my trance.
It passed, and then I was back to breathing hard through my nose. I slid
my tongue along the vein under his cock.

His thrusts became faster, harder. His cock was pulsing, and I knew he was on the edge. I reached up and played with his testicles like they were Chinese therapy balls. A trick I picked up from a pal back in my clubbing days. "Agh," he cried. I tightened my grip until I felt him spasm and a warm flood hit the roof of my mouth. I kept my face still, allowing him time before he pulled out. Then I walked to the bathroom, found the sink, and spat. I removed the crinkled paper lid from a water glass and filled it with tap water. Gargled some and drank the rest. I checked myself in the mirror. My face was flushed, red and white. My hair mussed all to hell. My cock was still at attention.

Cisco was seated at the edge of the first double bed. He looked more awake, his dark eyes fever bright. His eyes weren't focused on mine, but on a different part of my anatomy. "Does someone need relief?" he asked.

"Could do," I said.

"Then come here," he said. "I've got just the thing."

I stood before him, my bare feet prickly against the carpet. He still had his socks on. They looked silly. He reached for me. Turned out, he did have just the thing.

☼

When I woke in the dark, with an arm around me, I panicked. Where was I? What had I done? Then I remembered. Cisco. Hotel room. Sex. Sleeping. His thigh pressed against the back of mine. It was hot. Too hot. His breath tickled the hairs on my nape. I drifted off thinking that, as Christmases went, this had been pretty good.

Four hours later, the sky was still dark, but it was time to get up. I needed to get home and change. My attempts at stealth weren't good enough. Cisco rolled to his side in a fluid move that told me he'd be good in the field. "Oh, hey," he said, his voice thick.

"I'm gonna get a move on," I said. "I need to change before work."

His rubbed his dark hair. "Right. You need a ride?"

"I'll grab a cab," I said.

"I guess I'll see you in a few hours."

"Yeah." Cisco was on until the 30th, when he got four days off.

"Um, you'll keep this quiet, right?" he asked.

I shoved my feet into my boots. "Sure."

"I could get in trouble," he said.

"How? I'm a consenting adult." I grabbed my coat.

"I don't want anyone accusing of us playing while we should be working."

"I think I can manage to keep my hands off you at work," I said.

He pulled back the sheet. My mouth got dry. "You sure?"

"I'll see you later," I said, running away before he could read my expression. I assumed it was hungry.

His low laughter followed me until I closed the door.

CHAPTER THIRTY

My fear that things might be awkward at work with Cisco was unfounded. We kept it all about Cody as we chased more false leads and reviewed, again, Sharon Donner's past for clues about her present location. She'd been born in New Hampshire, gone to junior college in Boston. Worked as a medical secretary for four and a half years. Married Samuel Donner, a certified public accountant from Connecticut. They lived in Wethersfield for several years, and moved to West Hartford in 1990. Aaron was born in 1991. Samuel died in 1994 of heart failure. Died by the water cooler. Luckily, he had a large life-insurance policy that provided well for Mrs. Donner and Aaron. She did some transcription work for extra income. Her home was still in West Hartford. The FBI had eyes on the place. She hadn't been near it. She hadn't visited her sister. Her parents were dead.

We went back to co-workers. None had heard from her in years. Ditto for her college friends. We did glean interesting details from both groups. Sharon had been "sick, a lot." She'd spent a lot of time in her college infirmary. "She had terrible headaches, but then sophomore year it switched to stomachaches and odd pains in her hands. Maybe she had carpel tunnel syndrome, before they knew what it was." Two of her co-workers said that Sharon had been "plagued" by illness. "She'd come in, looking terrible, but insisting she could work," one said. "Half the time, she'd be sent home. Sharon seemed annoyed. She'd prefer to be at work, she said. Where she could feel useful. Frankly, I think she liked the attention."

Wright and Mulberry had worked the more recent friends and acquaintances. Their reports showed that Sharon's "sicknesses" almost completely disappeared once Aaron was born. Of course, Aaron was a very sick child. She spent "half her life in hospitals," one church friend had said. The church friends speculated she must've been off her head with grief over Aaron's death, to commit a kidnapping. Details didn't support that theory. Sharon had been upset in the wake of her son's death, but months later she appeared to be coping. She participated in church groups, completed work assignments, and volunteered at the hospital. The hospital volunteer coordinator had confided that Sharon's manner was sometimes "off." She'd be solicitous and kind most days, but sometimes snappy and quick to take offense. She had less than modern views on Jews and blacks, and the supervisor had warned her to keep such views to herself.

She had no other properties. Her car, a 1994 Lexus, hadn't been spotted. She had healthy bank accounts. Fairly regular ATM withdrawals that indicated weekly shopping expenses. Checks for legitimate services: locksmith, car garage, home insurance, groceries. She was one of those women who held up the grocery line writing a check. Figured.

Finnegan was in. He and Wright had swapped shifts. He offered a running stream of commentary on our chief suspect. "She bought more craft supplies. How many craft supplies does one lady need?"

"Maybe it was for church stuff," I said.

"Yes, because what people need are more hand-knit toilet-paper covers," he said.

"Toilet-paper covers?" I asked.

"The kind with the Barbie doll stuck in the middle, so the knit part looks like a skirt."

"You're kidding me," I said.

"Nope. Hey, Dix, you know those Barbie-doll toilet-paper cover thingies, right?"

Dix came around the corner, traces of powdered sugar on his lips. Courtesy of the holiday treats some citizen had given us. "What are you on about now?"

"The Barbie things that old ladies have in their bathrooms."

"My mom has one," Klein said.

"See!" Finny pointed at Klein. "Told you!"

"She won't get rid of it," Klein said. "It has sentimental value." He peered at Dix's lips. "Where's the Stollen?" Dix pointed. Klein walked away.

Bank statements. Phone records. Employment records. Parking tickets. Midafternoon, Finnegan looked up, rubbed his strained eyes, and said, "Shoot me. Through and through. Shoot me. I swear to God if I have to read one more mundane detail of this woman's life . . ."

"Cheer up, Finny. It's quitting time." It was, for him. Despite the kidnapping, people still had schedules. Maybe if we had a genuine lead, an actual sighting, it would be different. We didn't. Besides, the FBI was on it. We were the backup dancers on this one. Technically, the FBI doesn't "take" cases from local law enforcement agencies, but we'd become the B team. We knew it. Everyone did.

Finnegan left with the last of the Stollen, "compensation pay" for the headache he'd incurred reading Mrs. Donner's crabbed handwriting on complaint letters she'd sent to her cable television provider. "Who *writes* letters to RCN?" he asked. "Those fuckers don't pay attention when you're yelling at them on the phone."

"Hey, Chief, could you take a look?" Cisco handed me a folder marked "Church Interviews."

"Sure." Hadn't Finnegan reviewed this? Had there been a problem? I took the folder to my office. Sat down and leafed through the contents. Yes, these were the interviews Finny had checked. Wait. What was this at the back of the folder? A credit card? I picked it up. No. The heavy plastic rectangle was a hotel-room key. A Post-It on the back said, "If you want to stop by tonight, here's a key." There was Cisco's phone number. Looks like I had plans tonight.

Concentrating on paperwork became more challenging, but I made it through my last hour and a half. "Stay safe," I called as I left.

My answering machine blinked. Had I checked it this morning? I pressed Play. "It's Mom. Where are you? I've called twice to wish you a

Merry Christmas. I know you worked today, but you should be home. Call me. Let me know you're safe. We worry about you."

Damn it all. Yesterday had been Christmas. I'd meant to call my parents. Then we'd gotten the hotel tip and then I'd been busy and forgot. Better remedy the situation. I'd tell Mom I'd gotten held up at work. I wouldn't tell her about Cisco. I kept that part of my life from my parents. They knew I was gay. Celebrated the fact. The minute I introduced a man to them, Mom would start planning our civil ceremony. Okay, maybe she wasn't that bad. I wouldn't know. I'd never tested her.

The second message was from Damien Saunders. "Happy Christmas, Thomas. I know you're working, but perhaps you'd like to get a drink, later. Tonight or tomorrow or whenever." A week ago, I'd have returned his call; even as I worried he'd sideline me with another gay cause. Didn't matter now. I had plans, with Cisco.

I called my mother and assured her I was alive. Asked about her Christmas. Heard a long story about the upstairs neighbors' baby. Told her about the false lead. She told me I was a good boy for helping the abused mother and son. "Good boy." Not a phrase she used often on me.

I checked my watch. Decided it was too early to visit Cisco. Instead, I did some weights. I'd set up a bench in the guest bedroom. I knocked out a series that left me gasping and sweaty. In the shower, I rubbed my torso with soap. I didn't have a six-pack. I had a four-pack. Normally this didn't leave me feeling inadequate, but Cisco's body was something else. Then again, he was younger. How much younger? Six years, maybe.

I debated shaving. Decided against it. Instead, I slapped aftershave on my two-day beard. Brushed my teeth. Put some gel in my hair and tousled the front. Used my nice deodorant. Looked for clothes that fit well without screaming, "trying too hard." Threw a clean uniform in a duffel, in case I spent the night. I called a cab, because someone would recognize my car in the hotel parking lot. The FBI was installed there. They'd put two and two together.

Small-town cabs were nothing like their city counterparts. Mine was a minivan driven by a guy older than my dead grandfather. I had to shout my destination at him. He kept the radio on at a level slightly below ear-bleeding. The radio was done with carols. Now everything was the "Best of 1997." As far as I could tell, 1997's best was a lot of rap music and Elton John singing about dead Princess Di.

Was Cisco expecting me tonight? I hadn't said anything on my way out. Hadn't wanted to make it awkward, or risk anyone overhearing. Maybe I should've waited another day.

The driver dropped me at the hotel's entrance. I walked through; head high, nodding at the staff like they should recognize me. I got upstairs. Knocked twice. He opened the door. His outfit from earlier was gone, replaced by sweats and a tank top. God, he looked good. Criminally good. I thought about booking him right there. Hand-cuffing him. Maybe my eyes showed the direction of my thoughts. Or maybe it was my pants. Either way, he pulled me in as he said, "About damn time."

CHAPTER THIRTY-ONE

Cisco left for North Carolina on the 30th. On the 31st, I caught up on all things I'd let slip, like clean clothing. I dropped two bags of laundry at Suds. Lucy stood behind the counter, her Goth face requiring less powder in the pale winter months. "Long time no see," she said. *The Alienist* lay facedown on the counter in front of her, its spine creased.

"Sci-fi?" I asked.

She looked at the book. "No. It's about Teddy Roosevelt and a shrink trying to catch a serial killer. 'Alienist' is what they used to call psychiatrists, way back when."

"Sounds like sci-fi to me."

She hauled my laundry bags around the counter. "Sunday okay for these?" She paused. Looked at my rumpled clothes. "Make that Saturday afternoon."

"None of your lip, missy."

"You sound like my gran sometimes. You know, I think she's looking for a new Bingo partner."

"Bingo isn't a paired game."

"It is the way she plays it."

"Nate in?" I asked, pointing at the door that joined the Laundromat to the bar.

"He's prepping the bar." She checked her wrist. Lucy wore a man's watch. The dial's face covered her thin wrist. "Should be slicing lemons now."

He wasn't slicing lemons. He was slicing limes. His hands cut perfect circles from the small fruit. One, two, three, four. He stopped cutting and looked up. "Hi, Chief." Not many people in the place. Late for lunch. Too early for dinner. A few committed drinkers at the bar. "What can I get you?" he asked.

"You said you used to work construction, yeah?"

"Of course. I'm a full-blooded Native, aren't I?" That's what folks in Idyll said. That Nate was 100 percent Nipmuc Indian. He found it amusing. He'd told me he didn't think anyone was 100 percent anything these days. "What are you working on?"

"I'm trying to pry up my kitchen floor. Parts of it are coming up, but the rest is adhered with some sort of superglue."

"What's under the floor?"

"Wood. Not sure what kind."

"Linoleum on top?"

"Yup."

"Hmm. I can come by tomorrow and take a look. You're up on Cotswold Road?"

"Yeah, 148," I said.

He nodded. "Anything else?"

I pictured my black-and-pink-tiled bathroom, the stupid cabinet pulls, and the nonfunctioning fireplace. "Yeah, but let's start with the floor."

"Tomorrow morning okay? Work is busy today."

Of course. Tonight was New Year's Eve. Biggest bar night of the year.

"It can wait a few days," I said.

"How about 9:30 a.m.?" Apparently Nate didn't believe in time off.

"Sure. Thanks."

"Don't thank me yet."

After I'd done a punishing series of crunches, push-ups, and pull-ups, I took a long, hot shower. Then I settled myself into my recliner and toasted myself with a drink. Praising my own wisdom in having taken New Year's Eve off. Let the others handle the drunks tonight. I reviewed a copy of Sharon Donner's finances. The money puzzled me. She hadn't touched her credit or ATM cards. What was she living on? How was she paying for food or gas or toothpaste? They'd been gone over a week. I checked her November credit card statement again. Gas charge, movie rental, restaurant bill, dry cleaning, craft store, gas station.

Then I reviewed her November bank statement. Groceries, house insurance, auto garage, church donation, pharmacy, groceries. Nothing unusual. She'd continued to pay her bills as if she'd continue living in the house that she'd abandoned. Property taxes, insurance. Nothing that signaled she planned to up and leave. The feds had searched the place and found no luggage and lots of empty hangers in the closet. Not everything was gone, though. The place still had plenty of belongings, from kitchen mixers to jewelry to pancake-batter mix.

I turned on the TV and watched as New Year's Eve celebrations swept across the world. There were fireworks and musical artists and actresses in tiny dresses shivering in the cold with bright smiles pasted onto their faces. Young men I didn't recognize sang and danced and wished everybody a fantastic 1998. 1998. God, where did time go? The year 1988 felt like it was behind my shoulder, about to tap me, but it was far behind and long ago. I sipped the last of the Scotch. It was too early or too late to be getting maudlin.

"No one likes a maudlin drunk," Rick used to say.

I once asked him what sort of drunk *did* everybody like, and he said, "Ah, Tommy. You ask the big questions, you do."

Rick. Dead. As dead as 1997 now. I'd have toasted him, but my drink was empty and that would have been disrespectful. Only thing worse than a maudlin drunk is a disrespectful one.

※

As promised, Nate arrived at 9:30 a.m., a battered metal toolbox in hand. He carried a thermos in the other. His eyes hopped from the peeling linoleum to the world's ugliest avocado fridge to the kitchen table with the scarred edge. He didn't say a word. He set the thermos on the counter, the toolbox on the floor. He bent and examined the yellow-and-white linoleum. "I've seen this before. In my auntie's house, years ago."

Sounded about right. My house had a lot in common with many aunties' homes.

He crab-walked forward and tugged at a peeling linoleum strip. It came up another quarter inch. "Hmph. This will take time and patience to remove. What have we here?" He peered at the exposed floor beneath the linoleum. "Hmm. Looks like hickory. That's good."

"Yeah?"

"If you can get this crap off without destroying the wood, you could have yourself a real nice hardwood floor. Assuming you like wood." He paused. Chuckled. Was he making a joke? He held a hand up. "Sorry. That came out wrong. Or right. Anyway, what else you got?"

"I hate these things," I said, pointing to the cabinet pulls. "Keep scraping my knuckles on 'em."

He stood and examined them. "They're shallow. Whoever lived here had little hands. These'll be easy to replace. MacDowell's over in Willington sells hardware. Doorknobs, drawer pulls. You might start there." He surveyed the room. "What else?"

"You ready for the world's worst bathroom?"

Nate rarely smiled. His poker face was permanent, but he looked intrigued. I led him down the hall to the bathroom. The black and pink tiles, the pink soap dish, and the round glass vanity lighting did it. Nate's mask cracked. His eyebrows twitched and he bit his right index finger. "This is amazing."

"That's one word for it."

"This place belongs in a museum."

"Thanks, Indiana Jones," I said.

He shook his head. "You don't have another bathroom do you?"

"No, why?"

"Because when you redo an entire bathroom, you need to find another place to shower and use the toilet."

"Hadn't thought about that."

"Not surprised." He caught my look and said, "I mean, how can you *think* in here? It's so loud."

"You get used to it after a while." I had. I'd lived here almost a year. The pink no longer made me flinch when I turned the lights on.

"Okay. Let's leave this room. It's gonna take me some time to think about."

We returned to the kitchen. Nate looked at the floor. My eyes were on the fridge, calculating whether I needed to visit the grocery store. Eggs, cheese, and suddenly my thoughts skipped a beat. Sharon Donner wrote checks at the grocery store. And at the pharmacy.

"Nate, how many checks do you write a month?" I stared at the fridge's metal handle. It was loose at the bottom. Had to be careful I didn't yank the sucker off each time I opened the fridge.

"Checks?" He tugged again on the linoleum. "Not many."

"If you paid for most everything with checks or credit cards, why would you withdraw so much cash each week?"

"Huh?" he said.

Why hadn't we seen it sooner? If Sharon Donner didn't need her weekly ATM withdrawals for food or gas or medicines, what was she spending it on? I moved into the living room and began rifling through the bank statements. They went back ten months. She'd begun the weekly withdrawals in late August. Two hundred dollars each week. For twelve weeks. That was, what, $2,400? Not enough to go underground for long, but it would give her a start. Had she been planning it since August?

"She's been working this for months!" I shouted.

"Chief, I'm gonna head out." Nate's voice seemed far away. "Looks like you got another problem to solve."

She'd been stockpiling cash so that she'd have it available once she took Cody.

"This is gonna break it open," I muttered.

"Bye, Chief!" Nate called. I waved at him, my mind miles away.

I moved to my recliner and thought, rocking a little, trying to work it out.

CHAPTER THIRTY-TWO

On the twelfth day of 1998, I found myself mired in paperwork. Agent Waters had taken all the information about Sharon Donner's finances and was using it to construct a timeline. Other agents were pursuing sightings. That meant I was back to regular work, sorting through the station's citizen complaints. There'd been a marked increase. Some were a by-product of the holidays. People got upset about things like tickets and even warnings issued by the police during the happiest time of the year. When I'd finished those, I found myself facing something I'd been putting off. My car graffiti. Finnegan told me he was still pursuing his own line of inquiry, but his slumped shoulders and voice told me he hadn't had luck fitting any of our callers into the frame. My suspect list was down to three names.

Burns
Dix
Klein

All were left-handed, or, in Klein's case, ambidextrous. I stared at the names. None of the men hated me. Not openly. But that's what this was all about, wasn't it? Striking at me from the shadows. Attacking me the way my prank callers did, under a veil of anonymity. I tapped my pen against the list. One of these men had spray-painted "FAG!" on my car. Had put a magazine with naked men in my mailbox. The college edition. Had that been a dig at my family of college professors? Or simply the issue he'd found at the local gas station? My hand stopped tapping the pen, the idea making itself known to my fingers first. The college edition. What was the issue month? December. I'd gotten it in October. That issue wouldn't have hit the newsstands yet, which meant my guy had a subscription or access to one.

The names shimmered before my eyes. I slammed a fist onto the desk. It hurt, but not enough. I wanted to break glass. Instead, I tucked the list into my drawer, finger-combed my hair, and stepped into the hall. Yankowitz nearly collided with me, his arms around a cardboard box. Jinx trotted behind him. "Hi, Chief," he said. "Bringing some things in for Jinx to work with. Sniff tests."

"Sounds good."

Jinx stopped at the sound of my voice. Tilted his head. I walked past, unable to take comfort in the dog. I needed to do this first. He sat at a desk, filling out a report on a car accident. "Hey," I said. He looked up, his dark eyes surprised.

"Need me?" he asked. He stopped stabbing the keys with his index fingers.

"Yes." I turned and walked to my office. He followed. "Close the door."

He did. I sat. His eyes darted to the chairs. He didn't sit. "What's up?" he asked. He stood, hands together, as if uncertain what to do with them. Those hands. They'd stolen evidence and used it to deface my car. To insult me and embarrass me.

"I know you did it." He had to lean in to hear me.

"Did what?" His voice was good. Not nervous. His eyes were another story, and if he squeezed his hands any harder he'd break a finger.

"You put the *Playgirl* in my mailbox and you defaced my car."

"What? No, I—"

"Klein, don't add lying to your list of sins."

He flushed. It wasn't admissible evidence, but it worked for me.

"You stole evidence from the Evidence room and used it to spray-paint hate speech on my patrol car. You defaced police property."

"I . . . it was a joke. Not a good one, but—"

"Stop." My voice was big. Loud. They'd have heard me, out there. "I don't care why you did it."

He looked to the window, toward the winter sun. I pictured him as he must have looked when he'd first joined the force. Eager, fresh-faced, like Billy. He'd wanted to protect and serve. To feel good, like he had at the bank. To be a hero.

"It was a joke," he said. "The magazine. I thought it was funny. That it would get some laughs. But one of the guys saw me do it, and then, I had to," he swallowed. "I had to tag your car in case he thought—"

"Thought you owned the magazine?" I asked.

He bobbed his head.

"You didn't have to do that," I said. He hadn't. He could've told me about the magazine, or told the other cop to fuck off. He hadn't needed to spray-paint "FAG!" on my car. "You'll resign, immediately."

He stumbled back, as if I'd pushed him. "But, I—" He gulped. "Chief, I'm sorry. Really, I am. I know it was stupid, but, please, don't fire me."

"I'm not firing you. You're resigning. If you don't, I'll press charges. You could do time. Maybe not. I don't think you want to take that gamble."

"When would I leave?" Would, as if he had options, choices.

"Today. You'll leave my office, give your notice to Mrs. Dunsmore, and turn in your gun."

He bit his lip. Those nice teeth. Good for smiling. He didn't have much to smile about now. "What about the guys? What will I tell them? Do I have to tell them—"

"The truth?" I imagined Klein announcing he'd been the one to tag my car. Pictured the men's reactions. Awkward silence, a few raised brows, and some strained well wishes. "No," I said. "You can tell them you have a family emergency."

"Don't you want to know who the other cop was?" he asked.

"Did he spray-paint my car?"

"No," he said.

"Then, no, I don't." Better not to know.

"What—" he stopped. His hand went to his belt. It would be weeks, maybe months before he stopped reaching for things on it that weren't there: his walkie-talkie, his gun. You gave all that up when you retired, or got kicked out. Klein hitched his shoulders. "Okay then."

He was the only other gay cop on my force. Or had been. Within minutes, he'd be unemployed.

"Good-bye, Klein," I said. "Good luck."

He checked me for sincerity. Didn't find it lacking. So he turned and opened the door and walked out. I counted to eleven and then punched the desk again. This time I scraped a knuckle and felt my chest loosen, a fraction. Enough to breathe.

CHAPTER THIRTY-THREE

Things change, bit by bit, but looking back, time compresses it all and it seems as if things were always the new way. Klein's absence was noted, gossiped about, discussed, conjectured. Finnegan and I had a brief conversation about it. He came to my office and asked, "Klein? Really?"

I said, "He admitted it."

He jammed his hands into his pockets and toed the carpet. "I never would've thought. Well, I guess you showed me, huh?" He looked up, ready for my I-told-you-so.

"I wish I hadn't," I said, and we'd left it there.

After nearly three weeks, it quieted, and the space that used to contain Klein was no longer empty. Not because we'd filled it, but because no one saw the Klein-shaped hole anymore. It was as if he'd never been.

Sweet Dreams was closed. Valentine's Day was approaching, and the store had been dark since January 20th. The rumor mill had it that the owners had broken up, and they were fighting over who owned the store. I drove past it, the freshly painted interior dark, the candy growing stale, the front door sign reading "Back in Ten Minutes!"

Cody Forrand was still here, even though he'd been gone six weeks. Outside local shop windows, his smiling face greeted you. You couldn't visit the post office, the library, the schools, or our station without being confronted by that wide grin. There was a billboard on Route 84 with his giant smiling face on it, startling me as I drove to Home Depot. I saw his face at Suds and at the grocery. I noticed the posters, wind-torn, water damaged, and sun-faded, yellowing, their edges curled with age and exposure. News stations had stopped running the story. The *Idyll Register*'s coverage dropped to a paragraph. When I spoke to the

Forrands, their voices no longer spiked. They were in the gray zone, expecting the worst but hoping for the best despite knowing the odds weren't good.

Outside their house, trees were wrapped in yellow ribbons. Wright told me yellow ribbons had been wrapped around Idyll trees back in the Gulf War, a symbol to soldiers, a prayer for their safe homecoming. Other trees in the neighborhood sported similar ribbons. They snagged your eye like a fish hook, the bright fabric unexpected and sharp in the dull afternoon light. The Christmas decorations were down. The ribbons stayed up.

The feds had moved back to New Haven yesterday, the first of February. They were still assisting, but their aid came in the form of phone calls and faxes. On the phone, I could feel Waters's anger. "Where the fuck did she go?" she asked. "She didn't have enough money saved to disappear for long." I had nothing to give her. We'd found no proof of Jane Forrand's involvement in the kidnapping plot. We were stuck, like dinosaurs that fell into those pits and stayed there, forever. Our minds were on Cody, always. Waters told me she had a couple dreams where she'd almost found him. I told her I tailed a car one day, certain the kid in the back was Cody. I drove sixteen miles before I got a good look at him. I then drove back sixteen miles, cursing all the way.

Cisco and I no longer saw each other. We'd met up at his hotel the last night of his stay there. He told me he had an early morning the next day. Subtext: go home, Thomas. I took the hint and left. I'd suggested we meet for drinks. He'd said he'd call. He hadn't. He probably had someone back in New Haven. Several someones.

Things change by inches. Like the vinyl flooring of my kitchen. I sat, my back against the lower cupboards, cutting the linoleum, shallowly, with a box cutter. I'd moved the living room TV so I could watch it from the kitchen floor as I pulled up strip after stubborn strip. Nate had showed me how in a ten-minute demo that he'd made look easy. Half the time, my strips tore in half, the glue exerting its ancient grip. I dug my knife in, too hard. Pulled it back toward me. I was supposed to cut away from my body, but I found it impossible. What's the worst that could happen? The knife would yank toward me? Sever my jugular? I'd die as I'd lived, with a crappy fucking floor.

On TV, an actor playing a cop kicked a door in. A front kick, using the flat of the ball of his foot. "Idiot." I scored the linoleum. "Back kick exerts more force." You could break your foot kicking the door the way he had.

The linoleum peeled up and away, exposing the cracked, brown glue below. I'd have to wash it up with soap and water, according to Nate. Several times. No wonder I'd never seen my parents engaged in the art of home repair. They were smart people. Also, they'd always had a super in their building.

A new show came on. One of those true-crime dramas with terrible re-creations of crime scenes. I found these harder to watch than the make-believe nonsense. I set the box cutter down. A face I knew came on screen. Blond hair, brown eyes, more makeup, and a slightly fuller face, but it was her, Jane Forrand. Why? Ah, the National Center for Missing & Exploited Children. I turned the volume up. The man beside her outlined the circumstances of Cody's disappearance. Cody's picture came on screen, the one I saw every day. If we never found him, he'd be locked in amber, smiling forever. This was the picture that defined him. It seemed wrong. That a boy's life should be reduced to one picture, a picture he'd probably hated dressing up for and having his hair spit-combed for. It wasn't him. It was an ideal.

"Please, if you have any information, call the number down below." Mrs. Forrand looked good. It was television, of course. They had hair and makeup pros. I'd seen her at her worst, sleep-deprived and anxious. This was the first time I saw her as others had: pretty, charismatic. She'd wanted to be an actress, to be on television. What a terrible way for her to get there.

What was it Cody had said about the TV show? They'd almost been on TV. The *Sally Jesse Raphael* show. I wondered. Maybe I'd ask Wright to look into it. He didn't have anything better to do at the moment.

It ended. A denture-cream ad came on. I found a channel showing a sports week wrap-up and returned to my flooring. Another half hour, and I'd call it quits. One third of the floor was bare of linoleum. It didn't look better. Wouldn't until the glue was gone. I'd get there. Inch by inch. I dug my razor-blade tip into the plastic surface of the lino-leum. The blade cut down and in, destroying the past, making way for the future.

The vacant patrol position created by Klein's resignation was posted. Résumés came. More than I'd expected. The résumés made me feel old. Two years' experience. Fresh out of the academy. We winnowed the pile. Interviewed candidates. All men except one. She had the least experience, seemed the most nervous, her hands cold and clammy. I'd sorted her into the No pile before she'd finished telling me why she wanted to police our small town. Another candidate blew his shot when he made a joke about killing deer with his patrol car. I'd hit a deer last year. It hadn't been funny. The three finalists were all different and yet the same. None of them gay. I could tell.

The mayor tried to roadblock the new hire. Argued at a town meeting that we'd blown our annual budget and could wait to hire another patrol person. This, then, was his revenge for our arresting his buddy, Mr. VanWyck. Though nothing had come of it. No prosecu-tion. Surprise, surprise. Mr. Neilly argued that we'd blown our budget investigating a murder and abduction, and that this increase in major crimes meant we needed more, not fewer police. They traded verbal blows until the other selectmen waded in and got a vote. Three to two in favor of the hire.

Mr. Trabucco was behind bars, again. Captain Hirsch had discov-ered several charred-to-hell-and-back magazines. I'd not been hopeful, but a few readable words—"boys" and "playground"—and one and a half pictures of a naked minor were enough to lock him up, for now. We had technicians trying to read the charred magazines with cutting-edge instruments. Maybe we'd get more, maybe not.

My cupboards had new handles. I'd taken the old ones off and lived with the inconvenience of opening them by pulling on the lower corner. This might've gone on forever, but Nate stopped by to check my floor progress. He saw the bare cupboards and asked, "How long?"

"Two weeks." It had been three.

"MacDowell's is open until six," he said.

MacDowell's was a barn-like building filled with housing supplies from old copper tubs to rows of metal radiators that reminded me of my city schooldays. The drawer pulls were in giant baskets near bins of doorknobs and clothing hooks. It made me think of how many homes there were in the world. Were most of the homes that had shed these doorknobs and tubs and radiators and door knockers and lamps still standing?

Baskets were filled with small flowered porcelain circles, wide curves of metal, copper pulls shaped like birds. So many, too many. A man in flannel watched me stare long enough that I looked up and said, "What?"

"Need something?" he asked.

"Pulls for my kitchen cabinets."

"What material?" He came nearer. I saw his right hand was missing a ring finger.

"Doesn't matter so long as it doesn't scrape my hand up."

"Gotcha. These'll never do that." He pointed to a basket full of knobs.

A lot of them were froufrou. "Got anything more basic?"

He dug through them and grunted. Moved on to the next basket. "How about this?" He dropped it into my palm. The metal was cool, the color almost gold. It weighed more than I expected. It was a star. Five points.

"How many are there?" I asked.

"How many you need?"

"Ten."

He found nine in the basket. The almost-gold winked at me, and I realized that the stars looked like old-time sheriff badges I'd seen on

TV as a boy. I'd had one. A fake metal star I'd pinned to my chest. I'd made Johnny play felon and locked him in our bathroom after processing him at the kitchen table. Dad laughed when he saw I'd taken his prints. Mom didn't when she realized I'd rolled Johnny's fingers in a red stamp pad she owned. The ink didn't wash off easily. Johnny's fingertips were a dull cherry red for a whole week.

I looked through the adjacent bin. Nope. Two more bins to search. My helper wandered away. I didn't notice, too busy rifling through drawer pulls. Who needed a drawer pull shaped like Massachusetts or California? The bins yielded nothing. There were only nine. I'd have to choose another. Something plainer, maybe a copper circle or square. I was prepared to tip them back into the basket when I saw it. It sat atop the wall hooks. I grabbed it. The tenth star.

At home, I discovered that if I centered them, the stars covered the two holes my removed pulls had left in the wood. I hadn't thought to take measurements. Stupid. I used a measuring tape and marked in pencil where the drill hole should go. The drill was fun to use, whizzy and fast. It took me two hours to install them all, with a break for a pizza and beer. Midway through the project, the phone rang.

"No one wants you here, gay wad. Leave town."

"How about you come over here and make me leave?" I said.

The caller hung up.

I stood atop my linoleum-free floor, still dark with glue in a few stubborn spots. The air smelled of wood shavings and hot metal. The stars didn't shine so much as wink, in the right light. It wasn't a big change. Small bits of metal, ounces of material. It felt like more. I could hear Rick in my head say, "So you've decided to stay, have you now?" He was using his gossiping gran tone.

"Shut up," I said. To him and to myself.

Why make a big deal out of drawer pulls?

CHAPTER THIRTY-FOUR

The line for Animal Control snaked outside the office, into the hallway. The office was open the second Saturday in March. So that's when everyone came. Just my luck. Behind me, I heard footsteps, light and fast. A child, running. "Come on! We have to get the tag for Gretel!" I knew that voice. Anna Forrand, her hair in a braided bun, came barreling toward me. Behind, her parents walked, hand in hand, small smiles on their faces.

Anna stopped shy of my toes. "Oh," she said. "Do you have a dog too?" She peered up at me as if we were old friends.

"A police dog, but it's not mine," I said.

Her parents' faces changed the moment they saw me. Their smiles descended; their lips thinned. They winced as if I'd hit them. I wished I'd made Yankowitz file the paperwork, or Billy. Anyone else might have been better.

"Hullo," Peter Forrand said. He put his hand on Anna's shoulder.

Jane Forrand nodded at me. Her stomach was a ball under her wool dress. Her hair was in a bun that matched Anna's. It made her look younger.

"You got a dog?" I asked.

Peter said, "Yes. Anna's wanted one for years and . . ."

"Now seemed like a good time," Jane said, her voice cheery.

Anna's smile revealed a missing front tooth. "It's a New Year's present cuz Mom said I'd been extra good this year."

"What kind of dog?" I asked.

"A cocker spaniel," Jane said. "We had them growing up. Sweet dogs."

"Her name is Gretel," Anna said. "I'm going to teach her tricks." Gretel, from her favorite fairy tale.

269

"There hasn't been any news?" Peter asked. He knew the answer. We kept them updated. Waters checked in with them too.

"No," I said. I wouldn't tell them of the tips we got, the cranks who saw the posters and called in false confessions or claimed they'd seen Sharon Donner at Disney World, or at their office party, or in London.

Anna said, "Cody wanted a dog. When he comes home, he can help walk her and brush her." Her voice trembled, uncertain. She wanted assurances we'd find him. Bring him home. Should I lie to her? It was one thing to withhold hope from Cody's parents. Another thing to make an eight-year-old girl miserable.

"Anna, honey, why don't you go fetch us a pamphlet about rabies vaccinations?" Jane asked. "Can you spell rabies?"

"Of course!" Anna ran past the people in line, ducking inside the office to stand before a tall wooden display.

"She's still sure he'll come home," Jane said. Her breath hitched. "But all the news, it says after the first few days, the chances . . . and it's been almost three months." She shuddered.

"There, now," Peter said. He rubbed her upper back.

Her hands cupped her stomach. "I picture him running through the front door every day, his cheeks all red."

Peter looked away, tears in his eyes. "Here comes Anna," he whispered. Jane straightened. Her hands fell from her stomach.

"Here's the pamphlet!" Anna cried. She held it up in triumph. Loose strands escaped the tight coil of her hairdo.

The line moved forward two steps.

"Where did you get your dog?" It was the only question I could think of not related to Cody.

"A breeder outside Farmington," Peter said.

"How old is she?" If the line didn't move much faster, soon I was going to exert a cop's privilege and skip to the front of the line. This small talk was excruciating.

"She was nine weeks when we got her!" Anna said. "So she's . . ." she mouthed the numbers until she said, "nineteen weeks!"

"Very good," I said. "You want a job balancing my checkbook?"

"Maybe you can help Mom," Peter whispered, giving Anna a nudge and a wink.

"Hey!" Jane said. "Not fair. Math's never been my strong suit."

"I know, darling. I was funning." He kissed her temple.

"I'm going to drop off some papers," I said. "Good luck with your puppy, Anna."

"Thanks! Maybe you can visit and see her sometime." She swayed, side to side.

"Maybe." I wouldn't. I couldn't. Hell, I hated driving near their home. The trees, still dressed in yellow ribbons and bearing water-stained Cody posters, reproached me.

I skipped ahead of the ten people before me, dropped the folder on the counter, and said, "K-9 paperwork." Before Mrs. Jethro could scold me, I was out of the office and in the hall, walking away from the Forrands.

In my office, I rifled through the latest tips about Cody Forrand. Not one looked legit. Peru? Nebraska? The last one was worst. Allegedly he'd been seen outside his house, sitting in the plastic playhouse he shared with his sister. I balled the paper in my fist and threw it. Not at the wastebasket, but at the wall.

"Whoa!" Yankowitz said.

Jinx bounded for the paper ball and clamped his jaws around it.

"*Lass los*," Yankowitz said.

Jinx dropped the ball and stared at it.

"*Komm her.*" That sounded a lot like its English equivalent. Jinx bounded to Yankowitz.

"*Sitz.*" Jinx sat, eyes on the now-damp paper ball.

"Thanks for dropping off the K-9 sheets. I had to get Jinx his distemper shot."

"I ran into the Forrands. Anna got a dog on January 1st. A belated Christmas surprise."

"What kind?"

"Cocker spaniel. Named it Gretel."

"Cute," he said. "Shelter dog?" Yankowitz was a big advocate of shelter animals. Skylar was a shelter dog.

"Um, no, from a breeder."

"A breeder?" His tone made Jinx shift and watch his face. He dropped his hand to the top of Jinx's head and rubbed between the dog's ears. "How old is the puppy?"

"Nineteen weeks. Why?" Yankowitz was frowning hard. This wasn't normal. Even Jinx picked up on it. He watched his owner, the paper ball a forgotten temptation.

"They got a puppy at the start of the year?" He mouthed numbers, like Anna. "Nine weeks old when they got her?"

"Yeah. Why?"

"Nothing." He shook his head. "It's just unusual to get a purebred puppy on short notice. They had perfect timing."

"Perfect timing," I repeated. Nothing else he said would've made my neck hairs go full alert. "Ten weeks back from New Year's Day was ..." I looked on my desk for a calendar but all I had was 1998; 1997 was left to time. "Very late October. Wait. When would a breeder advertise puppies?"

"Good breeders often don't. Most have waiting lists." He worried a spot on his utility belt. "You know the breeder's name?"

"No, but they said it was in Farmington." Nine weeks before New Year's Day. They hadn't mentioned getting a dog. Hell, Jane had seemed downright afraid when Skylar first showed up at their house to look for Cody. I'd assumed she was anti-dog. Then again, spaniels were smaller. She'd grown up with them. What if it hadn't been the breed, though? Who was afraid of golden retrievers? What if she'd been afraid of what Skylar could do? Track her missing son.

"Can you look into it? Find the breeder and find out how and when the Forrands acquired the dog?"

"Okay," he said. "Sure."

"Do it soon."

His glance asked questions I didn't answer. He and Jinx left. I walked to my plant. Stared at its leaves and thought hard. Maybe they'd planned to get a dog for Christmas all along. Maybe they'd gotten a call from a friend who knew a breeder.

Maybe Wright had news. I found him typing a report, one slow finger-strike at a time. A toothpick stuck out of the left side of his mouth. Watching was agony. This must've been what it was like for Johnny, when we were kids, doing homework. Having to watch me struggle through European history. Although, honestly, when was the last time someone asked me about the monarchies of Europe? Never, that's when.

"Enjoying the show?" Wright asked out of the side of his mouth.

"Not at all. It's excruciating."

"Sorry to disappoint." He struck the *e* and the *n*. "You want something?"

"Any news on the Forrand case?"

He stopped typing. Looked up. "What? No. Why? You hear something?"

"No."

"Then why are you over here?" He sounded more annoyed than usual. Maybe trouble at home. That wouldn't be unusual, not for cops.

"For the scintillating conversation. What about the TV show? Any news there?"

"They said they'd call." It didn't sound like he planned to check in.

"Where's the number?" I asked.

He withdrew the toothpick from his mouth and pointed it at several stacks of folders on Finnegan's desk.

Finnegan's desk was, at the best of times, a biohazard. It wasn't the best of times. I sat in his seat after I checked it for sticky substances; I pushed aside lollipop wrappers, cigarette ash, and a blackened banana peel to get my hands on the first stack. When I found the folder, I took it to my office.

Getting through to the person I needed, the booker for *Sally Jesse Raphael*, wasn't easy. I was transferred five times and listened to Muzak for twenty-two minutes. It paid off, though. Gabriella Montrose remembered the show about sick kids. She'd booked the guests. "Jesus," she said, "that show was a frigging nightmare. I told them, never again. Arranging travel for a kid who is *allergic* to sunshine? I need a cigarette just thinking about it."

"What about Cody Forrand, and his parents?"

"Cody," she said.

"The boy who can't feel pain."

"Ah, him. Seriously, that kid was the most normal of the lot. Running around, hamming it up. Cute, too. But he wouldn't sit still long enough for us to tape him. Like I said, pretty normal." This comment rang true. Everyone acted like Cody was a nightmare because he ran wild, but if he hadn't been sick, if he'd been a boy who knew what pain was, wouldn't he have been like me? A rambunctious kid who'd rather run than sit still.

"What about his mother?" I asked.

"Her." The way she said it told me they'd not gotten along. "She acted like her son was the goddamn star of the show. Kept making demands, and kept asking questions about how she'd be shot. From this camera or that? Her left side was her best, and could we get that one?"

"She had acting ambitions, once upon a time," I said.

"No fucking kidding," Gabriella said. "I thought she was going to destroy the green room when she found out we'd cut them from the program. I made sure a security person escorted them from the building."

"What about her husband?" I asked.

"He wasn't there, as I recall. Just her and the boy. I swear, if Sally ever tries another show like that—I don't care how good the ratings were—I will quit!"

"How did Cody react to being cut from the show?"

"Him? I don't think he cared, either way. But as they were getting ready to leave, the mother said, 'This is the last straw. I'm done.' She said it to her son. Poor kid. He kept saying, 'I'm sorry,' and she said, 'It's too late for sorries.'"

I leaned against my seat. Maybe Jane Forrand had planned the kidnapping with Sharon Donner? Mrs. Donner got a new son, and the Forrands got their old life back. Not exactly, but they had Anna, their smart, desperate-to-please daughter, and a new baby on the way. Plus, a puppy. Hansel and Gretel, without Hansel. Wasn't that what the terrible, storybook parents wanted? Fewer mouths to feed.

CHAPTER THIRTY-FIVE

Yankowitz found me tossing junk mail into the recycling bin. "Chief? I got back from Farmington." He'd found something. It was in his voice. "The breeder, Mickey, said the Forrands asked about puppies in August. They were in luck because he had plans to breed a new litter. They reserved one."

"When?"

"Mid-October, when the dog's pregnancy was confirmed."

"Before Cody went missing."

"They gave a deposit December 18th," he said.

"Between the first and second kidnappings." When Cody had returned home. Maybe they'd decided they wanted a dog, on top of two kids and a third on the way? No. I'd seen the way they lived. There was no way a puppy fit into that home.

"Seems like an odd decision," he said. "Taking on the responsibility of a pet with two kids, one of 'em so sick."

"It's worse than that. They knew Cody wasn't staying. They planned it."

"They helped Mrs. Donner?" he asked.

"Yes, but we need more. Wait. Who reserved the puppy and paid for it?"

"I didn't ask. I assumed it was both parents."

"Call the breeder. Confirm it."

I called Agent Waters. She was out, but Agent Mulberry was in. I told him about the puppy and the TV show. He didn't think it was damning evidence, but he agreed to review the Forrands again, beginning with their first statements about Cody's disappearance.

"You mind if I do some digging?" I asked. Yes, it was Idyll's case. However, I needed the feds' help, and I didn't want to step on anyone's sensitive toes.

"What did you have in mind?" he asked. I told him, and he said, "Door-to-doors? Please, be my guest." He paused. "You know, if it was them, they actually had me fooled. I've seen my share of bad parents, but they're in a new class."

Were the Forrands worse than parents who beat their kids, who neglected or molested them? Were they worse than parents who murdered? Were they the same? We wouldn't know until we found Cody Forrand. Knew if he was alive, or dead. Then we could judge them.

Lord, preserve nosy neighbors. Keep them safe from harm and watch over them. At 4:35 p.m., I found Geraldine Howard, who lived directly across the street from Sharon Donner. She'd greeted my introduction with a curt, "I've already answered questions about that woman." When my questions included new photos, of Peter and Jane Forrand, she grew curious. She invited me in, muted her television, and offered me tea.

She looked at the pictures long and hard. "This one." She waved the photo of Jane Forrand in her hand so that the photo buckled, "She stopped by."

"Once? Twice?"

She twisted the photo to look at it again. It was from the press conference. Jane's face was startled and pale. "Several times, mostly in the fall. October, before Halloween, it was. She had a boy and girl with her, but after that she came alone."

"And him?" I pointed to the picture of Peter Forrand.

"Never saw him."

"How long did she stay when she visited?"

"Oh, I couldn't really say." She ducked her head. Played shy. "I don't spy on my neighbors."

"Of course not. Only, you might have looked outside to check the weather and seen her car still in the drive, after an hour or more." I'd give her excuses. I'd hand her a bucket full of them, if only she'd say what she'd seen.

"She stayed at least three hours. I know because *One Life to Live* was beginning when she left, and she'd arrived during *The Price Is Right*. Twice she came and stayed about that long."

Where were the kids during this time? School. Right.

"Were they good friends?" I asked.

She leaned back. "Now, how would I know a thing like that? It's not as if I listen at keyholes."

"No, no. I wondered if, when you saw them, they seemed chummy."

She moved her lips as if swishing mouthwash. "I wouldn't have thought so. Mrs. Donner, she was a queer bird. Always off to church with her little boy, always talking about her burdens and how God never gave you more than you could handle. Pious." She spat the last word. "The other woman, she was younger and not churchy."

"What makes you say that?"

"It's how she struck me."

"They got along?"

"The younger one yelled at Mrs. Donner once, in the drive. Something about her not doing something right. She seemed upset."

"Do you know when that was?"

"Jennifer escaped from an elevator shaft, and John convinced Susan not to kill herself."

"Suicide?" What was she talking about?

"On *Days of Our Lives*. That show is spiraling out of control. Honestly. I think they've got monkeys writing those scripts."

I jotted this down. Maybe someone could figure out what date that episode had aired. "And you only saw the children the one time?"

"Yes. The little boy, that was Cody Forrand." She didn't make it a question.

I nodded. "Yes."

"So she took him then, Mrs. Donner? Abducted him after her boy died?"

"Did you know her boy, Aaron, well?"

She snorted. "Not hardly. She barely let him out of the house. Claimed his 'condition' made it too dangerous. Too dangerous to ride a bike, too dangerous to play on the slides, too dangerous to swim. Poor mite. Always at church or the hospital."

"You remember when he died?"

"Yes. I saw the ambulance and police come. Sirens fit to split your ears."

I thought back to the medical report. "Did you notice anything odd, before the ambulances?"

"Just the light."

"The light?" I asked.

She pointed to the picture window. "His bedroom faced the street. Second floor. The light flicked off and on, several times, like someone was flipping the switch."

The fuse had gone. The air-conditioning unit turned off. The fuse? Had it controlled the whole room? I wrote fast, words blurring. "You're sure about the light?"

"Yes. Later I thought how it seemed almost prophetic, the light flickering, like the last little bit of Aaron before he departed this world."

"Do you know how long it was before the ambulances came? The lights flickering?"

"Least an hour. I'd gone to the grocery and back. I was unpacking when the sirens started up. I dropped a box of cereal."

"Right. Thank you, you've been most helpful."

"Well, I'm no busybody," she said, puffing her chest. "But what's the world coming to when one doesn't *watch out* for one's neighbors, am I right?"

I stuffed my notepad in my pocket and stood. "I couldn't agree more."

⛥

Agent Waters listened to my summarized interviews with Sharon Donner's neighbors. Several had identified Jane Forrand as a visitor of Mrs. Donner's, though none had been as helpful as Geraldine Howard. Waters asked, "So, how would it have gone down? They agree to give Cody to Mrs. Donner? Why didn't he ID her after the first grab?"

"Maybe he only saw the mask. She drugged him with the cocoa. Maybe he never got a good look at her."

"Or maybe Mommy told him not to tell," she said. "Wait. Didn't Wright say his parents would answer for him during interviews? You think both parents were in on it, right?"

"Peter didn't visit Mrs. Donner. Still, it's hard to imagine he didn't know."

"Impossible," she said.

"Although it seems he doesn't know she was cheating on him."

"Are we sure about that?" she asked. "Sure his vasectomy didn't fail?"

"How can we be sure without a paternity test?" I asked.

"That might be a useful tool," she said.

"I'm not sure we can get one without consent."

"Do they know that?" she asked.

"Probably not." I began to see how Waters had gotten to where she was. "By the way, a couple of the guys' wives and mothers are fans of *Days of Our Lives*. Two of 'em said that the episode with the elevator escape aired December 18th."

"So after the first grab went wrong," Waters said. "You think Jane Forrand went to bawl Sharon Donner out?"

"Makes sense," I said.

She said, "Let's hope we don't have to explain it to a judge. Right now, it's all conjecture. Circumstantial. We'd never get a trial, much less a conviction." Her frustration was audible.

"Yeah." The Forrands had plotted their child's abduction while they hung his stocking and talked of Christmas presents with him. They'd led us as if our noses had strings. Anger rose up again like bile. Those fuckers had given their child to a woman who might've been involved in her son's death. They'd handed him over like a gift, while weeping on camera and calling us incompetent in our search efforts. I'd see them in handcuffs. I would give them something to cry about.

"Chief, call!" One thing I appreciated about Mrs. Dunsmore. She didn't yell. Didn't need to. And now I never knew whether "Chief, call" meant it was for me or aimed at me. I snatched up the phone.

"Chief, this is Mike Shannon."

"Hey, Mike. How are you?" Was this a social call?

"Good. Wanted you to know. We got some prints off your kidnap car. Hairs too."

"That's great." Two and a half months after they'd been taken. Just about right.

"It's some young guy, Mark Farraday. Report is headed your way, but I wanted to give you the scoop."

"Thanks, Mike. I appreciate it."

I had Billy run Mark Farraday through the system. He was twenty-two years old. Busted for being involved in a hit-and-run at which the driver had left the scene of the crime. Farraday was a passenger. Born and raised in Chaplin, Connecticut. Chaplin, where everyone knew their neighbors.

I called Waters. She perked up at the news of Mike Farraday's prints. "Guy from Chaplin, huh? I like that. Hey, how did you get the report already? I don't see it."

"I've got friends," I said. Left it at that.

"You think this Farraday kid knows the Forrands?"

"He must."

"Damn," she said. "We need to get him in here."

"Mind if I watch?" I asked.

"If that's what you're into," she said, laughing. "Absolutely."

CHAPTER THIRTY-SIX

The FBI interview room looked proper, with wooden chairs, a heavy table that could seat six, and a two-way mirror. The room was wired to tape audio and video. A few subtle logos here and there reminded you where you were at all times. Even the folder Waters had in front of her had the FBI seal on it. Plus Mark Farraday's name, big and bold, on the front.

Mark Farraday was a lanky kid with big hands and big brown eyes. Maybe his eyes were so big because of the terror he was experiencing. His eyes flittered from the folder with his name on it, to Waters, to me, and then to the mirror. When he'd shown up, alone, Waters and I had heaved sighs of relief. He hadn't lawyered up. Now he sat, scared, watching us like we were big bears about to devour him.

"Hello, Mark," Agent Waters said. "Thanks for coming. Like I said, I'm hoping you can help us with our inquiry into Cody Forrand's abduction." She leaned on the last word, abduction. Subtle, and effective. Mark swallowed, hard, and audibly.

"Cody was taken on December 22nd. We've determined he was driven in a silver Toyota Camry belonging to Arlene Pearl, of Barkhamsted. Mrs. Pearl reported her car stolen when we found it parked on Weymouth Avenue."

Mark watched Agent Waters turn pages in the folder. He couldn't quite read what was on the pages, but he strained forward as far as he could.

"The crime technicians processed that car and found DNA that matches Cody Forrand. They also found fingerprints." She looked up, at him. "Your fingerprints."

"Mine?" His voice cracked.

"Yours," she said. "Can you explain that?"

"I think I need a lawyer," he said.

"I think you need to tell us where you took Cody Forrand before I charge you with federal kidnapping." This time the emphasis was on federal.

"I didn't drive him anywhere," he said. "I swear. I just stole the car. I didn't know they were going to move Cody in it. I like Cody. He's a great kid. Really." His words emerged all at once, leaving him breathless.

"Why did you steal the car?"

"She asked me to," he said.

"She?" I asked.

"Mrs. Forrand. Jane."

I fought back the smile that spread inside me.

"Jane Forrand asked you to steal this car," Waters said.

"A car. One that wouldn't be reported stolen anytime soon. I do landscaping, and I'd worked a job in Barkhamsted a month back. I knew Mrs. Pearl had a car she barely drove. I figured it would work. I didn't know they meant to use it more than once."

"You stole it more than once?" Waters asked.

"She needed it more than once. She didn't tell me why."

"And you didn't ask?" Waters didn't bother to hide her skepticism.

"She was very upset, especially the second time. She'd been through so much, what with Cody going missing. Plus she and Mr. Forrand were having trouble." He spoke Mr. Forrand's name with the deference you pay to one's elders whom you met when a child. Yet he called Mrs. Forrand by her first name.

"Why did you steal the car for her?" Waters asked.

"She asked me to, plus she paid me. I needed the money. I owe so much in student-loan money, and work was slow, before all these winter storms hit."

"She paid you?" Even better, from a prosecution perspective. "When?"

"October. She said she'd pay half upfront, before she needed the job done, but she didn't have that much."

October. Waters and I shared a look. Bingo. We now had evidence of her planning as far back as October.

"How much did she pay you?"

"One hundred and twenty five dollars."

"You took one-twenty-five for a four-hundred job?" I asked, critical.

"She paid me another way." The red spread down his neck. Another way, huh?

"She had sexual intercourse with you?" Waters made it sound cold, clinical.

"It wasn't like, I mean, I didn't do it because of that. I've been in love with her since I was sixteen. And she said her husband never touched her anymore. That she felt ugly and old, and that I made her feel special. She's a beautiful woman. She's just had a tough life, taking care of Cody."

Wow. This guy might as well have "patsy" tattooed on his forehead.

"She's pregnant," Waters said. "Did she tell you?"

"What? No. I heard rumors." Of course he had. In a town like Chaplin, probably everyone knew. "I assumed she and her husband made up."

"So you didn't consider that the baby might be yours?" she asked.

"What? No. She was on the pill. She told me."

"You might find this difficult to believe," Waters said dryly, "But she lied."

Mark Farraday unraveled. He babbled about not being ready to be a father, and how would he support a child, and why would she do this to him? We let him rant for a few moments before we insisted on getting a full statement from him. He was only too happy to oblige, especially when Waters spelled out his criminal charge options and what the power of cooperation might mean for him. He forgot his teenage fascination with Jane Forrand in the face of federal charges and pending fatherhood.

Once we had the statement, Waters and I conferred. We had enough to grab Jane Forrand, to get a warrant to search her house. But would a search tell us where Cody was? Would coming at her with a full-frontal attack guarantee we'd find him?

"I can get Wright in," I said. "To help." I knew better than to offer Finnegan.

"No," she said. "We keep this small. We've been the ones talking to them lately. We'll keep it that way. Coffee?"

I took her up on the offer and discovered that if my tax money was being misspent, it certainly wasn't on the FBI's coffee budget.

There is no such thing as the perfect crime. No matter how carefully someone plans, no matter how detailed the bank schematics or how trained the sniper, mistakes happen, and evidence exists. A loose thread from a jacket, droplets of blood, an unexpected witness, or plain old bad luck. Detectives work hard, but sometimes it's the little unexpected gift the universe throws at you that breaks a case open. That explodes the otherwise-perfect crime, leaving bits of plans and better futures scattered like shrapnel.

Gretel was an eager, face-licking, silky-eared pup that jumped on me as soon as I stepped inside. After she'd slobbered over my proffered hand, she went at Waters, who said, "Stop!" in a tone that made Gretel yip, and back away.

"Come, Gretel!" Anna called, patting the front of her pants. "Come here!"

Gretel ran to Anna and licked her face, making Anna laugh and say, "Stop" in a tone that guaranteed Gretel wouldn't. Happy family.

"We have some news," Agent Waters said. She stood with her hands at her waist.

She slid her eyes to Anna and Gretel and shook her head at Peter.

"Anna, take Gretel out back, will you?" Peter said.

"She just went out."

"Anna, remember what we agreed upon? You'd take Gretel for walks."

"Okay," she said. "Come on, Gretel!" She gathered her coat and a turquoise leash.

"Hat!" Jane called. "It's freezing out there."

Anna grabbed a pom-pom hat. Gretel pranced, her nails clickety-clacking on the floor. Anna had to calm her before she could attach the leash, then she took Gretel out the front door.

"Stay near the house!" Jane yelled.

"A young boy was found recently, dead. We think it may be Cody," Waters said.

Peter's face tightened. Jane's hands covered her mouth. She squeezed her eyes closed. "No," she whispered.

"Are you sure?" Peter asked. His voice broke.

"No. That's why we came. We'd like you to come to the station and look at some pictures."

Jane sat on the sofa. "No," she said, shaking her head. "It can't be him."

"Where is he? I mean, his body," Peter asked. His voice shook.

"At the state medical examiner's office."

"It may not be him," I said. "That's why we need you to come and look at the photos first."

"What about Anna?" Jane asked.

"She can come too," I said. "Officer Yankowitz is at the station. He's in charge of the K-9 unit. He can teach Anna some dog tricks with Gretel."

"My boy," Jane said, wiping her eyes. "Is it him?" She had real tears on her cheeks, but she'd studied acting. She ought to know how to cry on command.

"It won't take long," Waters said, as if this was an objection they might raise.

"We'll get our coats." Peter hesitated, as if unsure what coats were.

Waters had to say, "Let's go then" to prompt him to fetch their coats.

Jane's coat didn't zip around her newly popped-out belly. Her husband's hand was on her back as she walked. "Anna!" she cried. "Anna!" For all the world, she sounded on the verge of a breakdown.

Anna came around the corner, her cheeks red as apples, her breath coming in pants, like her dog's. "Where are we going?" she asked. Gretel danced around her feet.

"We need to talk to the police. Come along," her mother said, extending her arm.

Anna raced past, toward the car. She opened the rear door, and Gretel jumped up and in. Anna seated herself beside the dog. Peter guided Jane, holding her elbow, as if she were frail.

Waters tilted her head, a signal. She got into her SUV and pulled in front of the Forrands. I took backup, behind them, in case they ran for it. Gretel rode with her face pressed to the rear window, delighted. Anna stroked her fur. Anna, the focus of her parents' attention for the first time in a long time. How would her life change today? The Forrands followed Waters, signaling every turn they took.

When we got to the station, Yankowitz was ready. He gave Gretel a treat, which she gobbled in two bites. "Want to teach her to sit and roll over?" he asked Anna.

"Really?" She looked at Gretel with doubt.

"Really. Come on. We'll use Mrs. Dunsmore's office." He winked, as if he was being naughty. She giggled and followed, no backward look to her parents.

When she was out of sight, Jane asked, "Where are the pictures?"

"Let's go to the interview room. No chance of Anna seeing them in there," Agent Waters said. She ushered Jane in front of her. I stepped forward, bisecting Peter from his wife.

"Peter, I need you to look at photos as well," I said.

"Yes, with my wife."

"Alone," I said. "If you're together, the chances of misidentification increase; but if you both independently say 'no' or 'yes,' we'll feel that much more confident."

He frowned. "But—"

"Look, I have no desire to subject your wife to the morgue if we don't have to. It's not clear the body is Cody's. Understand?"

He gnawed his lip. He didn't understand, but I was standing too close, crowding him. It made him uncomfortable. He stepped away and said, "Okay. Where?"

I took him to my office, away from the interview room where

Waters was showing Jane pictures of a seven-year-old boy's corpse. The pictures had come from a cold case that Waters had grabbed. The dead child resembled Cody. Same build, brown hair. Blue eyes, but that wasn't evident from the photos. The boy rested on his side, eyes closed, hair dirty with bits of twigs and leaves. Abandoned in the woods, like Hansel.

I sat in my chair, and he sat opposite, scanning the desk for the promised photographs. I didn't have any. Peter wasn't getting the same questions as Jane.

"Peter, when did you decide to get Gretel for Anna?" I asked.

"What? Where are the photos?"

"Answer the question, please."

"The dog? Um, New Year's Day. Jane said it would help Anna, to have a pet, what with Cody being gone."

"Yes, but what if he came back? Could you really handle a dog?"

"I didn't think it was a great idea, but Jane said when Cody came, we could re-examine the situation. If it didn't work, her sister could take Gretel. Jessica loves dogs."

"Right. So you found a dog two days before the new year?"

He heard my skepticism. "Jane knew a breeder who had puppies. A buyer had fallen through and he had one puppy available."

"How convenient," I said.

"Look, what's this got to do with Cody? I want to know. I want to see him."

"So do we," I said. "Your wife put down a deposit on your puppy on December 18th. She'd contacted the seller about the dog in August."

"That's not right," he said.

"The seller remembers, and he has a check receipt, from your account, dated December 18th. We've seen it."

"I don't see what that has to do with Cody."

"Do you know someone named Mark Farraday?" I asked.

He nodded. "He used to do lawn work for us when he was a teenager."

"Mark Farraday's prints were on the stolen car used to abduct Cody."

"Did *he* take him? Mark Farraday?"

"No. He stole the car. Because your wife paid him to."

"What? Stop it." He stood. "Why are you saying these things? Jane didn't have anything to do with Cody's kidnapping. She's his mother!"

"Sit down, Mr. Forrand." I used my perp tone. He sat. "This is Mark Farraday's confession." I pushed the paper to him. "In it, he states that your wife promised him four hundred dollars to deliver a stolen car to a parking lot in West Hartford."

"Four hundred dollars? We don't have—"

"Yeah. She didn't pay the full amount. Instead, she paid one fifty and, uh, 'bartered' for the rest." I let that sink in. "Did you think the baby was yours? With your vasectomy? Did she tell you it was?"

His face got red, and he clutched the edge of the desk. So hard his knuckles turned white. His jaw clenched. He looked one blink away from a seizure. "I knew the baby wasn't mine. She said she made a mistake." The words came out hollow. He glanced down at the paper. Blinked. He read a few lines. His fingers released their grip on the desk. "She loves Cody," he whispered. "She's moved heaven and earth to find him."

"I can't help noticing that she looks very happy these days."

He shook his head. "It's the baby, the hormones. She's not . . ." He stopped. Read more of Mark Farraday's statement. His face lost color.

"The thing is, Peter, your wife has been visiting Sharon Donner since early this fall. I think they planned this months ago."

"Why?" He closed his eyes. As if he could shut it out. "No, that's crazy. Jane loves Cody. She wouldn't help with his abduction." He stood up. "We're leaving. You're crazy. She wouldn't—"

I interrupted. "From what I saw, you two had a nice life back in Chaplin. Great house, two kids, active life. Until Cody's frequent injuries and hospital visits got the neighbors talking, huh? Your life was never the same after him, was it? You lost your job. Had to downsize."

He deflated. "It's not his fault. He didn't choose to have a rare genetic disease."

"He didn't. And right now I'm worried about his safety. I have reason to suspect Aaron Donner's death may have been aided by his mother."

"She *killed* him?" He leaned back, stunned.

"The FBI is investigating his death. If she harmed Aaron, what might she do to Cody?"

"Where is she?" he wailed. "Where has she got him?"

"That's what we'd like to ask your wife." The thought knocked him sideways for a second. His wife, who'd bartered away her body, had also traded their son, for freedom. She might know where he was. Had known all this time. "Agent Waters is interviewing her now, but if Jane won't tell her, we'd like you to ask her." I stood. "Stay here. I need to check on something."

I walked to the interview room. Heard the murmur of voices within. I knocked on the door. Waters exited a minute later. Her pursed lips told me things hadn't gone well. She closed the door and said, "Nothing. When I asked about her meetings with Sharon Donner, she told me she'd visited to keep her company, that she was worried about her after Aaron's death."

"Did you mention Farraday?"

"No. The minute his name comes up, she'll shout for a lawyer. I can't have that."

"What about the pictures? How'd she react?"

"She held them up close, real close. Then came the waterworks."

"She positively identified him?" We'd taken bets. I'd thought she would; Waters didn't. Waters thought she wanted to milk the missing-son story. I thought a dead son was safer. People stop looking for dead kids.

"You were right. She seemed relieved. How did it go with her husband?"

"Good. Pretty sure he's sold on it."

"But will she tell him where Cody is?" she asked. "She's got ice water in her veins, that one. Once she'd worked her way through half a box of tissues, she asked when they can have the body. She started talking funeral details two seconds later. Sounded like she was planning a fucking wedding." Waters didn't curse a lot. She hated Jane Forrand. Maybe it was a woman thing, or a mother thing. Ever since we'd figured out Jane's involvement, Waters had wanted her head on a spike.

"I'm going to go back in there. Ask a few softballs. Let her think we're getting ready to take her to the morgue. You prep Peter, yeah?"

"Yeah."

Peter was pacing the floor of my office. He stopped when I came in. "Can I see Jane now?" he asked.

I said, "We need to know where Cody is. We've only got one shot at this. If she asks for a lawyer, we're lost. We have zero leads on where Sharon Donner took him. We need that information. If you step into that room and start screaming, she'll never give it to us. You need to be calm."

"Calm! You've just told me she helped plan my son's kidnapping. That she's known where he is for months."

I waited him out and said, "You're Cody's best chance to make it home."

"How am I supposed to get her to tell me?" he asked.

"Why not say that you saw the Farraday confession when I left the room? That you pieced together her involvement." I watched him process this. "And then you have to do something that might be hard."

He looked up at me. "What?"

"Say that you'll help her. Offer her your support. Say you'll back up whatever she says. Say you need to know where Cody is. Do not let her tell you it's safer if you don't know. Insist."

He rubbed his hair. "I don't know if I can. She gave our son to a murderer!"

"Shhh. Anna's in the building." I wasn't worried that Anna would overhear. I was concerned her mother might.

"We'd like to record the conversation." I got out the mini tape recorder. Our interview room wasn't wired for sound. When Peter talked to Jane, we wouldn't be able to hear a word. Waters had campaigned to bring them to the FBI building, but I'd thought it would spook Jane too much.

Peter took the mini recorder from me. "Do you think he's alive?" he asked.

If I told the truth, he might decide an intact family meant more than his dead son. "I don't know," I said. "I'd like to find him, and bring him home, either way."

He exhaled a shaky breath and scrubbed his face with his palms. "Me too." He hit the record button on the mini tape player. Then he slipped it into his coat pocket. We walked to the interview room. I knocked on the door and waited. Waters opened it. Jane Forrand sat, hands in her lap, forward of her pregnant belly. Her cheeks were tear-stained.

"Waters, can I, uh, grab you for a minute?"

Peter stepped inside and stood beside his wife.

Jane asked, "Where's Anna?"

"Learning how to make Gretel roll over." I couldn't have Anna here. Jane would never admit to being involved with Cody's kidnapping if Anna were present.

Waters exited the room. Peter looked toward his wife. The door closed.

Waters's eyes had dark shadows. Neither of us had slept much. We ran on coffee, adrenaline, and hope. "It's in his hands now," she said. She walked toward the coffeepot. Stared at the half-full glass container. "What do you think his chances are?"

"I'm not sure if he's up to it," I said. "Even if he is, why should she tell him? She might lawyer up. Refuse to talk."

"He's her husband," she said.

"The same husband she cheated on. Same husband whose kid she gave to a possible child killer."

"True, but I don't know, I think she needs him. She wants the happy family. Husband, two kids, nice home. She had it before, and she can have it again, but not without him. She can't slot Farraday into his place."

We looked toward the interview-room door. Not that we wanted to see anyone step out. It was too soon. If either of them left now, we'd failed.

Waters followed me to my office. We sat and placed bets, more bets, on where Cody was. Waters thought he was in state. I thought not. His face was plastered on posters. It had been on TV. There was the billboard. I couldn't imagine he would go unreported if he were here. I was thinking Canada. Wasn't hard to get there. All you needed was a driver's license and a reason. "Holiday trip" would do.

"I hate waiting," Waters said. She checked her watch.

"We're ready to go if he gets the info, right?" If Peter extracted a location from his wife, I wanted us to hit the ground running.

"They're waiting on my call." She pulled her mobile phone out and squinted at the display. "Come on, come on," she muttered.

"If wishes were horses, beggars would ride," I said.

"What does that—oh," she said. "I get it. You telling me to be patient?"

I laced my hands behind my neck and stared at the ceiling. "I'm saying you can't hurry it, so why dwell on it?"

"You're the most laid-back city cop I've ever met," she said.

"It's the small-town living. It's changed me."

"Really?"

The ceiling was made up of square panels dotted every half-inch. There were thirty-six holes in each panel. I'd counted them, several times. "No," I said. "I know I can't change the outcome. We're going to have to wait."

"Ah, a fatalist," she said, as if it explained everything. Fatalist? That's the problem with the feds. Too much schooling.

"Close your eyes and take a nap," I said.

She scoffed at my suggestion. I counted the holes in the ceiling tiles. The half tiles in the far right corner had only eighteen holes. Huh. Never noticed that before. I looked at Waters. She peered at her phone. I returned my gaze to the ceiling.

"Waiting is the bread and butter of police work." Rick used to say that, to rookies when they'd complain about why couldn't we search the suspect's home now, or why did we have to wait on the lab for the results?

I must have drifted off. Because when I heard the knock, I had to open my eyes and close my mouth. Billy stood in the doorway. "Mr. Forrand wants to see you," he said.

Waters jumped to her feet. "Where's Mrs. Forrand?"

"With Anna."

"Send him in." I checked my shirt for drool. Hoped to hell I hadn't snored.

Peter Forrand came in, his face a decade older. He reached into his pocket and held out the recorder. "Thimble Islands," he said. Waters took the recorder from him. "Jane said he's on the Thimble Islands. She begged me not to tell you. Said he'd be happier on his own, without two siblings. She—" Tears fell. He shook his head, unable to continue.

"Did she confess? To planning the grabs?" Waters asked. He nodded. She smiled, a tight, small smile. "We'll send a team for him now." She squeezed Peter's elbow.

"Can I come?" he asked.

"Stay with Anna," she said. "We're going to arrest Jane. Anna will need you."

"Can you, can you not do it in front of Anna?" He rubbed his mouth. "I don't want her to see that."

"Billy!" I called. He ran into the room moments later. "Get Mrs. Forrand. Make sure her daughter stays with Yankowitz," I said.

A minute later, Jane appeared, clutching her coat to her stomach. "Can we go now? Anna hasn't had lunch, and I'm not feeling well. We can do the identification later, can't we?" Her plea seemed grotesque. Her willingness to claim a dead boy as her own.

Waters said, "Jane Forrand, you're under arrest for the abduction of Cody Forrand." She put the cuffs on Jane, in front of her protruding belly.

Jane twisted her hands. "What are you doing? Peter! Tell them! Tell them what a mistake they're making!"

Peter closed his eyes against the image of his pregnant wife in handcuffs.

"Peter! Call a lawyer. Jacob What's-His-Name. The guy you played basketball with." Jane was breathing hard. "Peter, are you listening?"

Peter opened his eyes. "Call him yourself," he said. He walked out of the room.

CHAPTER THIRTY-SEVEN

I drove behind a caravan of FBI vehicles, my hands tight on the wheel. The car rocked slightly, due to forceful winds and our speed. Yankowitz sat in the passenger seat. We were listening to a copy of the tape recording, finally learning what happened between Peter and Jane Forrand in that interview room. Behind us sat Skylar. We had a coat belonging to Cody for scent, plus a cadaver dog belonging to the FBI. Hope for the best; plan for the worst.

The tape was near the beginning, a few moments after Peter had entered the room with Jane. "I said the boy in the photos was Cody," Peter said, his voice low.

"Yes," Jane said. "I, I think so too."

"I saw Farraday's statement," Peter said, his voice unsteady. Wow. He'd jumped right to it.

"What statement?" Jane's composure slipped. She hadn't known we'd found Farraday.

"About the car, and about you and him." He sighed. "I don't care why you lied about who you slept with. I know we've been . . . It's been so hard with the kids and everything. Janey, I have to know."

"Know what?" She was feeling her way, uncertain.

"I can't protect you if I don't know what to say."

Silence.

"Please," Peter said. It sounded genuine.

A shaky breath, hers, most likely. Then a rumble. He must've touched the recorder. "Tell them you knew about the affair with Farraday. That I told you and begged forgiveness," she said.

"What about the car? Farraday said that you told him to steal the car Cody was abducted in."

"We'll say he got angry when I broke it off. That he had a hand in the abduction."

"Did he?" His voice was soft, almost inaudible.

Ahead, the FBI vehicles took the next exit. I followed.

Jane said. "Baby, I'm so sorry." Her voice caught. She cried. He let her.

"Where's Cody?" he asked, his voice soft. What that must've cost him, I could only imagine.

She sniffled, but said nothing.

"Janey, where's Cody?" His voice was harder.

"He's with Sharon," she said. "Safe, with Sharon. She loves him, you know. Like her own son." Peter said nothing. "And she has money, plenty to care for him. She always did." There it was, envy. Envy that Sharon had money. Jane did not.

"Where?" Peter said. "I need to know, in case they ask questions. In case they start to get close. We can redirect them, right?" He was too eager. She must've sensed it.

"It's safer for you not to know," she said. A rustling. She must have hugged him. The noise was terrific. Skylar barked.

The road ahead was rougher, less well-paved than the highway. I glanced at the speedometer. Eighty miles per hour.

"Janey, tell me where Cody is," Peter said. There was steel in his words.

"I can't. If you don't know, you can't slip up. If you don't know—"

"If I don't know, I can't move on. Please." Peter's voice broke. "Just tell me. Tell me and I can sleep at night, and we can, we can move on."

She hesitated.

"Please, Janey, please. I need to know." His voice dropped to a ravaged whisper.

Maybe it was the grief in his tone, but she told him, "The Thimble Islands. They're staying at a house that belongs to some guy from Sharon's church. He doesn't live there. No one does in the winter. It's a safe place. Cody is safe. I promise."

"Does the church guy know about Cody?"

"No. She made a copy of the key without his knowing. The cops were all over people Sharon knew. He hasn't said anything. He doesn't know. They're just going to stay there another month. Maybe less now that we have this boy."

"The boy in the photo?" Peter asked.

She was close to him. Her voice louder now. "We'll do just as you said. We'll say the boy in the photos is Cody. They'll stop looking. We can start again, fresh. Like when we were first married. I'm sorry, Pete, but it was so hard. You don't know what it was like, being stuck at home, day after day. Having to keep Cody from hitting Anna with a golf club or doing stunts. We were always in the hospital. One day I saw this haggard-looking woman across the street, and a second later I realized it was my reflection. I didn't recognize myself. Poor Anna never got my attention because Cody was always leaping off the picnic tables and jumping off the swing sets. He'd never stop. I asked him; I *begged* him. I couldn't do it anymore." Her voice broke.

"Why didn't you *tell* me?" Peter asked.

"I did, but you always told me it would get better when he got older. It *wasn't* getting better. And the house was always a disaster. I just wanted a break."

"Why didn't you tell me what you were planning? All this time, I had no idea."

"It was safer, baby, for you, and us. I was going to tell you. I just needed things to quiet down."

"But I thought he was dead!" Oh no. He'd lost his temper.

"He's not. He's fine. You know how much experience Sharon has with his disease. I promise. He's fine, just fine." Another rustling. Another embrace.

He took a moment. "So we bury him? This boy?" He must've pointed to the photo.

"People will stop looking for Cody. Sharon will take good care of him. She has more resources, and far more time. It will be okay, you'll see. I did this for *us*, sweetheart, and for Cody. He'll have her undivided attention. If we stick together, we can get through this," she said. "Trust me. I love you." A kiss. And silence.

"I'd better get this over with," Peter said.

"What?" her voice pitched up. Worried.

"Tell them I'll go to the morgue and identify the body."

"Oh, okay. I'll take Anna home. We'll have dinner ready when you get back." Another noise from the microphone. She'd hugged him again. She whispered, "I love you. More than anything."

Yankowitz said, "I can't believe her." He shook his head.

Peter said, "Back soon." The door opened. The tape went click. He'd turned it off.

We drove, in silence, lost to our own thoughts until ahead of us, the cars braked, pulling off into a turnout. Agents got out of cars, pulling binoculars from their vehicles and putting them to their eyes. Scanning the islands for signs of life. We got out of the car and were assaulted by chill winds, pushing us. The islands looked small, their bases pink rock, covered with scrub and wind-whipped pines. A few had homes. Many were barren.

Yankowitz had told me that most of the islands were uninhabited. Two were home to stone quarries. One had produced the rock used in Grant's Tomb and the Lincoln Memorial. The largest island, Horse Island, was owned by Yale University.

"There it is," Yankowitz said, pointing. "Yale operates it as an ecology lab."

In summer, it was probably lovely. Now, it was cold, and the waves were white-capped. Not a nice beach day. The March winds blew the agents' hair every which way. I exited the car. Agents milled in small groups, conferring. We had to figure out which island Cody was on before we set off. Agent Waters stood near Mulberry, who looked at a map. "My money's on Money Island," Mulberry said, tapping the map. The paper flew up and nearly escaped his gloved hand. "Damn wind."

C'mon, God, give us a sign. One sign. He's just a kid.

"Money has the most houses," Yankowitz told me, pointing to another craggy shape rising from the sea. "No one lives there after fall."

"No one lives on any of these after Labor Day most years," Mulberry said. "I got a sister in Stony Creek." Stony Creek was the town behind us. "She says in the summer it's crazy down here. Everyone going to their summer homes. Tourists out on water taxis." He lifted a pair of binoculars and scanned them, left to right. "Wouldn't know it now."

Sea spray made the air cold and damp. A group of feds tromped over, dressed in tactical gear, their black, heavy boots rattling loose pebbles. "Fred saw a thin trail of smoke there," one said. He pointed.

Mulberry said, "What did I tell you? Money Island."

"Do we know which house?" the fed asked.

"Not yet," Waters said. "We sent agents to interview members of her church, but so far they've not found him."

"What do you think?" the fed asked. "Wait for the intel?"

My pulse accelerated. Sharon may have killed her son. If Cody was alive, he was in danger. Knowing exactly where to go was a huge tactical advantage, though.

"No," Waters said. "We follow the smoke. Is everyone ready?"

"Let me get Skylar," Yankowitz said.

"She okay on boats?" Waters asked.

He said, "The challenge will be to keep her from swimming." We all shivered at the thought of that freezing saltwater.

Yankowitz led Skylar down the dock to the second boat. The first carried Waters and the SWAT guys. The loud gurgle of the engine and the back-and-forth to maneuver out of the dock had me clutching a rail.

"Not a sailor?" Yankowitz asked. He stood, legs loose, not seeming to mind the salty spray attacking his face. Skylar sat, ears peeled back by the breeze.

"Which island?" I asked, looking at the islands, some so small you could fit ten people on it, others miles across. I was guessing Money Island was one of the bigger islands.

Yankowitz said, "There," pointing.

I blinked against the spray and focused on his pointer finger. Money Island was ahead, several islands between it and us. I could see a row of houses near the waterfront. Whoever had spotted the smoke had sharper eyes than mine. I couldn't make it out. The cold nipped at bits of exposed flesh, and I was thankful once again for my new hat. The boat rocked up and down, up and down. I fought a surge of nausea.

I would not get sick. I would not. I clutched the railing harder and breathed out my nose. As we got closer, the agents got on the radio. Had a confab about which dock to land at. There were several, but not many could accommodate our big boats. We puttered, watching the first team disembark their boat and prep. After minutes bobbing on the water, we pulled into a dock several hundred yards away. The boat jolted forward, and I nearly fell. My death grip on the railing saved me.

Skylar barked, the noise sharp. Yankowitz silenced her with a command.

We waited while they got everything ready and secured the lines. Then we filed off the boat, onto a worn deck, splintery and gray, that creaked beneath our combined weight. God, I hoped we wouldn't fall in. I hurried off it, onto the rocky soil, to glance at the houses. Some were simple cottages; others were grander summer homes with huge windows and large decks.

"That way." An older fed named Chuck, pointed. "The smoke is coming from there. We'll wait for the alpha team to secure it." We followed in their wake, walking a path between two houses. The wet sand felt unsteady. I kept scanning the area. There. The yellow house four hundred yards ahead and to the right. From its chimney curled a thin strip of smoke.

The team divided and approached fast and low. They looked ready for war, armed with flash grenades, a rammer, and plenty of guns. There was enough stopping power to take down the entire island if it had been filled with people. The only sounds were of shrieking birds and the hiss of sifting sand across the ground.

We watched and waited as they covered all entrances and exits. I was too far back to see them break in the door, but I heard it. Heard their yells and then a woman's scream. We waited, shifting, trying to see better, craning our necks and squinting while we waited for the all clear. It came minutes later. We surged forward, rushing toward the house. Waters stepped outside and called, "He's not inside. She won't tell us where he is."

"He is with God!" Mrs. Donner yelled from inside the house. Fuck. With God? My skin prickled.

Yankowitz unsealed the bag holding Cody's coat. Knelt and proffered it to Skylar. He gave her the search command. Skylar sniffed it and went to attention. Then she turned toward where we'd come from and set off.

"You want the other dog?" a fed behind me asked. The cadaver dog. If Cody was with God, it was the dog we needed.

"Give them a minute," I said. Yankowitz followed Skylar back the way we'd come. I walked in their wake. Skylar padded along the sandy road, headed past where we'd docked. I looked toward the boats, bobbing on the ocean. Christ, what would we tell Peter Forrand?

Skylar paused and headed away from the docks, toward the island's interior. Scrubby pines protected us from the worst of the wind. Ahead was a shed. Probably used to store swimming equipment and summer furniture that would grace a patio four months from now. All the summer people, drinking beers from ice-filled coolers, and rubbing sunscreen into their pale skin. Would the dead, kidnapped child intrude on their summer fun? Would Money Island become known as the island where Cody Forrand died?

Skylar trotted around the shed and barked twice. Yankowitz hurried to the door. "Good girl." He reached into his pocket and gave her a treat.

I peered through a small window, but the crusted salt and dirt made it impossible to see inside. The door was locked with a simple lock, the kind kids put on their school lockers. It was fastened high, at shoulder height. Fuck. I ran back toward the house. "Crowbar!" I shouted. "Crowbar!"

The guy who made it to me first said, "What?"

"We need a crowbar!" I pointed to the shed. Skylar was digging at the dirt near the door.

The fed's eyes went wide. He ran back to the others. When he returned, he brought a team of six. The first levered a bar between the lock's hasp and yanked hard. Nothing. He tried again, and the door-frame broke, leaving the intact lock outside. He pushed the door open with the flat of his hand. Skylar barked. Inside, it was dim. I saw kayaks with yellow life vests inside. Two Adirondack chairs stood to the right.

"He's here!" The door breaker called. A second later, "Medic!"

I rushed forward, after the medic. Inside, the first fed knelt by a small white figure I'd mistaken for driftwood. Twisted to one side, his back to us, I hadn't recognized it for what, for who, he was. Cody. His right arm hung at a wrong angle. Broken. His face turned toward us. His left eye was swollen, bruised. His lip split. His body thin, so much thinner than when I'd last seen him. His eyes looked enormous in his pale face. His hair was matted. The medic covered him with a shiny foil blanket and put two pairs of socks onto his bare feet. "Hell," I heard the medic whisper under his breath. "His arm." He crouched before him, uncertain how to move him.

I stepped forward and scooped him up, mindful of his arm. Cody's eyes locked onto mine. "Chief," he said. His voice cracked.

"You should watch his arm," the medic said.

I strode forward, anxious to get him to the boat so we could get him to the hospital. "He can't feel pain," I said. But I could. Every stumble, every jounce, hurt as I held him to my chest.

"Where's Mom?" Cody asked. He looked around at the men in their black body armor and shrank into me. Couldn't feel pain? Maybe not physically. He was in for a world of hurt when he found out what his mother had done.

"Your family will meet you at the hospital. You're safe." I took big steps and tried not to jostle him. He was so light in my arms. His face against my chest was cold.

I said, "Is there an ambo on shore?" We needed to race him to the hospital. We couldn't lose him, not now that we'd found him. *God, you listening? If you let him die now, I'm not going to church again, not ever.*

"Yes, and a team at Children's is expecting him," Mulberry said. "Go to the first boat," he said, correcting my course. I'd headed to the boat I'd come in on. "It's faster."

The medic wanted to set Cody on a bench but worried the movement would disturb his broken limb. "I'll hold him," I said. Cody was shivering. I tucked the foil blanket about him a fraction higher. And though the boat sped off, hitting waves hard and bouncing more than during the initial journey, I didn't loosen my grasp on him.

CHAPTER THIRTY-EIGHT

Suds was empty except for Nate and me. He handed me my mug of coffee and slid the *Idyll Register* across the bar. "Cody Forrand Found!" A picture of Cody, propped in his hospital bed, took up half the page. Next to it was a photo of me carrying him in my arms off the boat, to the ambulance.

"Nice picture," he said.

I pushed the paper away. "Fucking feds. They love their photo ops." Agent Waters was behind that. She'd tipped off the press. If it went well, she wanted coverage. Mine was the photo dominating the papers. She'd told me she was happy to be in the photos with her arm on Sharon Donner's, leading her into custody. "Your photo makes you a local hero," she'd said. "Mine makes me the woman who nailed a monster, and a clever monster to boot." A nice memento to show the bosses when promotion time came around. Waters would do all right.

To show I could play nice, I'd given the FBI almost all the credit for the solve, though I held back some for Yankowitz and Skylar. They deserved it for finding Cody.

"You hear anything about Sweet Dreams?" I asked Nate. The store was still shuttered.

He frowned. "David and Charles are still at war. Sharleen is representing her dad. She says he's lost weight. I saw Dave yesterday, and he didn't look so hot. He's renting a place in Willington. It's a shame."

I hadn't known a lot of gay men who had partners for life. That wasn't my scene. But I'd liked Charles and David. They'd presented an alternate possibility . . . and now they didn't.

"What's going to happen to him?" Nate tapped the photo of Cody. In it, Cody smiled, but his face was a mess. Hard to conceal the beatings Sharon Donner gave him.

"He'll go home in a week or so. His foot got frostbitten and his arm was broken and healed badly. They had to re-break it to reset the bone."

Nate winced. "Ouch."

"He can't feel pain," I said.

"Right. That's hard to imagine. Still, even if it didn't hurt—" He rubbed the bar top hard. "What's going to happen to her?"

"Sharon Donner?" Her face had been front-page news too. Woman of a dead kid with CIPA steals another. The press loved the idea that she'd killed her son and was looking to do the same to Cody. I'd seen her neighbor, Geraldine Howard, on two TV interviews, talking about how she'd never liked Sharon Donner and had always thought she was up to no good.

"No. Cody's mom. What'll happen there?" he asked.

"It's up to the prosecutors now."

"Do you think she'll do time?"

"Yup." I finished my last swallow of coffee. "People love a woman in distress. Pretty mom with a kidnapped kid, around Christmas? They loved it." I shook my head. "People hate things, too. And the only thing they hate more than a mother who hurts her child is to be taken in, to fall for a scam. She did that. She made them feel stupid. No jury will forgive her for that."

Nate said, "God Bless America," and then, "Refill?"

The hospital seemed like an oasis of calm compared to the last time I'd been inside. Two days ago, it had been doctors yelling, nurses running, and Cody on a bed, two steps from death. Today, he sat up, a Lego truck kit on his lap. His battered face was a mess. His arm was in a cast. And his foot was wrapped. The foot they were afraid they'd have to amputate. What had they done?

Peter sat next to Cody's bed. He stood when I came in. "Sit," I said. "Just came to check on Cody. How you doing?"

Cody said, "Chief! I got the Lego truck kit!"

"That's great, buddy."

Peter said, "Looks like Santa found it after all." I raised my brow and he mouthed, "Donor." Ah, so it wasn't the original kit. The one Mrs. Forrand had bought and given to Mrs. Donner to lure Cody into the stolen car.

"How are you feeling?" I asked.

Cody shrugged. "They took two toes," he said.

Oh no. So they hadn't saved his foot, not entirely. Two toes. He'd be okay with three, wouldn't he?

"Cody will need some physical therapy, later," Pete said.

"Where's Anna?" I asked.

"Home, with my parents," he said. "She's been teaching Gretel tricks."

"Kimberly," Cody said. He tried to lock two plastic bricks together with one hand.

"Kimberly?" I asked.

"The dog's name," Cody said. "We changed it to Kimberly, like the pink Power Ranger." Poor Anna. Once again forced to give way to her brother. What chance did she have now? He'd been kidnapped, starved, beaten, rescued. Featured on the cover of newspapers and magazines. She'd always be number two in that family.

"Where's Mom?" Cody asked.

I shot a look at Pete, and he shook his head. "She's still traveling, pal. Hey, maybe after lunch we can watch *James and the Giant Peach*."

Cody nodded. "Can I have ice cream?" he asked.

How could he want ice cream after he nearly froze to death? He didn't feel it, that's how. Cold took his toes, but it didn't hurt. Funny. I didn't think I'd be eating ice cream anytime soon.

"Sure. Chocolate?" Pete asked.

"Yeah," Cody said.

"You want to help me make the truck, Chief?" Cody asked me. I dragged a chair over and stuck bricks together for a half hour, until Cody's eyes closed and he fell asleep.

"He's still recovering," his father whispered.

"How are you doing?" I asked.

He grimaced. "I'm getting there. The worst is when he asks for Jane. I didn't know what to tell him the first time, so I made up some story about her going on a trip. I know I'm going to have to tell him, eventually. But how?"

"Has he said anything about her involvement?" I asked.

He squeezed his eyes shut. Exhaled shakily. "She prepped him for the first grab. Had told him all these stories about the Power Rangers and their base and how, if he was a very good boy, he might get to visit someday." He opened his eyes and stared at the floor tiles. "After we got him back, she told him that Power Ranger secrets couldn't be shared and it was okay not to tell anyone, especially the police, about their base or what they did."

"Jesus," I said.

"Yeah. I still can't believe she just gave him away." He pulled the blanket higher over Cody. "Do you think she knew about Aaron? That his death wasn't an accident?"

"No." In truth, I didn't know, but no one else had suspected murder. And as much as I loathed Jane Forrand, I wasn't certain she'd have given Cody to a murderer. A religious nut? Yes. A killer? No. Maybe it was a fine distinction, but I suspected it wasn't to Peter Forrand.

"It's funny, but his missing toes, his arm, those don't worry me as much as what he'll hear on the playground about his mother. The things other people will say. I don't know how to shield him."

"He's a tough kid," I said, hating the words as I spoke them. They were empty. Sure, Cody was tough, but that was because of his medical condition. That same protection didn't extend to his feelings.

"Is there anything I can get you?" I asked.

Peter Forrand gazed at his sleeping son. "A time machine?" he said, offering up a weak smile. A time machine, sure, only how far back would he go? To before the first kidnapping, before Cody was born, before he met Jane?

I found a copy of the *Idyll Register* photo on my office door. A gold star was stuck above my head. I took it down and headed for my wastebasket. Thought twice. Put it atop my desk. A bark brought my head up. "There he is!" Dix called. "Man of the hour!"

Ah, so Yankowitz was getting it too, the hero treatment. "Man of the year," he called back. I heard the smile in his voice. A few months ago, Yankowitz had been the meter maid who couldn't drive, the butt of jokes. Now he was the guy who'd found Cody Forrand. Quite an upgrade.

"Jinx!" I said.

The German shepherd came bounding into my office. I reached into my cabinet for the box of treats I'd picked up. "Here you go." I set a treat on the floor and watched Jinx destroy it in two bites.

Yankowitz came in a moment later. "Hey, he hasn't earned that yet."

"No?"

"He needs to work on his responses. Yesterday he didn't signal on a find."

"Must be hard for Jinx, living with Skylar now that she's a media darling."

"Hardly. Jinx still rules the roost."

"Things okay?" Now was the time for him to tell me if the guys were playing too hard, if he'd had enough of the hero treatment.

"Sure, though I wish the reporters would stop calling. Lindsay's getting tired of answering the phone."

"It's only been two days. They'll lose interest. Some disaster will make you yesterday's news."

"Good. It's weird having people ask you so many personal questions. I had a reporter ask what my sign was and if I was single."

"No wonder Lindsay's annoyed."

He smiled to himself. "I didn't tell her that. I'm not stupid." He looked at the newspaper photo on my desk.

Jinx barked, once. Mrs. Dunsmore appeared. I told Jinx, "Good dog."

"Good morning," Mrs. Dunsmore said. She went straight for my plant and said, "This thing is dying of thirst! I'm glad you're here," she said to Yankowitz. "I got off the phone with the mayor. He wants to have a parade."

"A parade?" I asked. Another parade? For what?

"For Cody Forrand. To celebrate his return and to honor our two heroes." She looked from Yankowitz to me. "Skylar too," she said.

"It's freezing out. No one is gonna come outside."

"We'll have it in early April," she said. "Once Cody's arm has healed."

"What do I have to do?" Yankowitz asked. Great question.

"Be on a float, with Skylar. Toss out candy. The usual."

"Do I get to throw candy too?" I asked.

She sized me up. "Maybe we'll let you ride in a convertible, beside the mayor."

"Couldn't we do something else?" I asked.

"There will also be a fundraiser."

Parades meant extra work details, and setting out detour signs for the parade route, and a thousand other trifling, stupid details I'd hoped we could avoid until Memorial Day. "Why don't they do the fundraiser without the parade?" I asked.

"Because people like parades. Gives them a chance to dust off their uniforms, play music, march in formation," she said. "Gives businesses a chance to look good, by volunteering materials and funds."

"I don't see the point—"

"Of course you don't," she said. "If you thought for one moment beyond your convenience and considered other peoples' needs, you might. The Forrands are going to need money. Plenty of it to pay Cody's bills. And for daycare or a sitter, since they lost their mother. Neighbors will pitch in for the first month or two or five, but then they'll get busy with their own lives. That family needs long-term help, and that means throwing a parade, getting press, and asking people to give."

"Let me know when you need me," Yankowitz said, stepping backward slowly, eager to escape her increasingly angry words.

"Thank you, Jim." Her voice fell an octave.

Yankowitz left and Jinx followed.

I said, "Look, I get that the Forrands need money. Fine, we'll have the parade. It's gonna mean a lot more work, and I'd rather not be hailed as a hero."

"It's not always about you," she said.

"Pardon?"

She put her hands on her hips, "You're not always the victim, you know."

"The victim?"

"You act like you're the most put-upon man in Idyll."

"I'm sorry. Did someone else have their car covered with hate speech?" Where did she get off with her attitude?

"You should've thanked Klein for that." Of course she knew it was Klein. Had she always known? Had she hidden that fact from me? "His act won you more loyalty than you'd have gotten without it."

"I should be grateful?" Jesus. She really was a hard case.

"You should stop acting like you're better than the rest of them."

"Better? How do I do that?"

"By putting them in their place, day after day."

"I'm their boss."

"Yes, and you should lead by example, instead of shaming them with their lack of knowledge. They're small-town cops. They do small-town policing, and it's not always rescuing cats."

"Forgive me for trying to teach them a thing or two."

"Teach all you want, but don't be condescending when you do it. And maybe find it in your heart to forgive them when they mess up. Everyone does, including you."

"I'm assuming this lecture has a point."

"Billy is still walking on eggshells around you. Smile at him once in a while. Don't make him fear for his job every damn day."

"I don't."

"You do!" With her free hand she rubbed the crucifix around her neck.

"As if you don't judge," I said. "With your cross."

She stopped rubbing it and held it out. "This?"

"You started wearing that the day after I made my 'announcement.' Don't think I didn't notice."

"Wrong. I started wearing it two days *later*, when my niece was diagnosed with cancer."

"Oh," I said. Belatedly, "I'm sorry about your niece."

"I've also been wearing it to remind me to be patient, to remind me that God has a plan and it contains everyone."

"Even me?" I asked.

"Even you."

"I don't care if you hate that I'm gay," I said. "I can handle that. Don't you—"

Her bark of laughter stopped me. "Hate you because you're gay? You really are blind. My niece, Valerie, the one with cancer, had an older brother, Leo. Sweet boy. Loved baseball and roller coasters. Used to spend nights with his sister at my house when his parents went out. When he was in college, Leo told his parents he was gay. They disowned him. Took away his money for college, refused to help him find a place to live. He stayed with me for seven months, working at the ice-cream parlor, saving money. Then he moved to California. I was so worried about him, but he got a job at an art gallery, made friends. Used to send me postcards. He was happy. And then, in 1985, he got sick."

AIDS. That was how gay men got sick at that time. So many.

"He was far gone, and they didn't have treatments like they have now. Doctors were afraid to care for him." She shook her head, her eyes bright. "I flew out to California, and he . . . oh, how he looked. Like a scarecrow, balding, and with sores on his face and lips. But his eyes, they were bright, and he told me that he'd been happier than he ever expected to be. He thanked me for helping him find his way West, and for not giving up on him. For staying in touch. For never suggesting the way he lived was sinful and wrong." She brushed her eyes and said,

"You don't know anything, Thomas Lynch. The problem is you think you know *everything*."

She walked out before I could defend myself or think of a cutting retort or apologize.

I got out of my chair, restless. Decided to visit with my detectives, who were also less than delighted with me. Neither had been included in the FBI's special op. I'd asked to bring them on, but although Waters liked Wright, she claimed there wasn't a place for him. Finnegan, she said, "wasn't vital."

They sat at their desks, Finnegan smoking, Wright chewing gum and telling Finny some New Year's story involving drunk twins.

"Hey," I said.

They said, "Hail the conquering hero" in unison, like they'd been practicing.

"Knock it off," I said. "Look, I know you're annoyed with me." Wright looked at his cuticles. Finny stared at the space where the air purifiers used to be. I missed them already. "Look, it was the FBI's call. For what it's worth, I wanted to include you."

"That and fifty cents will get you bus fare," Finny muttered.

"I'm sorry," I said, thinking of Mrs. Dunsmore. Of her accusation that I acted as if I was better than everyone. I didn't believe it, no matter what she thought. "I'm really sorry you didn't get to join me on a seasick ride across a choppy ocean."

"Yankowitz said you nearly lost your lunch," Wright said.

I was willing to play ball. "Why don't boats move like cars?" I asked.

"Because the ocean moves, dummy, unlike a highway," Finnegan said.

"Ohhhhh," I said.

"Hey, what's the deal with the Farraday kid?" he asked. "He going to be indicted?"

"Not on kidnapping charges," I said. "He stole the car without knowing why Jane Forrand needed it. He'd had a crush on her since he worked for her as a teenager."

"So because he was getting paid and laid by her," Wright said, "he wasn't likely to ask questions."

I nodded.

"The thing I can't wrap my head around," Finny said, "is why did Mrs. Donner return him after the first grab?" He picked up a pencil and gnawed at it like a damn woodchuck.

"The boat she planned to use was out of gas. Someone at the dock spotted her. She interpreted this to mean that the Lord had decided the time was wrong."

"So Cody wasn't loopy when he told us about the boat," Wright said.

"No, but if you remember, it was his mother who suggested the 'boat' was a ride outside the grocery store."

"Is Mrs. Donner bat-shit crazy?" Wright asked. "Or just playing?"

"Beats me."

"What about Jane Forrand?" Finny asked. He set his tooth-marked pencil down.

"I think the *Sally Jesse Raphael* show was the final straw. She'd finally turned her nightmare into a TV opportunity and Cody blew it."

Wright said, "What I don't get is why she thought getting pregnant would help."

"She might've thought her husband would get over Cody's disappearance faster with a baby on the way. Or she wanted another perfect family, this time with a kid she knew wouldn't have CIPA."

Finny asked, "What'll happen to her baby? Once she gives birth?" He crumpled a piece of paper and tossed it in the air.

"I'm guessing they'll do a paternity test," Wright said. "If I were Peter Forrand, I'd insist."

I said, "Peter Forrand says if the child is his, he'll sue for sole custody and raise it."

"Even if it has CIPA?" Finny asked. I nodded.

"And if it's Farraday's?" Wright asked.

"No idea." Mark Farraday didn't seem like he was eager for fatherhood.

"That plumber story she tried to sell us was pure fairy tale, wasn't it?" Wright asked. "I always thought it seemed convenient."

He'd never said so to me, but I let it go. "Looks that way. I think she stole it from the Victoria Fitzgerald playbook. She used that case to sow suspicion and prejudice her husband against the police."

"Worked a treat, too," Finny said. He rotated his neck. "Any word on Cody?"

"He lost two toes." Both detectives winced. "Otherwise, he's looking better."

"Poor kid," Wright said. "You think Mrs. Donner was going to kill him?"

Finnegan said, "'Course she was. You saw the pictures. He wouldn't have lasted another week out there."

"She got angry when she realized how public the kidnapping was made. She thought she'd be able to rename Cody, take him someplace far away, and have another son. But then she saw her face on the news and realized it wouldn't be so easy," I said.

"Can the feds prove she killed her son?" Wright asked.

"Last I heard, they wanted to exhume him, test for traces of poisons or drugs in his system. Thing is, if he died of hyperthermia, it's going to be tough to prove she caused it." I thought of what Geraldine Howard had told me, about the flickering light coming from his room before Aaron died. What if he'd been signaling? Trying to get someone's attention while his body shut down?

Wright interrupted my dark thoughts with, "They've got her for Cody, anyway. I don't think her 'the Lord told me to do it' act will work on a jury."

"Well, if you'll excuse me, gents, I have 1997's crime report to complete for the next town meeting," I said. "As you know, we're full of it these days. Must be that terrible city influence I keep hearing about." I jerked my thumb to my chest.

"Ooh," Finny said. "Life of the hero, huh?"

"Life of a paper pusher, more like." I returned to my office, hoping they resented me a little less.

When a trio of knocks at my door came at 4:50 p.m., I thought about not answering. *Coward.* I called, "Come in," and in came Agent Cisco. He closed the door behind him. I didn't know what to say.

"Hello," he said. He stood in place, looking around my office as if it was new. "Rescued any abducted kids lately?" Cisco hadn't been around when Waters and I laid the groundwork and executed our plan. He'd been on another case. Some human-trafficking thing involving money wired via computers. Tech stuff.

"How's life?" I asked.

"Not bad." He chafed his hands. "You?"

"Can't complain." God, this was awkward.

"I wanted to see if maybe you'd like to grab dinner."

"Dinner?" I sounded like a parrot, a very stupid parrot.

"Or maybe you're busy." He seemed uneasy.

"No, I'm free. I just need to finish up a few things," I said.

"Great. Look, I'm sorry if I—" He cleared his throat. "Waters saw you, leaving our hotel. She reamed me out for getting involved with you. Said it was bad to mix with local law during an ongoing investigation. Told me I needed to think with my other head and not be seduced by every handsome man I met."

"Waters called me handsome?"

"She transferred me off the case, to teach me a lesson. Now that the case is over," he stepped closer, "Mom's not watching."

"You sure she hasn't put a tracer on your car? Maybe a bug on your phone?"

He grimaced. "Not funny. She really is a control freak."

"Give me a half hour?" I tried to recall if I had aftershave at the station. I had a clean black shirt hanging on the back of my door. I could change into that.

"Okay. Meet at Quinn's?"

"Sounds good," I said.

After he left, I counted to twenty, slowly. Then I rifled my drawer and found deodorant, aftershave, a comb, and a spare pair of underwear, socks, and jeans. I changed in the locker room, after I'd checked that it was empty. I buttoned my black shirt and brushed at a smudge on my cheek.

The door squeaked open. Billy stepped inside. He saw me at the sink and stopped.

"You coming in?" I asked.

"You mind?"

God, *was* he scared of me? Had I made him that way?

"Billy, you work here. You can come in anytime."

He said, "I was gonna brush my teeth. I've got a date after work."

"Girl from the video store?"

He slammed his locker shut. "How'd you know that?"

"Small town." I'd overheard Finnegan making remarks.

"Great. That means Mom knows, and she'll be asking questions at Sunday dinner."

I unbuttoned my top shirt button. Better.

"You got a date?" He lowered his eyes to the sink. For a moment, he'd forgotten. That my date would involve another man.

"Matter of fact, I do," I said.

Billy squeezed paste on his toothbrush. "Good luck," he said. His cheeks were aflame.

He was trying. I needed to reward the effort.

I met his gaze in the mirror.

"Thanks, Billy, but I don't need luck." I winked and left the room, whistling.

ACKNOWLEDGMENTS

Thank you is a phrase that is lovely and warm, but it falls short of expressing what I mean. I want something larger and richer to tell these folks how much I appreciate them, owe them, and love them. *Thank you* is the best I have, though.

So many thank yous to my agent, Ann Collette, who is a tiger fighting for and with me, and whom I trust when she tells me she loves my work, because she doesn't suffer fools or poor prose! Equal thanks to my editor, Dan Mayer, whose good opinion means the world to me. I feel lucky to have him looking over my shoulder.

Thanks to friend and critiquer Elizabeth Chiles Shelburne, who took time from her busy schedule to read my fledgling work. It's much better because of her.

I owe tons of thanks to Jamie Severson, who does everything, including laser-cutting, painting, marketing, and author wrangling. She's also a terrific person. Ride or die, girl.

Belated thanks to Peter Ruggiero, who let me interview him about life in Connecticut during the 1990s. Thank you for sharing your time and wit with me.

Gratitude is due to Lynne Barrett, who taught a session on plot at the Muse & Marketplace conference that was helpful and stuck with me, given the recurring Hansel and Gretel theme in this story.

An orchestra of thanks to Joe Murphy, who read my reviews for me, so that I'd believe everyone loved my work, which was hella kind.

Special thanks to Karen Brennan and Jeff Hawson, dear friends who helped copyedit *Idyll Threats* and didn't complain that it's the worst possible way to read your friend's book. Promise I won't do it again!

Big canine hugs to the original Skylar, who inspired her namesake. Thanks for all the doggy comfort, you big, sweet dog.

So much appreciation is due for my fellow Novel Incubees and my SSB authors who've been supportive and helpful and funny. To all the very generous mystery writers who welcomed me into their weird, fantastic group with open arms. I've come to learn that people who think about how to kill other humans are some of the nicest people you'll meet. Special thanks to Lisa Alber, Cindy Brown, and Bill Cameron, who made me feel at home in a city where I knew no one.

Big ups to all the booksellers who hosted me or recommended my books to their buyers. Special thanks to my local indie, Porter Square Books, and to Gary, who always greets me as a "bestselling author," which is a stretch my ego appreciates. And thanks to librarians everywhere. You're wonderful. Keep fighting the good fight.

A very special thank you to Mercedes Hightower, who wrote the world's most effusive Goodreads review of *Idyll Threats*. Writing this book wasn't always easy. So I printed your review, Mercedes, and hung it near my desk. When I was tempted to not write or to stop early, I'd look at your words and say, "Mercedes wants another book, and she deserves it." You're part of why this work exists. Readers, never doubt your power. Your enthusiasm for an author's work matters. It urges us on.

To my friends and family, whom I love, and who love me in return, everlasting thanks.

To my partner, Todd, you're funny and smart and I love you.

ABOUT THE AUTHOR

Stephanie Gayle's *Idyll Threats* is the first book in the Thomas Lynch mystery series. Stephanie's fascination with crime began when she attempted, at age four, to outsmart a policeman. After flirting with the idea of becoming a defense attorney and then working a few weeks as a paralegal, she decided writing crime fiction would be more satisfying—and fun. Her first novel, *My Summer of Southern Discomfort*, was chosen as one of *Redbook*'s Top Ten Summer Reads and was a Book Sense monthly pick. She has also published stories and narrative nonfiction pieces, including two Pushcart Prize nominees.